PRAISE FOR

THE CASSANDRA PROJECT

"The plausibility of the story will thrill any conspiracy theorists while the accuracy and thoroughness should satisfy the science fiction fan in us . . . In the end, *The Cassandra Project* is more than just a science fiction novel. Jack McDevitt and Mike Resnick have created a credible mystery with just enough historical influence to make you think—wait, this could have really happened?"

—Examiner.com

"McDevitt and Resnick take us along on a well-written ride through all sorts of backdoor deals and hidden secrets before they tell us what really happened . . . as they rewrite history in a way that doesn't conflict with what we think we know."

—*The Florida Times-Union*

"*The Cassandra Project* paints a new history for NASA. The novel explores where NASA has been and where it is going. It wraps that history in a thrilling mystery that, in part, provides an explanation for what the Watergate scandal was really about."

—*Orson Scott Card's InterGalactic Medicine Show*

"The apparent cover-up conspiracy at the heart of [the novel] is peeled back layer by layer through an elaborate series of plot twists and turns." —*The Press-Sentinel*

continued . . .

JACK McDEVITT

"The logical heir to Isaac Asimov and Arthur C. Clarke."
—Stephen King

"Jack McDevitt is a master of describing otherworldly grandeur."
—*The Denver Post*

" 'Why read Jack McDevitt?' The question should be: 'Who among us is such a slow pony that s/he *isn't* reading McDevitt?' "
—Harlan Ellison

"You should definitely read Jack McDevitt."
—Gregory Benford

MIKE RESNICK

"Resnick is thought-provoking, imaginative . . . and above all galactically grand."
—*Los Angeles Times*

"Nobody spins a yarn better than Mike Resnick."
—Orson Scott Card

"Mike Resnick is a journeyman in a world of apprentices, one who knows his craft. His name on a book guarantees a solid story and believable characters, constructed with imagination and grace."
—Raymond E. Feist

"One of the most daring and prolific writers in SF. There's no subject he won't explore, and he always delivers."
—David Brin

THE
CASSANDRA
PROJECT

Jack McDevitt
and Mike Resnick

ACE BOOKS, NEW YORK

THE BERKLEY PUBLISHING GROUP
Published by the Penguin Group
Penguin Group (USA) LLC
375 Hudson Street, New York, New York 10014

USA • Canada • UK • Ireland • Australia • New Zealand • India • South Africa • China

penguin.com

A Penguin Random House Company

THE CASSANDRA PROJECT

An Ace Book / published by arrangement with Mike Resnick and Cryptic, Inc.

For information, address: The Berkley Publishing Group,
a division of Penguin Group (USA) LLC,
375 Hudson Street, New York, New York 10014.

ISBN: 978-0-425-25645-9

PUBLISHING HISTORY
Ace hardcover edition / November 2012
Ace mass-market edition / November 2013

PRINTED IN THE UNITED STATES OF AMERICA

10   9   8   7   6   5   4   3   2   1

Cover photo of "moon" by David Huntley/Shutterstock Images;
illustration by S. Miroque.
Cover design by Rita Frangie.

For Barry Malzberg,
who has been a good friend to us both

ACKNOWLEDGMENTS

We are indebted for the assistance of Walter Cuirle and David DeGraff, who managed the special effects. And to our editor, Ginjer Buchanan.

1

It was probably a sign of the times that the biggest science story of the twenty-first century, and probably the biggest ever, broke in that tabloid of tabloids, *The National Bedrock*. It might have gone unnoticed had an enterprising reporter not launched it into the middle of a press conference intended to be a quiet, nostalgic celebration of NASA's accomplishments over a span of sixty years. And to get everyone's mind off the fact that the Agency was now looking at a closing of the doors. In any case, when it first happened, nobody recognized it for what it was.

NASA's public affairs director, Jerry Culpepper, was in total control, fielding questions, returning glowing responses, admitting that, yes, we knew the Agency had fallen on hard economic times, as had the rest of the country, but there was much to commemorate, much to feel good about, and that was where our attention should be focused on this historic day.

It was July 20, 2019, exactly fifty years since Apollo XI had touched down on the Moon. Jerry stood before a large canvas depicting Neil Armstrong, Michael Collins, and Buzz Aldrin, gathered around a control panel, looking down at a lunar landscape. Jerry, carried away by the emotions of the day, was riding with them.

The event was being held just off the lobby, in a room that

would be dedicated to exhibits from that first landing. Space helmets, moon rocks, astronaut uniforms, and the logbook (signed by each of the astronauts) would be on display. Photos of a Saturn V, a lunar module, the Kennedy Space Center, the Sea of Tranquility, adorned the walls. "They set a high standard for us," he said, speaking of the eighteen astronauts who'd made the six lunar flights. It was a statement he immediately regretted, because it overlooked the legion of men and women who'd ridden the big rockets before and since, who'd put their lives on the line and, in some cases, had made the supreme sacrifice. He thought about correcting himself but could see no way to do it gracefully. So he moved on, talking without notes, and finished with a line he'd often used in guest appearances: "As long as we remember who we are, they will not be forgotten."

He looked out over his audience and spread his hands. "Questions?"

Hands went up all over the room. "Diane." That was Diane Brookover, of *The New York Times*.

Jerry didn't care much for Diane. She was okay in a routine social setting, but she enjoyed trying to make him look foolish. Of course, that was true of reporters in general, but she was particularly good at it, especially when she smiled. She was smiling then. Whatever. Best to get her out of the way early. "Jerry," she said, "why does the government need a NASA Hall of Fame when they already have one for the astronauts? I mean, aren't you really putting this thing up simply to distract attention from the fact that NASA's closing down?"

"We're not closing down, Diane," he said. "It's true, we've entered an era of austerity. No one's denying that, but we'll still be here when your grandkids show up to take one of the tours. Look, there are good times and bad. That's inevitable. We'll ride this one out, as we always have. As to the Hall itself, the astronauts have, since the beginning, been our go-to guys, the people out front. The problem is that they are *so* significant, and *so* visible, we tend to miss others who've also made major contributions—the scientists, the engineers, the computer specialists. We're a team. We've always been a team. From the first day, back in 1960. Without the support people, the ones behind the scenes, the achievements of the past sixty years would never have happened. So the Hall of Fame is a way for us to recognize *everybody*, including some major contributors the public has never really known about."

Jerry was quiet and shy except when he had an audience. Then it seemed as if a different personality took over. He smiled easily, connected with everyone, and enjoyed his work. It was a valuable capability, especially in those rapidly darkening times.

The hands went up again. He looked over at Quil Everett, from NBC. Quil was tall, lanky, prematurely gray, with a vaguely British accent. "Jerry, where do you think NASA will be in ten years?"

Jerry glanced at the ceiling, as if NASA were headed for the stars. "Quil, if you can tell me what the fiscal situation will be for the government, I could probably answer that question with some precision. If we get the resources, I think you'd be surprised at what we might accomplish. If not, at the very worst, we'll be right here, waiting for the future to arrive."

Barry Westcott, from *USA Today*, was next. "Jerry," he said, "when Gene Cernan brought the last Moon mission home, he was turning out the lights on the entire American manned space effort. Wouldn't you agree that's exactly what happened, just that it's taken a long time for us to realize it? The biggest thing we've done since has been to send robots around the solar system."

That brought a deadly silence. "Let's keep in mind," Jerry said, "that it wasn't Cernan who turned off the lights. It was Richard Nixon. The Agency was ready to move on. But we were caught in a war, there was no money available. And the truth is that we had a president who really didn't care that much." That was over the line. He wasn't supposed to criticize presidents, past or current, but thinking about Nixon always got his blood pressure up.

And the moment arrived: Warren Cole lifted a hand. Cole was from the AP, and he was seated in his customary spot up front, frowning, staring down at something on his lap. It looked like a copy of one of those garish tabloids.

"Jerry," he said in a warning tone, "have you seen the current copy of *The National Bedrock*?"

The press officer smiled politely. "No, I haven't, Warren. Guess I missed it this week."

"They have a story about some of the material put out by NASA a few days ago."

The Agency had released a mountain of documents, audios, and videos going back to its first year, tracking the history of the U.S. space effort. Jerry had been looking through them that morning. Building his sense of what might have been. He'd seen a copy of the original 1960 message distributed through the armed forces seeking volunteers for an astronaut program. The video of John Kennedy speaking to Congress in 1961, promising that we would land on the Moon before the end of the decade. Walter Cronkite describing the liftoff of Apollo XI. And boxes of documents recording everything, from ordering the upgrading of computers at the Johnson Space Center in Houston to detailed reports on the losses of the *Challenger* and *Columbia*, and the deaths of Roger Chaffee, Virgil "Gus" Grissom, and Edward White in a training accident.

"There's a lot of stuff there, Warren," he said. "Is there something specific you're interested in?"

He got to his feet. "May I play something for you? From the audios?"

"Sure. But keep it short, okay?"

Cole held up a gooseberry. "They recorded part of a conversation between Sidney Myshko, who was the commander on one of the early lunar flights, and Mission Control. It was an orbital mission in January 1969. Six months before Neil Armstrong landed on the Moon. There's only a minute or two, and it's packaged with a lot of other communications. But this one segment is particularly interesting. The first voice is Myshko's. And you should be aware that the mission at that time had reached the Moon and was in orbit." He thumbed the device.

MYSHKO: *Houston, approaching launch point.*
HOUSTON: *You are go for launch.*
MYSHKO: *Four minutes.*
HOUSTON: *Copy that.*
MYSHKO: *It's incredible, Houston.*
HOUSTON: *Keep in mind we are going to lose communications when you pass over the horizon.*
MYSHKO: *Roger that.* (Pause) *We are in the LEM. Ready to go.*
HOUSTON: *Good luck, guys.*

Jerry frowned. He couldn't get past the first line. *"Approaching launch point."*

"Jerry, this is supposed to be strictly an orbital flight. And it's several months before Apollo XI. But they're talking as if they're getting ready to go down to the surface."

"That can't be right, Warren."

"Want me to play it again?" The place had gone dead silent.

"Please."

"We are in the LEM." The LEM, the Lunar Excursion Module, was the vehicle that would have served as the lander had they been going to the surface. *"Ready to go."*

"Warren," said Jerry, "there's obviously a communications breakdown there somewhere."

Cole lifted the gooseberry. Stared at it. "I guess. Can you explain how a breakdown like that could have occurred?"

Jerry tried laughing. "I'd say it was a joke. In case any reporters were listening."

"Seriously, Jerry."

"All right. Look, this is the first time I've heard this. So I have no way of knowing what was going on. I suspect they were just rehearsing. We all know how these flights are. You do everything as you would on the actual mission except land. That's not hard to believe, is it?"

"It just seems very odd."

There'd been two other test flights to the Moon after the Myshko mission. One commanded by Aaron Walker in April, and Apollo X, by Thomas Stafford, in May. Then Apollo XI had launched, and the world changed. "Warren, these details are a bit before my time."

"Mine, too, Jerry."

There was a rising buzz in the room. Cal McMurtrie, seated behind Cole, was asking Cole if it was true, was that really in the package, where was it exactly?

"Well," said Jerry, "there's obviously been a gaffe somewhere. It's probably just a ground-based test run of some sort. Is it dated?"

"January 14, 1969."

"Let me check on it, and I'll get back to you." He looked around the room and picked someone who traditionally gave him no trouble. "Sara."

Mary Gridley was NASA's Administrator. She was a decent boss even though hers was a purely political appointment. As, for that matter, was Jerry's. She was waiting for him out in the corridor. "What the hell happened?" she said. It was less a question than an accusation. Mary was tall, taller than he was, and she had a voice like a drill. She was one of the smartest people Jerry had ever known and fully capable of manipulating anybody to get what she wanted. But she concentrated her efforts on making NASA work rather than centering them, like other bosses in Jerry's experience, on her own career. She had little tolerance for screwups. And it was evident from the look in her eyes that somebody had screwed up. He was pretty sure he knew who it had been.

"You saw the press conference?" he asked, knowing damned well she had. But he needed a moment to organize his defenses.

She pointed back down the passageway in the direction of her office. Then she spun on her heel and Jerry—though he walked beside her—followed her back. She didn't say anything more until the door had closed behind them. Then she exhaled. "Jerry," she said, "that was supposed to be a celebration out there."

It was indeed. Jerry had expected to spend the morning talking about moonwalks and robot missions to Jupiter and Voyagers and the International Space Station. He'd been ready with Buzz Aldrin's famous line about not getting so lost in cleaning up social messes that we forget about the stars, and Neil deGrasse Tyson's comment that he was tired of driving around the block, boldly going where hundreds had gone before, and that he would gladly sign on for a ride to a new world. He'd had a dozen other quotes ready to go that, somehow, hadn't shown up. "I know—" he said. "I didn't expect—"

"Jerry. You let the situation get away from you. Anything like that happens again, just admit there's a misunderstanding somewhere and *move on*. Don't stand there talking it to death. That business with Sidney Myshko—"

"I'm sorry, Mary."

"I thought you were smarter than that." She sighed. "Don't *ever* let them take control of the conversation. Anytime you do that, you're going to lose." She sat down behind her desk and shook her head. "We'll need to find out what happened, if we can, and put out a formal statement. The damned thing's already gone viral."

"You're kidding," he said.

She touched her keyboard, and the display lit up. She'd done a search for *Sidney Myshko Jerry Culpepper*. The screen showed 28,726 postings. He leaned forward to get a better look:

When Did We Really Go to the Moon? NASA Spokesman Culpepper Hasn't a Clue

Confusion at NASA: Government Can't Get Its Facts Straight

These Are the Guys in Charge of Space Shots?

Did Somebody Land on the Moon Before Armstrong?

Conspiracy Theorists Back in Force

It Was Neil Armstrong, Dummy

Jerry stopped at his secretary's desk on the way into his office. "Barbara," he said, "get Al Thomas for me, please."

He went inside, closed the door, and collapsed into a chair. *Amazing how trivial stuff becomes such a big deal. Especially in government.*

The office walls and the desk top were covered with framed pictures from his career. Jerry standing beside President Cunningham at a NASA dinner. Jerry chatting amiably with the governor of Florida. Laughing it up with Senator Tilghman. Shaking hands with Jon Stewart. Jerry was up there with all kinds of celebrated people from the political and entertainment worlds. But there wasn't a single photo of an astronaut.

There weren't any astronauts anymore. Hadn't been for years.

He'd been watching the news before going down to the luncheon. Ironically, he'd left the TV on, and it was now running an old *Star Trek*. Captain Kirk giving orders to raise shields and man battle stations.

His alert dinged, and the *Enterprise* blinked off and was replaced by Al Thomas's amiable features. "Hi, Jerry," he said in his trademark baritone. He sounded like an action-movie star. In fact, he was a skinny little guy with thick glasses. "I was about to call you."

Al was in Huntsville, where he oversaw NASA's archives.

"You saw the press conference?"

"I heard about it."

"What happened? Where'd that thing come from?"

"I don't know. I have my people going back over the record now, trying to figure it out."

"Was it really in the package?"

"Oh, yes. I was hoping it wouldn't be there. It would save a lot of work. The records from that era aren't exactly digital. Something like that can be hard to find. We'll need a little time."

"Who was the CAPCOM?" The guy on the Houston end of the transmissions.

"Hold on a second." Al was thumbing through documents in a folder. "Here it is. Frank Kirby. I thought that was his voice. He was there for most of the missions during the lunar era."

"Assume it *is* their voices, Kirby's and Myshko's, is there any way that could have happened? Might it have been, for example, a practice run-through of some sort?"

Barbara's radio was playing in the outer office. Sounded like the Downtowners singing about women and bullet trains. "Sure," Al said. "It could have been anything. Probably, they were just screwing around during off time, playing out what they desperately would have liked to do. All those guys wanted to make the landing. But sure, it had to be something like that."

"Okay, Al. Look, let me know if you get something more, okay?"

"Absolutely, Jerry. Umm—are they upset over there?"

"It'll pass. Mary doesn't like it much when the organization looks silly."

"Yeah. They're on my case here, too. I can't believe they actually expected me to vet all that stuff." He sounded rattled. "Anyway, I'm sorry we made a problem for you."

Jerry wondered whether he should mention the incident in the NASA blog. He didn't want to do anything to extend the story, but he'd be perceived as ducking it if he didn't say *something*. He started a response, *It doesn't take much to excite the media.* Then deleted it. It's never a good idea to attack the reporters. He grinned. Especially if you're a public-relations guy. Maybe substitute *public* for *media.* Yeah, that might do it.

Barbara's voice broke in: "Jerry, you have a visitor."

He glanced at his calendar. Nothing was scheduled. "Who is it, Barb?"

"Morgan Blackstone."

Blackstone? The overhyped cowboy billionaire who was always talking about taking America into space? What the hell could he want with Jerry? "Okay," he said, as if Blackstone stopped by every day, "send him in."

He tapped his keyboard and brought up a proposal Mary had made for an unmanned Mars mission. It had gone nowhere. He was gazing steadily at it, pretending to be absorbed, when the door opened. He held up a hand, busy at the moment, have a seat, be right with you. Jerry tapped the display a couple of times and made a face. Then he looked up.

He was accustomed to dealing with people in high places, but he felt immediately intimidated. Blackstone was one of those men who could walk into a party at the White House and take over the room. He towered over Jerry, who, at five-eight, disappeared easily into crowds. An irritating smile suggested he was bestowing a favor merely by being there. Thick black hair and an unruly mustache added to the cowboy mystique. He obviously worked out a lot, and he walked like John Wayne. He'd have looked perfectly at home with six-guns strapped to his hips.

Despite all that, Jerry could have tolerated him except that the son of a bitch made a habit of criticizing NASA. The Agency was a waste of government funding. Bureaucrats bound for Mars but traveling by dog cart. A few weeks ago, on *Meet the Press*, he'd commented that NASA had gone to the Moon a half century ago, come home, and been sitting on the front porch ever since.

Jerry did not normally rise when men came into his office. But somehow he found himself on his feet. "Please," he said, "have a seat, Mr. Blackstone." He indicated the wing chair, which was his preferred location for visitors. It was a bit lower than the other chairs. "What can I do for you?"

Blackstone ignored the chair. "You can start, Jerry, by calling me 'Bucky.'"

"It's a pleasure to meet you, Bucky." The billionaire came forward and shook his hand. Jerry leaned back on the desk, and Blackstone finally sat down. "How's everything going with Blackstone Enterprises?"

Blackstone nodded. "Well enough," he said. "I guess the truth is that we're having an easier time than NASA."

"You probably don't have all the facts," Jerry said. "We're doing all right."

His visitor nodded. "Every time the government has a problem, they cut your funding."

"We're still here."

"I'm glad to hear it, Jerry." He cleared his throat. "I suspect the country will always be in good shape as long as NASA is here and functioning."

"We like to think so, Bucky." Blackstone glanced back toward the outer office. The Downtowners were doing "The Frankford El." The volume had gone down, but it was still audible. He signaled surprise that Jerry would permit such moonshine. "Guilty pleasure," Jerry said. "What can I do for you?"

Blackstone smiled benignly. He understood perfectly. We all have weaknesses. "I saw the press conference this morning," he said.

Jerry nodded. "Odd story, wasn't it?"

"Oh, yes." He sat back, relaxed, crossed his legs. "More years ago than I care to remember, I did public relations for the Stanfield Corporation. Nothing at the level you're operating at, of course. But I remember how unnerving it could be. You were always at the mercy of the unexpected."

"That's certainly true."

"I thought you handled yourself pretty well, Jerry."

"Thank you."

"Were you able to find out how it happened? The conversation between Myshko and ground control? What was it, some sort of test run?"

"Probably. We haven't tracked it down yet, Bucky." He didn't feel comfortable using the man's first name. "But I can't imagine what else it could have been."

"Of course. I thought maybe it was a hoax. That somebody added it to the information released by NASA."

"At this point, we just don't know. We'll figure it out."

Blackstone leaned back and shook his head. "Strange things happen." He had dark, piercing eyes, narrow cheeks, and a no-nonsense manner.

"I guess," Jerry said. "Did you come in for the press conference? I didn't see you in the room anywhere."

"No. I was up talking to your boss. Afterward, I went down to the cafeteria for lunch. I always like eating here. You never know whom you might meet. Anyhow, that's where I saw it. Just the last fifteen minutes or so."

Jerry wasn't sure how to respond. So he made a sound deep in his throat and nodded.

"Jerry, I know your time is valuable, and I don't want to take it up unnecessarily." Blackstone smiled, and much of the hardness went away. "Despite what we'd like to see happen, we both know NASA's time is done. Over. There's a lot of pressure right now by the corporates who feed off NASA to keep you going, and that's the only thing keeping it afloat."

"I'm not sure I agree."

"It's okay. We can debate it another time. At the moment, we both know UPY and MagLev and all the rest of them have made a fair income selling Saturns and test vehicles and God knows what else to the government for sixty years. They're not in the same league with the armaments industry, but there's still a lot of money involved. Today, though, times are changing. The government's under a lot of pressure. Next year's an election year, and the public is up in arms. They've had it with billions spent for a program that doesn't do anything. You know as well as I do that the Hall of Fame is a diversion, the latest step in a general shutdown."

"That's not going to happen, Bucky."

Blackstone shrugged. Jerry's opinion was of no consequence. "The president's going to have to show more progress in cutting costs than he's been able to do so far. He's even going to go after the Pentagon, I hear. You really think he won't be coming after you? After NASA, that is?"

"They've already hit us pretty hard. We're still here, though. We'll still be here when I retire."

Blackstone's eyebrows rose, and an amused smile appeared. "You know, Jerry, the truth is that, okay, you need public funding at the start for something like a space program. You have to have it. The project's just too big, the risk too great, for any individual company. But once you get it off the ground, the best way, the way that's always worked most effectively in this country, is to turn it over to private industry. If Nixon had done that in, say, 1973, it's hard to say where we might be by now."

Jerry didn't really want to get into an argument. And in any case, he knew there was some justification for what Blackstone was saying. So he held out his hands, suggesting that the future was anybody's guess. "How about some coffee, Bucky?"

"Thanks," he said. "But I should be on my way."

"Okay."

"If we're ever really going to get back to the Moon, put together a manned expedition to Mars, do anything like that, it will be a private entity that does it, probably a group of corporations. I came here today to talk with Mary Gridley about some areas where we can help each other. And I watched you in that press conference when they asked you about the Myshko flight.

"You handled yourself pretty well, Jerry. NASA will never get to Mars. You know that as well as I do. But *we* will. Blackstone Enterprises. If you're interested, when we leave, we'd like you to come along."

"You're offering me a job?"

"I need a good public-relations officer. I have a good one in Ed Camden, but I'll admit to you that he doesn't believe in what we're doing. I need somebody to be the face of the organization, a true believer. Someone who understands that we belong in space. That we have to get clear of this world if we're ever going to be more than simply a lot of people sitting around watching television. That we'll continue to evolve as a civilization."

"Bucky," Jerry said, "I appreciate the offer. It's very kind of you."

"But—?"

"I'm committed here. I just don't agree that a single corporation or a corporate group can manage a project of this size. I think that, if the United States government can't do it, if NASA doesn't do it, it's not going to happen."

"Jerry, the future's with us."

"I wish you luck. But you'll have to show me."

"We will. In any case, the offer's on the table. But it won't be there forever."

———————

Jerry was the most visible person in NASA, save for the old astronauts. That was like being the biggest satellite in Earth orbit, except for the Moon. Nevertheless, Jerry got a lot of calls from strangers. Barbara deflected the majority of them. They tended to be from people asking how they could become astronauts, meet astronauts, or get astronauts to help out in various fundraising events. A few were from cranks who complained that NASA was spending too much money or wanted to know why we weren't on Mars. And some even wanted to report meetings with aliens or UFO sightings.

Occasionally, she passed one that mattered on to him. "From somebody named Harkins," she said. "He says he's a former Navy captain. And that it's important."

"Did he say what it's about, Barb?"

"Negative. Insists he'll talk only to you, Boss."

———————

The guy was easily in his eighties. White hair brushed back, bifocals, cracked voice. But he sat straight up in a leather chair, his wrists draped over the armrests. "My name's James Harkins, Mr. Culpepper," he said. "I used to fly choppers for the Navy."

Jerry could see the flickering light of a fire in the background. "Yes, Mr. Harkins, what can I do for you?"

"I'm not sure that what I have to say will be of any interest to you. But I think it's time for someone to know. I watched you earlier today."

"Okay. What did you want to tell me, sir?"

"I was aboard the *Kennedy* when it picked up the Myshko team. There were three of them on board, of course." The other astronauts had been Louie "Crash" Able and Brian Peters.

Jerry had a sinking feeling. Whether it was a suspicion that he was about to hear something that would undercut his convictions or because he was going to discover that Harkins wasn't as sane as he looked, he couldn't be sure. "You actually helped pick them up?"

"No. But I was on deck when they were brought in."

"All right. So what did you want to tell me?"

"Maybe nothing, really. Nothing that makes any sense. But it's always bothered me, and I'd just written it off until I heard about that radio exchange. Between the capsule and ground control."

"What did you see, Captain?"

"We pulled three astronauts out of the water, Mr. Culpepper. They all had bags with them. Well, no big deal about that. It's what you'd expect. But one of them stumbled coming on board and dropped the bag on the deck. I don't remember which one it was."

"And—?"

"A couple of rocks fell out."

"That's it?"

"Mr. Culpepper, these guys were riding a Saturn rocket. Weight mattered. Why would any of them take along a couple of rocks?"

2

Had he accepted Blackstone's offer, Jerry would have been perceived by his colleagues as betraying the organization. And betraying *them*. It would be an admission that he believed NASA's mission had effectively ended. That the future for the organization had run out. It would also, he thought, be a betrayal of himself.

He loved working for NASA. Loved what it stood for. The ongoing lack of funding, which continued year after year, decade after decade, was frustrating. Infuriating. He was not a little kid, was not affected by idle dreams of flying to the Moon so we could say we'd done it. He believed relentlessly that humanity had to move on or slide backward. That the planet was becoming too crowded. That there were practical reasons to establish a foothold beyond the home world. He wasn't sure precisely what the nature of that foothold should be. But he knew that it required the presence of an active United States.

But somewhere down the line, we'd sold out.

Jerry had worked on several political campaigns, including the gubernatorial and presidential runs of President Cunningham. He'd done public relations for Ohio State, for the Pentagon, and for the Carmichael & Henry law firm. In all those situations, everyone on board had understood that they were there to sell a product. His colleagues in the various government agencies felt the same way. The connection was strictly business. Even the political campaigns. There'd been no sense of destiny in the wind, of inevitable disaster if Laura Hopkins had made it into the Oval Office instead of George Cunningham. They all pretended to believe the fate of the nation rested on the election, but everybody knew that the nation would survive however the vote tally went. But with NASA, it was somehow different.

Cape Canaveral was the gateway to the world beyond. That was where it was all supposed to happen. And if they'd been a little slower to roll out the future than everyone had expected, it wasn't the fault of the Agency. The money, and the political will, had never been there. They'd gone to the Moon, and somehow, for the politicians at least, the luster came off. There was nowhere else to go. Mars was too far. Nobody cared about robot missions. Nobody cared about orbiting telescopes. Consequently, NASA had been left to its own devices. No politician dared close it down, though, because the space agency had somehow become inextricably interconnected with America. But they left it on a subsistence diet. Jerry's packing up and heading out to Blackstone Enterprises, Inc., would ruin his reputation with those who understood what the Agency represented. And these were people he cared about. Blackstone wanted nothing so much as to bring down the Agency.

Jerry sat in his office watching rain clouds roll in from the west. He'd taken the job there with some reluctance. Mary had been George's campaign manager in Ohio and later an active participant in his successful run for the White House. At the president's suggestion, she'd hired Jerry, who'd come to the Cape without enthusiasm. Everyone knew the Agency was a ticket to nowhere. But his attitude had changed during his two and a half years on the Space Coast. He'd become a certified true believer. If we were to get off world, Jerry knew, NASA was indispensable.

Barbara's voice broke through the clouds: "Jerry, Al's on the line."

Returning Jerry's call. She put him on-screen, and he smiled uncomfortably. "I checked the transmissions, Jerry," he said, staring down at a piece of paper on his desk. "They are correct." Al was close to retirement, and he looked it. He was tired and ready to go. His skull gleamed in the light from a lamp.

"Okay."

"I'm sorry. I wish I could have warned you. But there's just no way. We don't have the people—"

"It's all right, Al."

"Is there anything else?"

"Actually, yes. I need a favor. Can you send me the complete record of the Myshko flight? The communications? Everything?"

"Sure," he said. "But I can probably have one of my people do a search if you just tell me what you're looking for."

"I'm not sure what I'm looking for, Al."

"You'll know it when you see it?"

"Exactly."

He nodded. Frowned. "Jerry?"

"Yes?"

"Look, I can tell you you'd be wasting your time. I've read through the transcripts. I think they were just screwing around, Myshko and the CAPCOM."

"You're probably right, Al. If they were, though, I need to know about it."

"Okay." He sucked in some air. "You'll have it before you go home tonight."

The Myshko mission had lifted off January 11, 1969, and returned January 21. Their objective had been to test various equipment and take pictures. The operation did *not* include sending a lunar module, manned or otherwise, to the lunar surface.

We are in the LEM. Ready to go. You couldn't really mistake the meaning. But it had to be a joke. Myshko no doubt grinning in the cabin, and Frank Kirby, the CAPCOM, getting a good laugh on the ground.

It was a gag they'd shared. Nothing more than that. Couldn't be anything more.

Except that Captain Harkins believed he'd seen a couple of rocks.

After the comment about the lander, there'd been no more exchanges for about forty minutes, until the ship emerged from behind the Moon, and transmissions became possible once more. Then they'd talked about position and course and life-support status and fuel usage. No further mention of the LEM.

In less than an hour, it was back behind the Moon. When it emerged a second time, they returned to exchanging routine data. Everything was working fine.

But there was a different voice speaking from the ship.

The new voice spoke with Kirby. It was all routine stuff. Position. Calibration of something or other. Fuel levels. Jerry did not hear the original voice as the vehicle moved across the lunar face. Then it slipped behind the Moon again. He moved ahead until it was back in the visible sky. Still the new voice. Ditto on the next pass. And on the next.

He checked the accompanying data, which informed him that the second speaker had been Brian Peters, the command module pilot. He was the guy who, in an actual landing, would stay behind while the commander and the LEM pilot went down to the surface.

It continued that way for twenty-seven orbits. Peters's voice was the only one on the circuit. Peters reporting all was well, keeping Mission Control updated on life-support status, occasionally commenting on how beautiful the home world was.

Then, without warning, almost fifty hours after he'd last been heard from, Myshko was back. "Houston, Crash thinks he may have spotted some ice in the north," he said, "but it's probably just a reflection. Reaction control hasn't been what we'd expected, but we'll give you details when we get home. We've also got a busted strut. Other than that, we're good."

Myshko did most of the talking on the way back, as he had on the flight out. "Crash" was Louie Able, the LEM pilot. He apparently never got near the onboard comm system.

Barbara came in to say good night. She was a good-looking brunette, mother of two boys, six and seven, both of whom had told Jerry they wanted to be astronauts so they could go to Mars one day.

Jerry had never married. Never found the time, really. Or maybe it was that the one woman for whom he would have been willing to give up his freedom had dumped him. He'd never really gotten over that. Consequently, he didn't allow himself to get serious about anyone. But there were evenings—and this was one of them—when he'd have liked to have someone to go home to. Someone special.

He lived in a third-floor condo north of Titusville off Route 1 near the Brevard Community College. On restless nights, he tended to work late. There were always people wandering around at the Space Center, the dedicated types he'd felt sympathy for when he'd first arrived, people who seemed to have no lives outside the Agency. Somehow, through a process he didn't understand, he'd become one of them.

So he strolled through the building that evening, talking to technicians who were trying to solve this or that problem because they claimed they couldn't sleep with it hanging over their heads. Or with security people. Or with accountants working late.

A tour group was wandering through the new Hall of Fame. There were about twenty of them, led by one of the guides, a young woman. She was talking about Gus Grissom, Roger Chaffee, and Ed White. It sent a chill through him, reminding him of the sacrifices NASA's men and women had been willing to make. He was feeling some regret that he hadn't accepted Blackstone's offer. And that realization, coming while he walked through a place dedicated to NASA's heroes, induced a sense of guilt.

Maybe he'd been taken over by the mission, and maybe *that* was what deserved his loyalty, rather than the Agency.

Funny how your footsteps have a louder echo at night.

Jerry would have liked to talk with one of the astronauts on the Myshko flight, but its commander and Brian Peters had both been dead more than a decade. Myshko had succumbed to cancer just after the turn of the century, and Peters, a few years later, had lost a battle with clogged arteries.

Louie Able had died four months ago, ironically, in a plane crash. He'd been eighty-six.

But Frank Kirby, the CAPCOM, was still around.

The CAPCOM, or capsule communicator, was the principal ground connection with an in-flight mission. An astronaut was usually selected for the assignment, on the assumption that no one was better qualified to handle a problem in space than somebody who'd been there.

Jerry had met Kirby about a year ago, when he'd sponsored a visit to NASA by a group of elementary-school students from Orlando, where he lived. It had been no more than an introduction, and Jerry had carried away no memory of the man save that he'd seemed happy surrounded by the kids. Kirby had been retired more than twenty years, but he'd apparently stayed active in the community. He was a member of the Friends of the Library, he'd led an effort to improve recreational facilities for children throughout the city, he'd been involved in a campaign to promote safety for the blind by upgrading traffic-light technology. And he was a volunteer at a shelter for battered women.

When, the following morning, Jerry mentioned his name to Mary, she said yes, that she'd had a chance to talk with him when he'd been at the Space Center. "He's a decent guy," she said. "But I hope you're not leading up to what I think you are."

"It would be interesting," Jerry said, "just to sit down and talk with him. Hear what he has to say."

"I think," she said, "it would be a good idea to leave it alone. You show up out there, and he'll know exactly what you're after. If there was anything going on, I don't think he's likely to open up to a guy who just appears on his doorstep. Let it go, Jerry."

But Jerry wasn't going to be put off that easily. "I was going to suggest," he said, "that we bring him here. Give him an award of some kind. It would be a very nice public-relations move. In fact, it's something we should have done years ago. We'd get a lot of good publicity by recognizing the community work of someone connected with NASA. We could bring him in for an award luncheon, give him a plaque, and it would cost nothing. This is a difficult time for us, Mary, and it would remind the public of the kind of people we have working here."

They were in her office. The blinds were pulled against a bright sun. Mary sat for a moment without moving, then literally snickered at him. "Jerry, do you think Kirby would be so dumb that he wouldn't know what it was all about?"

"Well, you'd be surprised what people will buy into when you tell them stuff they want to hear. No, I think we'd have no trouble getting away with it."

"Okay, let's say this guy, who used to be a Navy pilot, who was one of our astronauts, doesn't have a brain in his head. He comes up here to accept an award. Do you think he might figure it out when you start asking him about Myshko?"

"I'll be careful. I can manage it so *he* brings up the topic."

She clearly did not approve of the idea. "Jerry, may I ask you a question?"

"Sure."

"Are you saying that you think Myshko might actually have landed on the Moon? And then, for reasons unknown, they kept it quiet? Is that your theory?"

"Of course not. But *something* happened."

"*What?* What could possibly have happened?"

"I don't know."

"If they landed, if they actually went down, what possible reason could they have had for covering it up?"

Jerry started thinking again about Blackstone. Maybe he should reconsider. Maybe he should jump over to Bucky's outfit. It would be easier if Blackstone himself weren't so despicable. "Maybe they were embarrassed that Myshko took things into his own hands. It would have been a public humiliation."

She shook her head. "Preposterous. They'd have been embarrassed, yes. But landing somebody on the Moon would have far outweighed that."

"What's wrong with giving ourselves a chance to find out? You want to spend the rest of your life wondering whether, maybe, something *did* happen?"

She took a deep breath. Put her tongue in the side of her cheek. "All right," she said, "set it up. But, Jerry—"

"Yes?"

"Don't do anything to embarrass us."

The first task was to find a name for the award. Jerry spent several days googling NASA personnel, active and retired, looking for someone who had made a serious contribution to the public welfare. Mary suggested he limit the search to astronauts, but he couldn't see any reason to do that. Aside from those who had landed on the Moon, or those who had died in the performance of their duties, no one else, not even among the remaining astronauts, was familiar to the public. The reality was that the public had never shown any interest in flights that didn't get beyond Earth orbit.

He considered naming the award for Kirby, but that would have been *too* obvious.

Then he found Harry Eastman, the perfect pick. Harry was a retired computer expert who'd spent thirty years with the Agency while simultaneously doing yeoman work for disabled children in Texas. Harry had set up a foundation to raise public awareness of the issue. He'd brought in film and sports celebrities and had accompanied them when they visited hospitals and special needs centers to talk to the kids, shake their hands, and give out souvenirs. The Eastman Foundation became a major fund-raiser for eight or nine charitable organizations. Jerry also liked the name: The Eastman Award had a ring of elegance.

He called Eastman and told him how much he admired what he'd been doing. "NASA would like to promote this kind of work, Harry," he said. "We'd like you to support an annual prize, the Eastman Prize, to someone connected with us. For outstanding contributions to special-needs kids. Or battered women. Whatever fits. "

"I'd be honored," Harry said, speaking from Houston, "but the foundation doesn't really have money to spare. How much would it cost?"

"Just the price of the plaque, Harry. In other words, zero."

"That's very kind of you, Jerry."

"Well, I wouldn't kid you that we're being entirely selfless. We expect to get good publicity out of it. And we've a few people who've been doing the kind of work you have. Not on your scale, but—"

"Let's make it happen," he said.

"Excellent. We'll want you to come in for the first presentation. On our dime, of course."

Harry laughed. He was lean, with gray hair and the kind of narrow, introspective features Jerry associated with people who'd been through painful experiences and hadn't quite gotten past them. He wondered how all the time Eastman had spent with damaged kids had affected him. "I'll be there. When's it happening?"

Jerry asked his deputy, Vanessa Aguilera, to make the call to Kirby. Best was to keep his distance from the project and not let

Kirby know he was involved. "Tell him," he said, "that we wanted to do something special during the opening weeks of the Hall of Fame. And Mary suggested recognizing people associated with the Agency who've been doing public service. Something not having to do with space technology. So we came up with the Eastman Award."

Vanessa was gone about ten minutes, then came back to tell him that Kirby had accepted. "He was excited," she said.

"Excellent," said Jerry.

Vanessa had soft brown hair and large blue eyes. She loved her job and was worried, like everyone else, that the organization was going under. *It's nice*, she was fond of saying, *to be doing work that matters.* If the Agency shut down, *when* it shut down, she didn't want to land eventually with a lumber company or in an Amtrak office doing accounting or answering phones. "He doesn't look well, though," she said.

"How do you mean?"

"Well, he's pretty old. He's in a wheelchair, and he was having a hard time breathing."

"I'm sorry to hear it. Sounds as if he's gone downhill since last year."

"He commented that it seems to be a last-minute arrangement."

Damn. That meant he suspected what was behind the award. Jerry was momentarily surprised that he'd agreed to come if he'd figured it out already. But then Vanessa eased his mind: "He thinks you want to get to him before he passes."

"Oh." Maybe they'd caught a break.

"He seems like a nice guy," she added.

The first Harry Eastman Award would be made at the new Hall of Fame, on the last Thursday of the month, which was three weeks away. Jerry handed most of the organizing details over to Vanessa, issued special invitations to people who'd played a major role in NASA's activities over the years, invited the media, and put together some appropriate remarks for Mary.

He settled back into his normal routine. He oversaw his blog, which was usually written by an intern; contributed to the NASA online presence; coordinated speaking engagements for the

Agency's representatives; made appearances at the University of Georgia and at the University of Central Florida in Orlando.

The LEM story turned into a two-day gag line. Fortunately, it had no traction. Nobody believed there was anything to it. How could there be? Even Warren Cole, when he came by on an unrelated matter, laughed about it. "It's a pity, though," he said. "What a story that would have made."

They were seated in the downstairs dining room. Cole was enjoying a plate of fish and fries, while Jerry, always conscious of his weight, settled for a grilled chicken salad. "You're really disappointed, aren't you, Warren?"

"I can't get disappointed about something I never believed in the first place. Did you find out what they were talking about?"

"Not really. It has to have been a joke."

"Yeah. Pity. It's a story I'd have killed for."

Cole was one of several reporters Jerry used to get stories out. It was always helpful to give someone an exclusive, even if you were planning a formal announcement a day or two later. It was a way of making reporters happy and keeping them on your side.

In this case, though, Jerry had his own motive. "On the subject of Myshko and the LEM," he said, speaking casually, "did you know who the CAPCOM was on the ground?"

Cole thought about it. Shrugged. "Before my time." He studied his fish and fries. And shrugged again. "Why, Jerry? Does it matter?"

"No." Jerry took a large bite of his salad, chewed, and looked out the window. It was a gray, chilly day.

"Then why'd you bring it up?"

"His name's Frank Kirby."

"He's still alive?"

"You got the handout on the Eastman Award?"

"Yes."

"Kirby will be the recipient that night."

Cole was prematurely bald, with a ridge of brown hair around his skull. He squeezed his forehead, rubbed his temples. "The story's dead, Jerry. You're not trying to bring it up again, are you?"

"Of course not. Though I wonder if he knows how close he came to giving the media the story of a lifetime."

Cole made a face like a guy with a toothache. "I think I'll leave it alone."

Jerry smiled. "I'm in favor of that, Warren."

"Have you mentioned this to anybody else?"

"No." Jerry made a science of knowing the media people. Cole would say nothing to anyone. And on the day of the luncheon, he wouldn't be able to resist. That would open the door.

When they'd finished eating, Jerry picked up the tab.

3

Morgan Blackstone looked out the window of his office and was well pleased. Off to the left, covering two acres of ground, was Blackstone Enterprises. To the right, thirty floors high and seeming to reach for the sky, was Blackstone Development. Between the two was the least impressive and most important of his businesses, Blackstone Innovations.

It was amazing, he reflected, what one forty-two-inch bosom could lead to. He'd seen the possessor of that bosom on the beach when he was barely twenty years old, talked her into posing nude in his studio (not that he owned one, but he rented a friend's unused garage), and when no one would pay him what he thought was a fair price for his photos, he decided to publish them himself. He talked some acquaintances into pooling their money—he'd never had trouble raising money—and two months later published the first issue of *Suave*. He'd shared a dorm room with best-selling hard-boiled mystery writer Chuck Bestler's son, got him to invest, and he in turn got Bestler to write the lead story. Blackstone had paid Bestler with 5 percent of the magazine, and Bestler, seeing gold in them thar hills, got all his friends in category fiction to contribute, at which point the magazine was a hit, and Blackstone, who barely knew one end of a camera from the other, hired a pair of top photographers who had their own stables of forty-two-inch models. And long before his twenty-second birthday, Morgan Blackstone was a multimillionaire.

He'd never liked his name, so he created a new *persona*, dressed like a cowboy (but in cowboy duds created on Park Avenue in Manhattan) and signed all his ads and editorials "Bucky." The name and image stuck, and he was "Morgan" only on contracts and tax returns from then on. By the time he turned twenty-three, Blackstone was bored with the magazine. He knew there were more important challenges out there, and he never wanted to become the eighty-year-old embarrassment Hugh Hefner had become, a withered old man pretending he was thirty-five and assuming that people still cared about his notion of the Good Life.

There were a lot of interesting little wars going on, and a lot of puppet governments received hundreds of millions of dollars from their dark masters (or, in the case of the United States' clients, their light masters), and he saw no reason why he shouldn't supply some of their needs. So he put up a million dollars of his own money, then quickly raised another fifteen million (this time as high-interest loans rather than for pieces of his company) and was soon supplying arms to all interested parties.

When he saw the negative publicity his business rivals were receiving, he sold out his interest before any of them could come to stand on his broad shoulders.

Next came the invention of an engine that would run on water. It didn't work, but he let Saudi Petrostock, National Dutch, China National Offshore Oil, American Petroleum, Royal Abu Dhabi, and Kuwaiti Oil Resource pool a quick two hundred million and buy it from him to keep it off the market.

He began casting around for his next business, analyzed his successes, and decided he'd pretty much followed "Wee Willie" Keeler's old dictum from a century earlier: "Hit 'em where they ain't." No one had started a successful men's magazine for a decade and a half before *Suave*, no one had had the chutzpah to supply weapons to warring banana republics in *this* hemisphere, and no one had blackmailed or terrified the auto companies in more than half a century. You had to go all the way back to Tucker, which wasn't quite the same thing since Tucker's car actually worked.

So Blackstone cast around for some other place where "they" weren't, and it wasn't long before he realized that the average state was a good five billion dollars in debt, and some of the larger spendthrifts, like California and Illinois and New York, were each well over fifty billion in the hole.

How could they raise money in a hurry since the federal government wasn't about to bail them out? Easy. They'd legalize gambling. There'd be a hue and cry from some of the more religious sections of the electorate, but some politician would point out that even churches hosted bingo games to raise money, and besides, the alternative was bankruptcy. And within a year, spreading money around various state capitals where it would do the most good, he had built luxury casinos in North Dakota, New Mexico, South Carolina, and Wyoming, and was the major stockholder in a fabulous new racetrack in Montana.

And when the dust had cleared five years later, he was no longer a millionaire, or even a multimillionaire, but had risen to the level of billionaire, and figured to amass his second billion in less than a year.

He looked around again, applying the same principle, and tried to determine where they weren't hitting 'em that year. The landscape was covered with enterprises and innovations, and for the first time, he couldn't spot his next move.

Until he looked *up*.

Then he knew. There was the biggest untouched target of all. Men had walked on it in 1969, and the stars were ours. A colony on the Moon by 1990, on Mars by 2010, then the moons of Jupiter, and surely by 2030 we'd have found a way around Einstein's theory and would be on our way *rapidly* to the stars.

Science said it couldn't be done, that there were laws that governed the universe—but Blackstone knew he came from a race of lawbreakers. Tell a man something can't be done, and he'll set about proving you wrong out of sheer cussedness.

Mars, the outer planets' satellites, the Oort Cloud, the stars, we'd reach them all. But first, the Moon. The government never had any interest in it, except for reaching it before the Russians did. We'd turned our backs on it a long time ago, and it was time to get that colony built. There'd be a mining section, and a low-grav hospital for heart patients (he'd figure out how to get them there, all in good time), and an astronomical observatory, and a refueling point for trips to Mars, and maybe Venus if he could develop space suits that could withstand the heat. Then on to Io and Europa and Ganymede.

And because he knew that this was his last great business venture, because he knew he would spend the rest of his life on it, Blackstone determined not to be just a figurehead but to learn it from the ground up. He spent time in the Public Relations Department, acquired some basic lab skills, even underwent training as an astronaut (though he hated the word and wanted his own term for it, preferably something that incorporated the word *Bucky* or *Blackstone*).

He even considered running for office on a platform of going back into space. Name recognition was no problem; he was a handsome, self-made billionaire, and he and his two ex-wives, both as eye-catching as Miss 42, were featured every week in the supermarket tabloids. But as a senator, he'd be one of one hundred, and he would have to convince fifty very independent—and often very foolish—men and women to vote with him, then hope the House could find 218 members in agreement, and further hope that the president didn't veto whatever initiative he'd launched. He could run for president, of course, and he was sure he could win, but it would take three or four years of organizing and money-raising. He didn't want to take three years away from the Moon to organize a political campaign, and while he could pay for the campaign out of his pocket, he didn't want anyone saying that he bought the presidency.

So, instead of becoming a member of the government, he decided that his best course of action was to *rival* the government, to do what it was too broke or too reluctant or too timid to do, to go back to the Moon and claim it for Blackstone Enterprises (and, incidentally, for the United States of America).

At first, the Congress ignored him, and the press made fun of his ambitious new project. That lasted about six months, until his first successful suborbital flight. By the time a year had passed, a Blackstone ship had made an orbital flight—after all, the technology had existed for half a century—and suddenly Congress decided that he meant business and was in dire need of congressional oversight.

He decided otherwise, only to find himself the object of a scare campaign. He wanted to put missiles on the Moon and fire them at our enemies. The public approved. But he might miss and hit Omaha or Charlotte or Seattle. The public laughed. He had made a secret pact with Hector Morales, the crazed dictator of Paraguay, and had promised to take him to the Moon before his downtrodden masses could rise up and kill him. And put him where? asked the public.

Finally, the government backed off and tried a new approach. "We're incredibly proud of our dear friend and outstanding citizen Bucky Blackstone," they announced, "and we'll do everything we can to help him."

"You can start by getting the hell out of my way," Blackstone had answered through his spokespeople.

"We're on *your* side," said the government. "We have all kinds of knowledge and experience to share with you."

"Keep it," said his spokesman. "And," added Blackstone, "I'll bet you a million dollars I reach the Moon before you do."

And, finally, the government realized that it was not dealing with its notion of a team player, and left him alone. They tried to convince the media to do the same, but even the president's most fawning sycophants in the press couldn't resist story after story of the cowboy billionaire who spit in Washington's collective eye and got away with it.

Everyone at Blackstone Enterprises cheered and congratulated each other. Well, everyone except Blackstone himself. He knew how quickly a winner's fortunes could change, especially in the financial and political arenas.

They needed something more. Everyone loved the notion of a cowboy's defying the government, but he couldn't do it every day, and it would soon become boring if he tried. And he could look ahead and see that he'd be a hero the day he reached the Moon and became the first man to walk on it in more than fifty years—but a month later, unless they found some purple people eaters, it would be a big yawn, just as it was the first time. People just didn't go crazy with enthusiasm at the sight of some rocks, no matter how far away they came from.

But then came these tiny hints about the Myshko flight. Microscopic hints in the beginning . . . but they didn't go away. *Something* wasn't kosher about that mission.

The problem was that it had occurred in 1969. It hadn't been mentioned in half a century. It didn't halt or even slow down the

Apollo XI mission. It had never been mentioned as anything more than it was: a pre-Moon-landing mission, a mission that reached the Moon but never landed, never even intended to land. If they saw anything dangerous, anything out of the ordinary, no one said anything. If they saw any reason for Neil Armstrong not to take a giant leap for mankind, either they never reported it, or else no one took it seriously, and indeed the Apollo XI mission went like clockwork.

Finally, Blackstone called in Ed Camden, who had been his primary spokesman for a year.

"Have you heard anything more about it?" he asked, lighting a cigar and offering one to Camden, who passed.

"About what, sir?"

"The Myshko mission, of course."

Camden shook his head. "I've spoken to my former colleagues at NASA and elsewhere, and no one knows anything. Most of them think it's a totally false lead, that your friends in the Pentagon and the White House are trying to divert you from your purpose."

"They're doing a damned good job of it," admitted Blackstone. "I'll tell you the truth, Ed. All logic says nothing happened because there sure as hell weren't any consequences, and we live in a universe of cause and effect. No effect? Then there was probably no cause."

"Well, there you have it, sir," said Camden.

"It seems so," agreed Blackstone. Suddenly he frowned. "But damn it, Ed, nobody in the Pentagon or NASA is subtle enough for this to be a ruse. Their idea of distracting me would be to release a description of a four-armed fifteen-foot-tall green man riding a thoat, or whatever the hell Edgar Rice Burroughs called it." He paused, took another puff of the cigar, grimaced. "*Something* happened on that Myshko mission, something they don't want us to know about." Suddenly he got to his feet, strolled over to the window, and stared up at the sunlit sky, wishing the Moon were visible. "But what the hell could it be that didn't keep Myshko from returning to Earth, didn't stop any of the Apollo missions, and yet needs a continuing fifty-year cover-up?" He shook his head. "God, it sounds crazy just describing it!"

"That's why we haven't uncovered anything," said Camden. "It *is* crazy."

"No," answered Blackstone adamantly. "I've always listened to my gut, and my gut tells me something happened, something they don't want me to know."

"You?" repeated Camden, surprised even after all these years at his boss's ego.

"All of us," conceded Blackstone. "Everyone." He paused and stared off into space, as if at something only he could see. "And I'm going to find out what it is."

"How? We've pulled just about every string we've got."

"Culpepper."

Camden looked around, frowning.

"It's a man, not a vegetable," continued Blackstone.

"Oh? The guy from NASA?"

Blackstone nodded. "Jerry Culpepper. He's a good man."

"He's a loyal man," said Camden. "He spouts the company line."

"True."

"Well, then?"

"He's also a moral man. Eventually, he won't be able to spout this nonsense any longer."

"You know that for a fact?"

"I'm a pretty good judge of character," answered Blackstone. "I offered him a job."

"My job?" demanded Camden.

"Something similar." Blackstone shrugged off the other man's obvious concern. "I can keep you both busy."

"When does he start?"

"He turned me down," said Blackstone. He relit his cigar. "It was too soon. When he can't stand the pressure any longer, he'll come over here. Another month, another half year, certainly less than a year. And when he comes, he'll confirm what we find out or intuit in the meantime."

"I don't like it," said Camden. "I've been loyal to you for all these years . . ."

"If I was firing you, Ed, I'd tell you up front," replied Blackstone. "You know me well enough to be aware of that. But something happened that they don't want anyone to know about, and they've kept it secret for fifty years. Now suddenly it's starting to seep out. They're going to clamp down, and clamp down hard. That's obvious."

"Then what's this all about?"

"They're going to have to tell Jerry what happened, so he doesn't inadvertently give us enough leads so that we can find out ourselves."

"I don't follow you."

"If Myshko was eaten by Moon lizards, he couldn't say it jokingly, and he couldn't firmly deny it. The first would start people thinking, and the second would start them digging."

"But Myshko came back," Camden pointed out.

"That was just an example, Ed." Blackstone made no attempt to hide his disgust with his underling for not being able to follow his train of thought. "Don't try so hard to convince me that I *should* replace you."

There followed a few awkward minutes. Camden didn't know what to say, and Blackstone began feeling guilty about humiliating him. He finally sent him back to his office and spent the rest of the afternoon pacing his own restlessly, trying for the hundredth time to dope it out: *What are they hiding, and why are they hiding it at this late date? What could possibly have happened that would still affect anything? If it would make a flight to the Moon more dangerous, why won't they tell us? They know I'm going to send up a manned flight within a year. Surely they can't want an American ship, which will be viewed as an American mission by everyone outside the country, to blow up or crash because of something they* could *have told us about and decided, for some reason, not to. So if the mission won't be endangered by our lack of knowledge, what is so goddammed important that they're lying like rugs?*

They *had* to be lying. That was the one certainty. But about what?

He had to force himself to look at it logically.

The ship took off. Check.

The ship circled the Moon. Check.

The ship returned to Earth on schedule. Check.

What the hell could have happened?

He walked to the window and stared out—and up—again. And suddenly he began to get excited. It was almost there, almost within his mental reach. He stood perfectly still, trying to stem his excitement, to just concentrate on the problem—and finally he *had* it!

He knew what had happened, why they had lied—and if he couldn't force the president to tell the country (and he was sure he couldn't, because the president would never admit to lying to the electorate), and he couldn't get Jerry to show him the data he needed, he was going public with what he thought had happened and making the government confirm or deny it before he took off.

Yes, he concluded mentally. To hell with a pair of pilots and three scientists. This was important enough to lose a scientist and add a billionaire cowboy who had figured it out.

4

Jerry was on hand to greet Frank Kirby when he came through the doors of the Hall of Fame. Despite what Jerry had expected, he did not appear feeble. He was permanently confined to a wheelchair, but his voice was strong, and he shook hands with the grip of a professional wrestler. "Jerry," he said, smiling broadly, "it's good to see you again."

"And you, Frank. Welcome home."

He'd been accompanied by several family members although his wife had remained in Orlando. "Janet asked me to say hello," he said. "She wanted to come but just wasn't up to making the trip."

He introduced a son and daughter-in-law, and two grandchildren, both probably in their thirties. Mary came over, and they did another round of introductions. The son, whose name was also Frank, thanked Mary for arranging the event. "Dad has done a lot for Orlando," he said, "since his retirement." Ordinarily, Jerry knew, she would have passed credit for the idea to him, but on this occasion she let it go. Best not to connect him with the award.

They strolled into the main dining area, where Kirby got a surprise: Several friends from his NASA years had been brought in. They surrounded him, laughed, offered toasts, shook hands, embraced, introduced family members, and talked about the old days. A gray-haired woman leaning on a cane flashed a wide smile. "It's good to see you again, Frank," she said. "How many years has it been?"

Frank shook his head. "Too many, Myra."

The VIP table waited at one end of the room, with places set for ten people. A tabletop lectern had been set up. Harry Eastman was already seated, talking with the operations director. Jerry wandered away from the group and sat down in back with Takara Yoshido, a systems designer.

Gradually, the guests drifted in. Mary got Kirby placed and took the seat beside him. The Orlando mayor was also present, as well as Laurie Banner, the president's science advisor. Several representatives from organizations that had benefited at various times from Kirby's support were present. Florida's Senator Mayville was across the room, engaged in a spirited conversation with Eugene Cernan.

"You and Mary did a good job, Jerry," said Takara. Her features took on a dreamy aspect. "It's a beautiful gesture. I like to think that someday maybe I'll be up there to receive the Eastman Award."

"What are you doing now to qualify?" Jerry asked.

"I was looking at Frank's résumé," she said. "I have a Girl Scout troop. I guess I'd have to step things up a bit."

"It's a good start, Taki."

A few reporters, including Cole, were scattered around the room. A TV camera in back would capture the event for the NASA Channel.

Everybody settled in. A few people went up to the head table for autographs or simply to shake hands with the guests. Eventually, the food began to arrive, baked salmon and roast beef, fortified with beets and potatoes and coleslaw. The low hum of conversation was interspersed with clinking silver. Kirby seemed to be enjoying himself, caught in an animated dialogue with Mary on one side and Cernan on the other.

Dessert consisted of chocolate cake and vanilla ice cream. And, finally, it was time for the ceremony.

———

Mary stood, welcomed everyone, and got her first laugh by saying there was a rumor that a manned flight to Mars had entered the planning stage. It was an inside joke, the sort of thing NASA had consistently heard from a range of administrations, usually coming shortly before more funding cuts. "We're also being told," she added, as the room quieted, "that we may even be able to bring them back."

She asked each of the special guests to stand and be recognized. Each got a round of applause. Then she brought Harry Eastman to the microphone to make the presentation.

The plaque, which was wrapped in purple cloth, was already stored out of sight at the lectern. "You all know Frank," he said. He looked in Kirby's direction, and the former astronaut raised a hand to the audience. "He's ridden the shuttles, but he never flew higher than when he reached out to help the children of Orlando." He read a list of the recipient's accomplishments. Then he produced the plaque, removed the cloth, and carried it over to where Kirby was seated. Mary handed him a microphone. Then she and Cernan moved away to make room. "I'm honored," Eastman said, "to present the first Harry Eastman Award for Civic Achievement to Frank Kirby."

Kirby received the trophy, took a moment to study it, and smiled. "Thank you, Harry." They shook hands. He raised the award so everyone could see it. "I'm indebted not only to Harry, who's been a friend for a long time, but also to Mary Gridley. To my former colleagues at NASA, who were so supportive for so many years. And to everyone who's helped out in Orlando." He put the award on the table. "But everybody knows I'm not alone. There are a lot of people who are doing far more than I've ever been able to. And some of them are in this room. There is an enormous number of kids who are in trouble. Who need our help."

He spoke for several minutes, mostly about the plight of children growing up in poor areas. Then he reminisced briefly about the state of NASA. "I've been away from my old job a long time," he said. "But this is still where I live. When I was growing up, we assumed that by the time we'd entered the twenty-first century, we'd have Moonbase and be well on our way to establishing a colony on Mars. We thought we'd be safe from any single catastrophe. Safe in the knowledge that the human race would survive. More important, perhaps, we understood that going off world was more than a safety measure. More, even, than a dream. It was part of who we were. The only real question was whether our generation would manage it, or whether we'd be remembered as the people who got to the Moon and then forgot how we'd done it."

A murmur ran through the audience.

"I guess we know how that turned out."

Someone up front wanted to know what had prompted him to start his charitable work, whether he'd been doing anything like that during his astronaut years. One of the computer guys asked whether he thought we'd ever get back to the Moon.

"Of course we will," he said. "Look, I know what you're thinking. That I'm a pessimist. And I am. But only in the short term. Eventually, we'll do what we need to. Maybe we'll even take the grand tour. But it'll be our grandkids who do it. Not us." Mary's hand touched his arm. "At least not me. I don't expect to see much more happen during my lifetime.

"But look at some of the people who are here tonight. Then ask yourself whether we're going to be satisfied with retiring to a front porch for the rest of our days." He asked if there were more questions.

A woman who identified herself as a physicist from the University of Georgia insisted on throwing cold water on everything. "Human beings can't survive in a zero-gravity environment," she said. "Eventually, we're going to have to face the reality that we're effectively earthbound."

The audience got restless, and there was some whispering. "You're talking about an engineering problem, Professor," Kirby said. "If that's the biggest hurdle we have to get over, I'll be grateful."

Jerry didn't know who she was, or how she'd gotten her invitation. He suspected she was a plant from higher up. Sent there for the express purpose of lowering expectations.

Warren Cole's hand went up. "Mr. Kirby," he said, "you were CAPCOM for a couple of the pre–Apollo XI flights. On one of them, Sidney Myshko reported that he was in the LEM and ready to go. And you replied 'Good luck, guys.' Can you explain what was going on?"

Kirby looked up at the overhead, then gazed out toward the entry doors. He shook his head. "Damned if I can remember what that was about. I know we said that. I mean, I heard the recording, so I know it happened. But it was a long time ago, and it's hard to remember specifics. I can tell you that we used to joke around a good bit. Sid was always saying how if he got up there, he was going to take the LEM down, and I suspect that's what it referred to. But it's obvious it had no real significance." He smiled and pointed toward a young woman seated off to one side.

But Cole stayed on his feet. "Follow-up, Mr. Kirby, if I may. There was a period afterward of more than fifty hours during which all your conversations were with Brian Peters. More than two days, sir. What happened to Myshko?"

Jerry could not entirely contain a smug sense of satisfaction. Cole was performing up to expectations.

Kirby's manner stiffened, and the smile faded. "I guess I should remind you that I wasn't in the capsule. I had no way of knowing why one person was on the microphone and not somebody else. It's not something I would have given any thought to."

He went back to the young woman.

"Which," she asked, "gives you a bigger sense of satisfaction, Mr. Kirby, riding a rocket, or helping a disabled kid?"

"That one's easy," he said. "You get a lot of satisfaction from giving a hand to a child. Riding a rocket has always scared me. And I don't want to speak for anyone else, but I'd be surprised if there's anyone who ever sat up on the nose cone of a Saturn V who wouldn't tell you the same thing. No, I'll play ball with the kid anytime."

———

When it was over, Kirby and his family and Harry Eastman were given a tour of the Hall of Fame. They saw a LEM and a model of the Space Station, made it onto a mock-up bridge of the command capsule, watched a 3-D film documentary explaining where NASA hoped to go during the next decade and why humans had to establish an off-world presence.

Jerry strolled over to where Kirby was talking with a couple of NASA people. When they wandered off, Jerry said how impressed he was with Kirby's charity work. "When the foundation first indicated it wanted to give an award," he said, "we had no idea what you'd been doing. It's an incredible story."

The wheelchair was powered, and they moved closer to a wall filled with three-dimensional photos of astronauts hopping across lunar turf, Saturn rockets soaring through sunlit skies, and shuttles docking at the Space Station. "So how," Kirby asked, "did you come up with *my* name?"

"We went online. Ran every name we could think of." Jerry shook his head. "You have a pretty good record, Frank."

"Thank you. That's very kind of you. It didn't seem like all that much to me. I was just trying to help. I mean, you know what they say, if you retire and head for the couch, they bury you the following year."

He liked Kirby. The explanation he'd given Cole had been reasonable enough. Still, it wasn't the only issue. He glanced up at an image of a command capsule coming over the rim of the Moon. "By the way, Frank—"

"Yes?"

They stopped in front of the picture. "I wanted to apologize for the newsman. He's from the Associated Press, and he tends to be a bit pushy sometimes."

"It's okay," Kirby said. "No big deal."

"I have to admit, though, he's got me curious. Was Peters really the only guy you were talking to during that *fifty* hours?"

"I don't know, Jerry. This is something that happened a half century ago. I was talking to whoever I was talking to. What difference does it make?"

They exchanged stares. "Frank, a Navy pilot who was present when they were bringing the astronauts on board the carrier at the end of the flight said one of them was carrying *rocks*."

Kirby's features hardened. "What is this, Jerry?" he asked. "A setup of some kind? You bring me all the way down here to put me through this?"

"No, of course not, Frank. I'm just curious, that's all."

He'd given the plaque to his son, Frank, Jr. Now he looked around, saw him, and waved him over. When he arrived, Kirby took the plaque from him. "Here, Jerry, you can have it back. And if we weren't in polite company, I'd tell you what you could do with it."

"Frank—"

"And I'll tell you something else." Everybody was staring at them now, mouths open. "Just back off this thing, okay? Do yourself a favor. Back off."

———————

Fortunately, Mary didn't see it happen. But a few minutes later, Jerry was called to her office. "What the hell happened?" she said.

He tried not to look guilty. "I'm not sure."

"What's *that* supposed to mean? Damn it, Jerry, I told you not to embarrass us. Did you know the whole thing got recorded? It's out there now." She waved in the general direction of her computer. "I wouldn't have believed you could be so dumb."

"Listen, Mary—"

"What?"

Her eyes sliced into him. "Look, doesn't it suggest anything to you that he got so upset?"

"It suggests he didn't want to discuss it." Her mouth tightened. "It suggests he thought it was silly. Did you set that reporter on him?"

Jerry was having a problem breathing. He'd never seen her so angry. "Not—"

"—exactly," she said. "Well, that's really good. What the hell is this business about rocks?"

"I got a call from a retired helicopter pilot. He says one of the Myshko astronauts dropped some rocks on the carrier deck."

"Rocks?"

"That's what he said."

"As in Moon rocks?"

"No way to know, Mary. Not sure what else—"

She took a deep breath. "Where's the plaque?"

"In my office."

"All right, Jerry. Fix the problem."

"I'm not sure I can."

"Find a way. And be grateful you still have your job."

———————

Jerry didn't think it would be a good idea to call Kirby's cell, so he tried the hotel. But they'd apparently checked out before coming to the luncheon. Maybe it was just as well. Let him cool off on the ride back to Orlando.

Mary was right, though: The incident was all over the Internet, the public-relations director for NASA being hammered by Kirby, who was being described by everybody as a person who was very popular and gracious and a champion of the downtrodden.

But why was he so upset? If it was really nothing, just some sort of lame joke between himself and Myshko, wouldn't he simply have laughed it off?

Barb's voice came through the fog: "Jerry, you have a call from Bill Godwin. He says he's the producer of *Koestler Country*."

That couldn't be good. NASA's public-relations director never got invitations to appear on cable TV. Even astronauts didn't get invitations. "Put him through, Barb."

Godwin appeared on-screen. He was a long, angular guy with a polished scalp and a white beard. "Jerry," he said, "how are you?" On the few occasions Jerry had seen him, he had radiated serenity. A nuclear war could have broken out, and Godwin would have remained perfectly relaxed. He smiled and somehow managed to suggest that he and Jerry were old friends. "We wanted to invite you to appear on the show."

"Bill, I'm seriously tied up."

"Come on, Jerry. You can make time for us. I mean, that's your job, isn't it?"

Damn. He didn't have an easy way out. "When did you have in mind?"

"Well—" Godwin delivered a smile. "How about tonight?"

"You normally restrict the show to political guests, Bill. What would we be talking about?" He wasn't sure why he bothered to ask.

"What the future looks like from NASA's point of view. And, of course, we'd be interested in knowing what the dustup was between you and Frank Kirby today."

"The show originates in New York, doesn't it?"

"Yes, that's correct."

"There's no way I could get there."

"Oh, you wouldn't have to, Jerry. We have people in Florida. They could come in and set you up, and you'd do the show from your office. Or even your home, if you like. Your call."

"I think I better pass. I'm seriously on the run at the moment."

"Okay. Sure. Whatever you want. But I have to tell you that

we'd have no choice but to make an announcement that you declined an invitation to appear."

"Come on, Bill. You're not really going to make an issue of this, are you?"

"Jerry, the guy gets a community service award, then gives it back before he's even out of the building. It's a human-interest story. And I know you want to explain your side of this."

"Have you invited Mr. Kirby?"

"We have. But he won't be able to make it."

"Are you going to make an announcement about *that*?"

"No need to. Look, we'd like to have him. But you're really the guy we want. You're at the center of this."

Jerry stared out at the sky. It was growing dark. Approaching rain. "What time?" he asked.

———————

Mary stiffened. "Al Koestler?" She stared at him out of the monitor. "I don't think that's a good idea, Jerry. There's no way you can win."

"If I'd ducked, you know what they'd have said."

"I know." She looked down, scribbled a note to herself. "Okay. Do it." Her features softened. "You'll be all right. Koestler's just a windbag."

Limit the damage. It's all you can do.

———————

They would do the broadcast from Jerry's home. It was a good choice. It had been a long day, and he needed to get away from the office. He ate at his favorite restaurant, Dixie Crossroads Seafood in Titusville, but never tasted the food.

The TV crew arrived shortly before seven and began setting up. Mary called to reassure him. "You'll get through it all right, Jerry," she said. "Just hang loose."

A makeup guy patted powder on his nose and cheeks. Then a young woman explained about the lights on the cameras and how he should talk to the lens. It was all stuff he knew, that anybody knew, but he let her go on. "You won't be on until the second segment," she explained. Her name was Shirley. Unlike Koestler, she seemed reasonable, and he would have preferred to have her conduct the interview.

A bright moon was visible in the trees. While Jerry stared out at it, they moved the wingback chair away from the window and put it beside a desk, then set up a camera so that the desk would occupy the background. As eight o'clock approached, a young man who seemed to be the director suggested he sit down in the chair. Jerry complied.

He'd done interview shows before, during his years as a campaign front man. But nothing on this scale, nothing on cable news that would go out to the entire nation. And never confronting a loudmouth host whose primary goal was to make his guests look silly.

Then it was time. Shirley switched on the monitor, and he watched the intros to *Koestler Country*. Koestler appeared, relaxed in a book-lined studio. He was in his fifties, sporting a smile that suggested the rest of the world was deranged but he would set it straight. He had thick red hair and always dressed casually. Tonight, it was a light blue pullover shirt and an azure sports jacket. He was looking through a sheaf of notes as the camera panned in on him, and a piano played the show's bouncy theme. He looked up, suddenly aware of the presence of an audience. "Hello, Mr. and Ms. America," he said. "Welcome to *Koestler Country*." He smiled and laid the papers on a side table. "Tonight, we'll be looking at who really controls the environmental protections in the United States, why a former astronaut showed up on the Space Coast for a public service award from NASA and promptly gave it back, whether we're doing the right thing shutting down our military and naval bases around the world, and, finally, whether our continually advancing technology is destroying our kids' ability to talk with one another. Our first guest this evening is Eliot Kramer. Eliot is an economist and was a member of the last administration's corruption watchdog group."

Kramer walked in past a set of dark curtains. He wore an artificial smile. "Good to see you again, Al," he said, as Koestler rose to shake his hand. Then they both sat down.

"Last time, Eliot," said the host, "we talked about the degree to which corporations control the efforts to do something about the environment. Has that changed at all?"

"It has, Al. It's gotten worse. And in my view, it's time to put some of these people in jail."

"So, Jerry," he said, inviting him in, "what's happening with NASA these days?" Al Koestler was not a fan of the space effort. "Once you got beyond Earth orbit," he was fond of saying, "there's no point in continuing. It's cold, dark, and empty out there. No place to go. Nothing to bring back."

"We're still doing exploratory work."

"What, actually, are you exploring?"

Jerry was taken by surprise. He'd expected an immediate focus on Frank Kirby. "The outer planets. We've learned a lot these past few years."

"For example?"

"We have a pretty good idea why Uranus rotates on its side. You know that, right? That it's completely tipped over?"

"How would that affect us, Jerry?"

"Well, there is no direct impact. But—You *are* familiar with the term 'blue sky science'?"

"Of course. That's science that doesn't do anything for us. But it's fine. I just don't think the taxpayers should have to pay for it." He continued in that vein for several minutes. And finally took a long, deep breath. "NASA gave an award to one of its former employees this morning. It went to Frank Kirby for community service in Orlando, Jerry. Am I right?"

"Yes. That's correct."

"Kirby, I understand, has a long history of taking care of battered women and kids in trouble. A genuinely good guy."

"Yes. He is. We were pleased to have the opportunity to recognize all he's done."

"Let's play a clip. This took place shortly after the award ceremony." Koestler glanced up at a screen set back among the books. Jerry watched himself again talking with Kirby, watched the conversation morph into a confrontation, himself matched against a kindly man in a wheelchair.

Then Kirby shoved the plaque at him. *"Here, Jerry, you can have it. And if we weren't in polite company, I'd tell you what you could do with it."*

They froze the picture. "Jerry," said Koestler, "why would anybody care who was on the capsule radio?"

"It just seemed odd, Al. It was no big deal, and I was surprised he got annoyed."

"Is there a suggestion that Myshko and his partner, um, Crash Able—I love that name, don't you?—weren't *in* the capsule during that period?"

"I asked him about it simply because the AP reporter had asked. That was all. I thought maybe it was an interesting question. I didn't even know if it was true. Didn't realize that Frank was upset, or I wouldn't have said anything."

"Well, okay. But what was that about the rocks?"

"The rocks?"

"The Navy guy who said he saw one of the astronauts bringing back some rocks?"

"I think he said *with* rocks. *Rocks* is a code word. It's a Navy expression for being nervous. As in 'he was rocked by the experience.'" That was a stretch, but Jerry hoped it would get him past the question.

"Why was Kirby so upset, do you think?"

"I just don't know. I'm certainly sorry I brought it up."

"But he was angry at *you*. You say you don't know why?"

"No, I don't. I guess there was a misunderstanding of some sort."

"In what way?"

"I'm not sure, Al. I'm really not. The only thing I can say is that I have a great deal of respect for Frank Kirby, and I want to take advantage of this opportunity to apologize if I gave offense. And obviously I did." Jerry looked directly into the camera. "I'm sorry it happened, Frank. And I'd like to make it right."

Mary called him minutes after the show. "You did good, Jerry. I thought you came away from it about as well as you could. Let me know if you hear from Frank."

Kirby called the following morning. "I'm sorry," he said. "I shouldn't have blown my stack like that." He looked down at Jerry from the TV screen, which was mounted beside a picture of Jerry and Myra Hasting, editor of *The Florida Times-Union*.

"It's okay. It was my fault, Frank."

"Let's just forget it, okay?"

"Yes. That's a good idea. You'll be wanting your award back, I hope." Jerry grinned.

"That would be nice, yes."

"I'll ship it this afternoon."

"Thanks, Jerry. And one other thing?"

"Sure."

"That business with Sidney Myshko. Forget it, okay? It's just confusion over a bad joke."

Jerry was grateful to put it aside and get back to his normal routine. Fortunately, the media have a short memory. The disappearance of Sidney Myshko from the Apollo transmissions all those years ago needed precisely two days to drop out of the news. Then, as he was getting ready to quit for the day, he got a call from Ralph D'Angelo. Ralph was a friend from Jerry's days at Wesleyan University. He was a columnist for *The Baltimore Sun*.

"Long time," Jerry said. "How you been, Ralph?"

"Still working, Jerry." He hadn't aged well. Ralph looked twenty years older than he actually was. His hair was gone, his forehead was wrinkled, his eyes were glazed. Jerry suspected he had health problems. Or worse.

"I hear you. These aren't exactly the best of times."

"I've noticed. Listen, I have a question for you."

"Sure."

"You know Aaron Walker retired here? The astronaut?"

Aaron Walker. Jerry needed a moment. He was one of the early Apollo guys. Had been on a test flight, the one immediately after Myshko. "I didn't know he'd gone to Baltimore," Jerry said.

"A few years ago, he walked into a liquor store right into the middle of a holdup. Got killed."

Jerry recalled the story, of course, though not where it had happened. "Yes," he said. "I remember. Sad end for a guy like that."

"He left a journal. You ready for this? In the journal, he says he landed on the Moon."

"He wasn't on any of the flights that landed, was he?"

"Not according to the record."

"Well, okay. Then there's a mistake somewhere."

"It's *his* writing, Jerry. We've checked it. Anyhow, what with this other stuff about Myshko, we're going to use it. I can send you a copy if you like."

"Ralph, it's a false alarm."

"Well, I wanted to give you a chance to comment. Why don't you take a look at what he said? You should have it now. I can wait."

The journal entry was dated April 21, 2009:

Hard to believe it's been forty years since my stroll on the lunar surface. Oops, forgot I'm not supposed to say that. Wonder what that thing was, anyhow?

"What do you think?" said Ralph.

"Is that it?"

"The context is interesting."

"How do you mean?"

"He was describing a day at the ballpark. He'd gone to the Orioles-Yankees game. He gave up when Robinson Cano homered in the seventh. It gave the Yankees, I think, a 9–2 lead. He got up and left.

"That night he commented on it in his journal: *'That was it. I'd had enough. Sitting up there when I should have been out somewhere celebrating the biggest event of my life. Of anybody's life.'* Then he tosses in the line *'Hard to believe . . .'*"

"Where's it been all these years?" Jerry tried to sound skeptical.

"Jane said she'd forgotten he kept a journal. She found it after he died. She'd never really looked at it, beyond reading about when he'd first met her mother. The mother's been dead a long time. Then when this stuff started about Myshko, she got curious and went back to it."

"Who's Jane?"

"Jane Alcott. His daughter. His only child, in fact."

"Who has the journal now?"

"I do."

Jerry looked out at the launch towers. "How does the entry read for April 21, 1969?"

"There isn't one. We have an entry for April 3, describing his feelings, his anticipation, for the flight. Then there's nothing until May 2. Three days after he got back."

"On April 21, they were orbiting the Moon?"

"Yes."

Jerry was getting a cold feeling in his stomach. "So what's the May 2 entry say?"

"Just how glad he was to see his family again. To be back on solid ground. That sort of thing"

"What does his daughter think?"

"She says she never noticed the ballpark line. She says she was not a baseball fan."

"I think Amos Bartlett's still alive," said Jerry. Bartlett had been one of Walker's crew.

"We called him," Ralph said. "Bartlett was the command module pilot. He told us it must be a mistake. Or a joke."

Jerry nodded. Of course. What else could it be? "That should settle it," he said.

"Do you have a comment, Jerry?"

"Sounds to me as if Walker was dreaming. Thinking about what might have been. Maybe he'd lost touch with reality. Started making up stuff for his journal."

"Is that the formal NASA response?"

"No. I'd guess, Ralph, at this point, that we're strictly no comment."

––––––––––

Jerry went immediately to the archives. For more than seventy hours, while the capsule orbited the Moon, Bartlett's voice had been the only one heard from the capsule. On the way out, and during the return flight, Walker had dominated the conversation. And occasionally, Lenny Mullen, the LEM pilot, could be heard.

But for almost three days, Walker and Mullen had been silent.

It was a rerun of the Myshko recordings.

5

Bucky Blackstone was in New York when the news broke. He made three quick calls, one to Ralph D'Angelo, two more to D'Angelo's editor and his publisher—both longtime acquaintances if not exactly friends—and when he was done, he had no doubt that the diary mentioned a landing.

But that was ridiculous. The most important event in human history, and they covered it up for half a century? It made no sense. Even if the government had some reason for a cover-up, how the hell could they get the consent of the crew? There wasn't a schoolkid anywhere in the Western world who didn't know the names of Neil Armstrong and Buzz Aldrin. How could you convince any landers who predated them to forgo that glory? And even if they agreed at the time, why would Myshko and the others keep quiet for twenty or thirty years—or fifty, if any of them were still alive?

He rubbed his chin absently, staring at nothing in particular, and frowned. No one had landed on the Moon before Armstrong. If they had, it would be a triumph, not a secret. We were in a race with the Russians, and Sputnik had predated everything we'd done. We couldn't have been sure that Khrushchev and the Russians weren't secretly working on their own Moon landing. If we *could* have touched down, we *would* have.

Don't forget those Kennedy memos that came to light back in 2012, he reminded himself. JFK didn't give a damn about science. All he was concerned with was the prestige of beating the Russians to the Moon. And if Harvard John didn't care about the scientific breakthroughs, you could be sure that Landslide Lyndon and Tricky Dick didn't give a damn either. To all three, the only important thing was getting there first, so of course they wouldn't hide the accomplishment.

So why did Aaron Walker write that in his diary?

Think, Bucky! he told himself. *You've already bought half an hour on CNN and Fox News to offer your version of what happened and what's being covered up, and to challenge the government to prove you wrong. You'd better be damned sure you're right, or no one will ever listen to you again.*

One thing is certain: Walker didn't write it as a joke. A lot of social mores have changed over the years, but diaries are still private things. He never expected anyone to read what he wrote—so why did he say that?

He checked his Rolex. Thirty-three hours before he had to speak on television. That didn't give him a lot of time.

He had come with a skeleton staff—Ed Camden; his longtime secretary, Gloria Marcos; and his bodyguard, Jason Brent. (Bucky thought of himself as a pretty fit specimen, more than capable of taking care of himself—but when you're a billionaire, you're a target for kidnappers and all the disgruntled rivals you beat, which is to say bankrupted, on the way to your fortune. He hated the thought of traveling with an entourage of bodyguards the way so many others of his economic stature did, so he'd chosen Brent, a one-man wrecking crew who was a crack shot, a karate champion, and had the fastest reaction time he'd ever seen.)

Bucky summoned all three of them to his suite. Well, to the huge living room of the presidential suite. Jason would never agree to stay down the corridor with a locked door between them, and slept in the adjoining bedroom.

"What's up?" asked Camden.

"You heard the news?" said Bucky.

"Yeah," replied Camden. "I wonder what the guy was smoking."

Bucky turned to Gloria. "You think anyone'll believe it?"

"Why not?" she answered. "Hell, a third of the public doesn't believe we ever landed. Why shouldn't another third believe we landed more often than we said?"

"I'm going in front of fifty million people tomorrow night," said Bucky. "I'd like to think I'm not about to make a total fool of myself."

Jason Brent looked puzzled. "I don't see a problem, Boss. I assume you're going to give your version about why Kirby wouldn't accept that award."

"He accepted it the next day," noted Camden.

"Even so, something's going on, and the Boss is going to give his version. Thing is, whatever it is, they've kept it a secret for fifty years, and that's if anything happened at all. So what if he's wrong? Who will know? Or put it this way: If something *did* happen, and he's wrong about what it is, the only guys who can contradict him and prove he's wrong are the same guys who have been lying about it for fifty years. He's not NASA's enemy, so why would they reverse course just to embarrass him?"

Camden considered what Brent had said and finally turned to Bucky. "He's got a point, you know."

"Look," said Bucky. "We're going to the Moon. If I wind up looking like a buffoon over this, every single thing we find, everything we learn, everything we announce to the public when we return, will be suspect because I'll have proven how easily I can be bamboozled."

"Then why not just ignore it, cancel your airtime, and pretend it never happened?" said Camden.

"Because *something* happened," said Bucky decisively. "I don't know what, though I've got a pretty good idea. And if I'm right about what it was, it's essential that NASA come clean before we actually launch our Moon mission." He paused, looking from one to another. "Doesn't it bother any of you that they've been lying to the public for half a century? And that it's got to be about something major, something *important*. If it's minor, there's no need to still be keeping it secret. If it was just some stupid glitch that could embarrass or humiliate them, hell, 80 percent of the public wasn't even alive then, and just about anyone who could be embarrassed is dead by now."

"That's an assumption, Bucky," said Gloria. "A logical one, but still an assumption. You know the government: It lies about something, usually something trivial, every five minutes. "

"I just explained why it's *not* trivial," said Bucky.

She shook her head. "You just explained why you *think* it's not trivial, and it was a logical answer—but what has logic got to do with the government? You say everyone's dead, so why not reveal whatever it was if it was trivial? I say there have been so many lies and cover-ups, why go to the trouble of exposing this one if everyone involved is dead and most of the public can't even remember the Apollo missions?"

"Okay," said Bucky, "I've listened patiently. I haven't heard anything to make me change my mind. Now we're going to spend the next day and a half trying to find out what the hell happened. Clearly, Ralph D'Angelo has either gotten possession of the diary, or he's made a photocopy of it."

"Why?" asked Brent.

"Because he's an hour from Washington, and he had to be under a lot of pressure to keep quiet about this," explained Bucky patiently. "So he had to protect his ass, and that means either the diary or a photocopy, with some expert already authenticating Aaron Walker's handwriting." He paused. "We need a copy of whatever he's got."

"Don't look at me, Boss," said Brent. "I don't leave your side, not for anything."

Bucky turned to Camden. "Okay, Ed. Get on the next flight down there, and don't come back without it."

"And if he doesn't want to part with it?" asked Camden. "I can't bust down doors the way Jason can."

Bucky sighed deeply. "We're not criminals, Ed. I don't want you to beat it out of him."

"Then what?"

Bucky stared at him. "You're working for a billionaire. What do *you* think I'm going to suggest?"

"How high can I go?"

"Gloria, D'Angelo's not syndicated, right? He just works for *The Baltimore Sun*?"

"That's right."

"What's the most he could be making?"

"Week, month, or year?"

"Per year."

"Without being syndicated? No more than $130,000, probably a little less."

Bucky turned back to Camden. "A quarter million ought to do it."

"And if he wants more?"

"Tell him you have to see it to decide if it's worth more."

"And then?"

"Then decide."

Camden walked to the door. "I'll get back to you as soon as I can."

Then he was gone. Bucky lit a Havana, took a couple of puffs, and walked back and forth in front of his desk, thinking. Finally, he sat down.

"I need to talk to Jerry Culpepper," he announced.

"Culpepper?" repeated Gloria. "Even if he knows what happened, which I, for one, doubt, he'll never tell you."

"We're on the same side," replied Bucky. "He just doesn't know it yet."

"What makes you think so?" asked Brent.

"His job is disseminating information." Gloria and Brent just stared at him, puzzled. "Don't you see?" he continued. "Everything he's built in his career depends upon his credibility. If they're lying to him or feeding him false information, they're destroying the one thing he trades on: his veracity. If he *knew* he was lying, that would be different, it'd be his choice—but my reading of him is that he's an honorable man. Hell, you saw what precipitated that *brouhaha* with Kirby: He wanted to know what happened." Another pause. "He's on *our* side. One of these days, he'll figure it out. In the meantime, I need to talk to him."

"If he's lying or ignorant, why?" asked Brent.

"So he'll know he's got a home here if they ever kick him out," answered Bucky. "Sooner or later, the truth will come out, and they're going to need a fall guy—and as Humphrey Bogart would say, he's made to order for the part."

Brent shrugged. "You're the boss."

"If we're all agreed on that, set up a face-to-face for me."

Gloria went to her much smaller desk, and a moment later Jerry Culpepper's image appeared on Bucky's computer screen.

"Hi, Jerry. Did I catch you at a busy time?"

"These days, those are the only times I've got." Jerry smiled. "What can I do for you, Mr. Bucky?"

"Bucky," Bucky corrected him.

"Bucky," said Jerry. "Do you mind if I ask you a question?"

"Be my guest."

"Your given name is Morgan. Why Bucky? The press has dubbed you 'The Cowboy Billionaire,' but unlike all the Texas oilmen I've met you don't wear a Stetson and boots, so why . . . ?"

"You really want to know?" asked Bucky with a smile.

"That's why I asked."

"It's for Buck Rogers. I always wanted to be an astronaut."

Jerry smiled. "Really?"

"Is it so hard to believe?" asked Bucky.

"Not at all. There were days that I was John Carter of Mars or the Gray Lensman. Earth was never big enough for me."

Bucky chuckled. "I *knew* we had a lot in common."

"I'm not so sure," said Jerry. "Your pin money could eat my life savings for breakfast."

"Come to work for me, and we'll do something about that."

Jerry smiled and shook his head. "I've got a contract, Bucky."

"I have the best lawyers in the country, and I'll pay court costs if NASA sues."

"I appreciate the offer, truly I do," said Jerry. "But I have to honor my commitment. What would you think of me if I broke it?"

"As disappointed as I am, I admire that," replied Bucky.

"So is that what this call is all about?"

"No, though of course I'd be thrilled if you came over to our side."

"*Are* we on different sides, Bucky?" asked Jerry.

"I hope not."

"Everyone at NASA is rooting for you to accomplish all your goals in space and hopefully awaken enough interest that we can get sufficient funding to get back in the race," said Jerry. "You're our best hope, so why should you be on the opposite side?"

"Because *you* may know something that *we* need to know," replied Bucky.

"Oh?" Jerry arched an eyebrow. "What?"

"I don't know," admitted Bucky. "But I have a feeling that Aaron Walker could answer that, and maybe Ralph D'Angelo, too."

Jerry tensed visibly. "Why do you think *I* know anything about it?"

"I said Aaron Walker knew," said Bucky. "*Do* you know anything about it?"

Jerry exhaled deeply. "I wish I did."

"I believe you. For now."

"I haven't been told not to dig," said Jerry. "There's no place I can't go, no file I can't see, no one I can't talk to. But . . ."

"But if it's hidden well enough, what they let you do makes no difference."

"What the hell could it be?" said Jerry, forcing a shrug. "We landed. We came back. All but one mission went like clockwork—and when Apollo XIII screwed up, nobody made any attempt to hide it."

"Can you take a word of advice from someone who's older and been around a lot longer than you, Jerry?"

"I'm all ears," replied Jerry sincerely.

"Protect your ass. When whatever it is comes out, they're going to hang you out to dry."

"Me? I'm the most loyal employee they've got."

"You're the most *visible* employee they've got."

"Look," said Jerry, "whatever happened or failed to happen, I'm sure it was decidedly minor. Probably just a lousy turn of phrase when you come right down to it."

There was a long, uncomfortable pause.

"But?" said Bucky. "I sense an unspoken 'but' at the end of that sentence."

"But this is my organization and my country, and while I may be as curious as you, if they want it kept secret, I'm ethically compelled to keep it secret."

"If they're lying to the American public, of which you were a member last time I looked," said Bucky, "I think you're ethically compelled to find it and bring it out in the open, whatever *it* is."

Jerry shook his head. "We're on opposite sides on this one, Bucky. My best advice to you is to leave it alone."

"And my best advice to you is that the last person you ever want to lie to is—"

"You?" interrupted Jerry.

"Yourself," said Bucky, breaking the connection. He turned

to face Gloria and Brent. "He'll come over when the time is right."

"If someone lets the cat out of the bag, who cares if he comes over?" said Brent. "And if they don't, he won't."

"He's a moral man," replied Bucky. "They're few and far between in this business, but they're always predictable. The bigger the secret, the more he's going to feel betrayed and ill-used."

"Let's see if it *is* a big secret," said Gloria.

Bucky grimaced. "You haven't been listening to me. It's big."

"How big?"

"You know what I think?" said Bucky. "I think some member of Myshko's team died when they were orbiting the Moon and NASA kept it quiet until they could find out what caused it. Remember, we were racing against the Russians, and that would have been a huge blow to our prestige."

"You really think so?" asked Brent.

"It makes sense. Obviously, it was either from natural causes or some problem they could pinpoint and fix, because the other Apollo missions all took off on schedule. But by then, they'd lied for a couple of months about the death, and they didn't want the publicity that would accrue if it came out."

"Why don't you call the White House and ask?" asked Brent. "I know you're on speaking terms with the president."

"All billionaires and religious leaders are always on speaking terms with any president," said Bucky. "But what can I do? Get him on Skype or the vidphone and ask him why he's lying to the American public? Besides, he may not even know about this. As far as I can tell, it's pretty well confined to NASA."

"If it's anything affecting future Moon flights, he must know about it, or why aren't we going back?" asked Gloria. "Hell, they *all* knew about it—Carter, Reagan, Clinton, the Bushes, Obama, all of them. They all gave lip service to the space program, then did everything they could to emasculate it."

Bucky shook his head. "You're looking at it the wrong way. They were politicians, not scientists—even Carter. The only thing the Moon meant to them was the prestige of reaching it before Russia did. Well, we reached it—and then the only thing it meant to them was billions of dollars that they'd rather spend on their own programs. They were probably thrilled when private industry started doing suborbital flights a decade ago. It meant the last pressure was off them to do it. NASA's moribund; it just doesn't know it yet."

"Then why are *we* going into space?" asked Brent.

"Because we don't give any more of a damn about science than *they* did. They went for prestige; we're going for profit."

"From the Moon?" asked Brent, frowning.

"From the Moon, and the asteroids, and the moons of Jupiter and Saturn. It won't happen this year, or this decade, but we can see the money in orbit up there, so we won't pack up and stay at home the way the government did after it beat the Russians."

Suddenly Brent grinned. "You think there are any Moon men up there?"

"Not yet," said Bucky. "Ask me again in a few months." He got to his feet. "Is anyone hungry?"

"It's awfully early," said Gloria.

"That isn't what I asked."

"If you want to wait for Ed to contact you, we can have room service feed us right here," suggested Gloria. "They have a splendid menu."

"It'll take him at least another ninety minutes to get to Baltimore, even on my private jet. and he'll probably have to negotiate the bribe for another half hour, maybe more. I could do with a walk, and a nice Greek meal—saganaki, dolmades, pastitsio, and top it off with some baklava for dessert."

"I could go for that," acknowledged Gloria.

"Let's choose a joint with belly dancers," suggested Brent.

"Let's choose one with the best menu, and if they have belly dancers, so much the better for you," said Gloria.

"Fair enough." Brent turned to Bucky. "Boss, if we're gonna walk, or even take a cab . . ."

"I know," said Bucky with an unhappy sigh. "The shaggy black wig, the shades, and the cane."

"Why let 'em know that they're looking at a billion dollars on the hoof?"

"It's been a dozen years since I was worth *a* billion," said Bucky, heading off to the closet and bringing out his wig, his sunglasses, his hat, his light overcoat, and his cane. "Am I properly generic now?" he asked a moment later.

"You look like the local dope peddler and his muscle," said Gloria, as he walked over and stood next to Brent.

"Okay, let's go sell some crack and have dinner," said Bucky, leading them to the door.

It was a sumptuous meal, and there *were* belly dancers. They spent two hours in the restaurant and, against Brent's wishes, walked back to the hotel rather than take a cab.

When they got there, they found an urgent message to contact Ed Camden. A moment later, his image was on the screen, staring at his employer.

"What's up?" asked Bucky.

"You're not going to believe this," said Camden, a troubled expression on his face.

"Try me."

Camden held a battered leather book up to the camera. "This is Aaron Walker's diary. It cost you $300,000."

"I assume from your urgent message that it was worth it?"

"You underpaid."

"Oh?"

Camden nodded. "Yeah."

"Okay, what did my three hundred grand buy me?"

"Let me read you an entry from January 19, 1979."

"Go ahead."

Camden turned to the proper page. " *'Ten years and nobody's even hinted at it. I can't believe Washington could keep a secret for so long.'* "

"That's it?"

Camden shook his head. "Here's December 1986. *'It's almost seventeen years, and still not a word of it. I must be one of the few guys left who knows the truth.'* " Camden turned to another page. "And January 19, 1988: *'Another year of silence. Just amazing.'* "

"Let me guess," said Bucky. "January 19 is the anniversary of when the Myshko flight took off?"

Camden shook his head and smiled. "Almost."

"Son of a bitch!" exclaimed Bucky. "It's the anniversary of when it would have landed!"

"Give the man a cigar," said Camden.

6

Jane Alcott lived with her husband and four kids in Sparrows Point, Maryland, outside Baltimore. They occupied a two-story white frame house with a large front yard in a neighborhood filled with trees. They were within a few blocks of Chesapeake Bay, the kind of place Jerry would have liked to settle down in if he'd had a family. He arrived in the early evening, as the sun was slipping below the horizon, and couldn't help thinking how much easier his life might have been had he been living out here doing public relations for one of the TV channels and living with Mandy Edwards, the only woman he'd ever really cared about. But she was a long time ago.

He still thought about her when life got quiet. He was over her, finally. Or at least that's what he told himself. Two years ago, she'd earned a Ph.D. in astrophysics. Now she worked for NASA in Houston. She was one of the reasons he'd joined NASA, with the possibility their paths might cross. In any case, she knew how high he'd climbed. Undoubtedly, she saw him now and then doing a press conference, or on the Agency's TV channel. He liked to think she regretted tossing him aside.

Now, in a rented car and under a bright moon, he pushed her out of his mind as he cruised down F Street and turned south onto Ninth. He passed more trees and sculpted lawns and broad driveways. The house numbers were hard to see in the dark, but Alcott had described the house, red brick with green shutters and two white cars in the driveway. The post light was on. He spotted it, parked, and looked around to assure himself there were no reporters in the area. Then he climbed slowly out of the car and started up the walk. A dog was barking somewhere, and a couple of kids next door were taking turns missing long shots at a basketball hoop mounted over the driveway. Basketball, he thought, was never really out of season. A cool breeze blew in off the Bay. He took a deep breath, thought again how the smart thing to do would be to go home and forget the whole thing. No matter how this played out, he was going to become a target for everybody's jokes. A comic figure representing an agency that belonged to the past.

He climbed a set of wooden steps onto the front deck. Lights blinked on, and the door opened before he reached it. A middle-aged woman, with dark hair and a nervous smile, looked out at him. "Mr. Culpepper?"

"Yes, ma'am." He could hear excited kids and sound effects inside. A war game in progress.

"Come in, please." She opened the door wide. The combat was coming from another room. "I hope you don't mind the noise."

"Not at all," Jerry said, walking into a tastefully decorated living room. A pair of vases filled with flowers stood on a table near the window, framed by lush, raven-colored drapes. The furniture was leather. Pictures of family members, mostly children, dominated the walls. A photo of Aaron Walker, in a commander's uniform, occupied a spot between the flowers.

She indicated a chair. "Make yourself comfortable, Mr. Culpepper. Can I get you something to drink?"

"No," he said. "Thank you very much. And my name's Jerry."

"I know. I've seen you on TV." She sat down on the sofa. "I'm Jane."

"Pleasure to meet you, Jane."

"You've seen the journal, right?"

"Yes, I have."

"I don't think I have anything to add. I was surprised by the entry. Jolted, as a matter of fact."

"I understand you'd never really looked through it before?"

"No, sir. Umm, Jerry. I've had the journal since my father died. Never really opened it until recently. He was living with us. Here. He had a room in back. A whole wing of the house, in fact."

"You must have been very proud of him, Jane."

"Oh, yes. He was a remarkable man. I miss him." Her eyes fluttered. "You would have liked him."

"I'm sure I would." He commented on how attractive the home was, and the neighborhood, then got to the point: "Do you have any idea what he meant by that passage?"

She leaned back and shook her head. She was an attractive woman though there was a sadness in her eyes. A sense, perhaps, that something incredible had happened in her father's life, and she'd somehow contrived to miss it. "No. I came across it about a year ago. We were housecleaning, trying to make some room, and we started throwing a lot of stuff out. And we discovered the journal. Actually, I'd known that he kept one because I'd seen him sometimes writing in it at night, but I'd forgotten. Then I opened a box, and there it was. Along with some of his books.

"I sat down and looked through it. But I didn't see much that interested me. Most of it was a record of visits with friends and family members. He'd been keeping it ever since college. I went back and read the sections about Mom, how he'd first been attracted to her, and all that. And some of the stuff about his Navy days."

"Yes," Jerry said. "He was a naval pilot."

She smiled. "A naval *aviator*, Jerry. Those guys are something else. They get insulted if you call them pilots." The kids' voices were getting louder. She got up, excused herself, and went in to make peace. While she was gone, Jerry looked more closely at some of the photos. In one, Jane posed with a man in a dark suit. Her husband, presumably. Something about him suggested that he was a lawyer, but it turned out he was a political consultant. The kids were between six and twelve, two of each gender. It was young male voices creating the nearby clamor.

Then they went quiet, and two boys came out into the living room, looking sheepish. Jane introduced them. They seemed subdued at that point. She'd probably told them that Jerry was directing the next Moon shot or some such thing.

"I'm sorry," she said. "They get carried away sometimes."

They went back to their game, and Jane reclaimed her seat.

"Where were we, Jerry?" Her brow wrinkled, and she looked down at the rug. "Oh, yes, courting my mom, and some of the Navy stuff—he got shot down in Vietnam. Made it back out to sea, fortunately, before he had to bail out. He got picked up by a destroyer." She sighed. "A month later, he was back at it."

"Did you read about his time as an astronaut, Jane?"

"Yes. Though only after that business about Sidney Myshko came out. I'd never really looked at it before that. I knew when he came back from the Moon mission that they'd gone down in the ocean, of course. He was picked up by a destroyer again. But until recently, I wasn't much interested in looking at the NASA entries because he always seemed kind of disappointed that he didn't get to do one of the landings. On the Moon. And I—just—didn't need any more of that."

"He was depressed by it?"

"Well, I wasn't born yet when it happened. In later years, it wasn't a subject he wanted to talk about. I used to ask him what it had been like, flying to the Moon, but he always changed the subject. So after a while, I just let it go."

"Why'd you decide to send it to the newspaper, Jane?"

She blushed. "*You* were responsible for that. I saw you on the news. And that reporter started asking about the Myshko mission, whether they'd landed or not. Not that I thought anything like that had happened, but I remembered that remark. About how he had gone strolling on the lunar surface. Then I saw how little he had to say in the journal itself about the flight. The ball-game entry was fifty years after that mission."

"That would have been nice, wouldn't it? Had he been in Apollo XI?"

"Oh, sure, Jerry. He would have loved to be on the flight with Neil Armstrong. To actually get a chance to walk on the Moon. But—" She shrugged. "It didn't happen. At least, I think it didn't happen."

"So what do you think the journal entry was about?"

"I have no idea. I was hoping you might be able to tell *me*." Jerry had no answer.

She leaned forward in her chair. "Do you think it's possible? That he actually landed on the Moon?"

"Jane, I don't think it happened. But at this point, I'm not sure of anything."

"I probably shouldn't have called *The Sun* about that ball-park entry. I didn't stop to think."

"You wanted it to be true?"

Her lips widened into a smile. "Yes. I'd love to find out that it actually happened. Dad would have been unhappy with me, wouldn't have approved of my going to the newspaper, but I couldn't see that it would do any harm."

"I agree."

"I didn't create a problem, did I? By calling the paper?"

"I don't think we need worry about that."

She looked over at her father's photograph. "I never knew him to lie. And he wasn't the kind of man who'd get carried away by his imagination. I really wish he were here today. I'd like to ask him to explain it."

———

Jerry never learned how Mary found out about his visit to Sparrows Point. "But I want us to stay out of it, Jerry. Is that clear?" She was parked behind her desk, pushed back in her chair, her eyes full of anger.

Jerry didn't do well in confrontations with superiors. With anybody, for that matter. He was inclined to be polite and agreeable. "I've been careful," he said.

"You mean the reporter who gave you the story wasn't the one who told you where the daughter lived?"

"Well, yes. In fact he was."

"So the press knows we're trying to find out what this woman knows, right?"

"Well, Ralph knows."

"And Ralph's employer is—?"

"Okay. So I guess I screwed up."

"Jerry, they haven't gone with the story yet. But you can be sure your buddy would like to know why we're interested."

"I told him it was a false alarm."

"Of course you did. And that's why you wanted to talk to the daughter, right?" She closed her eyes and pressed her lips together. "You might as well have told him we're doing a cover-up. That something really *did* happen."

Jerry tried to look like a guy who'd been caught in an impossible situation. "*He* called *me*. I didn't go to him."

"What difference does it make?"

"All right."

"Don't touch it again, Jerry. You understand me? If anything else comes up, check with me. I'll handle it."

Staying out of it might not be easy. Jerry got a call that afternoon from a woman who identified herself as Cary Blankenship. Cary was in her eighties, but she still radiated energy. She was seated in a lawn chair in front of a potted tree. "I used to work for NASA," she said. "I was only a technician. I did pretty routine stuff. But I remember something that always seemed odd."

"What was that, Cary?"

"Just before the Moon flights, the landings, they had something called the Cassandra Project. Don't know what it was. It was a big secret. Very hush-hush."

"Did you ever find out what it was about?"

"No. In fact, we weren't even supposed to know there was such a thing."

"So why's that odd?"

"Because we didn't normally do secret stuff. I mean, the equipment, sure. A lot of that was classified. But missions? That just didn't happen. We were pretty public. Some of the technology was classified, but having a project that nobody wanted to talk about, that was a first. Well, not quite a first, but it was unusual. Later, when we were involved launching spy satellites and stuff, things changed. But it wasn't like that in 1969."

"*Cassandra* was a mission?"

"I wouldn't swear to it, but I sure had that impression."

Jerry ran a search, but no reference to a NASA Cassandra Project showed up. He decided it was of no consequence and had just gone back to work when he got a call from Brian Colson, the host of *The Brian Colson Show*. "Jerry," he said, "how are you doing?"

A chill ran down Jerry's spine. No way this could be anything other than bad news. "Fine, Brian. What can I do for you?"

Colson was a big, intimidating guy. His show was billed as news and opinion, but mostly it consisted of his launching attacks on politicians he didn't like, or even ones he *did*, or at least claimed to. It was hard to guess why anyone went on his show. But Jerry figured that if you could stand up to Colson, you could win a lot of points with the party bosses and even with the voters. And, of course, you also went on if you had a book to sell. "Jerry, we're having one of your friends on tonight." He paused, probably to give Jerry a chance to fill in the name.

Jerry resisted the impulse. "Who's that, Brian?"

"Ralph D'Angelo. That's an interesting story about Aaron Walker's journal. *The Sun* will be going with it tomorrow."

A chill ran down Jerry's spine. "I can't see a story there anywhere, Brian."

"You think Walker was just making it up? Maybe drinking or something?"

"About what?"

"Come on, Jerry. Do you want me to read you what he says?"

"I don't know, Brian. He must have been joking. He was probably doing what we all do, making up something he wished had happened."

"Good enough. You want to come on the show tonight and say that?"

Turn up on *The Brian Colson Show* tonight and go looking for a new job tomorrow. "It's not worth the time, Brian. Mine or yours. Not that I wouldn't enjoy talking about current projects. But this Aaron Walker story—"

"No reason we can't talk about some of the current stuff you're working on."

"Brian, thanks, but I have to pass. I'm buried at the moment."

"You know what really rings my bell about this, Jerry?" It was an expression he used all the time on his show. Everything rang his bell. "When he said, 'Oops, forgot I'm not supposed to say that.' "

———

Jerry told Mary about the invitation and warned her that *The Sun* would be running the story.

She took it well. "Can't say I'm surprised," she said. "Well, you did the right thing. Probably. Staying off the show."

Jerry thought about calling Amos Bartlett, the lone surviving member of Walker's crew. But an online blogger had already asked him about the mission, about whether they'd gone down to the surface. He'd denied the story. Moreover, if Jerry followed up, it would very likely get back to Mary.

He skipped dinner that evening. He wasn't hungry, and it was just as well. He could stand to lose a pound or two. He retreated to his condo and opened all the windows. It was a cool, pleasant evening, and he needed to hear the distant rumble of the sea. That soothing sound tended to put everything in perspective. He understood quite clearly that Neil Armstrong had been the first man to set foot on the Moon. Everything else was an urban legend. But it was precisely the kind of story the media love to feed on.

He watched the news. Watched an episode of *The Shadow*, a guilty pleasure that allowed him to escape reality for an hour. Then, at eight, he switched over to Colson.

Colson routinely did three segments. On that evening, the first concerned a once-popular actor who insisted on beating his wife, taking drugs, and generally raising hell. He'd thrown a young woman with whom he'd been sleeping through a window several evenings before, then tried to punch out the cops who came for him. His guest was the network's Hollywood reporter. When they broke for commercial, he advised everyone what was next: Did the Moon landings happen the way we were told? Or is NASA hiding something?

When they came back after the commercials, Ralph was seated across a table from Colson. They were already deep in conversation, none of it audible to the viewer, which was the standard routine. The host raised a hand ostensibly to signal his guest that they were live, faced the camera, and the sound came back. "After fifty years," he said, "are we hearing a new story about the Moon landings? Our guest this evening is Ralph D'Angelo of *The Baltimore Sun*. Ralph, why are there suddenly doubts about who was first man to land on the Moon? Is it anything we should take seriously?"

Ralph laughed. Shook his head. Indicated, before he said a word, that he had no idea where the truth lay. He described the Eastman Award luncheon, and they played the clip of Warren Cole asking about the exchanges between Myshko and Mission Control, played the exchanges themselves, played Myshko's incomprehensible comment: "We are in the LEM. Ready to go."

And Mission Control's equally inexplicable "Good luck, guys."

If they weren't leaving the capsule, why wish them luck?

Which was exactly the question Colson asked his guest.

Ralph made a face. Shrugged. "It makes no sense, does it, Brian?"

They stayed with it for a few minutes, while Colson tried to imagine any context that would explain the exchange. There was none. Then they moved on to the rocks. Jerry's face became warm. Why hadn't he kept his mouth shut? "Is there any truth to the story?"

"Jerry Culpepper says it happened."

"So who would be carrying rocks in a space capsule?"

"That *is* strange, isn't it?" said Ralph.

And finally, to Aaron Walker's journal. They posted the extract:

> . . . *forty years since my stroll on the lunar surface. Oops, forgot I'm not supposed to say that. Wonder what that thing was, anyhow?*

"What *thing* do you suppose he's talking about, Ralph?"

"If we could answer that, maybe we could figure out the rest of it, Brian."

"You know," the host told his audience, "if the journal entry was all there was, I'd write it off as a joke. Or something Aaron Walker wrote after maybe drinking too much. But—"

"I know, Brian. We're beginning to get a pattern."

"You said you had something else."

"After the story appeared yesterday, I called a reliable source at NASA."

"And what did your reliable source say?"

"I showed him the journal. He asked me where it had come from. Well, that was Jane Alcott, of course, Aaron Walker's daughter. And I understand he flew down and went out to talk to her."

"The source did?"

"That's correct, Brian."

Colson looked out at his audience. "We invited Ms. Alcott onto the show, but she declined. I should also mention that we asked NASA's Jerry Culpepper to appear with us here, but he also ducked." He inhaled. Nobody on the planet could inhale like Colson. "Look, folks," he said. "We don't know what's going on, but something clearly is." He smiled. "Maybe they sighted aliens on the Moon." He thanked Ralph for coming in, then turned back to the camera. "Closing out this evening, Senator Jennifer Baxter will talk to us about her bill that would make group marriage legal. Stay with us."

Everybody at the Space Center must have seen the show, and copies of the *Sun* were everywhere. When Jerry showed up for work next day, some grinned, others looked away, and a few, without going into detail, assured him everything would be all right. Barbara wished him good morning while she tried very hard to behave as if nothing unusual had happened. And Vanessa did her best to stay out of the way.

He did *not*, however, get called into Mary's office.

He'd been worried that it would morph into another big story, that the morning would be filled with calls from reporters. There were several, but it didn't become the avalanche he'd feared.

He settled into his routine, putting together a press release on the Heynman telescope, whose launch had been postponed twice. It was now rescheduled for next year, but nobody believed it would actually happen. The Heynman was designed to do spectroscopy in the far and extreme ultraviolet spectral ranges. He wasn't sure what that meant, but he plugged it in for the media. When it was finished, he sent it to Barbara for distribution to the mailing list and started prepping for the annual Florida Librarians luncheon, which was being held that day in Titusville. Jerry had accepted an invitation to be guest speaker. He half expected Mary to direct him to send Vanessa in his place. But it didn't happen.

Under normal circumstances, having an audience was just what he would have wanted to bring him out of his funk. But not this time. He sat in his office, staring into a void. After a while, he got up and pulled the blinds against the late-summer sun, which was beating down on the space complex.

Barbara came in. "Did you see *The Herald* today?" she asked.

"No," he said. *The Herald* was the Titusville newspaper.

She touched the keyboard and made an adjustment. An AP story was headlined: EARLY SECRET MISSIONS TO THE MOON? "I thought you'd better know before you went to the luncheon," she said. Her tone was sympathetic.

"Barb," he said, "I'd have been surprised if they *weren't* running it." He turned it off.

At the luncheon, he would begin by talking about why librarians were essential for an advancing society. That would win over the audience. Then he'd bring in the future. Why we needed a functioning space program. Satellite communications. Navigation. In time, we'd put up energy collectors and use them to provide global power, to get us past this primitive age that was so dependent on fossil fuels. We would also be able to provide protection against asteroids. And, ultimately, there would be Moonbase and Mars. And who knew where we'd go from there?

He pulled an index card out of the box, picked up a marker, and wrote reminders on the card: CHALLENGES. COMMUNICATIONS. GPS. COLLECTORS. ASTEROIDS. MOONBASE. And, finally: KIDS. He always ended the same way: "I envy the kids being born today. Imagine what they're going to see during their lifetimes. All that's needed is for us to make it happen."

That always got a strong reaction. He wished he believed it.

——————

The luncheon went smoothly. There were only two questions about the news stories, both suggesting it was impossible to imagine how such an idea could be taken seriously. Jerry, of course, explained that he never ceased to be amazed at what people were willing to believe. "We don't read enough," he added. Afterward, he stood talking to several of the librarians, watching the crowd file out. He wasn't paying much attention to the conversation until one of them, a gray-haired man in a light blue jacket, asked him how it felt to be famous.

"I'm not famous," he said. He didn't need any modesty there. He got periodic speaking engagements and showed up on TV occasionally, like for the press conference that had started it all. He'd once believed he might live a life that would warrant an autobiography. But that dream was long past. He'd never really done anything. He'd never lifted off on a mission, never pulled anybody out of a burning building, never served in the military. Once, in high school, he'd driven in the tying runs with two out in the ninth inning of a playoff game. That had been the peak moment of his life.

"Sure you're famous," said the man in the blue jacket. He was short, stocky, with a thick waist. He wore a white open-collared shirt with a Tampa Bay Rays logo emblazoned on the pocket. "Modesty, Mr. Culpepper, is, I guess, what we expect of true greatness." He smiled. Kidding, but he meant it.

On his way back to the Space Center, Jerry thought about it. To most people, he probably did look like a celebrated figure. A man who held press conferences. Rode first class on planes. Appeared as a guest speaker at local luncheons. Look at me, Ma. I'm on top of the world.

He would like to accomplish one thing of significance in his life. Perform one truly memorable act, so that people would remember him. He didn't need a monument. A footnote would be nice. He'd helped get President Cunningham elected. (Jerry remembered when he was just George.) But that was about it. And who'd remember a political wonk?

Gerald L. Culpepper. The man who revealed the truth about the Moon missions.

The truth. What was the truth?

He knew. Armstrong had been the first man on the Moon. A few other miniscule details were being misinterpreted because they made an interesting story.

And that was all it was.

Amos Bartlett, who'd been Aaron Walker's command module pilot in 1969, lived outside Los Angeles. Jerry sat a long time staring at the TV. Finally, he decided what the hell and made the call. It rang four or five times, and a woman answered. "Hello," he said, "is Mr. Bartlett there?"

"Just a minute, please." No on-screen picture. Well, that wasn't unusual when a stranger was involved. She could, of course, see *him*. "Who should I tell him is calling?"

Jerry sighed. This might not go well. "Jerry Culpepper," he said. "From NASA."

"Okay. Hold on a second." He heard a door open and close, and the woman's voice again: "For you, Amos."

Jerry listened to the wind blowing against the side of the

building. Tree branches moved. Then the TV picked up a picture of Amos Bartlett. He was close to ninety, but the guy still looked okay. Tall, lean, with a full head of white hair, he could have been on his way out to play a round of basketball. He leaned casually back against a desk top while he gazed at Jerry. "Hello," he said. "What can I do for you, Mr. Culpepper?"

"Mr. Bartlett." Jerry tried to sound casual. At ease. "I have a couple of questions I'd like to ask."

"Go ahead." He sounded vaguely hostile.

"You were the command module pilot for Aaron Walker back in '69."

"Why don't we cut right to the chase, Mr. Culpepper?"

"Okay."

"You want to know if anything happened on the lunar flight?"

"That's correct. Aaron Walker left a note in a journal—"

"I know about the journal." His voice took on an edge, and his eyes narrowed. "I don't know what he meant by it, but I can tell you it was a routine flight. Nothing out of the ordinary occurred. Okay? Anything else?"

"Why is the question so irritating?"

"Look. I don't mean to be rude, Mr. Culpepper, but I'm sure you understand how silly this is. Do you have anything else?"

"Amos. Is it okay if I call you that?"

"What exactly is it you want from me, Mr. Culpepper?"

"If I can get a release for you, will you tell me what happened on that flight?"

It was only there for a moment, a brief quiver, teeth sucking his lip, eyes suddenly focused somewhere else. Then he came back. "If you've anything serious to ask, I'll be here."

Bartlett broke the connection.

———

There was no one left at NASA from the 1960s. In fact, Jerry knew of only one person living on the Space Coast who had been part of Agency management when Apollo XI went to the Moon: Richard Cobble, who'd been one of the operational people during the glory years. Cobble, until recently, had been active in a support role, serving with the Friends of NASA, a group of volunteers who helped wherever they could but mostly threw parties. Increasingly, during recent years, they'd taken to talking about the "good old days."

Jerry checked Cobble's record. He'd arrived at the Agency in 1965 as a technician. Eventually, he'd risen to become one of the operational directors.

"He's out bowling," a young, very attractive woman told him. Probably a great-granddaughter. "I'll let him know you called."

Cobble returned the call just as Jerry was leaving to go home. It was obvious that, wherever he had been, it had had nothing to do with bowling. He was in his mideighties. Unlike Amos Bartlett, he looked it. His eyes had no life left in them, and his shoulders were bent with arthritis. His jaw sagged, and he drooled as he looked out of the TV at Jerry. "How's life over at the Center?" he asked. "I haven't been there for a long time."

"It's quiet," said Jerry. "Not a whole lot happening."

"I know. It's sad. I never thought things would go this way."

Jerry kept him talking for a few minutes, about the state of space travel, about what might have been. And, when he thought Cobble receptive, he asked about the Myshko and Walker missions. "We keep hearing rumors that they landed in '69. Before Armstrong. Richard, does that make any sense to you? At all?"

"No," he said. "I can't imagine why they'd have wanted to do it. I mean, I know that the guys in the ships would have liked to make the landing. But they weren't going to go down without NASA's okay. And they didn't have it. Even assuming one of them had been a maverick, how could they have kept it quiet for a half century? We've both worked for the government, Jerry. You know how the government is at keeping secrets."

"Is there any way it could have been done without your knowledge?"

Cobble was seated in an armchair. But he didn't look comfortable. He started to say no, stopped to rearrange himself, and started again. "Look, Jerry, anything's possible. I wasn't actually in a position during that year, during '69, where I had a handle on things. Is it possible they could have done it? Sure, it's possible, but do I believe it? Why don't you ask me if I believe in Area 48?"

"I think it's Area 51, Richard."

"Whatever."

"Okay. Thanks. If you think of something, let me know, okay?"

Barbara stuck her head in. "Anything else, Jerry?"

"No, Barb," he said. "See you Monday."

The phone rang. It was Cobble again. "There *was* one thing, Jerry. There was something back then, I think it was the same year, '69, they called the Cassandra Project."

"Cassandra?" That was the project Cary Blankenship had referred to.

"Yeah. I'm pretty sure it was '69. Anyhow, I'm not sure it ever really existed. I just remember the name because there were rumors. But I don't recall anybody who actually knew anything about it. So—Oh, hell, it's probably my imagination. My memory doesn't work very well anymore."

"Do you know anything about it, Richard?"

"No. Just that—Well, let it go. I don't know what I'm talking about." He clicked off.

Barbara was still standing in the doorway. "Who's Cassandra?" she asked.

Jerry googled it. "I think she was the Greek woman who could tell the future." There were multiple entries. "No, I guess she was Trojan," he said.

There was also a Cassandra software system, a Cassandra school for actors, a Cassandra chain store that sold furniture. But of course there was nothing connecting the term with spaceflight.

"So she could predict the future," Barbara said. "Any reason why NASA might name a project for her?"

Jerry read the entry. "Maybe there is. Nobody ever believed her."

7

Bucky hated having facial makeup applied. Every time he went on television, they put it on him, and every time he objected, they explained that everyone, even the president, even the pope, wore makeup for television. And every time they told him that, he rattled off thirty or forty current baseball and football players who didn't wear makeup during postgame interviews (and he'd occasionally toss in a mud-spattered jockey who'd just ridden a winner on an off track). It didn't make any difference; as much as he complained, they applied the makeup. He drew the line at their wanting to damp down his hair and then blow-dry it to make it look thicker.

"I am not Cary Grant!" he would snap. "I don't have to look like a romantic lead."

"Cary *who*?" was the usual response from the young makeup artists.

He would update it to Burt Lancaster, then Sylvester Stallone, who weren't quite the romantic stars Grant was, but after that he was out of names because he'd been too busy the past thirty years to watch any films and see who women were swooning over these days.

Jason Brent leaned against a wall, looking vastly amused.

"You're supposed to be protecting me," growled Bucky.

"I'd rather watch you squirm."

"You're fired."

"That's the fifth time this month," noted Brent amiably.

"I guess I'd better not fire you again this month. You'd never think to start counting the fingers on the other hand."

Brent chuckled. "Come on, Boss. It's just makeup. They put it on you every time, and you bitch every time. It hasn't done you any harm yet."

"They're supposed to be *listening* to me, not *looking* at me," muttered Bucky.

"Then make it a radio address."

"You're fired again."

"You can't," said Brent. "Not until you hire me back first."

"I don't mind having a deadly killer in my employ," said Bucky, "but if there's one thing I hate, it's an uppity one."

Brent laughed again, and this time Bucky joined him.

Ed Camden entered just then, couldn't figure out the joke, and waited patiently for them to calm down.

"Anything more?" asked Bucky at last.

"Like what?" replied Camden. "You saw the damned diary."

"Have you checked to see if anyone else kept diaries?"

"Bucky, most of them are dead, and the handful who aren't are spread all the hell over the country, probably the world, and I just got the damned diary the day before yesterday."

"Have you talked to Aaron Walker's shrink?" persisted Bucky. "Was he prone to delusions?"

"He didn't *have* a shrink," said Camden.

"You checked?" said Bucky, surprised.

"I haven't worked for you all these years without knowing a little something about how your mind works," replied Camden. "No shrink, no aberrant behavior, no DTs, no nothing."

"Damn!" said Bucky. "I have to address, I don't know, thirty million people in a few minutes, maybe forty million . . . and all I've got is guesswork and supposition."

"What are you going to say?"

"I'm still thinking about it."

"You know . . ." began Camden.

"Yeah?"

"You could still cancel it. They've got DVDs and films they can run on a minute's notice, probably even some old Sid

Caesar or Ernie Kovacs kinescopes, any number of things for emergencies."

"I paid for the time," said Bucky adamantly. "I'm going on."

"You're going to make some crazy statement in front of zillions of people. Why?"

"Crazy?" demanded Bucky.

"It'll *sound* crazy," persisted Camden. "Myshko played golf on the Moon. They smuggled a woman aboard the ship. They brought back a little green man. Whatever it is, whether you wind up being able to prove it or not, it'll sound crazy—and we're planning a Moon trip in just a few months, for all I know even sooner."

"Your government has been keeping a secret for half a century," said Bucky. "It's time to bring it out into the light of day."

"We don't have proof of anything yet."

"Then I'll encourage some viewers to help find the proof."

"Bucky, you'll encourage forty-three wackos. The remainder of the forty million will think you're crazy or a clown."

"Let 'em," said Bucky.

"Think of what it'll do to our Moon shot!" urged Camden. "Weren't you the guy who didn't want it to look like you were easily bamboozled?"

"I've decided that this is more important," answered Bucky. "And it'll get more people interested in what we're doing."

"They'll think it's being orchestrated by a looney tune!"

Bucky shrugged. "I repeat: Let 'em."

"I don't know how many years you've spent building your reputation," said Camden, "but it'll only take one telecast to destroy it."

Bucky stared at Camden for a long moment. "That's the way I was thinking yesterday. I was wrong."

"In what way?"

Bucky smiled. "Who's going to fire me?"

Camden stared at him uncomprehendingly.

"Who's going to say I can't go to the Moon?" Bucky continued. "I think what I'm going to suggest is correct. But if I'm wrong, the only thing that will change is the public's perception of me, and since I'm never running for political office, I don't give a damn about that. You'll still have a job, none of my corporations will miss a step, we'll still send a rocket to the Moon, the IRS will still harass me every year. The only people it might affect are Jason and his crew. If everyone thinks I'm a harmless idiot, there'll be fewer attempts to kidnap or kill me."

"There have only been two since I came to work for you five years ago," noted Brent.

"Good," said Bucky. "Then if I'm right, you can apply for early retirement."

Brent laughed again, and Camden just shook his head in defeat. "Well, I tried," he said at last.

"And believe it or not, I appreciate it," said Bucky. "You're trying to defend my image. The thing is, my body may need protection from time to time, but I've reached the point where my image can take care of itself." He paused. "Whatever we find, whatever we see and experience up there, we're going to bring back proof, and once we do, what they think of me will have nothing to do with the importance of anything we find."

"All right," said Camden. "Do it your way. Hell, you always do."

"That's why most of my staff has been with me for years. I never have anyone to blame but myself."

"So what *are* you going to say?"

Another smile. "Why don't you listen?"

And another sigh. "I will."

Gloria entered the dressing room.

"Ah! A fourth for bridge," said Bucky.

"I'm glad to see you're not nervous," she said. "I'm just here to tell you you're on in six minutes."

"Who's introducing me?"

She frowned. "You never said anything about that. I assume one of the announcers from the network."

"That'll be okay," replied Bucky. "Though I'd have loved to have had Jerry Culpepper do it."

"It'd cost him his job."

"I know," said Bucky. "Then he'd have no compunctions about coming to work for me."

"I never know if you're kidding or not," said Camden.

"Tell him, Gloria."

"Half the trick is never letting them know if you're kidding," she replied.

"Right," agreed Bucky. He stood up and looked at himself in the mirror, adjusted his tie, studied his face, and ran his fingers through his hair. "So it won't look like they groomed me right before I came out," he explained, then looked around. "Now where did I put that damned book?"

"You mean the diary?" asked Camden.

"Yeah."

"I know you paid good money for it, but if you hold it up in front of the camera, you'll cost Ralph D'Angelo his job."

"He won't go broke before he finds another," said Bucky. Suddenly he stood still, shrugged, and turned to the door. "What the hell. You never know when we'll need a friend in Baltimore." He stepped out into the corridor. "Which way do I go?"

"I'll take you," said Gloria, grabbing him by the forearm and leading him away from the dressing room.

"Hello, Mr. Blackstone," said the director, as Bucky reached the soundstage. "Would you prefer to be seated or standing?"

"Makes no difference." Bucky scanned the soundstage. "I don't see a desk or a chair, so I'll stand. Where do you want me?"

"Over here will be just fine," said the director, indicating a spot. "I'll have the teleprompters move over to—"

"Don't bother. I don't use them."

"The anti-Obama," said the director with a smile.

"I never use a prepared text, so there's nothing to read."

The director looked dubious. "You mean you're just going to speak off the cuff to thirty million people?"

"Forty million," said Gloria.

"However many," said the director.

"Yes, that's what I mean," answered Bucky.

"I've covered six presidential campaigns," said the director. "No one does that."

"Maybe that's why we have so many problems," said Bucky. "Tell me when you want me to stand there, and have someone give me a countdown when I get there."

He found a folding chair and sat down, totally relaxed, while those who knew him and those who didn't marveled at the total lack of tension in his face and his bearing. Presidents who addressed the country every week were usually immersed in their notes, or practicing their opening lines to themselves, three minutes before they went on camera. But as Bucky had mentioned earlier, he wasn't running for any office, and there was no one who could take away what was his.

"All right, Mr. Blackstone," said the director. "Take your position, please."

Bucky stood up and walked over to the spot where he'd been instructed to stand.

"Very good. Look into whichever camera is showing the red light."

"I'm looking into this one," said Bucky, pointing to the closest of the three cameras. "You do whatever you want, but that's where I'll be looking the whole time."

"Please, Mr. Blackstone! I'm the director!"

"And I'm the guy who's paying for the airtime. As long as everyone remembers that, we'll get along fine."

"I doubt it," muttered the director.

"Then I'll buy this network and get along fine with your replacement," said Bucky, and, suddenly, the director fell silent.

A makeup woman came up to wipe a couple of drops of perspiration from his forehead. He simply shook his head no, and she made a right turn and walked away.

"Twenty seconds," said the director.

Bucky cleared his throat.

"Ten."

The countdown continued to zero, and he heard a voice say: "At this time, we bring you a special address from Morgan Blackstone, the owner of Blackstone Enterprises."

You could have added Blackstone Innovations and Blackstone Development, thought Bucky irritably as the red light flashed on.

"Good evening, ladies and gentlemen—and select politicians," he added with a smile. "I'm Morgan Blackstone, and I'm here to talk to you about something important.

"First, a little background. Since the last Apollo mission, it's been close to half a century since man has set foot on any world except our own. This is little short of shameful. Earth is part of a solar system, a number of planets in orbit around a star. It's estimated that there are more than one hundred billion stars in our galaxy, which we know informally as the Milky Way. And it's estimated that there are more than one hundred billion galaxies in the universe. Since the creation of the Hubble telescope, we are learning that more stars *have* planets than do not. There are over a billion G-type stars in the Milky Way, which is to say, the same type of star our Sun is. And all this is a roundabout way of saying that there's a lot of real estate up there, probably a lot of it habitable, and, somehow, we've lost interest in it.

"Yes, I know, every president has found better things to do with the money that should rightfully have kept NASA flying to Mars and the asteroids and the moons of Jupiter and Saturn. And even NASA officials admit that a hungry child or a sick senior needs that money more than they do, so it has become incumbent upon private industry and entrepreneurs to continue man's exploration of space. There have been a number of successful manned orbital flights, and as many of you know, my own corporation is planning to make the first manned landing on the Moon since the end of the Apollo program, which means since more than two-thirds of you were born."

Bucky paused and stared into the camera, ordering his thoughts for a few seconds, then continued: "All this is background, information that you can find on the Internet, or see on any newscast, or read in any local newspaper on the unlikely assumption that your community still *has* a local newspaper.

"What I'm about to tell you next, however, is something you won't be able to find in any of those places, no matter how hard you look. I'm telling you because the government is going to do everything they can to discredit me once this talk is over. They *may* try to keep us from taking off for the Moon though they have no legal right to, and when I bring back proof of what I'm about to tell you, they will put the entire machinery of the government to work trying to convince you that I'm a flake or a con man."

He put on his most open and trusting face. "I'll leave it to you to decide. Just remember: They work for *you*, not the other way around. I won't let them bully me, and you must stand up to them, too."

Now came the fatherly smile. "All right, I know you weren't expecting anything like this. I'm going to give you a minute to come back from the kitchen, the bathroom, wherever some of you have wandered off to, and then I will tell you something that your most trusted public servants have been hiding from you for all or most of your lifetimes."

He fell silent and signaled Gloria for a glass of water, which she promptly brought to him. He wasn't the least bit thirsty, but he wanted to be doing something during his minute-long break, if for no other reason than that people just tuning in wouldn't think they were watching some idiot who was too nervous to say anything and just stared dully into the camera.

He counted the seconds as he toyed with the glass, handed it back to Gloria—who again walked in a kind of half squat so she wouldn't be seen on camera—and once again faced the red light. "I trust you're all back," he said. "Now I have a question for you. What were the first words spoken by the first man to set foot on the Moon?"

He paused to give them time to mouth the answer. "I'll wager all of you said, 'One small step for man, one giant leap for mankind.' Am I right?"

He smiled, the way a schoolteacher might smile. "I regret to inform you—oh, *how* I regret it—that that answer is not correct. 'One small step for man' were the first five words spoken by Neil Armstrong—*but they were not the first words spoken by the first man on the Moon!*"

He waited for the impact of what he had said to strike home.

"That's right," he continued. "Apollo XI was *not* the first American ship to land on the Moon, and there is an excellent chance, almost a certainty, that a man named Sidney Myshko, and not Neil Armstrong, was the first American to walk on its surface. *That* is what the government has been hiding since 1969!"

He had to pause again for the buzzing among the studio staff to die down.

"I have had near-certain proof of this in my possession for more than a day, but I—and others—have had our suspicions about it a lot longer. I will be making certain things public once I'm sure that innocent parties are insulated against the fallout.

"I have one more announcement, and that is that *I* will be on the ship that flies to the Moon this summer, and I will bring back further proof of what I said. Hopefully, I can also determine *why*, when we were in a race with the Russians to reach the Moon, we went out of our way to hide all proof of our initial landing, only to then make Apollo XI's accomplishments available to the entire world as they were happening.

"Whatever the answer is, whatever the reason for the cover-up—and make no mistake about it, *cover-up* is the right term—it happened almost half a century ago, and the reason is surely no longer valid. It's my own guess that the secret is like most Washington secrets, kept by inertia rather than necessity.

"And that, ladies and gentlemen, is what I wanted to say to you tonight. Either I or one of my spokesmen will be available to the press starting tomorrow. Thank you for your attention, and good night."

"You have seventeen minutes left!" hissed the director in a panic.

"I bought them, they're mine. Run a test pattern until the half hour's up."

The director frowned. "What's a test pattern?"

"Ask somebody," said Bucky, walking off the soundstage.

Brent hustled him to a waiting limo, accompanied by Gloria and Camden. It peeled off just before the paparazzi could surround them.

"Back to the hotel?" asked Brent.

Bucky shook his head. "We're registered there under my name. They'll find us in five minutes. Have the driver take us over to a nice hotel in Jersey, and get us a suite and a couple of rooms in your name."

"Right," said Brent, sliding the glass barrier behind the driver's seat and giving the instructions to the chauffeur.

As they drove, Camden turned on the small TV in the passenger section. "They won't break into basketball, or any of the sitcoms, but I'll bet you're on every cable news show."

He switched the channel, and suddenly the president's press secretary was facing the camera.

"No, of course it's hogwash," she was saying. "There are always paranoid conspiracy theorists out there. You think being a billionaire disqualifies you from buying into this drivel?"

Another channel, and the vice president was speaking: "Next thing you know, he'll be telling you that Obama was born in Kenya and that George Bush was a cokehead."

Another, and this time it was the Majority Leader of the Senate: "We don't need another witch hunt at this time, and especially for such an unlikely, make that impossible, witch. Mr. Blackstone has made a fool of himself, which is his privilege, but he has also doubtless convinced a number of gullible Americans, as well as America-hating foreign powers, that our

government has propounded the most unbelievable lie for half
a century. Accordingly, I am instructing my staff to return all of
his campaign contributions . . ."

"Turn it off," said Bucky.

"It bothers you?" said Camden. "You had to know what their
reaction would be."

"No," said Bucky. "It bores me. Every one of them is protecting a secret they don't even know exists. I've never been a fan
of sheep."

Camden turned it off.

They drove the rest of the way in silence. Brent registered
them at an upscale hotel, made sure Bucky had his face buried
in a handkerchief as he walked through the lobby, and a couple
of minutes later the four of them were ensconced in the parlor
of the presidential suite.

"See what room service has and order enough for the four of
us," Bucky told Gloria, and she picked up a menu, studied it for
a moment, then walked to the phone and ordered.

"Well, at least we're free and clear for the rest of the night,"
said Camden, relaxing on a leather recliner.

"You really think so, do you?" asked Bucky, amused.

"Sure. The press is probably still nosing around the last hotel."

"I wasn't referring to the press."

And ten minutes later, a bellhop knocked on the door.

"What can I do for you?" asked Camden, opening the door.

"Is one of you a Mr. Blackstone?" asked the bellhop.

Camden was about to deny it when Bucky spoke up. "One of
us is," he said.

The bellhop walked over to Bucky and held out a silver tray
with an envelope on it.

"You're in the habit of hand-delivering notes, are you?"
asked Bucky.

"From this particular source, yes, sir," said the bellboy nervously. He turned and left the room before anyone could tip him.

"So what have you got?" asked Brent.

"Why guess?" asked Bucky, opening the envelope, unfolding
the letter, and staring at it. "They're *good*, I'll give them that."

"What is it?"

"From the White House," answered Bucky. "Received four

minutes ago. That means they knew we were here about a minute after we walked into the suite."

"And the message?" asked Gloria.

"About what you'd expect," said Bucky, laying it down on a coffee table for everyone to see. The stationery said: Office of the President, and the handwritten note read:

Bucky—

We have to talk.

George Cunningham

"So are you going to talk to him?" she asked.

"Sure," replied Bucky. Then he smiled. "Eventually."

8

A presidential visit to the Space Center was a rare event. The last one had occurred in 2011, when Barack Obama and his family followed through with their plans to watch the launch of the *Endeavour* despite receiving news that the mission had been scrubbed because of problems with a heater system. It was, probably, an appropriate conclusion for what some described as man's most epic achievement.

But George Cunningham was coming. "He's going to stay overnight," said Mary.

That was a surprise. "Will Lyra be with him?" The First Lady.

"No," she said. "She's on a peace mission to the Middle East." She grinned. The First Lady, like most presidential wives in recent years, was an active player in the administration. And Lyra had proven herself a decent diplomat. But peace in the Middle East? That was a loser's game. "He wants to stay at the Beach House."

The Beach House was an unassuming cottage out on the Space Center shoreline. In another era, it was where the astronauts and their families stayed before a mission. It was where they'd said good-bye to each other. But that was a long time ago. Now it served primarily as a conference center. "He can't stay there," Jerry said. "The place doesn't even have a bedroom anymore."

Mary glanced briefly at the ceiling. "Last time I looked," she said, "he was the president. He can probably stay wherever he wants."

Jerry shrugged. "Okay. I'll talk to Tom." Tom Bergmann, who'd refitted the place.

"No. He wants it as is. Don't touch anything."

"But—"

"Jerry, the president has a taste for history. The word we got is that he'll sleep on the sofa. Leave it alone."

"You're sure?" Presidents don't sleep on sofas.

She sighed. "Stop pushing."

"All right." He looked out at the palm trees. "Why's he coming? Going to announce a flight to Mars?"

"They didn't say. My best guess is that he's going to try to boost morale. You know how he is. Or maybe he just wants an excuse to stay over at the Beach House."

"I hope," Jerry said, "he's not coming in to close us down." That was a dumb thing to say, and they both knew it. If he was shutting the doors, he'd do it from the capital.

"That's not really fair, Jerry. He's done what he can for us."

"I expected more."

"Let's try to be reasonable. Anyhow, I want you to arrange a press conference for him. We'll use the theater at the Visitors' Center."

"Okay."

"He'll be coming in Saturday morning." Four days. She smiled. This White House never gave you much warning.

─────────

Ordinarily, assisting with the preparations would have been at the top of Jerry's priorities, but he'd allowed the business with the Myshko and Walker missions to obscure everything else. Nevertheless, he had Vanessa set up the theater for the press conference. That would have the additional advantage of allowing a formal luncheon. Earlier in the day, the president would make an appearance at an orphanage. There would also be a Saturday evening reception. Jerry was charged with putting together a guest list.

He was trying to organize everything when Mary called. "He wants to attend services Sunday morning at the First Presbyterian Church in Titusville. Do you by any chance know the pastor?"

"No," said Jerry.

"Okay. Contact him. Let him know what's going to happen. Find out what time the services are, okay? We want something around nine o'clock. Whatever's close to that, we'll go with. Tell him there'll be some people who will want to talk to him about security details. They'll be in touch."

Cunningham was routinely accused by his political enemies of showboating. He was, they charged, always visiting schools and shelters for battered women and A.A. meetings. They said it was okay up to a point, but they charged he did it for purely political reasons and therefore debased the very institutions he claimed to be helping.

It was all politics. Jerry knew the president well enough to entertain no doubts about his judgment and his intentions. He believed he had a responsibility to help where he could, and he enjoyed doing so. "If I can remind people," he'd told Mary in Jerry's presence one evening, "that these organizations need their assistance, I'm going to do it. Any way I can."

The remark had stayed with him. Now, while he returned to assembling the guest list, he found his thoughts wandering back into history. To the Beach House and those long-ago Apollo flights. What had Myshko and Walker and their crews been thinking when they gathered out there with their families?

———

It probably wouldn't have occurred to him to broach the Cassandra business with the president had Mary not cautioned him about bringing it up. "I know you, Jerry. I know how your mind works. And I'm warning you: Don't even think about it."

If something *had* happened here a half century ago, the president would be aware of it if anybody was. And he immediately began imagining himself confronting Cunningham. "Mr. President, what really happened on the Moon back in 1969?" Sure. "And while we're at it, what about that Roswell business?"

You couldn't get past the absurdity of it all.

The president came in on a Marine helicopter, designated Marine One. It descended onto the shuttle landing pad, where it was met by a small delegation of NASA executives. Ordinarily,

Jerry should have been among them, but Mary found something else for him to do. She wanted him to set up a teleconference with people at NBC to arrange a tour of the facility by a group of TV celebrities. It could have been taken care of at any time over the last few days, but Mary had sat on it, set the timing to coincide with the arrival of the White House delegation, and pulled it out of her pocket at the last minute. "Forgot about meeting them," she'd said. It was a lame explanation, as she knew it was, as she intended it to be. She was sending a message: Keep your distance while he's here. Do nothing to remind him of the Moon-landing story. And especially, if you get close to him, don't bring it up. In fact, don't get close at all.

The entertainers were the cast of the popular science-fiction series *The High Country*, which was set in the distant future and pictured a well-funded NASA running flights all over the solar system. It had debuted as a three-part special, in which the world was threatened by an inbound asteroid. The asteroid, when last tracked, had been in a harmless orbit. Someone had apparently deliberately diverted it onto its lethal trajectory. (It didn't seem to occur to the scientists in the series that it could have bumped into something, that the diversion could have been accidental.) They found the bad guys, who, despite various false leads, turned out to be not aliens, but deranged humans traveling back from the future. Their motivation for trying to destroy the planet was never made clear.

The lead characters, a scientist who'd developed a high-powered laser to be used to take out the asteroid, and a team of astronauts under the command of a Russian captain, Ivan Kolchevsky, played by the immensely popular Boris Vassily, got the job done in classic fashion. The special effects were spectacular. Everybody loved it, and the show morphed into a weekly series. It was not bad theater. The astronauts operated out of Moonbase. The world's premier orbiting telescope was saved in a hair-raising episode in which one of Captain Kolchevsky's team very nearly took the long plunge into the atmosphere. In another episode, scientists discovered life at the lunar north pole. Then a mission to a space station being assembled near Ganymede turned into a rescue effort for a ship that got into trouble when a jealous boyfriend seriously injured the pilot.

If the series was less than brilliant, it *did* avoid the usual

chases after space aliens that the general public had come to
expect from TV science-fiction shows. In the case of the lunar
microbes, for example, it examined the social consequences of
the discovery and set off a real-life debate about the literal truth
of the Bible. Another episode demonstrated how a united effort
to expand the human role in space advanced the cause of peace.
(Arab and Israeli occupants living at the Ganymede station had
to cooperate in order to survive after a massive power failure.)
One show got involved, hilariously, with a virtual exercise intended to determine what the gender makeup of a crew should
be on a flight to Uranus. The conclusion seemed to be that no
type of crew, encased for a year or two with only each other,
could possibly avoid major disharmony. To put it gently.

Jerry recorded it every Tuesday and usually watched it the
same night. So, apparently, did everybody else at the Space Center. Engineers, computer specialists, astronauts, personnel managers, even the guys who swept the floors and manned the
cafeteria inevitably discussed each episode the next day. For
Jerry, for all of them, it was both exhilarating and painful. *The
High Country* was an alternate world, where they were reminded
once each week what NASA, given the chance, might have been.

By the time Jerry had finished talking with NBC, the president was tucked away in the director's conference room. Secret
Service guys stood guard at the door. When Jerry approached,
they eyed him suspiciously and signaled that he was not authorized to enter. He wouldn't have made the attempt in any case,
of course. He'd never really considered looking for an opportunity to open up to the president about his concerns. That would
be career suicide. Jerry knew President Cunningham to be a
hardheaded realist. There was no way he'd be taking any of it
seriously. Unless, of course, he had inside information.

That was a possibility.

But Jerry was inclined to believe that the president, like most
people, bought the official story. And the reality was that no
compelling evidence had surfaced to demonstrate that view
wasn't accurate. All he had were hints. Missing voices on old
recordings, a curious journal entry, barely recalled memories of
something called the Cassandra Project. If there were any truth
to the early landings, what could they have been about? In an
era when the U.S. was desperate to demonstrate its technologi-

cal superiority over the Soviets, what could possibly have accounted for pulling off a landing but then keeping it quiet?

Nevertheless, Jerry decided he'd watch for an opportunity. And with luck, he'd get a break. Maybe when the president saw him, *he'd* be the one to bring up the issue. Jerry wouldn't have to. And that would keep him out of trouble with Mary. After all, it had dominated the news for several days. Well, maybe not *dominated*, but it had certainly maintained visibility. And Cunningham knew he could trust his old campaign worker. It would probably only be necessary for Jerry to get close.

A small retinue of reporters accompanied the president to the Golden Apple Orphanage just outside Titusville. "No need for you to go, Jerry," Mary told him. "It's probably best that we maintain a degree of separation. I'd just as soon not remind him about the secret flights." She smiled, suggesting it was a joke, but she got her point across. So Jerry went back to his office and spent the rest of the morning staring out the window.

The presidential party returned just in time for the luncheon. Jerry was assigned a table in back, where he sat with several visiting NASA managers, people from Huntsville and Houston. Jerry had met them all before, but in some cases he needed a furtive glance at their badges to recall names. One of them, Grant Tyler, an astrophysicist, immediately brought up Myshko and Walker. "Hard to believe anybody could have taken any of that seriously," he said, apparently unaware that it was precisely how Jerry had been portrayed in the media. Or maybe he was just enjoying himself.

The president was seated at a rectangular table with a lectern at its center. It was set on a platform in the front of the room. Mary and three other NASA executives were with him. They seemed to be having a good time, trading stories and laughing at one another's jokes. It was one of Cunningham's considerable political strengths: He knew how to put people at ease.

Eve Harrigan, an engineer at Houston, sympathized with Jerry's situation. "It *was* strange, though," she told Grant. "I can understand why people might think something was going on."

Grant got the message and changed the subject.

The menu choice was between catfish and New York strip.

Jerry went with the catfish, accompanied by mashed potatoes and a swirl of vegetables that he couldn't identify. The conversation at Jerry's table wandered onto the subject that currently occupied everyone's attention: the future of NASA in an era of tight funding. The reality, of course, was that NASA had been put on hold during the Vietnam War, and had never really gotten off the dime afterward. Presidents came and went, promising great things, a new state-of-the-art vehicle, a return to the Moon, a Mars mission, a rendezvous with an asteroid. All the stuff they'd been doing on *The High Country*.

The catfish was good.

The waiters followed up with strawberry shortcake and vanilla ice cream. Jerry and his companions were still indulging themselves when Mary stood, went to the microphone, and adjusted it. She introduced herself, led a round of applause for the president, and welcomed the assorted guests. "Mr. President," she said, "we know you've always been intrigued by spaceflight. And I have no doubt you're going to help us move forward with plans to send a manned mission to Pluto."

She'd intended it to be funny, but a hush fell over the room, and she realized immediately the remark hadn't gone well, wouldn't be interpreted as she'd intended, but would instead sound like a criticism of the administration. But it was too late, and she did the only thing she could, turning it into an *oops* moment. "I have a talent for blowing my lines," she said, with a tight smile. That, at least, brought some laughs.

Cunningham waved to her. It was okay. She waved back, finished the introduction, and turned the microphone over to him. He thanked her and looked out at the audience. "If we could manage a voyage to Pluto," he said, "I can think of a few people in Washington who'd enjoy making a reservation on it for me."

That got more laughs. Everyone knew he was talking about the Speaker of the House. "Ladies and gentlemen," he continued, "I'm delighted to be here today. And I know that you're concerned about the future of the Agency, from which we expected so much and which we've supported so little. I can't help thinking that we might have made it to Pluto had we diverted even a reasonable fraction of the money we've wasted over the past half century and given it to you folks."

That brought a standing ovation.

"That's not to say that NASA hasn't accomplished an enormous amount. We've been to the Moon, we've sent robot vehicles throughout the solar system, we've put telescopes in orbit that have allowed us to look back almost to the beginning of time. That's not bad."

That produced another round of applause. But it had become more tentative.

Cunningham nodded. "I understand," he said. "It's not enough, is it? When we started recruiting our first astronauts, back in the late fifties, we were only talking about one thing: Putting humans in space. On the Moon. That was all we cared about." He stopped. Exhaled. "I suspect everyone here has seen the Stanley Kubrick movie *2001*. For anyone who hasn't, it's about a ship headed for Jupiter. If you read the book, you discover they were actually going to *Saturn*. This was a film made in the sixties. At the time, the notion of manned missions out beyond Mars didn't seem all that far-fetched. We were going to do it all by the beginning of the twenty-first century. But for a variety of reasons, we discovered we couldn't manage it. None of that can be laid at *your* door. Nevertheless, here we are. Stuck on the ground eighteen years after Arthur Clarke's astronauts headed for the outer solar system."

The president looked up toward the ceiling. Behind Jerry, ice cubes rattled. Somewhere, a chair moved. They were the only sounds in the building. "I wish I could tell you that's all going to change. But, unfortunately, the country remains in a financial hole. You know it, and I know it. But I can promise you this: Despite what you're hearing on the Internet, despite what the media are saying, we are not going to shut this agency down. It's not going to happen. NASA is not going away. You can carve that in concrete."

The applause was louder this time.

"And I'll tell you something else: It's possible that the world, several thousand years from now, will have forgotten a lot of our history. It may no longer remember there were two world wars during the last century. It may not recall the nuclear standoff during the Cold War years. But I can tell you one thing: As long as men and women live, they'll remember that we once walked on the Moon. And they'll never forget who did it."

That took off the roof.

Jerry watched the reporters crowd into the theater at the Visitors' Center and couldn't help feeling a brief twinge of jealousy. He couldn't have drawn enough people to fill the front row.

Mary suggested he stay away since his presence alone might be enough to elicit questions. He let her see he was annoyed, but he said nothing and went up to his office to watch on C-Span. Four other cable networks also provided coverage.

Most of the questions centered on continuing problems in the Middle East, on the growing Franklin Movement, "a penny saved," which was demanding that many of the social programs the president favored be closed down. Did he see any hope of healing the left-right split in the country? What had happened to the promise that NASA would be lifting solar-power collectors into space? How did he feel about Bryson Evers's comment that the biggest problem the world had was the one no politician would talk about—the enormous growth of world population?

"Well," said Cunningham, "we're talking about it, aren't we?"

The question had been raised by NBC's Quil Everett. "Do you agree that it's a problem for us, Mr. President? And if so, what are we going to do about it?"

It had been described as the new third rail. Cunningham hesitated. Everyone knew it was true. But a substantial part of the electorate still believed there was a moral obligation to have big families. And, historically, there was no give on the issue. Furthermore, next year was an election year.

"*Yes,*" said Cunningham. "Of course it's true. There's not enough food. Not enough fresh water. Countries are going to war over natural resources. And that's only the beginning."

He didn't explain what the administration planned to do, other than continue to look into the problem. It wasn't exactly a call to action, but his admission alone, Jerry knew, would grab all the headlines tomorrow.

The Myshko and Walker missions never came up. Jerry wasn't sure whether he was relieved or disappointed. He switched over to CNN and MSNBC to watch the comments by the assorted policy experts. Only one, Stu Krider, mentioned the earlier flights. "Yesterday's news, I guess," Krider said. He was the only commentator Jerry knew of who had treated the story as anything other than something to generate laughs.

Cunningham was given a tour of the Center that evening. He

stood beside one of the old Atlas rockets, admired a command module, and talked with a few astronauts who'd been brought in specifically for the event. Jerry was part of the group of nine or ten NASA people following him around. Now that the press conference was over, Mary had eased her restrictions. Eventually, as they emerged at the base of one of the launch towers, the president looked Jerry's way. Their eyes connected. The president smiled. "Hello, Jerry," he said. "Busy time for you, I guess?"

Cunningham had all the physical attributes of a leader. He was tall, broad-shouldered, with leading-man features. He was in his forties, the youngest chief executive since Jack Kennedy. People naturally liked him. His ratings, even during these difficult times, remained high. And the country absolutely loved the First Lady, Lyra, who might have been a beauty queen in her younger days. Lyra had a self-effacing sense of humor and, in the view of some, had been the most effective campaigner on either side in the 2016 election.

And then, without warning, Jerry's opportunity arrived. The president, still looking his way, smiled. "What's all the ruckus about the Moon flights, Jerry?"

The world stopped momentarily. A warm breeze was coming in off the ocean, and he could hear tree limbs moving gently. All conversation died. Off to one side, he saw Mary. Her gaze focused on him, her lips tight. No smile. No give.

"Don't know, Mr. President," Jerry said. "I guess some people get excited pretty easily."

Cunningham smiled and moved on.

Jerry stood, looking at a wall. Avoiding Mary.

Dumb.

Cowardly.

———

The reception went off smoothly. An array of former and current NASA people showed up to pay their respects. Jerry knew many of them personally. They wandered up to him with expectant smiles, generally restricting their comments to how good it was to get back to the Space Center, but they all looked at him with a glint in their eyes. He'd become one of those guys who believed in Roswell and the abominable snowman.

Of the few who mentioned the Myshko story to him, Larry

Jurkiewicz stood out because he'd preceded him as press officer. "You're out there all the time," Larry said. "It's easy to screw up. You say the wrong thing, and you're stuck with it." He looked genuinely sympathetic. "Just hang in, Jerry. After a while, it'll go away."

He wasn't sure precisely when it happened, but by the time the evening had ended, he had come to terms with his failure to bring the issue up directly to the president. It could have done no good. If Cunningham knew anything and wanted to make it public, he would already have done so. Since he apparently didn't know anything, there was nothing he could contribute to the conversation.

In the morning, he accompanied the presidential party to the First Presbyterian Church in Titusville. He sat quietly in back during the ceremony and listened to the pastor welcome his guests before speaking briefly on the requirement to love one's neighbor. "It isn't all about money," he said. Jerry remembered church visits during the campaign, when the preachers had routinely pitched thinly disguised messages at the candidate. We need to see that both sides of the evolution issue are taught in the schools. Or whatever. But the pastor's sermon, based on the directive to love thy neighbor, showed no sign of a political imperative.

When it ended, the Secret Service sealed off the church while the president left. By the time Jerry got outside, he was gone. The worshippers lingered for a time. The pastor, Adam Tursi, stood by the front door, shaking hands and talking with parishioners. Jerry overheard part of it: "I like him," Tursi said to a small group on the church steps. He looked amiable, with an easy smile, his gray hair ruffled by the wind. "The president seems like a good man. But I miss the sound of the launchings. I sit in my office, and the only thing I hear now is the birds." He glanced over at Jerry, apparently trying to figure out whether he knew him. "Birds," he said again, "and an occasional police siren."

An hour later, Jerry watched film clips at home showing Marine One lifting off from the space facility. Eventually, Mary called.

She smiled at him from the screen. "It went off like clockwork, Jerry. Well done."

9

Bucky was poring over the latest cost-analysis figures for the Moon shot when Gloria Marcos entered his office. "I thought I said I wanted to be alone for an hour while I read all this stuff," he said, making no attempt to keep the irritation out of his voice.

"It'll hold," she said. "Turn your television on."

"To what?"

"Any cable news channel. They're all running the same thing."

A well-dressed middle-aged woman was standing at a podium, answering reporters' questions.

"Who is she?" asked Bucky.

"Maria Carmody," answered Gloria.

"Should that mean something to me?"

"She's Sidney Myshko's daughter."

"And?"

"Just watch."

The question was garbled, and there were no microphones being passed around the audience, but Maria Carmody's answer was crystal clear:

"I repeat: My father never set foot on the Moon," she said adamantly. "Does anyone here seriously think he would have been the first man on the Moon and then spent the rest of his life not telling anyone, not even his only child?"

"Bucky Blackstone thinks it!" yelled a reporter, and the assembled journalists broke out in laughter.

"I am not convinced Bucky Blackstone has the capacity to think seriously about *anything*," she said. "I'm sure if he had his way, they'd be digging my father up to examine his feet for moondust."

Another outburst of laughter.

"She's killing you, Bucky," said Gloria softly.

"I haven't been up to bat yet," he replied.

"What was that half-hour address to the nation?" she shot back.

"Spring training," said Bucky. "Now be quiet. I want to hear this."

"Have you any message for Bucky Blackstone?" asked a reporter.

She stared into the camera. "Mr. Blackstone, I don't know you, and I don't know why you're doing this . . . but I implore you: If you have a shred of human decency, let my father rest in peace!"

"She's *good*," said Bucky softly. "I wonder if she believes all that, or if someone in the administration has coached her?"

"You don't coach tears like that in a woman who's never acted," noted Gloria.

"Assuming that I believe for a moment that every woman on Earth can't cry on cue, she could just be nervous," replied Bucky. "Or since she's new to this, she might not know enough not to look directly into those spotlights. They'll make *anyone's* eyes water."

"You're reaching."

He shrugged. "Maybe I am. But there's one thing I'm *not* reaching about: Washington has been lying since 1969."

Camden wandered in just then. "Oh—I see you're watching it. I was going to alert you."

Bucky turned away from the image of Myshko's distraught daughter. "What do *you* think?"

"Seriously?" said Camden. "I think I'm going to spend the next couple of months defending your sanity when I *should* be publicizing the Moon shot." He paused and stared at Bucky. "Can I be totally honest?"

"That's what I pay you for."

"No, you pay me to manipulate the press and the public, honestly when I can, dishonestly when I have to."

"I stand corrected," Bucky growled. "Go ahead and say what's on your mind."

"Okay." Camden stared at him. "I don't know why the hell you had to bring this up in the first place. Who *cares* if another American set foot on the Moon before Armstrong did? What difference can it possibly make at this late date?"

"I don't know," answered Bucky. "And until I *do* know, I'm going to keep digging, keep holding it up to the light and getting others to help me unearth the truth."

"The only others will be wackos who live for conspiracy theories."

"Like the wackos who believed that the president of the United States was covering up a break-in? Or perhaps the wackos who believed a different president of the United States was lying under oath, in court, about a sexual encounter?" Bucky allowed himself the luxury of a satisfied smile. "You know, sometimes—not always, not often, but *sometimes*—the wackos are right."

Camden sighed deeply. "Okay, you're not going to back off this thing. I'd better go prepare for the press." He held an imaginary microphone to his mouth, "No, he doesn't have long conversations with the ghost of Teddy Roosevelt. No, he doesn't spend a lot of time speaking in tongues. No, he hasn't asked me to put a leash on him and walk him out in the rose garden."

"I *like* the last one," said Bucky. "Be sure you use it."

Camden muttered an obscenity under his breath, turned on his heel, and left.

Bucky turned back to the television, but it was reporting the standings in the current golf tournament, and he shut it off.

"You really think she's a dupe?" asked Gloria.

He shrugged. "Who knows? But *something* happened, and they can deny it to Kingdom Come. All it'll do is make them look foolish when it comes out." He lit a Havana cigar. "Actually, that's the least of their problems. You're a senator. Do you go out on a limb for a president who's been caught lying? You're a governor. The president asks you for a favor: hold back on this, don't propose that yet, whatever. Do you accommodate a guy that the public no longer trusts?"

"But if you're right, *every* president since Nixon has lied about it."

"True," he agreed. "But they're not dealing with Congress or running for reelection. You've heard the old expression, 'What have you done for me lately?' The flip side is: 'Which of you has lied to me lately?' "

"Maybe all this publicity will convince President Cunningham to come clean—always supposing there's something to come clean *about*," said Gloria.

Bucky shook his head. "He's already denied that anything happened. That's his story, and he's stuck with it."

She stared at him for a long moment. "What if he's right?"

"He's not."

"What if he *is*?"

"Then I'm going to look damned foolish for a few months or a few years, but it won't affect the Moon shot."

She sighed. "I hope you know what you're doing, Bucky."

He smiled at her. "I hope so, too."

Gloria looked out the window. "It's starting."

"*What's* starting?"

She pointed at the various trucks and vans lined up at the building's entrance. "CNN, Fox, ABC, NBC." She frowned. "I don't see CBS yet."

"That's odd," replied Bucky. "They're in Cunningham's hip pocket. You'd figure they'd be first in line to make a fool of me."

"They just pulled up," Gloria informed him.

"Good," said Bucky. "I hate it when things don't make sense."

"If you want to avoid them," suggested Gloria, "you can take the elevator down to the basement, walk the tunnel to the factory, and I can have a car waiting for you."

"I'm not avoiding anyone. I'll let Camden talk to them for maybe five minutes, until the stupidest questions are out of the way, then I'll go down and meet them."

A tall, slender woman with incredibly thick bifocals stood in the doorway to the office and rapped her knuckles against the molding.

"Not now, Sabina," said Gloria. "He's just leaving."

"It's all right, Gloria," said Bucky, getting to his feet. "Come on in, Sabina. Did you find what I want?"

"Yes, sir, Mr. Blackstone."

"Kill the 'sir' and the 'Mister.' I'm just Bucky."

"Yes, Bucky."

"Good. I'll be back after I face the mad dogs of the free press," he said. "But start tracking him down. In fact, do it from here. Then I won't have to hunt you down to see how we're doing."

"All right," she said, looking around.

"There's only one desk," said Bucky. "Sit down and use it."

"Yes, sir . . . Bucky."

"Okay, I'm off to slay the dragons, or at least hold them at bay." Bucky walked to the door. "I'll be back when they run out of dumb questions and dumber threats. Gloria, get her set up on computer number three."

Then he was walking to the elevator. Jason Brent joined him as he left the office and fell into step behind him.

"Let me guess," said Brent. "You're gonna save Camden from the press?"

"Fair's fair. He thinks he's saving me right now."

"I don't suppose I can talk you into a Kevlar vest?"

"Not today," answered Bucky. "Hell, the ones who hate me most will have the most vested interest in keeping me alive so everyone knows I'm a kook and a liar."

"I never looked at it that way," said Brent. He smiled at Bucky. "Are you?" he asked, only half in jest.

"What difference does it make as long as your paychecks don't bounce?" replied Bucky. "But for what it's worth, something *did* happen up there on the Moon, and I am damned well going to find out what it was."

"You mean *we* are going to find out," said Brent.

"Not to worry," Bucky assured him. "No one's going to attack me on the Moon."

"Most of those guys from 1969 are dead."

"Most of those guys from 1969 would be in their nineties," said Bucky. "They're entitled."

The elevator reached the ground floor, and they got out, walked through the front entrance, and found themselves facing a dozen cameras and twice that many reporters.

Bucky stepped forward to where a series of microphones had been set up. "I trust Mr. Camden has been treating you all with the dignity and decorum that becomes your occupations?"

"We love you, too," said the reporter from *The New York Times*.

"They been getting vicious?" Bucky asked Camden under his breath.

"Anxious and eager, anyway," said Camden.

"Okay, take off. Then when I leave, they won't have anyone to talk to."

"Except each other," said Camden. "These days they'll interview each other, and that'll pass for news."

"Don't worry about what you can't change. I'll see you tomorrow."

Camden left, and Bucky faced the assembled reporters. "All right, ladies and gentlemen. Here are the ground rules. If you have a question, raise your hand. If you speak without being recognized, I won't answer. Second rule: If you ask the same question twice, or the same one someone else asked, I won't answer.

"Third rule: If you use any insulting pejorative toward me, this press conference is over, and none of my staff will lift a finger if your colleagues choose to tear you apart." He paused long enough to make sure his instructions had been heard and understood. "Okay, ABC first."

"Have you any comment on Maria Carmody's statement, or her plea to you to leave her father alone?"

"I've never even met her father," said Bucky. "My understanding is that he's been dead for quite some time, so I can hardly be bothering him."

"She denies that anything untoward happened on Sidney Myshko's January 1969 flight," said Fox News. "What have you to say to that?"

"That I'm sure it's a comforting thought to grow up with," answered Bucky. "How old was she when he flew to the Moon? And if he was a willing part of a governmental cover-up, do you think he'd have confided in a young daughter, however many years later?"

"All you're doing is uttering denials!" yelled CBS. "How about some facts?"

"You did not have your hand raised, sir, and I did not recognize you. I will answer no further questions or comments from you." Bucky turned to NBC. "You're next."

"You can't shut *me* up!" bellowed CBS.

"I don't have to," said Bucky. "Ladies and gentlemen, this press conference is suspended until you get the gentleman from CBS to agree to be silent for the remainder of it—and if he speaks out again after so agreeing, the conference is permanently concluded."

And sure enough, it worked. No one, not even a colleague, was going to cost them a story.

"Is there any proof that Sidney Myshko actually landed on the Moon?" asked CNN.

"Almost certainly," answered Bucky.

"That sounds like you're hedging."

"You want a stronger answer? Okay, yes, proof exists."

"Then where is it?" asked *The Chicago Tribune*.

"Beats the hell out of me," said Bucky. "I'm sure the White House could tell you, and I'm equally sure they won't. But if it didn't exist, they wouldn't be working so hard to cover it up."

"If it didn't exist," said MSNBC, making no attempt to keep the sarcasm out of her voice, "wouldn't they be behaving exactly the same?"

I hate questions like that, thought Bucky. Aloud, he said: "I have proof of a cover-up in my possession. We've only been investigating this for a few days, and I'm not prepared to make what I have public until we've unearthed every piece of corroborating evidence."

"What does the White House have to gain by lying about the landing?" asked *The Wall Street Journal*. "In fact, what did any of them have to gain?"

"That's what we plan to find out."

"This proof you keep hinting at," said CNN. "Can you at least give an idea what constitutes it? Is it a document, a photo, something in a computer? Or"—he tried unsuccessfully to suppress a smile—"could it be something on the Moon itself?"

"I have *some* of the proof in my possession," answered Bucky. "We've just started hunting for the rest."

"Will you be hunting on the Moon, too?" snickered MSNBC.

"Almost certainly."

"How do you know your crew won't be part of the cover-up?" continued MSNBC.

"I don't," answered Bucky. He paused and stared across the assemblage. "That's why I'm going on the flight."

Suddenly, there was excited buzzing, and, finally, Fox News raised a hand.

"Are you saying that you're going on the Moon flight expressly because you don't trust your crew to accurately report what they find?"

"What *is* there to find?" added CBS. "It's a big, empty rock."

"You, sir," said Bucky, pointing to CBS, "have already been told that I will not answer your questions." He turned to Fox. "In answer to your supposition—I hate to dignify it by calling it a question—I'm going because it's my corporation and I *can*. I trust my crew implicitly, but I want to see whatever's there with my own eyes."

"And if nothing's there?" asked *The New York Times*.

"Then I'll have had the trip of a lifetime, and every one of you will wish you'd been there instead of me."

"And if you find out you were wrong, won't there be any consequences?" persisted *The Times*.

"Yes, there will," said Bucky. "I'll have lost almost all credibility, and it'll be a long time before anyone believes me again. But the beauty of a free society is that I *can* make a fool of myself, and each of you can—and doubtless have—done the same and survived it."

He spent ten more minutes answering variations of the same questions, and the press started getting annoyed that he wouldn't give them the facts they wanted, or admit he didn't have enough proof to make such outrageous statements.

Finally, he closed it off, went back inside, and instructed Brent to lock the entrance so they couldn't follow him all the way up to his office, as he was sure they wanted to do. Then he and Brent rode up to the penthouse, where his office overlooked the city.

"I saw you on the tube," reported Gloria, when he entered the office. She smiled. "I'm amazed I haven't quit and reported you to the local asylum." Then: "Are you *really* going on the Moon flight?"

"I said so."

"When did you decide? Today? Yesterday?"

"The truth?" asked Bucky with a guilty smile. "When I had my last checkup four months ago and my doctor said my body could handle it."

"You never told us."

"That was four months I didn't have to argue with all my well-meaning staff members who thought the trip would kill me," replied Bucky. He walked over to his desk, where Sabina was staring at his computer screen. "How's it going?"

"I found one," she responded, looking up at him. "The *only* one—Amos Bartlett."

"He's the only survivor from two Moon flights?"

"That's right, sir. I mean, Bucky."

"If you know that, the press has to know it, too," said Bucky. "It's been two nights since I made that speech. They've got to have tracked him down. What has he said?"

"Not a thing," replied Sabina.

"Don't tell me he's a mute?"

"No, sir . . . Bucky. But he's very sick and can't have visitors. He's living by himself in an assisted-living home. When the press found it, they camped out there. The home got a court order to get them off the property, but they surrounded it, and he's been moved to a military hospital, where they *can* keep the press away."

"How sick is he?" asked Bucky. "Likely to die before we can reach him?"

Sabina smiled. "He's old, and he's infirm, or he wouldn't be in an assisted-living facility, but I don't think he's sick at all."

"Music to mine ears! Tell me why you think that."

"I did something that's probably illegal, sir," she said, so intent on her revelation she forgot to correct herself and call him Bucky. "I phoned the closest pharmacy to the facility on the assumption that that's where they'd get their prescriptions, pretended I was the home, and said I was just double-checking to make sure they'd transferred Bartlett's prescriptions to the hospital. They told me they'd transferred the Lipitor, but thought the hospital would be taking his blood pressure and might want to change the dosage on his Diovan."

"Cholesterol and blood pressure," repeated Bucky happily. "Hardly the sign of a dying man, especially since they didn't change the one and didn't seem to think the other was due for an instant change. Yeah, he's healthy, all right. The only question is whether he's in the hospital against his will or not."

"I can't tell that from the computer, Bucky," said Sabina.

"No, we'll have to ask him in person. Thanks, Sabina. You

used your brains and your initiative, and that's what I'm paying you for. You'll find a pleasant surprise in your next check."

"Thank you, Bucky," she said, getting to her feet. "It was a pleasure. Anytime I can help you . . ."

"I'll remember," he said, escorting her to the door. When she'd left, he turned to Gloria. "How much is she making?"

Gloria shrugged. "I don't know."

"Find out, and raise her two hundred a week."

"Right," she said, jotting it down in a notebook. "Anything else?"

"Find out what hospital they're keeping Bartlett in, buy Camden a plane ticket, and send him out there to talk to him."

"Just to talk?"

"If he'd like to come back here, and the hospital will let him go—don't forget, it's military—fine. But if he's got something to say, have Camden buy whatever he's got to say."

"He'll want to know how high he can go."

"Whatever it takes. I'd like to send someone else—Camden's face is pretty well-known—but he's as good as we've got at spotting someone who's lying."

"You want to send someone else, someone with a real brain who *isn't* known to anyone with a television set?" said Gloria. "Send Sabina."

He considered it for a moment. "What the hell—why not? Send her back up here, and I'll give her instructions—what to ask, what to look for, what to ignore. And what to offer."

Late that night, after he'd sent Sabina on her way, and Jason Brent had driven him home, he walked out to the deck behind his villa, drink in hand, and stared up at the full moon in the cloudless sky.

Well, I've got the whole country talking about it now, he thought. *I wonder what the hell really* did *happen up there.*

A growing excitement encompassed him as he realized that he was actually going to find out.

| 10 |

After Morgan Blackstone signed off, Jerry's phone started ringing. CBS, Fox, *The Orlando Sentinel*, *The New York Times*. What was his reaction to Blackstone's comments? Did Jerry really believe there'd been secret landings? Could he imagine any reason why there *might* have been?

Jerry tried to respond by saying the story was impossible to take seriously and he'd have to let it go at that. But nobody cooperated. If he couldn't take it seriously, what was the confrontation with Frank Kirby all about? "I just don't know what the truth is," he told *The Philadelphia Inquirer*. "The conspiracy theory makes no sense. So no, I don't agree with Blackstone. Sometimes I wonder if Walker and Myshko planned the whole thing just to give us something to talk about." And when *The Los Angeles Times* told him that was crazy, he agreed.

Jerry would have been grateful to see Morgan Blackstone just go away. Retire somewhere to a mountaintop and fade from view. No, not *fade*. Vanish altogether. Exit stage right.

He'd watched Blackstone's catastrophic TV appearance with a sense of growing horror. If the issue had been perceived as a trifle eccentric before, it was now outright lunacy. The guy came off as a thoroughgoing nutcase. Jerry had been munching a tuna fish sandwich when it started. Five minutes into the rant, he very nearly threw it at the TV. Then he began wondering whether this was how Mary perceived *him*. He and Blackstone were, after all, saying the same thing. But there was a difference. Jerry was more inclined to *imply* that something wasn't right with the official story. Blackstone had taken an earthmover to it. Furthermore, Jerry was known to the general public. His was the face of NASA. People knew who he was, and they had no reason to doubt his good sense. Everybody trusted him. Blackstone, on the other hand, for all his money, had never been a public figure. Now he was becoming one of the best-known people in the country. MSNBC delivered an instant poll showing that 98 percent of those polled could identify him, and that four out of five classified him as deranged. Or worse. One of the "political advisors" on CBS commented that he also had the effect of scaring people. "Look," he said, "they know this guy is going to be launching rockets."

And therein lay the problem. Blackstone had stirred up such a commotion that Jerry could not hope to pursue the matter quietly. *Thanks a lot, Bucky.*

Barbara was at her desk when he arrived at the office the next day. She looked at him with a mixture of dismay and sympathy. And there was something else, something in her tone that suggested she no longer saw him the same way. She'd been his secretary since his arrival. In fact, she'd been more than that: She'd been a friend. But when he walked in that morning, it was as if a gulf had opened between them. It wasn't that she'd grown distant. But as if they no longer knew each other.

Ordinarily, if a major NASA story had broken during the course of an evening, it would have been front and center when he came into the office. Jerry, did you see what they were doing in the Space Station? Or, had he heard about Commander Ryan and the stripper? But on this day, she'd simply looked his way, eyes half-averted. "Hello, Jerry," she'd said, with a weak smile. "How's it going?"

How, indeed?

Mary hadn't called yet. She couldn't have been happy.

He pushed back in his chair and focused on the photograph of himself and three Girl Scouts gathered in front of a test rocket in the museum. It had been taken only last month.

The kids were from Troop 17, based at one of the local churches. Suddenly, it seemed a long time ago. A happier time—

He was scheduled to interview Petra Bauer, a NASA physicist, later that morning. Jerry was a regular contributor to NASA TV. It was, in fact, the aspect of his job that he most enjoyed. His biggest laugh line always came when he claimed that his earliest ambition was to be an astronaut, but that he had a problem with heights. The line probably worked because people could see the truth in it. One look at Jerry told you he was not a charge-the-hill kind of guy. Mostly, Jerry was about getting along. He had social skills that wouldn't quit, a talent for making people like him. He was a good speaker, and he had a passion for spaceflight. As long as other people were doing it.

He was a perfect fit for his job. Or he had been until Sidney Myshko's long silence turned up.

Blackstone was convinced there'd been a landing. Jerry thought *maybe* it had happened. Something clearly had been going on. But he could not imagine any reason for the secrecy. *So explain yourself, Bucky. Come up with a theory. Give me a scenario that makes sense.*

His phone beeped. "Mary's on the line," said Barbara.

He picked up. "Good morning, Mary."

"You saw Blackstone last night?" She sounded tired.

"I saw him, yes."

"This thing just won't go away." He heard music in the background. Mary had a taste for symphonies. "I'd like very much to get rid of it, Jerry."

"I'm sorry it's been causing a problem."

"It isn't your fault. I'd probably have done the same thing if I'd been in your position. I'll admit that it's got me wondering, though. Still, I just want it to stop."

"What's the latest?"

"Armbruster and Collins, this morning. They're already talking about cutting back on our budget." Two members of Congress who'd based their careers on getting rid of what they called wasteful spending. NASA had always been near the top of their list. "The problem is that we're being associated with Blackstone. With this whole goddamned story."

Jerry listened to birds singing in the trees. Their lives looked so much better than his. "I got a lot of calls from the media last night," he said. "Asking for a reaction. But I backed off. Told them I didn't know any more than they did."

"Did they let you get away with that, Jerry?" Her voice hardened.

"Yes," he said. "Up to a point. They tried to get more. But—"

"Okay. Good. I think that's exactly the right tack. We need to keep a low profile for a while. Let Blackstone carry the ball." She paused, and he locked in on the music. Rachmaninoff, maybe? The classical composers all sounded alike to him. "By the way—" She frowned. Bad news coming. "I'm replacing you on the interview today."

He growled under his breath. "You really think that's necessary?"

"It's a precaution, Jerry. I think, for a while, the less the public sees you, the better off we'll be."

Jerry let her see he was unhappy. "Okay. Whatever you say."

"Later, when things calm down, we can go back to normal."

"Who's going to do the interview?"

"Martin."

Martin Moreau was the personnel chief at the Space Center. He outranked Jerry, and though Jerry would not have admitted it even to himself, he would be a good replacement. Well, adequate. He didn't have Jerry's style. Jerry's showbiz approach. But nobody did. Not along the Cape, anyhow.

Suddenly, he was looking at a depleted morning. He sat listening to the clock while his resentment grew. He thought about going up to Mary's office and offering his resignation. *That way you won't have to worry about my reminding people about NASA.*

Why did no one else care? Other than Blackstone?

Even Barbara had backed off.

"Jerry?" Her voice. "You have a visitor. A Mr. Collander?"

"Who?"

"Joseph Collander. Security just called. He's apparently down at the entrance. Says he would like to see you. "

"Did he say what about?"

"Myshko."

Another crank. "Tell him I'm out. Tell him I've gone to Egypt on a goodwill tour."

"Jerry, he says his father worked for us back in the sixties."

Jerry hesitated. He didn't want to get in any deeper. On the other hand—"Okay. Let me talk to him."

Barbara switched him over. "Dr. Culpepper?" The voice was thin. It seemed reluctant, hesitant.

"I don't have a doctorate, Mr. Collander," Jerry said. "What can I do for you?"

"Mr. Culpepper, my father was a computer technician for NASA back during the sixties and seventies. I might have something you'd be interested in hearing."

Jerry took a deep breath. "I'll be down in a minute."

———————

Joseph Collander did not match his voice. He was a big guy, the type who might have been a linebacker in his earlier years. He was dressed informally, which of course was standard along the Space Coast. Casual open-neck shirt with a University of Florida emblem on the pocket, and a Rays baseball cap. "Mr. Culpepper," he said, "I'm sorry to take up your time. I was watching that guy on TV last night. Blackberry or something—"

"Blackstone," said Jerry. He led Collander into a conference room.

"Yeah. That's it. And I know you were involved in it, too. The business about maybe somebody landing on the Moon before Neil Armstrong."

"What did you want to tell me, Mr. Collander?"

"Joe, please. And, to answer your question as honestly as I can, that press conference last night, I know this will sound crazy, but it reminded me of something my dad told me years ago."

"What's that?"

"You know that the first time we got a look at the back side of the Moon was when a Russian probe took pictures in, I think, 1959. We got some pictures ourselves during the sixties. They distributed them to the media, and they were big news for a while. Then we stopped."

"Making the pictures available to the media, you mean."

"Yes. My dad said they were still getting pictures, but nobody got to see them. Including my dad and the people working with him. There was no indication whether they'd been classified.

I mean, there wouldn't be any reason to classify them unless they'd spotted a Soviet base back there. Then, after a while, everything got back to normal."

"Your father was seeing the pictures again."

"Yes. There was never any explanation, or even an admission by higher authority that it had happened. In fact, he was told he was imagining it. And when he pushed a little, they told him to shut up."

"When was this?" asked Jerry.

"It was before my time, Mr. Culpepper. It always bothered my father that they'd do something like that and then lie about it. But he swore it happened."

"Can I get you some coffee, Joe?"

"No, thanks. It tends to keep me awake all day." They both smiled at the joke.

"Is your father—?"

"He died fifteen years ago."

"Is there anybody else you know of who could back up the story?"

"There were a bunch of NASA retired guys living around here at one time. They used to go to lunch together and everything, and I guess they still do. But I don't think any of the ones from my father's era are left now."

"Did you ever hear any of the others mention the censorship?"

"I really don't recall, Mr. Culpepper."

"*Jerry's* good."

"Jerry. Okay. But now that I think of it, I *do* remember something else. My dad said that when the analysts got access to the pictures again, there was still a problem. There was an area they were never able to see. It was never visible. As if the pictures had been cropped."

Jerry called Al Thomas at the Huntsville Archives. Al looked as if he was having a busy day. "What do you need, Jerry?" he asked.

"Al, during the sixties, we took a lot of satellite and probe pictures of the back side of the Moon, right?"

"We took some, yes. Mostly from probes."

"Were any of them ever withheld?"

"You mean classified?"

"Yes."

"Not that I know of. Hold on a second." He was back after about three minutes. "No, Jerry," he said. "The lunar pictures, all of the ones taken by the United States, were distributed to interested researchers as soon as they became available. There's no indication any of them were ever held back."

"Okay. Can you forward a complete set to me?"

"Jerry, that's a lot of pictures."

"It's important, Al,"

"Okay. I'll see what I can do."

Jerry glanced down at the note he'd written himself. "One other thing."

Thomas sighed. "What is it?"

"Mission parameters. I could use them, too. If it's not too much trouble."

"All right. I'm not really sure what we have. But I'll dig everything out. Are you in a hurry?"

————————

The pictures came in as Jerry was getting ready to leave for the day. There were hundreds of them, and they were all dated. He brought them up on his display and got lost among craters and ridges and bleak lunar plains. He looked for something, anything, that might have caused someone at a high level to conclude there was a problem. And he felt like an idiot doing it. He had been transformed into a geek at a science-fiction convention.

But there was nothing. No extended time period during which pictures were missing. No secret Soviet base. No automated rocket launcher filled with missiles. No vacuum-breathing Moon people living in a crater.

He read the mission plans. He examined maps of the far side of the Moon and tried to see whether any areas that should have been in the photos were missing. He went down and ate a quick dinner in the cafeteria. Then he went back to his office and looked at the maps some more.

The problem was he didn't really know what he was doing.

In the morning, he called Cal Dryden, a physics professor at the University of Central Florida. Cal was an enthusiastic supporter of NASA whom Jerry had met at a fund-raising luncheon a year earlier. A secretary told him Professor Dryden was in class, but she'd leave a message. Thirty minutes later he was smiling out of the display. He seemed to get heavier every time Jerry saw him. He'd grown a beard, which was probably a bad idea because it carried streaks of gray and made him look a few years older. Though maybe that was the effect he wanted.

"Hi, Jerry." He was seated in an armchair with a wall of books behind him. "What can I do for you?"

"Cal, I have some pictures of the back side of the Moon. From the late sixties. I was wondering—" How to phrase this? "I think they might be incomplete. I was wondering if you could take time to look at them for me."

Cal's brow creased. "What do you mean *incomplete*?"

"There might be areas that should be there but aren't. You know, where we have maybe both sides of a section of ground but the middle's missing."

"You want me to find the missing pieces?"

"I want you to determine whether there *are* any missing pieces."

"Jerry, you say these pictures are from the sixties?"

"Yes."

"So why would anybody care?"

"It's hard to explain, Cal."

He took a deep breath. "I assume it has something to do with the Myshko flight?"

"It might. I don't know. But I'd appreciate it if you'd keep this to yourself."

"Okay. But hell, Jerry, what's going on over there? You guys trying to start rumors about secret missions?"

"I can't imagine a better way to cut off what's left of our funding, Cal."

"Seriously."

"I think there's simply a communication breakdown somewhere. I'm trying to settle it now."

"Okay. Send the pictures. Do you have descriptions of what they're supposed to be?"

"I have the mission parameters."

"All right. Send those, too."

"One other thing, Cal—"

"Yes?"

"If you see anything unusual, anything you wouldn't expect, let me know, okay? But nobody else."

A wide smile appeared. "What did you have in mind?"

"I don't know, Cal. Anything odd."

———————

It was a Friday night. Jerry had been dating Susan Cassidy on and off over the past few months. Susan was a librarian in Titusville. She was not exactly gorgeous despite her raven hair and dark eyes. But she was smart, and she was the type of woman who grew more attractive as you got to know her. He was sitting with her at the Olive Garden on Merritt Island enjoying his spaghetti and meatballs when his phone buzzed.

Jerry was not one of those people who'd sit with a friend, or a date, and talk on his cell. But he saw that the call was from Cal. "This is important," he told Susan. "Bear with me, okay?"

She smiled and nodded. No problem.

"Yes, Cal," he said. "What have you got?"

"Not a thing, Jerry. Everything that's supposed to be there is *there*. I can't find any missing parcels of ground. The missions pretty much covered the entire area."

"You're sure."

"I ran them through the data file. Everything's correct."

"Okay, Cal. Thanks."

He turned the phone off, dropped it into a pocket, and said, "Sorry." Then he went back to the meatballs.

Susan's eyes drifted past him. She raised her wine, sipped it, put it back down. "Is there a problem?"

"No. Everything's fine."

"My experience over a lifetime, Jerry," she said, 'is that when people say 'everything's fine,' it usually isn't."

He grinned. Shrugged. "It's no big deal, Susan."

"Is Blackstone going to do another TV show?"

"It's not anything like that." He explained about the lunar photos.

"You think they saw something up there, and they were hiding it?"

"No. I don't." He tasted his wine while he thought about what he wanted to say. "You know, Susan, I'm always amazed at how easily we get sucked into crazy notions. I think we all have a predilection for fantasy."

"And this Cal didn't find anything missing?"

"No. Nothing deleted from any of the pictures."

She smiled. "That must be disappointing."

"What makes you say that?"

"Oh, come on, Jerry. Wouldn't you love to discover there's a big mystery of some sort going on? Something the government's been covering up for half a century?"

He laughed. "Listen, babe, my job's complicated enough. I don't need any mysteries."

"Jerry." It was almost a sigh. "Where's your romantic side?"

"That only shows up when you're in the area, Susan."

"Ah. Well spoken, Lancelot."

He lifted his wine to her. "I calls them the way I sees them, sweetheart."

"Of course. I'd expect no less." She touched glasses. "Jerry. About the pictures. There's another possibility."

"What's that?"

"Maybe there *was* something they didn't want anyone to see. So they *did* make them unavailable."

"But we have the pictures. There's nothing missing."

She shrugged. "Proves nothing. They could have photo-shopped them. Maybe they simply replaced them with other pictures."

The following day he called Cal again. "I hate to ask you about this," he said, as the professor began frowning, "but I need something else. It occurred to me that somebody might have replaced the original pictures. Photoshopped them. Is that possible?"

"Is it *possible*? Sure it's possible, Jerry. Almost *anything* is possible. You can't travel faster than light. And you can't travel in time. Except forward, one day at a crack. Otherwise, anything goes. What are you suggesting?"

"I'm not suggesting anything, Cal. But I want to eliminate the possibility that the original pictures were replaced. Is there a way to do that?"

"Sure," he said. "But listen, Jerry. First of all, I'm buried these days. And anyhow, even if I weren't, it's not my field of expertise. You want a professional for something like this."

"Can you suggest anyone?"

"I don't think there's anybody here who would qualify." He smiled. "Something like this, I'd take to NASA."

His old girlfriend still looked great even though the years had begun to pile up. She was African-American, a graduate of La Salle University in Philadelphia, and a rabid baseball fan. The Phillies, of course. She was the only woman Jerry had ever really loved. But the chemistry hadn't worked on her side. He'd been smart enough to make sure the breakup hadn't erupted into a cascade of hard feelings. And he'd stayed in touch, more or less. But he was reluctant to ask a favor. The rush of emotions that came from being near her had not abated over the years.

Last he'd heard, she was still single.

She smiled at him out of the display, told him she was glad to see him again, and asked how he was doing. "You seem to be making news," she added.

"Not sure how I got in the middle of it, Mandy," he said.

"Story of your life, Jerry."

He laughed. "It's just a series of communications problems."

"Okay." She gazed at him skeptically. Tilted her head. His heart started racing. It was as if he were back in high school.

"I could use your help, Mandy."

"What do you need?"

"I want you to look at some Moon pictures. The lunar surface. We have the dates when they were supposed to have been taken, by probes and satellites. In the late 1960s. And the locations. I'd be grateful if you could tell me if they are what they're supposed to be."

She looked at him. "How've you been doing, Jerry?"

"Okay," he said.

"Married yet?"

"No. Not yet. I've got a candidate, though."

"Good," she said. "Lucky woman."

That hurt. But he kept going. "How about you?"

"Been too busy, I guess."

The conversation trailed off. She was, he thought, trying to find a way out. She didn't want to do the lunar pictures. And she was uncomfortable in his presence. "Okay," she said finally. "But, Jerry, keep my name out of it. Okay?"

| 11 |

Bucky spent the night in the office. He didn't do it very often, but for those occasions when he needed to, a luxurious bedroom suite had been installed on the top floor—he hated calling anything in an office building a penthouse—complete with shower, steam bath, state-of-the-art sound and video systems, and fifty of his favorite books.

He *could* have had his driver take him home, but he'd have had to run the gauntlet of the press, which had left about a dozen members camped out in front of the building and another handful at the exit to the underground garage.

The most recent polls said that 80 percent of the public thought he was a flake, so why, he wondered, was the press still after him? Then he realized that a billionaire flake was probably worth more copy, vocal and written, than just about anyone other than (and, on some days, including) the president.

He spent half the night watching reruns of famed boxing matches, one of his passions. He saw the seventh round Long Count, Sonny Liston's first-round dive in Maine, Mike Tyson turning to putty when he realized he couldn't bully or terrace Evander Holyfield, Arturo Gatti and Mickey Ward three times in the squared circle to show onlookers what it was all about. He watched Max S weight of the Third Reich on his shoulders, collapse under it in less than a round, and Muhammad Ali show lightweights and bantamweights how to stick and run.

He was still sitting in his overstuffed leather chair when he woke up at five in the morning. The channel—clearly devoted to reruns that could be purchased for pennies, or at most dimes—was now showing Seattle Slew beating Affirmed in the only battle of Triple Crown winners, and Ruffian breaking down, and Man o' War running past all known reference points. He reached for the remote, turned it off, staggered over to the king-size bed, and collapsed on it, fully clothed.

He woke up at eight, showered, shaved, put on a pair of slacks and a polo shirt—when you own the company, anything you want to wear becomes the day's dress code—and considered going down to the building's cafeteria. Then he decided that if the press had managed to get inside, they'd be looking for him there since there was no way they could get up to the top floor—the elevators required personal codes for the top three floors. He checked the refrigerator to see what he had in the suite, and found some not-yet-stale donuts. He pulled them out, made some coffee, and sat down to eat, drink, and catch up on the morning's news.

Jerry Culpepper wasn't fielding questions that day, and Bucky wondered if they were hiding him, disciplining him, or if they'd let him go. He contacted Gloria, who had just arrived, and asked her to check on Jerry's status in case he was available. She got back to him five minutes later: No, he was still employed by NASA.

Too damned bad, thought Bucky. *I could really use that young man. He's got a rep, and he's Ed Camden without the paranoia and rough edges.*

He spent a few more minutes nursing a second cup of coffee, then got to his feet, walked down the corridor to his office, and entered it.

"Good morning, Bucky," said Gloria. "You look like hell."

"That's what I like: respect from an employee."

"Good mor— Would you rather I lie to you?"

seen you."

than I've ever

"God, it sounds *worse*," he muttered. "Go back to telling the truth."

Gloria laughed aloud. "You're a night person. You can't help it. But since you *are*, and you own the company, why do you feel you have to drag yourself into the office every morning by nine?"

He stared at her for a long moment. "I hate it when you ask questions like that."

"You want some coffee?"

"No, I'll float away. I assume Jerry Culpepper hasn't been fired since last we spoke?"

"No."

"Pity." He paused. "We're not at war with anyone?"

"No."

"No earthquakes, tornadoes, or hurricanes on the horizon?"

"No."

"Maybe I *will* go back to sleep." He was about to walk back out the door when her computer came to life.

"I don't think so," she said.

"Oh?"

"Sabina Marinova just entered the building. She wants an immediate meeting with you."

"Send her up," he said. Suddenly he frowned. "How the hell did she get back so fast?"

"She commandeered one of your private jets and pilots."

"How about that?" said Bucky. "She's already showing more initiative than Camden. I knew I liked that girl."

"I'd be careful about calling her a girl," said Gloria. "She's as tall as you are and probably twice as fit."

"I thought all women like being called girls."

"About as much as you like being called a boy by a member of my sex."

"I don't mind it."

"*You* don't mind that two hundred million Americans think you're as crazy as a loon," she shot back.

"Two hundred *fifty* million," he responded with a smile. "Unless Fox and CNN are both lying."

"Doesn't it bother you, Bucky?" she asked seriously.

"I'd rather they agreed with me," he said. "If I'm right, eventually they will, and if I'm wrong, then they *should* think I'm crazy."

She stared at him. "I suppose that's the kind of self-confidence it takes to make all those billions. Personally, it'd drive me as crazy as they thought I was."

He smiled. "I've been wrong before. I'll be wrong again." Suddenly the smile vanished. *"But not this time."*

There was a knock at the door. Gloria opened it and Sabina entered the office.

"Well?" said Bucky. "Did you see him?"

Sabina nodded. "I saw him."

"Is he still there?"

"He's probably safer there than anywhere else."

Bucky frowned. "Are there people out after him?"

"I meant from the press."

"Did he have anything interesting to say?"

"That'll be up to you to decide, sir . . . I mean, Bucky," said Sabina. "I have a video of our conversation. He doesn't know I took it."

"Clearly, you didn't hold up a camera or a cell phone," said Bucky. "What did you use?"

"Mr. Brent showed me how to outfit myself," she said with a smile, pointing to a button on the vest of her pantsuit.

"I'm surprised Mr. Brent knew," said Bucky. "Usually, he just beats information out of people."

"Really?"

"Not since he began working here—but I like to think he had a romantic past." There was a brief pause. "Can you show me the video now?"

"I can feed it through your computer or just project it against a wall," said Sabina.

"Start with the wall. Gloria might as well watch it, too, since I'm not competent to process it." She stared at him curiously. "Private joke. Let's see it, please."

She manipulated the button, a tiny window opened in it, and an instant later the image of a very old, very wrinkled man in a hospital gown appeared on the wall.

"I'm very glad you agreed to see me, Mr. Bartlett," said Sabina's voice.

"Why not?" he said. "You're not press, and you're not federal."

"I take it the past few days have been difficult for you?"

"For me and those in charge of me," he agreed, "no thanks to your boss."

"You mean Mr. Blackstone?"

He nodded. "Bucky Blackstone, right." Suddenly he smiled. "That was some speech he made the other night!"

"You heard it?"

"Of course I did. Everyone knew he was going to say something explosive about NASA. I wanted to see what it was."

"And now that you've heard it, what is your opinion of it?" asked Sabina.

"That he's asking for trouble."

"You mean by saying irrational things?"

Amos Bartlett stared at her. "If you say so," he replied at last.

"You're the only living member of the two flights that preceded Apollo XI."

"Clean living does it every time," said Bartlett with a smile that was interrupted by a coughing fit.

"Are you all right, Mr. Bartlett?"

"I'm fine," he replied. "Just had one too many cigarettes after dinner. Do you smoke?"

"No."

"Smart lady. I wish I could break the damned habit. Maybe I can in this place. They didn't look happy when I lit up."

"We're getting off the subject, sir," said Sabina. "What did you think of Mr. Blackstone's speech?"

"I think he's buying a mess of trouble."

"In what way?"

"You accuse the government of lying, you're asking for trouble."

"Yes, I suppose so," said Sabina.

"Of course, my bet is even the Congress doesn't know about this. Probably just the president, and maybe two or three others, tops."

"Say that again?" demanded Sabina, a sudden tension in her voice.

"Sure," replied Bartlett. "Your boss is buying a mess of trouble."

"I mean, what does the president know that even Congress doesn't know?"

Suddenly Bartlett got a haunted look around his eyes, which

began darting back and forth. "Presidents know lots of things senators and representatives don't know," he replied noncommittally. "That's why they're presidents."

"What does this particular president know about Sidney Myshko's flight?"

The haunted look became more pronounced. "Who said anything about Myshko's flight?"

"Morgan Blackstone did," answered Sabina. "That's what we were talking about."

"We were?"

"And you were about to tell me what you know about it."

"I was?"

"Yes, Mr. Bartlett, you were."

"Who sent you here, really?"

"Mr. Blackstone."

"You're sure?"

"I showed you my credentials before we started talking."

"How do I know they're legitimate?" he said. "How do I know you're not working for *The New York Times*?"

"Why would I be working for *The New York Times*, Mr. Bartlett?"

He stared at her again, then sighed deeply. "I don't know," he admitted. "I mean, hell, they own the Army, and the Army's got me locked away here."

"You don't mean *The Times* owns the Army?"

"Hell, no. I don't know what I mean."

"Then can we talk about the Myshko flight?" persisted Sabina.

"Why don't we talk about Neil Armstrong's flight? I mean, that's the one everyone wants to talk about."

"Not you and me," said Sabina. "We want to talk about Myshko's flight. And yours."

The haunted look morphed into a very frightened one. "We do?"

"We do."

"All right. But I want a cigarette first."

"I don't have any."

"Get me one, and we'll talk."

The picture went dead.

"What happened?" asked Bucky.

"I went out and bummed a cigarette off another patient, since I knew they wouldn't sell any in the hospital shop, and I was pretty sure the staff wouldn't be permitted to smoke."

"Makes sense."

"And when I came back with a cigarette, he'd closed and locked the door." She looked apologetically at Bucky. "It's my fault, sir. I forgot that he wasn't sick, that it was more like protective custody. It never occurred to me that of course he could walk across the room and lock the door."

"There shouldn't have been a lock on the inside, not in a hospital," said Gloria.

"Unless the army wanted one," said Bucky. "They could probably have rigged a dead bolt in ten minutes' time. It wasn't done with you in mind, Sabina; it was in case any members of the press got through, maybe disguised as an orderly."

"So is the video useful?" asked Sabina anxiously.

"Extremely," said Bucky. "He as much as admitted something happened up there. We'll give him a day or two to realize the sky isn't falling in on him, and then try again. You did good, Sabina."

"Thank you, sir," she said. Then: "What do you think really happened up there?"

"Just what I said the other night," replied Bucky. "I think Myshko was the first man on the Moon." He grimaced. "Most people think I'm crazy, which is their privilege. What bothers me is that the ones who believe me haven't asked the most important question."

"And what is that?" asked Sabina curiously.

"*Why* was Sidney Myshko the first man on the Moon?"

12

Jerry was prepping for his weekly press conference when Mary came by the office. She delivered an automated smile, no warmth in the eyes, and nodded as if they'd just agreed on something. More bad news on the way. "How's everything going, Jerry?" she asked.

"Okay," he said. While she took a seat on the couch, he added some trivia about issues that would probably be raised.

She listened, indicated she agreed with him, made a suggestion about the information they were getting back from the Mars rover. Then she smiled again. "Jerry, I'm not comfortable with this Myshko thing. It's just waiting out there now that Blackstone has gotten into the middle of it. I still can't believe he was dumb enough to get involved. It'll get him the publicity he wants, but that's purely short-term. In the end, it'll ruin his reputation. I've known him for a number of years. Thought he was smarter than that."

"I guess," he said.

"Anyway, he's made things a lot more complicated. I was hoping we could change the subject, get the reporters talking about something else. But that's not going to happen. So be ready for it."

Jerry heard a door close somewhere along the corridor. Then: "I'll do what I can to sidestep the issue, Mary."

She shook her head and focused behind him somewhere. "Unfortunately, I'm not sure you'll be able to keep them at a distance, Jerry. They're going to be pushing about Blackstone. And they're going to want to know what *you* think."

"We're not thinking of canceling the conference, are we?"

"No. No way we can do that. But I think this would be a good day for you to call in sick. Put Vanessa out there. Let her deal with them." Jerry didn't think much of the idea, and he made no effort to hide his feeling. "She's been a pretty good backup when we've needed her."

This had become a routine strategy lately. Bury Jerry. "Mary—"

"Did any of the reporters see you coming in?"

"No. I was here early this morning."

"Good."

"Mary, I don't think this is the way to go."

She sat back, and the lines around her mouth hardened. Mary had fought her way up in the hardscrabble politics that ruled the current era. No mercy. Go for the throat. Never lose sight of the next election. It was a world in which public relations was everything. Truth was defined by how many people bought into a given proposition. She didn't really care what had happened with the Moon flights a half century ago. The only thing that mattered was the effect they might have on NASA at the moment. What impact would result from his going out and standing behind that lectern? "Why not?" she asked.

"Nobody's going to believe I just happened to get sick today. In the wake of Blackstone's broadcast."

"Do we really care what they think?"

"Isn't that what this is all about? Mary, I can handle it."

She shook her head slowly. Not rejecting what he'd said but apparently wondering how they'd reached this point. "All right. But you're going to be walking a fine line in there. Just try to get through it without making things worse. Do you have some announcements to make?"

"Yes." He held up some index cards. "We have some new pictures of the Kastelone Galaxy—"

"The what?"

"The Kastelone Galaxy. It's actually *two* galaxies. Colliding. We've got some spectacular pictures. They're both bigger than the Milky Way."

"What else?"

"Three more exoplanets with oxygen atmospheres. The scientists think they're living worlds."

"Okay. That's good."

"And there's more evidence that the Sun is a double star."

"Really?" Finally, her features softened. "There's another *star* in the solar system?"

"It's a half light-year out, and it's too dim to see with the naked eye. But yes, it's there."

She shook her head. "I'll be damned. I'll tell you what we could *really* use right now, though."

"What's that?"

"A message from Alpha Centauri." She took a deep breath and turned her gaze toward a window. "Where are the aliens when you need them?" Jerry could hear birds singing. The truth was that the stories were not new, except for the second sun. He was just resurrecting them and would add a few details for the press. "All right," she said. "It's against my better judgment, but go ahead. Try to keep talking about that other sun. Keep the questions to a minimum."

———————

The press conference was routinely scheduled for ten o'clock. But on this day, Mary moved it back to eleven. The official reason given was that it was necessitated by an upgrade being done on the electrical system. The reality, Jerry suspected, was that Mary would not have been comfortable regardless of who was at the lectern, and she wanted it pushed as close as she could manage to lunch hour.

Jerry sent the graphics down to the pressroom projector and was getting his index cards together when Barbara came into the office. "Jerry," she said, "Dr. Edwards is on the line. I told her you were busy, but she says it's important. "

Jerry glanced at his watch. He had about five minutes. "Put her on, Barbara."

The line clicked as she made the connection. Then Mandy was on the display. "Hello, Jerry," she said.

"Hi, beautiful, what do you have?"

"Are you sure your people didn't screw up the dates?"

"The pictures don't fit?"

"Jerry, a *lot* of the pictures could not have been taken at the times indicated."

"You're sure?"

"Yes. Of course I am."

So there really had been a cover-up. Did that mean there'd been a *landing*? "How can you tell?"

"The shadows aren't right. Which means the Moon, at the time the pictures were taken, was in a different place than it actually would have been on the given dates."

"These are pictures of the far side of the Moon?"

"Yes."

"What about the near side?"

"The near side's okay. I didn't see any problems there."

"All right. What are the dates? Of the bogus pictures?"

"They run from the very beginning of the program until approximately May 1969."

Just after Walker's mission returned. "After that, they're okay?"

"That's correct. By the way, it's always the same general area."

"How do you mean?"

"There's a strip of ground that we never get to see. The photos that have been manipulated always exclude the same area."

"How big is it? Where?"

"It's about two hundred miles by eighty or so. Anyhow, I've marked it for you. You should have the package now. You can see for yourself."

Jerry looked at his watch. He was running late. "Okay, Mandy, thanks. I owe you."

"It's centered on the Cassegrain Crater."

"The *what*?"

"The Cassegrain Crater. It's a small one. Only about forty miles across. I can't imagine why anybody would be trying to conceal it. But, anyhow, there it is. And one more thing, Jerry."

"Yes?"

"I checked some Russian pictures from the same time period. They were cooked, too."

———————

Jerry was running late. Despite that, he walked slowly out of his office and nodded to Barbara. She was looking at him with a strange expression. "You okay, Boss?" she asked.

"Sure," he said. He left the office, went out into the corridor, and pushed the elevator button.

Somebody passed him. "Hello, Jerry."

A woman's voice. It was one of the computer wonks. He needed a moment to come up with her name. "Hello, Shelley," he said, as she disappeared around a corner.

The elevator doors opened and he went in.

He pressed DOWN. Checked his watch again, but the time didn't register.

There really *had* been a cover-up. But what the hell were they hiding? What *could* they be hiding? And the Russians as well?

The elevator descended past the fourth floor.

The third.

He should have gone with Mary's idea. Let Vanessa handle the press conference.

The doors opened at the second floor. Wally Bergen got in. Said hello. Jerry didn't usually care when people stopped the elevator to ride up or down one floor. But this time it annoyed him, and he almost said something.

"Ready for the reporters?" Wally asked with a smile. He was a little guy. Glasses. Smiled too much. He was always trying to be cheerful. Jerry didn't like nonstop cheerfulness.

"Sure," he said.

———————

There were about forty people crowded into the pressroom. Almost three times the usual number. Jerry walked to the lectern, waited for everyone to quiet down, and welcomed them in a tone that suggested nothing unusual was going on. He knew he should not make any reference to Blackstone, but he couldn't resist. "It's been a busy week," he said with a grin. Everybody knew what he meant, and it got some laughs. But it was a dumb start.

He described some improvements in scanners that had been mounted on the Valkyrie, a robotic mission that was approaching Jupiter. Then he went into his routine with the colliding galaxies, the exoplanets, and the second sun. He put the images up. They were spectacular. When he'd first seen the Kastelone pictures, he'd wondered what it would be like to live on a world in a place where stars were being knocked around in all directions. Were there living worlds, maybe even worlds with people on them, getting torn loose from their suns and dragged into the night?

Ordinarily, he would have mentioned that possibility to spice up the presentation, but now it was the kind of remark that would be used to confirm the notion that he was a kook. "Fortunately," he said, "we live in the Milky Way, which is a quiet, sedate neighborhood." He added a smile.

And, having used only about fifteen minutes, he asked if anyone had a question.

Everybody raised a hand. He looked around, hoping for a safe place to land. And pointed at Ellie McIntyre. Ellie represented the local magazine *Oceanside*. It was usually interested in topics that concerned coastal merchants. Like when would the next launch happen? Of course, launches were off the table, but the Space Center still brought in high-profile guests and ran presentations that drew a decent number of visitors.

"Jerry," she said, "what did you think about what Morgan Blackstone said last week?"

He laughed. Not anything to be taken seriously. "I'll have to let Mr. Blackstone speak for himself, Ellie," he said. "To be honest, I didn't see the show. I can tell you that, if anybody was on the Moon prior to Neil Armstrong and Buzz Aldrin, it would make a great science-fiction movie."

Diane Brookover, of *The New York Times*, was next: "Jerry," she said, "can you categorically deny that there's some sort of cover-up going on here? That we don't know the entire story of the Moon landings?"

"Can I categorically deny it? I wasn't here, Diane. Maybe we sent an early mission looking for oil, and we didn't want to tell anybody because—Well, I don't know." He was on a platform that was elevated about eighteen inches off the floor. He looked out over their heads. Saw one of the interns standing in the doorway. *Everybody* was interested. "The whole notion is so ridiculous, I don't know where to begin. Now, if we could, I'd like to move on and not waste any more time on this."

Someone who identified herself as representing Fox asked

whether there was evidence that there might actually *be* life on the exoplanets as opposed to there being worlds where the conditions were simply favorable?

"My understanding," said Jerry, "is that there's simply no way to know for certain but that the chemical mix in the atmospheres of two of the three worlds indicates a high probability of life. The third one—let me check my notes here—the third one is maybe one chance in four or five."

She kept her hand in the air. "So that makes how many worlds now with oxygen atmospheres?"

"I'm not up on that," said Jerry. "But I think this puts the count at about fourteen."

Barry Westcott, of *USA Today*, was next. "Jerry, the National Astrophysics Association has issued a statement thanking NASA for everything it's done over the sixty years of its existence. They give the Agency credit for a long list of achievements, the flybys, the telescopes, the analyses of Martian soil. The lunar flights finish pretty far down the list. And they only seem to count because they brought home some Moon rocks. It sounds like a eulogy. Is NASA finished?"

Jerry resisted his inclination to brush the question away as ridiculous. "I suspect we'll be here for a good many years, Barry. The country's space program isn't going away. Yes, we've fallen on lean times. But so has everybody else. This country isn't going to shut down its space program. That's just not going to happen."

He nodded to a young man on his right. Another stranger. "Mark Lyman," he said. "From *The Nation*. Jerry, where do you think we're going to be, as far as space exploration is concerned, in twenty years? Is there any chance we'll go back to the Moon?" Lyman looked as if he'd just graduated from college. A thin, reedy kid with unruly hair and a tone that sounded vaguely accusatory.

"Twenty years is a long time," said Jerry. "And none of us is very good at making predictions. I can tell you this much: If President Cunningham wants to see a return to the Moon, we can do it. All that's necessary is a willingness to pay for it."

"We could probably do that," said Lyman, "just by staying out of the next war."

A middle-aged battle-scarred woman on his left: "Tonya

Brant," she said. The columnist best known for unrelenting attacks on the administration and on right-wing politicians. "Jerry, the president was here a few days ago. When you asked him about the Myshko flight, how did he react?"

"Tonya," he said, "I never brought the subject up with him."

"Why not?"

"Because it's crazy. Deranged."

"He didn't mention it either?"

"He doesn't usually confer with me on matters of policy."

"But when wild stories are going around that reflect adversely on whether the government is telling the truth about something, I'd think he would be interested. I mean, he must have asked whether anybody here had any idea where this story had come from. If I'd been president—not that anybody would ever vote for me—I'd want to get a better feel for what's going on."

"Tonya, I just wouldn't have been able to help him in any event. The whole story is a baseless rumor. I suspect he has no interest in wasting his time on it."

"Okay," she said. He wanted to break away, to go to someone else, but she wasn't quite ready to let go. "Let me just ask you, Jerry. Point-blank. As far as you know, there's absolutely no basis to this story, none whatever, and no reason to believe the government is hiding something. Is that correct?"

"Yes," he said. "Absolutely."

He rarely skipped lunch. But his appetite had gone away, so he went back to his office.

Barbara smiled at him as he walked in. "Nice job, Jerry," she said. "I'm always amazed how you can push back at those people. The guy we had here before you always caved."

"I think you're being generous, Barb. But thanks."

"You had a couple of calls." She handed him two note cards. He glanced at them. They were requests from local TV stations for interviews. He did a lot of those. "You want me to schedule them?" she asked.

"Sure," he said. "Give it a few days, though."

A warm breeze was coming in through the windows. He had a corner office, with views of the Vehicle Assembly Building and Launchpad 39A. Hard to believe he'd ever thought he would want to be an astronaut. To ride an Atlas through the clouds. Now the prospect of simply sitting on one while it rested on the pad made him uneasy. He closed the windows and turned on the air-conditioning.

He sat down in front of the monitor and brought up the package of lunar pictures from Mandy. There were two sets. One consisted of the photos he'd sent her. The second showed him what the surface *should* have looked like on the designated dates. There were about seventy photos in each of the two sets.

To Jerry, every part of the Moon looked like every other part. Craters. Craters within craters. Dark areas referred to as seas. And jagged-looking mountains.

The first pair of pictures were dated October 7, 1959, ten years before the Saturn flights. They were the product of the Soviet vehicle Luna 3, the third spacecraft to make it successfully to the Moon and the first to get pictures of the far side. Both photos were purportedly of the same area, one as it *had* looked on the official record, the second as it *should* have looked. At first glance, he saw no difference between them.

Craters, rocks, ridges, everything seemed identical.

But Miranda had said the shadows were wrong. He studied them. Increased the magnification. And yes, the shadows were angled differently. In the photo she'd indicated as accurate, the shadows were slanted more to the left of the picture. It wasn't easy to see, but it was there. Other pictures showed similar discrepancies.

So it was true: The images had been falsified. And the Russians were part of it.

The area that had been doctored was centered on the crater she'd mentioned. Cassegrain.

She'd enclosed a few pictures taken in August 1969, which, she said, were valid. Those were by Zond 7. *Another Soviet vehicle.*

An attached comment read: *The Zond images, as far as I can tell, have not been doctored. Nor can I find anything afterward that does not seem authentic.*

What in hell had been going on?

Barbara's voice interrupted him: "Jerry, Mary wants to see you."

"Okay," he said. "Tell her I'll be right there."

He did a search on the Cassegrain Crater. There wasn't much. It was, of course, on the back side of the Moon, never visible from Earth. It was located in the south, close to the Mare Australe. And the Lebedev Crater. Jerry had never heard of either.

Cassegrain was named after a Catholic priest who, in the seventeenth century, designed and built a new type of telescope. And that pretty much summed up everything. Except that the name rang a bell somewhere.

Cassegrain.

Where had he heard it before?

He shrugged, got up, glanced out again at the launchpad, copied a couple of the pictures in Miranda's package, put them in a folder, and headed upstairs to Mary's office.

———————

"Come in, Jerry." She was seated behind her desk, turning over sheets of paper. Without looking up, she pointed toward one of the chairs. Jerry sat. She stared down at the paper and shook her head. "They want to change over the computers. Bring in Open-Book's quantums. You believe that?"

"They're expensive."

She looked up at him and rolled her eyes. "It's ridiculous. The ones we have are fine. I think we're getting pressure from Beaverbrook again." She was referring to Adam Barnett, a Maryland senator with a strong British accent. Barnett was on NASA's funding committee, and OpenBook was located in Baltimore. "Anyway, I wanted to tell you I watched the press conference. I thought you did a good job. Held off the wolves. Maybe by next week this will have gone away."

He showed her the folder. "I've got something here that you'll want to see."

"What's that?"

He got up, took out the pictures from October 7, 1959, and laid them on her desk. He had to stop a moment, check them again to make sure he knew which was which. "This one," the one on her left, "is the *official* picture."

"Of what?"

"The area around the Cassegrain Crater."

She shrugged. But she already had a sense of what was coming. "Okay. It looks like the Moon all right."

"The official picture is Russian."

"So what does it have to do with us?"

"The other one is what a picture taken on that date *should* have looked like."

She bent over and studied the photos. Looked back at him. "Are they supposed to be different?"

"Look at the shadows."

She sighed. "Jerry, what are we doing here?"

"Photos of this area taken through late 1969, from the very beginning until after the Walker mission returned, were switched out. By us and by the Russians. Whatever it's about, they're in on it, too."

She lowered her head into her hands. "Oh, God," she said. "Jerry, do you hear yourself?"

"Yes, I do. Mary, there *are* no photos of this area during that entire time period that weren't tampered with."

She took a deep breath. "What's different about them? Are you talking about the *shadows*?"

"Yes."

"It's hard to see a difference."

"I've forwarded the entire package to you. Look at them on your computer."

She brought them up on the display. Studied a pair. Moved to the next ones. "Has anybody else seen these? An expert of some sort?"

"Mandy Edwards."

She was nodding. "And she thinks the official pictures—"

"—are doctored. Yes."

She looked at more pictures. Wiped the back of her hand against her lips. "Okay," she said finally. "Maybe you're onto something. I don't know. If you're right, it's been kept quiet for a half century, and I can't see that anyone's been harmed by it. Can we just let it go?"

Jerry suddenly felt tired. "You know, I lied out there today."

"In what way?"

"Tonya Brant asked me point-blank whether I had any reason to believe the government was hiding something. I told her no. Nada. No way."

"Jerry—"

"I don't like lying. Especially to television cameras."

"Jerry, for God's sake, you've been in politics. You helped George make it to the state house. Helped him get to the Oval Office."

"That's *politics*, Mary. People expect you to shade the truth. It's part of the game. This isn't the same thing at all."

"Jerry, I wish we could just walk away from this."

"When I went in there this morning, I already knew about these." He picked up the folder. "But I wanted to save my job, so I just flat out lied."

"Jerry, this is all a misunderstanding of some sort. It's just a crater. For God's sake, what do you think they were trying to hide? What do you think they could *possibly* have been trying to hide?"

"I told you I don't know, Mary."

"All right, when you find out, let me know. Then we'll see whether we want to go further."

"No," he said.

"Jerry, I'm not asking you."

"I'm part of the cover-up now, Mary." She sat staring at him. "You'll have my resignation by the end of the day."

13

Barbara teared up and told him she wanted him to stay. Vanessa, who might have been looking at an opportunity to step in and take over, nevertheless seemed genuinely unhappy. The fifth floor was filled with friends, people he routinely ate lunch with, partied with, played bridge with. He'd enjoyed working with them because they were true believers. Most of his career had been spent in places where it was just a job and everybody understood that. Even when he was working on George's Ohio campaign, surrounded almost exclusively by volunteers, the level of enthusiasm had been different. Not that it had been at a lower level, but it had been aimed, not at putting a man everyone admired into the state house, but rather at winning a game, at being smarter than the other side.

He took time to stroll through the area, saying good-bye to everybody. They all wished him luck. Some said he was making a mistake and should reconsider; others thought he was making a smart move, getting off a sinking ship. When he'd finished, he returned to his office and began getting his personal gear together. His sweater. Some notes. His pens. He was taking the photos down off the walls when Mary came by and made a second appeal. "You don't really want to do this," she said. "Take twenty-four hours and think about it. Call me tomorrow and let me know. I'm sure we can work something out."

God knew he wanted to stay. To be here when NASA became what everybody had thought it would become. But he no longer believed it.

"Mary," he said, "this isn't politics. We're supposed to be a science-first organization. That's what brought me here, and it's the position I've taken since my first day. I don't cover up, I don't mislead, and it would be doing the organization a serious disservice to start now.

"Something strange happened fifty years ago. I don't know what it was, or even what it might have been. But whatever it's about, unless someone can give me a good reason to back off, something better than keeping my job, then I won't be part of what we're doing now. Of lying about it."

He handed her the resignation. Fifteen minutes later, he drove past the security gate onto the Kennedy Parkway, thinking how he'd never go back.

———

In an age of instant communications, a guy with the right kind of reputation didn't have to wait long for job offers to come in. In fact, they were stacked up at his website when he got up next morning. Half the corporations on the planet seemed to need someone to become the face of their operations. He received invitations from Bolingbroke Furniture, "Relax with the Elite"; from Kia and Ford; from Coca-Cola; and from Amnesty International. Harvard offered him a teaching position. The United Nations wanted him to join the Committee for the Elimination of Hunger (CEH). MSNBC invited him to join the band of commentators on *The Morning Show*. The State Department offered him a post as an assistant secretary. He had no experience whatever in foreign policy. So that might have meant somebody was hoping to keep him quiet.

The NFL needed a spokesman. They'd gone through a series of scandals, and they wanted someone, they said, with a reputation for integrity. He wondered whether they weren't just looking for somebody to distract the reporters.

Most of the positions would have brought in considerably more money than he'd been making with NASA. But he just couldn't get excited about moving cars or soft drinks. Or covering for the NFL's wayward millionaires. The State Department, he suspected, would find a way to send him to Outer Mongolia. Amnesty International sounded good, but the money was minimal.

Josephine Bracken called him as he was getting ready to go out to breakfast. She was with CUES, the Committee to Upgrade Energy Systems. It was another nonprofit. "We need you, Jerry," she said. Josephine had been an activist for twenty years. "We can't offer you the kind of money NASA was paying you, but look at the cause you'd be supporting. If we don't succeed in getting our message out, in getting rid of fossil fuels, the climate will deteriorate to the point there will be massive disasters. It's just a matter of time. There's no way we can continue to pour poison into the atmosphere before we get a major reaction."

"I'd like to help, Jo," he said, "but if you want the truth, I think people are tired of listening to warnings about the climate. Yes, it's going downhill. But it's been a slow process, and the deniers won't give up until the catastrophe hits. The fact is, nobody cares anymore. Most people don't even think about it. The problem's gone invisible."

"That's why we need you, Jerry. We need someone to help stir things up."

"Jo, I'm going to have to pass. I hate to say this, but working with your organization would just be a shortcut to a heart attack. I've had enough of lost causes."

She sighed. "Okay, Jerry. I hope you'll change your mind. If you do, give me a call, okay?"

He felt guilty about that. But he was convinced there'd be no serious effort to deal with the problem until the Atlantic rolled in over downtown Manhattan. He just didn't need any more frustration in his life. Better to go back into politics. Real politics, that is, the kind where you just find a way to beat the other side and put your guy in office. It was the sort of work he could live with. And, to tell the truth, that he enjoyed.

Jim Tilghman was up for reelection this year. He was running for his second term in the Senate. And he was a decent guy. Someone he could support with a clear conscience. The word was that he was unhappy with the way his campaign was being run. That meant a reorganization would be coming.

Jim was an old friend. If the stories about disarray among the troops were correct, Jerry would probably be hearing from him.

He went to Darby's for breakfast. It was a nice break. Darby's was down at Cocoa Beach, overlooking the ocean. He couldn't eat there on a workday; it was too far out of the way. But it was perfect for a Saturday. Or for somebody no longer gainfully employed. He pulled into a half-empty parking lot. It was already hot, and no breeze came in off the ocean. They were predicting a high over a hundred.

He went inside, decided he wasn't going to worry about his diet, ordered bacon and eggs and a side of pancakes. Then he sat there, waiting for his breakfast to arrive, looking out over the Atlantic and listening to the rumble of the surf. If Tilghman called, he would accept. Jim was from Pennsylvania, and even though Jerry didn't know much about the politics in the Keystone State, he was a quick learner.

Maybe this was going to turn out to be a break for him. He'd enjoyed working at NASA, but the reality was that, whatever might happen there, his career had stalled. There'd been nowhere for him to go. If he'd remained at the Space Center for the next two decades, he'd have still been doing the same job.

Jerry wasn't sure what he wanted to do with his life. He'd been a history major in college and had expected to launch a teaching career. That had seemed natural enough for him. He was one of maybe three kids in the speech class who weren't terrified of getting up in front of everyone and delivering a few comments on how they'd have responded, say, to the Cuban Missile Crisis. The instructor, Professor Clement, had cited a study tabulating the things that people feared most. Death had come in second. Public speaking led the way.

Jerry, though, was a natural. He loved performing.

Maybe eventually he'd run for office himself. Representative Culpepper from the great state of Ohio. He liked the sound of it.

There were more job offers waiting when he got home. He'd received invitations from two talk shows to sign on as a regular panel member. One was the politically oriented *Slippery Slopes*, but the other was *Dark Energy*, on the Science Channel. He wished he had the background to do the Science Channel, but he'd get lost as soon as they started talking about quantum mechanics or string theory.

There were a couple of feelers from politicians, both in Ohio, both in local races.

But if he was going to get back into politics, he might as well go for the top. Rather than wait for Tilghman, he decided to take the first step. He called the senator's office. The woman who answered identified herself as Sally. She obviously didn't know him. Neither his name nor his face. "How may I help you, Mr. Culpepper?" she asked.

"I'm a friend of the senator's," he said. "Is he available?"

"I'm sorry, sir," she said. "He's not here at the moment."

"Would you tell him I called?"

"Yes. May I ask what this is about?"

"I suspect he'll know, Sally."

"Very good, Mr. Culpepper. Thank you for calling." And the screen went blank.

Jerry looked at the time. It was slightly after ten. Ordinarily, at that hour, he'd have been getting ready for his appearance on the NASA Channel. Going over the topics, constructing some spontaneous remarks, coming up with optimistic assessments on current projects.

It was painful. The organization he'd served so well had forced him to leave when he was coming to its defense. Because he wouldn't allow it to get further sucked into this web of lies and doctored photos and whatever else.

———————

He called Ralph D'Angelo.

"I was about to call *you*," Ralph said. "What happened?"

"I was asking too many questions."

Ralph was in his office. He pushed back in his chair and rubbed his hands across his few remaining strands of gray hair. "Are you telling me there's actually something to that Moon story?"

"Yeah. Something happened."

"What, precisely?"

"I don't know, Ralph. But the photos of the Moon, the back side near the Cassegrain Crater, were doctored. All the pictures between 1959, which were the first ones, until after the Walker mission, were not what they were supposed to be." He explained in detail. "I can send them to you, if you like."

"So whatever was going on, the Russians were in on it, too?"

"Apparently."

"Jerry, that's crazy. That was the height of the Cold War. They wouldn't have cooperated with us on anything."

"I know. It makes no sense."

"You have any kind of theory at all?"

"I got nothing, Ralph. I can't imagine what the hell was going on."

"We could publish the pictures, and all that would happen is that NASA would say there must have been a mistake, it's a long time ago, who cares?"

"I know."

"All right. I appreciate your getting to me on this. But we're going to need something a little more substantial, Jerry. You know what I mean?"

———————

Jim Tilghman didn't return the call. Jerry knew he should take the hint, but Tilghman had told him any number of times how much he would enjoy having him around to work on his campaign. *You're just the kind of guy we need.* And, of course, there was always the possibility that his message had gotten lost in the stack, that Tilghman had never seen it.

He waited until Monday before calling again. He got someone else this time. Wanda. "This is Jerry Culpepper," he said. "I'm a friend of the senator's. Is he available?"

"I'm afraid not at the moment, Mr. Culpepper. May I have your number, please?"

Jerry sat through most of the morning, thinking maybe he should break down and take the NFL job. Then, shortly before lunch, the call came in. "Mr. Culpepper?" Wanda again. "Please hold for the senator."

Jim Tilghman had grown up in the Appalachians. He looked like a mountain man. He'd been an offensive guard at the University of Pennsylvania, spent two seasons with the Eagles before concluding that his Maker hadn't really intended him for pro football. (Jim was an intensely religious man, a quality that didn't hurt him with the voters.) He'd gone to law school, become a prosecutor in Harrisburg, and later a judge. "I want to apologize for not getting right back to you, Jerry. We've been buried around here and, to be honest, it just got away from me." His black hair was neatly combed, but his goatee was missing. He was somewhat ahead of schedule. Goatees, Jerry knew, were never beneficial during election years. "What can I do for you?"

"Jim, I guess you've heard I left NASA."

"Yes, Jerry. That's a pity. You were the perfect guy to have out front." He hesitated, as if he was about to say something more. But he simply repeated himself: "It's a pity."

"Well, it was getting uncomfortable for me."

"The Myshko thing."

"Yes."

"I can see how that could have happened. It was all a long time ago, Jerry, whatever it's about. Something like that makes everyone uncomfortable. Do you know anything that hasn't been made public?"

"Not really."

Another pause. Then: "So what can I do for you, Jerry?"

That should have told him. In the past, Tilghman had always been forthright about his interest in securing him for his staff. "I'm thinking about getting back into politics, Jim."

"Really? You planning on running for office?"

"No. I don't think I have the qualities to win an election for myself."

"I understand."

"Actually, I'd like to sign on to your campaign. If you think you could use me."

"Jerry, to tell you the truth, I don't really have a staff position open."

"Oh."

The senator's face reflected regret. "Wish I could."

"It's okay. I'm sorry to hear it."

"Jerry." Tilghman looked around, apparently checking to see whether anyone could overhear him. "I'd love to have you. But right now's not a good time."

"Why do you say that?"

Tilghman put his elbows on the desk and rolled his shoulders forward in what looked like a blocking position. "Jerry, you're connected with the stories about the Myshko flight. And with Blackstone. That puts you right in the middle of the Moon conspiracy."

"I never said there was a conspiracy."

"It's hard not to read it that way. And being on the same side as Blackstone doesn't help. Jerry, you're radioactive right now. I'd take you in a minute if that weren't the situation. But, listen, a lot of people owe me favors. I can get you something somewhere, if you like. The Scoville people are looking for someone like you."

"Scoville? What do they do?"

"Firearms distribution. I think I can set you up—"

Most of the offers were coming from public-relations firms. McCrane and Whitney. Dobbs, Bannister, and Huffman. The big ones. He'd make far more money with them than he'd ever get in a government job. But the prospect of writing commercials did nothing whatever for him.

He and Susan went back to the Olive Garden for dinner. And drank the wine. "The library could use you," she said with a smile. "Of course, we couldn't pay you the big bucks like NASA."

Thank God for Susan, he thought. That night he needed her. She felt like the only safe harbor in a world turned suddenly hostile. "I'd never given it much thought until recently," he said, "but most of the jobs out there, the stuff I'm qualified for, I don't really want to spend my life doing."

The dark eyes were fastened on him. "But you've always done public relations, Jerry. I thought you enjoyed it."

"That was before NASA. The job really meant something there. I don't know. I bought into the mission. Like, I guess, everybody else. Except maybe Mary and the rest of the people on the sixth floor. And to tell you the truth, I'm selling them short. It's the system, not the people. But I don't think I could make a living hustling toothpaste."

The pizza arrived. But Susan never looked away from him. When the waitress was gone, she finished her wine. "You know, Jerry, most of us don't get to move the world. Just maybe a very small part of it."

"You suggest I take a job with McCrane and Whitney?"

"Not necessarily. But you might want to lower your sights a little."

———————

In the morning he had a call from Leslie Shields, who identified herself as one of the producers at the Target Channel. "Mr. Culpepper, I can't flat out offer you a position with us. But we're preparing a series that we'll be calling *Serendipity*. We've put together some films depicting how we got lucky, how historical events very easily could have gone the other way. For example, I'm sure you know that George Washington, when he was an officer in the colonial militia, applied for a commission in the British army. The Brits didn't believe that colonials were especially competent, so they rejected him. Imagine a Revolution in which he's on the other side."

"Sounds interesting," said Jerry, wondering why they were calling *him*.

"Then there's the Kansas-Nebraska Act."

Jerry was a little foggy on that. "What about it?"

"At the time it was passed, in 1854, Lincoln had served one term as a member of the House. But he lost interest in politics and returned to Springfield and a successful law practice. He would probably have stayed there had it not been for the Kansas-Nebraska Act, which would have extended slavery beyond its original borders. So the idea is that we'd prep a film and bring in a historian. You and he would introduce it, and afterward, you'd do a discussion about the possible consequences. Had Lincoln not been in the White House, had there been someone more willing to compromise—say, Stephen Douglas—might the Civil War not have happened? And if so, where would we be today? And so forth."

"Sounds interesting," said Jerry.

"We feel it's a great concept. It's not the sort of issue that comes up in everyday conversation. Anyway, we'd like to have you come in and audition to host the show."

"Why me? Wouldn't you do better to get a historian?"

"No. We'll *have* a historian each week. We need someone to ask the questions that an ordinary person would ask."

"I see."

"I guess I didn't phrase that very well. Mr. Culpepper, we

need someone who can put himself into the mind of the viewer and move the conversation in appropriate directions."

Shields was blond, blue-eyed, about forty. She wielded the easy confidence of someone accustomed to success. To having people take her seriously. She flashed a convivial smile that promised good times ahead. The Target Channel logo, a bull's-eye pierced by an arrow, occupied the wall space behind her. "You'd enjoy the challenge," she said. "And the Target Channel is a good place to work. We have creative people and good management. You'd be at home."

"I don't think I'd be the right guy for the job," he said.

"We also have a show about the Revolution." She showed no inclination to let up. "If things had gone a little differently in the royal family, they'd have had a smarter foreign policy. The Americans would have been happy, and Lexington would never have happened."

Jerry thought about it. "No Revolution?"

"There'd have been no United States. We'd be like Canada."

NASA popped back up in Jerry's mind. "That might have been a distinct improvement," he said.

14

Jerry collapsed into a chair, switched on the TV, and sat back to watch the closing segment of *Koestler Country*. He didn't particularly like the host, but he enjoyed watching him hassle politicians. They were on commercial, so he changed over to ESPN, and dialed in the Cincinnati Reds. They were in the third inning and already had a four-run lead over the Giants. First good news of the day.

But he watched Big Charlie Tinker walk two in a row, sighed, and went back to *Koestler*. The host was sitting in his book-lined studio with Brandon Janiwicz, one of the policy experts they were always trotting out. Koestler wore a skeptical frown, while his guest was demonstrating his trademark smirk. "—which is very strange," Janiwicz was saying. He was pressing his fingertips together while gazing out of the screen with unrelenting skepticism. "It's just an odd coincidence, that's all I'm saying, that, at this particular moment, they had to pull him out of that assisted-living facility and run him over to Lackland. Where they've sealed him so nobody can talk to him."

"So what does that tell you, Brandon?"

"Well, I'm not a conspiracy guy, Al. You know that. But

obviously Bartlett's hiding something. I don't know what it is. But something's not right."

———————

Jerry killed the sound. Froze the picture, Koestler leaning forward with that shopworn smile that suggested he'd uncovered another piece of corruption, and Janiwicz amused that anyone could have expected to fool *him*.

Outside somewhere, somebody was trying, without success, to start a car.

Bartlett, of course, was the sole survivor of the two lunar missions that might, or might not, have touched down on the Moon. Jerry googled him.

———————

"Look, Maria," said Jack Marquetti, host of *The Morning Show*, "the guy's almost a hundred years old. And what have we got? The media going after him and claiming he's hiding from them in a hospital. I'd like to see how well Al Koestler will be doing at that age. What we're seeing here, and it embarrasses me to admit it, is the media trying to make a story where there is none. We have a deranged billionaire buying time to make silly claims, and sure, people get excited, and next thing we know everybody's talking about a conspiracy. Neil Armstrong wasn't first on the Moon. We've had it wrong all these years. It was really Harry Myshko."

"*Sidney*, Jack."

"Beg pardon?"

"His first name was *Sidney*."

"Whatever."

———————

Eddie Bancroft, the host of *The Eddie Bancroft Show*, pointed his index finger in the general direction of Air Force Colonel Max Eberhardt. "I'll tell you what I think, Colonel. It's not a coincidence that next year's an election year. This whole business is an effort by the Republicans to suck the president into a ridiculous story. To force him to make a statement. Then, when it all turns out to be a joke, no matter what he's said, he'll look

idiotic. Dumb. I mean, that's the only explanation that makes
any sense."

———————

Meredith Capehart, on *The Rundown*, scribbled something on
her notepad, waved the pencil at her audience, and frowned.
"I'm not supposed to mention this in public," she said, "but the
whole story was dreamed up by the media. Look, you have a
couple of nitwits, Bucky Blackstone and what's-his-name, Jerry
Culpepper, saying crazy things during a slow season. Of course
the media are going to run with it. What would you expect?"
She touched her earpod. Faked a look of surprise. "Wait one,
Louie, they're telling me archaeologists have just discovered a
working radio buried in the Great Pyramid."

15

George Cunningham loved fund-raisers. He got no greater pleasure anywhere than mixing with the party faithful, hearing the
enthusiasm when he walked into a room, seeing the gleam in
everyone's eyes, the hands outstretched to touch him. There was
nothing quite like telling those jokes on himself, like the one in
which the First Lady confessed to him that she'd fallen in love
with him because he'd looked so much like her family's pizza
delivery guy back in Ohio. "She loves pizza," he added. It always got a laugh.

The first requirement, if you want to succeed in politics, is
to stand for something. The second is to pretend to be modest,
to disguise yourself as an ordinary person. The guy down the
street. And to play that role to the hilt. Be an average American
with the right moral values. The kind of guy the average voter
would like to sit down with over some beer. Pull that off, convince the voters, and nothing will ever stop you.

Cunningham would have been delighted to be able to say
what he really thought, to be brutally honest with the voters, to
point out that the country couldn't go on forever watching the
dollar lose value. That we couldn't continue indefinitely packing
more people within our borders. He owed it to the electorate to
mention that sometimes the country needs a little socialism.

(That it's okay; we'll just call it something else.) And so on. That was all political poison. To stay in power, you had to play the game. But that didn't mean he didn't believe in country over party. Everybody *said* that, but Cunningham *believed* it. It was a position that often alienated his allies. But he'd do what he could to stay in power because it was important to keep his political opponents well away from the Oval Office. They were inclined to approach every problem with a hammer.

He was at the Hyatt Regency Century Plaza in Beverly Hills. There were some Hollywood people in the audience. Among them was Grant Barrin, the action star. Grant was at the far end of the president's table. You couldn't go wrong if the heroic types came out for you. Comedians were good, too. And leading ladies. But you couldn't do better than someone like Grant.

Within minutes after he was seated, they rolled out the dinner. Steak, mashed potatoes, corn, red cabbage, and apple sauce. George's kind of meal. He had never developed much of a taste for ethnic food. He was basically a meat and potatoes guy. Senator Andrea Gordon was on his left, and state party chairman Bill Merkusik on the other side. He expected to name Andrea as his running mate in 2020.

The party was anticipating problems holding on to its California House membership. And that became the topic during the meal. The voters were unhappy with the runaway inflation, and they wanted overseas bases closed down. The United States, many of them felt, had developed serious imperial ambitions, which it could not afford. The watchword in the 2020 election was going to be "time to come home." George would have loved to pull out and bring everybody back to the States. He'd already done some of that. But the country had made promises under previous administrations. And some places were inherently unstable. Leave, and people who had supported the United States would die. He didn't want that on his conscience. *The New York Times* was leading the charge against him. It was an easy enough call, he told Merkusik and Gordon, for *The Times*. They wouldn't have to live with the results when people started getting butchered.

Sometimes, he regretted having gotten into politics. He didn't like the life-and-death decisions that periodically faced him. Twice he'd stayed out of conflicts while his critics screamed for intervention. And he'd watched while dictators massacred thousands. Blood on his hands whether he acted or stood by.

Damned job. Sometimes, he was tempted to announce that he'd back off at the end of his first term. Let somebody else try his luck. If there were a graceful way to do that, he probably would. But it would hurt the party, and, consequently, damage a lot of the people who'd supported him.

———————

When they'd finished eating, Merkusik rose to applause, took his place at the lectern, and introduced him. The applause was deafening. Andrea smiled at him. Go get 'em, cowboy.

He shook hands with the chairman. "Thanks, Bill," he said, turning to the audience. He had to wait for them to settle down. When they did, he held up both arms. "I love California."

More cheers.

"Thank you," he said. "It's always a pleasure to be among friends." He told a few jokes about his early ambitions to break into the movies. "I always wanted to be a leading man," he said, looking toward Grant as if trying to suggest they would both have been in the same class. Grant smiled and pointed a finger. You and me, baby. And the laughs came. He stayed on message. The party would win big next year, he told them, but they couldn't do it without the efforts of the people gathered in that room. He thanked them, and expressed his hope for their continued support. He outlined his objectives for the second term. Social Security would be kept on track. The administration would continue its policy of closing overseas military bases deemed nonessential. "The problem we face," he said, "is that two decades after we were saying that history had essentially ended, we are still dealing with an unpredictable world. And, unfortunately, the very act of taking precautions sometimes tends to create more potential enemies. The really good news, of course, is that the destruction of the global nuclear stockpile continues on pace."

That line always got applause. Decades from now, if he was remembered for anything at all, he'd get credit for pushing, and finally bringing to fruition, the Nuclear Weapons Elimination Treaty. His father had been appalled that the world had stored tens of thousands of atomic bombs in its arsenals and, when the

Cold War ended, made no move to get rid of them. "There won't be a future," he'd told George one evening after they'd watched a scientist on the History Channel make dire predictions about the next half century. "Eventually," he'd said, "either by accident or design, one of them, or maybe a lot of them, will go off, and take three million people into oblivion with it. Once that happens, civilization will come apart."

The treaty had been signed in 2018, in Hiroshima. Remarkably, every nuclear-capable government on the planet had gotten on board. There'd been promises, some coercion, a lot of compromises. To make the system work, the United States, and everyone else, had granted unrestricted and unannounced access to I.A.E.A. inspectors. Passage had been branded a miracle, accomplished in the face of outrage around the world. He wished his father could have lived to see it.

Cunningham made it a point never to talk longer than twenty minutes. At fund-raisers, he'd found it best to cut off at about fifteen and turn the program over to the audience. So he assured everyone that, whatever it took, he would maintain a balanced budget. Then he asked for questions.

Clyde Thomason, a vice president at Paramount, wanted to know whether the president saw an economic turnaround coming. That led to a discussion about the administration's efforts to get inflation under control.

How had he managed to get the Koreans to agree to a peace treaty?

Was the United States going to get involved in the effort to get global population under control?

Were we going to continue sending aid to Cuba?

What was his reaction to Morgan Blackstone's comments?

That came from a guy near the front. Cunningham was pretty sure they'd been introduced at one time, and he seemed to recall he was a banker. But he couldn't remember a name. "Blackstone?" he said, stalling for time. Merkusik, who'd taken a seat beside the lectern, wrote the questioner's name on a slip of paper and placed it where the president could see it.

"To be honest, Michael," he said, "I really don't know how to respond to his comments. I think you'll have to ask him to explain a bit more. While you're at it, you might check with Mr. Blackstone to see if he knows what's going on in the Bermuda Triangle."

Bill Merkusik rode with him to the El Segundo Air Force Base. "Good show, Mr. President. You were great in there." He was heavyset, had lost most of his hair, and had a face full of wrinkles. Still, when he laughed, an entire room could light up. He was a physician though he'd given up the practice long ago. He'd hated the health-care system. Cunningham had promised reform, but hadn't gotten to it. It was complicated, and nobody really had a workable answer.

Without Merkusik, Cunningham knew, he would very likely not have taken California. And that would have cost him the race. "Thanks, Bill," he said. "They were a good audience."

"They believe in you."

"What's on your mind, Bill?" He'd seen a shadow in his eyes.

"Michael's question. About Blackstone."

"Yes?"

"Mr. President, it's becoming an issue. Blackstone lit a fuse last week. You're going to have to lay it to rest."

"Lay *what* to rest, Bill? There's nothing to tell."

"You're sure?"

"Of course I'm sure."

"Okay. Just be aware that Bucky has some friends here. And they trust him. Word's getting around that, well—"

"Look, Bill, I can't shut down a nonstory. The more I talk about it, the more credence it will get. Just relax. It'll go away on its own."

16

Bucky Blackstone spent the night in his bedroom suite atop the office building, had some breakfast brought up from the cafeteria, considered lighting a cigar, decided against it, poured himself another cup of coffee, and carried it down the hall to his office.

"Have you heard the rumors?" asked Gloria excitedly as he opened the door.

"We're at war with Latvia?"

"No, of course not."

"The Cubs won the pennant?"

"Stop being silly."

"You're right," said Bucky, sitting down at his desk. "It's much easier to believe that Sidney Myshko turned cartwheels on the Moon. Now, I could guess all day, or you could enlighten me."

"The word on the grapevine is that Jerry Culpepper resigned yesterday!" said Gloria.

"Have you tried to check it out?"

"Of course," she replied.

"And?"

"The grapevine is always right," said Gloria. Then she smiled. "You called that one, Boss."

Bucky nodded. "He's gone. He's a moral man. He could put

up with just so much lying and duplicity, and then he had to quit. He'll find working conditions here much more to his liking."

"You want me to try to get hold of him today?"

"No, that wouldn't look good, not for either of us. I'd look like I was buying off NASA's spokesman after starting all this controversy about the Myshko mission—"

"*You* didn't start it," interrupted Gloria.

"You and I know it, but most of the public never heard of it until I went on the air, and George Cunningham has the press in his back pocket. If he feels betrayed, and he will, that's the way the story will be played." He paused and looked out of the buildings that formed the bulk of his empire. "And Jerry won't look any better, not if he comes to work for me the day after he quits. We'll give him a couple of weeks, and then, to quote an Italian friend I never had, I'll make him an offer he can't refuse."

"What if someone else offers him a job first?"

"Then I'll outbid them."

She smiled. "It must be nice to be able to say that and not have anyone tell you no."

"People have been telling me no all my life," answered Bucky. "I got rich by ignoring them."

"So we just pretend Jerry doesn't exist for a few weeks, and then you dangle so much money at him, he can't say no?"

Bucky shut his eyes and sat stock-still for a moment. Gloria had worried the first few times she'd seen it years ago, certain he'd gone into an epileptic or catatonic trance, but by now she was used to it. It just meant her boss was getting an idea, and they usually worked out to his advantage.

"Let's not ignore Jerry totally," said Bucky. "See if you can get me a face-to-face connection with him."

"The press hasn't been able to get a statement out of him all day," said Gloria. "My guess is that he's not answering his landline or his cell phone."

"You're probably right," agreed Bucky. "Tell you what: Let's send him a video e-mail. Do we have his address?"

"Yes."

"Good. This way he'll read it when there's no pressure on him to reply right away."

"You don't expect him to get right back to you?"

"Of course I do. I just don't want him to feel pressure."

"What *do* you want him to feel?"

Bucky smiled. "Curiosity. He didn't quit NASA because of the truth. He quit because they're hiding it from him." He stared at his computer. "I never remember how to start the camera and microphone."

"Some astronaut," she said sardonically, walking over and activating the machine. "All right, just hit ENTER, look at the camera, and start talking."

Bucky did as she instructed, and a tiny blue light went on above the camera lens, showing that it was operating.

"Hi, Jerry," he said. "This is Bucky Blackstone. I'm not calling to offer you a job. That'll come later if you're interested." Suddenly he smiled. "I'm calling to offer you a proposition."

He paused for a moment to let that sink in. "One of the nice things about leaving this message rather than speaking face-to-face with you is that you don't have to contradict me for form's sake. I'll just assume you're issuing all the expected denials, okay?"

Bucky paused again, giving Jerry time to assimilate what he was saying.

"All right," he said after a few seconds had passed. "You know and I know that Sidney Myshko landed on the Moon. What I don't know is why, and I assume you don't either. I also don't know why the government and almost everyone connected with NASA feels obliged to lie about it, but that doesn't matter. I've found some additional material in Aaron Walker's diary, and one of my most brilliant and trusted assistants"—he frowned briefly, trying to remember her name—"Sabina Marinova, has interviewed Amos Bartlett. I've got a video of the complete interview." Suddenly, he grinned. "I'll bet you'd like to know what we've found in the diary. And I suspect you'll be curious about the video. Admit it."

One last pause to dangle the baited hook, and then it was time to reel him in. "Well, you can, Jerry. I may know a little more than you, but there's a lot more both of us want to know. I'm busy overseeing all the preparations for our Moon flight, and I just haven't got the time to follow up on it. Besides, everyone thinks I'm a billionaire crackpot, whereas you're a straight arrow through and through. So how would you like to do all the digging that you either couldn't do at all, or had to do when no one in authority was looking? No salary, I'm not hiring you, not until you're ready to sign on for the long haul. But I'll pay all your expenses, fly you anywhere you need to go, give you cash to slip to anyone who won't talk for free but will sing like a bird for money. Not only that, but I will loan you Serena—make that Sabina—Marinova, and since she *is* my employee, all of her expenses are covered, too."

Bucky looked at his watch. "Okay, Jerry. It's nine fifteen in the morning. Get back to me by six o'clock tonight. After that, the offer's no longer on the table."

He deactivated the camera and microphone, leaned back, and allowed himself his first cigar of the day.

"You really mean it?"

"Why the hell not?" responded Bucky. "His sources have to be different from ours. And he's got nothing to do for the next two or three weeks."

"If you're going to give him your most trusted superspy, you really ought to learn her name."

"Maybe I'll call her Lady X. That sounds properly mysterious, don't you think?"

"Why not?" answered Gloria. "After all, she's been a covert agent for, oh, maybe five minutes now."

He chuckled. "She's good, and since I didn't know she existed until a couple of days ago, I'm sure we can spare her."

"What if he doesn't *want* a covert assistant?"

"Then he doesn't have to have one," said Bucky. He shot her a smile. "But I'm not paying him to find a bunch of answers, then not share them with us. She can be his covert assistant or mine, but he's not working on his own until I know I can count on his loyalty."

Jason Brent entered the office. "Hi, folks. Anyone try to kill the boss yet?"

"It's early in the day," said Bucky. "Have patience."

"You sticking around here for a while?" asked Brent. "I thought I'd go down and grab something to eat."

"Be my guest."

"Until the cafeteria starts charging, that's what we all are," answered Brent. He walked back into the corridor and over to the elevator.

"Well," said Bucky, "what's on tap for today?"

"Nothing, really," said Gloria. "You want to inspect the ship?"

"Good God, no! I wouldn't begin to know what to look for. And I still have to learn the terminology. Can't be calling a hatch a door."

"Since you've announced that you're flying to the Moon, don't you think you *should* learn it?"

"There's time," said Bucky. "Right now, I'm more concerned with why someone stood on the Moon rather than what he called all the gizmos he used to get there."

"Well, you can always talk to Amos Bartlett."

He shook his head. "Once they figure out that Sabina's not a granddaughter or some such, it will have taken them two hours, tops, to find out who she works for, and they'll have Bartlett locked up tighter than a drum." He grimaced. "Besides, he told her what he knew. I don't think I could get any more out of him. Some people are too rich to bribe, some are too stupid, and some, like Bartlett, are too damned close to the grave to be able to use it. No, he's not the answer."

"The diary?"

"Been through it three times, all the way back to 1958. I guarantee there's nothing else there."

"Is there *anyone* who knows the truth, do you think?" asked Gloria.

"*I* know the truth," Bucky shot back. "Sidney Myshko was the first man to walk on the Moon. I just don't know *why*."

"Who would?"

He shrugged. "If I knew that, I'd have this thing solved by dinnertime." Suddenly he sat up erect. "All right. If I can't solve it, maybe I can put some pressure on someone who *can*."

"You mean Jerry?"

He shook his head. "I *hope* Jerry can help. He had to know some things we don't know for him to walk away from his job."

"Then who?"

He grinned. "Who's the one guy who can get things done when he wants to?"

"President Cunningham?"

"You got it in one. Set up a face-to-face with him."

"Oh, come on, Bucky," said Gloria. "You can't just call the White House and get through to the president. Only the presidents of China and Russia can do that."

"He'll talk to me," said Bucky with total self-assurance.

"What makes you think so?"

Bucky grinned. "Tell him I've got a conversation with Amos Bartlett on video, and I'll put it on the Internet in an hour if he won't talk to me."

"Would you?" she asked, frowning.

"I don't know," he admitted. "But the point is, Cunningham doesn't know either. Believe me, he'll talk."

And sure enough, five minutes later, the president's face appeared on Bucky's screen.

"Good morning, Mr. Blackstone," said Cunningham.

"Good morning, Mr. President. And you can call me Bucky."

"All right, then—good morning, Bucky." A humorless smile. "And you can call me Mr. President. Now what is so vital that our latest astronaut feels compelled to speak to me on such short notice?"

"I thought you might be ready to talk about the Myshko Moon landing."

"You'll want to speak to a science-fiction writer about that," responded Cunningham. "The first man to walk on the Moon was Neil Armstrong. I could recommend any number of history books on the subject."

"*They* would be the fiction books, sir," said Bucky. "I just want to know if I would find them under science fiction, or perhaps espionage?"

"Just what are you suggesting, Bucky?" demanded Cunningham.

"Just this, Mr. President," said Bucky. "You lost a good man at NASA because he couldn't stand up there and lie to the public anymore."

"Who are you referring to?"

"Jerry Culpepper."

"I know nothing of that."

"Of course you do," said Bucky. "You're a bright, competent man, and you run the country like I run Blackstone Enterprises. Little things—especially *important* little things—don't escape your attention. Now, as I was saying, you lost a good man. And NASA and the White House can spin the story any way you like, but the truth is going to come out. I'm in possession of Aaron Walker's diary, and at least twenty members of my staff plus a member of the press can testify as to what's in it. Now I'm aware that the FBI can bust in here and try to find it—"

"Your government does *not* break into private homes and businesses!" snapped Cunningham.

"Damned lucky for you I don't believe that for a minute, or I wouldn't vote for you next time around," said Bucky. "When it's important enough, you'll do what you have to do. But I also have a video conversation with Amos Bartlett, and it makes no difference if you steal that, because there are dozens of copies that have been dispersed all over the country, and the day I report that the original has been stolen—which would be a lie; the original is hundreds of miles from here—the others will all be available on the Internet within an hour. Which is why you agreed to speak to me in the first place."

"Just what is it that you want, Mr. Blackstone?"

"Bucky."

"What the hell do you want? If anything happened, it happened half a century ago, and I'm as much in the dark as you! I'm not hiding anything, damn it! I never even *heard* of Sidney Myshko until a month ago!"

Bucky stared at the president's image for a long minute. Finally, he said: "I believe you, sir. You are as ignorant of what happened as everyone else is. Now I have a question for you: Would you like to become informed?"

Cunningham looked suspiciously into the camera. "What, exactly, are you proposing?"

"I want to give you a copy of the video. I could send it over the Internet, of course, but it's too easy for pirates to swipe it and disseminate it. There have to be dozens reading, or trying to read, everything that comes and goes from the White House, and any company as big as mine has its share of would-be eavesdroppers as well. But if you will send an authorized member of your staff here to pick it up, I'll turn it over to him; and then you can see for yourself. And yes, I expect you to have your experts analyze it to make sure it hasn't been faked or tampered with."

"If I send a representative, then what?"

"Then I hope you'll be curious enough to start pulling strings," said Bucky. "And, surely, you have more strings to pull than I have."

"That's *it*?" said Cunningham. "You just want to pique my curiosity?"

"There's been a massive cover-up for fifty years," said Bucky. "We don't know exactly what happened or why it's been covered up. Your government—well, the tiny handful of members with any knowledge of this—are *still* covering it up. Wouldn't you like to know why? And if it's no longer important to keep it secret, wouldn't you like to be the president who pulled it out of a darkened corner and put a light on it?"

Cunningham stared silently at him, as if considering his response.

"I'm going to get to the bottom of this," continued Bucky. "I'm willing to spend every last penny I have to find out what happened and why. Right now, I'm a billionaire kook who's making ridiculous claims, but I can already back some of them up, and if I get to the bottom of this while you're denying everything, the press and the public are going to assume your government has been trying to discredit me out of malevolence rather than ignorance."

"All right," said Cunningham at last. "I'll send someone by with written authorization, signed by me, and I'll look at your video. But I make no promises."

"I haven't asked for any."

"No, you've just made veiled threats," said Cunningham. "I don't like you very much, Mr. Blackstone."

"That's a shame," said Bucky with a smile. "I really *did* vote for you, you know."

The president broke the connection.

"Well, this has been quite a morning of bribes, entreaties, and threats," said Gloria. "Isn't there anyone you'd like to murder before lunch?"

"Don't tempt me."

Bucky spent the rest of the morning okaying outlays for the ship's continuing construction and upgrading, had lunch with some visiting business associates from Japan, and got back to the office in midafternoon. He answered messages from Ed Camden, told Sabina Marinova to be prepared to go on a new assignment on a minute's notice, and refused interviews with three television stations, four radio stations, and two Internet news services.

He was reading over some financial statements from a small subsidiary in Nepal when his computer beeped and told him that he had a message waiting. He ordered the machine to play it.

Instantly, Jerry Culpepper's haggard face appeared, looking at if he hadn't had a good night's sleep in a week.

"Hi, Bucky," it said. "I got your message. If there are no crouching dragons or hidden tigers, I'll do what I can."

17

The president had taken the call from Blackstone at Camp David, where he and Lyra were, finally, enjoying a relatively quiet weekend. Usually, when Cunningham went to the presidential retreat, Ray Chambers manned the guns at the White House. But the chief of staff's wife, Paula, had grown increasingly close to the First Lady, so this time they'd *all* gone to Maryland.

Paula had been a literature professor at Ohio State. It was where she'd met Ray, when both were graduate students. Ray claimed she'd fallen in love with him on that first day and he'd eventually given in and agreed to a marriage. Paula, of course, had a different story. It wasn't hard to see where the truth lay.

Lyra was especially taken with her. "She is," she told her husband, "probably the smartest person anywhere near the White House." And, when he'd frowned, she'd added, "Except you, dear, of course."

Both women had been kept up to speed on the Moon flap, and all four were eagerly awaiting the arrival of Blackstone's video.

The delivery hadn't taken long. Less than three hours after the phone conversation, the White House messenger had been helicoptered in. They sat down in the main lodge, and Lyra opened the package, removed the video, and inserted it into the drive. There was no preamble, no explanatory comment by Blackstone, simply the date and time of the recording, seven days earlier, played against the sterile backdrop of a hospital corridor. Then they were looking at an old man propped up against three pillows in a bed. Ray checked the image against a photo. "It's Bartlett," he said.

Then a woman's voice: "I'm very glad you agreed to see me, Mr. Bartlett."

Bartlett stared up over the top of the screen. "He doesn't know he's being recorded," said Paula.

After that they fell silent while Bartlett rambled through his conversation with his unseen interrogator.

"My bet is even the Congress doesn't know about this. Probably just the president, and maybe two or three others, tops." His voice trembled.

Ray glanced across at the president, shook his head, and looked away.

"Who sent you here, really?" Bartlett asked.

"Mr. Blackstone."

"How do I know you're not working for *The New York Times*?"

When it was over, and they'd listened to the interviewer, Sabina Somebody, explain how she'd been sent for a cigarette, then locked out of Bartlett's room, they simply sat staring at one another. "Look," said Lyra finally, "this guy's probably certifiable. He thinks *The New York Times* has an army."

Ray agreed. "You ask me, George, Blackstone's got nothing."

"If this recording shows up in the media," said Paula, "it will convince everybody that something *did* happen during the mission. It can't be read any other way, except that Lyra's right, and he's deranged. But that perspective will get no traction unless you can do a second interview and demonstrate he's out of his mind. Do that, of course, and the country will end up hating you." She looked squarely at Cunningham.

"I agree," said the president. "We need to send somebody to talk to him. Find out what we're dealing with."

"Not a good idea," said Ray. "Too much is at risk. If we're seen taking this seriously, and it turns out to be as crazy as it seems, we'll be permanently connected with it. I suggest we tell the media we'd be happy to see Mr. Blackstone reveal whatever factual information he might have. In the meantime, the White House has more important things to do. And we keep our hands off it."

Cunningham shook his head. "If something really did happen during the Moon flights," he said, "I'd like very much to know about it."

"George, we've already talked to everybody who might have known something. They're laughing at us."

"We haven't asked *everybody*. Paula's right."

"George, please, stay clear of Bartlett. If it gets out—"

"Make it happen, Ray."

———————

Three hours later, they were on their way back to the capital in Marine One. Lyra and Paula sat talking quietly. Ray was reading through a Defense Department report. Cunningham stared out at the mountains, listening to the thrum of the blades. In the distance he could see a pickup moving along a narrow road.

The Moon, he knew, would be full that night. But he would have been happy if it never rose again.

18

"Okay," said Ray. "I've sent Weinstein to talk to him, but I still think it's a mistake." He was *not* happy. "George, we can still back away. If you pursue this thing, it's going to come back to haunt you. I can see the cartoons now. You'll be running around the Moon with a flashlight peeking into craters. 'Hello, anybody there?'"

Cunningham stared across the Oval Office at the pictures of his old friend Ruby O'Brien and himself standing outside an Iraqi schoolhouse, surrounded by kids. They were both in uniform. Ruby had died a few years later in an Afghan helicopter crash. Cunningham knew what it meant to be in combat, and those horrendous years in the Middle East had left him scarred. "So you're saying there's no chance it could have happened."

"What I'm saying is to just stay away from it. If it turns out that there was some kind of plot, you can congratulate Blackstone and give him a medal. If it goes the other way, which it almost certainly will, you'll be clear."

"I've been trying to do that, Ray. Stay clear. Ever since Culpepper started all this. But it keeps getting worse."

"Just ride it out."

"I don't see how we can do that."

"George, we're talking about a very old man. And yes, maybe he has lost his grip on reality. That's a much more likely event than secret Moon landings. I mean, look, this guy is very likely frustrated because he came so close but didn't get a chance to go down to the surface. So what happens? It eats at him for a lifetime. After a while, he invents his own reality. Let's just not get in any deeper. And by the way, you might have the Army tighten security a bit so nobody else can get to him. Do that, and in a few months, when Blackstone makes his flight and doesn't find a damned thing, the whole business will collapse. and everybody will be laughing at him. You want to be sure you're on the right side of this. George, let the voters think you're taking it seriously, and when it comes apart, your reputation will be gone. And I'm sure you noticed this will all be happening during an election season."

Where the hell was the hidden vault containing secrets to which only the president had access? He'd seen it in the movies any number of times. It contained the papers concerning the truth about the Kennedy assassination, what Lincoln had been told about the probable cost of a civil war, what had really brought on the Japanese attack in 1941, and the offstage deal between Kennedy and Khrushchev that had staved off a nuclear exchange during the missile crisis.

There'd been a rumor during the fifties that the Cold War had been a cover. NATO and the USSR were in an arms race, but not against each other. The arsenals were being assembled for use against invading aliens. Yes, they were on their way. The nuclear standoff between East and West had been intended to prevent panic while everybody got ready to present a united front.

Cunningham smiled. Good way to keep everyone calm. He tried to imagine what it had been like to live under the imminent threat of hydrogen bombs arriving at any time.

And then there'd been the Philadelphia Experiment.

So why wasn't there a provision to pass vital information from one president to another?

"Because," said Ray, "every president leaves office with stuff he hopes people will forget. Lyndon Johnson and George W. Bush got us into pointless wars. You think they want to explain how it happened?"

Ray Chambers was a tall, quiet guy. Glasses, thin hair, nervous smile, always carrying an umbrella. Cunningham had found him difficult to take seriously at first. He was virtually unknown to the public in an age when anyone affiliated with the president was subject to scrutiny. Even the White House chef. But Ray had somehow managed to remain invisible. It was one of several reasons the president liked him. Another was his supreme political instincts. Ray had, incredibly, remained behind the scenes while directing the campaign that had brought Cunningham an unexpected nomination, then a victory against the charismatic Laura Hopkins, whose early poll numbers had been overwhelming.

———————

Cunningham had not experienced an easy three years in the Oval Office. There'd been continuing problems in the Middle East as angry mobs overthrew dictators only to give themselves over to lunatics who were even worse than the guys they replaced. The United States was still plagued by debt. Unemployment was down, but not nearly enough. Energy costs had created a climate of ongoing inflation. The world had finally been forced to face the reality of a population growth that was outrunning resources. And oceans were rising as the poles melted.

"And now," he said, "we're dealing with lunacy on the Moon."

Ray nodded. "It's the derivation of the word."

Cunningham frowned.

"*Lunatic*. We used to believe moonlight drove people crazy."

His phone buzzed. "Mr. President, we have Stephen Goldman on the line."

Goldman had been the NASA director during the final two years of the Obama administration.

Ray backed out of the way as Goldman's intense features appeared on-screen. "Good morning, Mr. President," he said. "I guess I wasn't surprised to hear you wanted to talk with me." Goldman had been a political appointee, who'd been used to signal that NASA's days of usefulness were effectively over. Though, of course, he hadn't realized that himself.

"Hello, Steve," Cunningham said. "Yes. We seem to have fallen on strange times."

"The world's gone crazy, Mr. President. Blackstone's always been something of a crank. But this latest business is over the top even for him."

"So there's nothing to it?"

Goldman frowned. "Are you serious? Of course not. It couldn't have happened."

"Why not?"

"There's no way NASA could have kept a secret on that scale. It would've gotten out."

"While you were at NASA, Steve, you never heard about anything like that? No rumors? Nothing at all?"

"Nothing at all, Mr. President."

"Can you think of any situation that would have justified two secret flights?"

"No, sir."

"None?"

"Well, maybe if aliens were camped up there somewhere, and they'd told us to bring them pizza or they'd attack. Look, Mr. President, I knew some of the NASA people from that time. The only thing that mattered to them was getting to the Moon, and the only thing that mattered to the politicians was beating the Russians. There's just no way they'd have done a landing and not said anything."

———————

Cunningham was looking at a busy day. Even by White House standards. A Pentagon delegation was scheduled in at nine. Then there'd be a conference with his treasury secretary and his economic advisors. When that was finished, he'd be sitting down with a couple of governors and a small group of educators to try to figure out what was wrong with the school systems. The United States was still running weak numbers in contrast with other Western nations and China and Japan. American kids were at the bottom in almost every category. He knew what some of the problems were: Politicians devised educational systems as if students were in some sort of lockstep. The importance of parents in the success of kids was overlooked everywhere. There was still no reasonable system for grading teachers and rewarding the good ones.

Everything that might be done to help seemed to run into

interference from local watchdog groups who thought they had the answers. Or from politicians who saw a chance to convert the issue into votes. Or from teachers' unions. Or from advocacy groups with no experience in the field.

It went on like that all day. But he couldn't get his mind off Bartlett. He'd been briefed on the radio transmissions, on how only Bartlett had responded. On the strange notation by Aaron Walker stating he'd made his landing in April 1969. On the indications that something similar had happened on the Myshko flight. Thin stuff. Still, when you put it all together, and threw in the Blackstone videotape, it was hard to explain. And Blackstone did not seem like the kind of guy to back a dead horse.

Richard Nixon had been president in 1969.

Cunningham needed to talk to one of the inside people at the Nixon White House. But they were mostly gone. Had been gone a long time.

John Dean was still around. But he doubted Dean had been close enough to the president for something on this scale. There *was* someone else though—

———

He was in his quarters that evening when the call came through. No Skype this time. Just audio.

"Mr. President. This was a surprise." Everybody in the country knew that voice, still strong, still carrying the ring of authority after so many years. "What can I do for you?"

"Henry," Cunningham said, "how are you?"

"I'm well, thank you."

"Glad to hear it. I suspect we could use you here."

He laughed. "The world keeps getting more complicated, doesn't it?"

"It seems so. I don't suppose you'd consider coming out of retirement?"

Another hearty laugh. "I think you have a very efficient secretary of state."

"Yes. John's quite good." He paused. Music drifted in from the next room, where his wife, Lyra, was playing a board game with the girls. "Did you see Blackstone last week?"

"No, Mr. President. I'm aware, though, of what he said."

"You were National Security Advisor to President Nixon when we landed on the Moon."

"That is correct."

"Would you care to comment on Blackstone's assertions?"

Outside, he could hear the wind in the trees. "No. I have no comment."

"All right, Henry. Would you be good enough to tell me what's going on?"

The girls giggled. Anna said something, and they were all laughing. He went over and closed the door.

"Mr. President, surely you're not taking any of this seriously?"

"I just want to get at the truth."

"I see." The wind picked up, then went away. "Mr. President, at the time I was a bit too busy with foreign affairs to become involved in Moon flights. May I offer you a piece of advice?"

"You may answer my question, Henry. That is *not* a request."

"If I had any knowledge of the matter that contradicted what everyone already knows, you may be assured I would not hold it back. You've established yourself as an effective president, sir. You're the man the country needs in these turbulent times. Please do not do anything to damage that perception."

"Henry—"

"Mr. President, stay away from this absurd business. You have nothing to gain. Even if Blackstone were correct, a curious premise in itself, it cannot harm you or the country. Your obligation is to preserve the respect the nation has for you."

"Then whose concern is it?"

"No one's. And that is my point. Stay away from this matter. Very likely nothing will ever come of it. If it does, it is best that you remain at a safe distance."

19

Milt Weinstein was known in the trade as a fixer. He didn't like the connotation, because to him it sounded as if he fixed horse races and baseball games, but in truth he had almost no interest in either of them. What he fixed were political problems—leaks, indiscreet statements, bimbo eruptions (odd how quickly that became an accepted political term), and the like.

He wasn't thrilled with the thought of going to Los Angeles to speak with a ninetysomething astronaut who hadn't said anything that could embarrass his employer. In fact, he had no idea what kind of answer he was trying to elicit from Amos Bartlett. For all he knew, he'd be trying to have a conversation with a drooling, incontinent old man who barely remembered his name, let alone his Moon flight.

But he'd been ordered to go by Ray Chambers—and Chambers was close to the president, so here he sat on a commercial airliner, in economy class yet, reading some news magazine that was two weeks behind where he was and wondering how long it had been since they had stopped selling booze in those cute little bottles.

Finally, he landed. As he picked up his suitcase, he automatically looked around for someone in a chauffeur's uniform holding up a sign with his name on it, and then remembered that, of course, there wouldn't be one, not when he was traveling incognito. He then spent a couple of minutes wondering why the hell a man who was unknown to 99.99 percent of the public had to travel incognito in the first place.

He walked out of the building, waited patiently in line for a cab, and gave it the name of his hotel. When it arrived, he gave the driver an extra twenty to stay put for a few minutes. Then he went to the front desk, got his key, and tipped a bellhop to take the suitcase up to his room while he went back out and climbed into the cab again.

Then it was off to the military hospital, a dull, rectangular, unimaginative brown building. The cab pulled up to the front door, let him off, and sped away while he walked through the glass doors that opened automatically when they sensed his presence.

He stopped at the front desk and got the name and room number of the general who was in charge of the facility, and was then given an escort to his office. The sign on the door told one and all that this was the office of Major General Samuel H. Glover. The young sergeant who had accompanied him knocked on the door, waited for a gruff "Come!" from the other side, then opened it and stepped aside as Weinstein entered.

The general looked at him with a total lack of interest.

"Yes?" he said.

"General, my name is Milton Weinstein. I believe I'm expected?"

Glover frowned at him. "Is there something wrong with you?"

"I'm here to speak with one of your patients. I'm just checking in to announce my presence and make sure there won't be any hassles."

"Which patient?"

"Amos Bartlett," said Weinstein.

The frown deepened. "Press?"

Weinstein shook his head. "Absolutely not."

"Then what's your business with him?"

"Actually, I work for your boss."

"General Landis?"

"*His* boss," said Weinstein with a smile. He pulled his White House pass out of his wallet and handed it to Glover.

"Are we to assist you in any way?"

"No. I just want to make sure I won't be stopped or have to go through a mile of red tape."

"All right," said Glover. "I'll have the young man who brought you here escort you to Bartlett's room. But first, you will stop by this room"—he scribbled down a room number on a piece of paper, then handed it over—"and dictate and sign a statement that you have been sent here by the president of the United States. If you are telling the truth, no one else will ever see the statement or know of your visit unless you choose to make it public." Another frown. "But if you're lying, or here under false pretenses, I can promise you a long, not very enjoyable stay in another government facility not too far from here—Terminal Island."

"Understood," said Weinstein.

He turned to the door, prepared to open it, only to find his sergeant standing there. He escorted him down the corridor to the office indicated on the paper. When they arrived, Weinstein dictated his statement to a young officer at a computer, waited for it to be printed out, and signed it.

"All right," he said, turning to the sergeant. "I'd like to see Bartlett now."

"This way, sir," said the sergeant.

"Can you tell me anything about him?" asked Weinstein, as they walked to an elevator.

"I know he flew one of the Apollo missions, sir, one of the ones before we landed on the Moon."

The sergeant punched the button for the elevator. It arrived, and they got in and started up. "Anything else?" asked Weinstein.

The sergeant shrugged. "Just that he was moved here to keep him away from the press."

"Why?"

"I really don't know, sir. He seems a nice old guy, but of course I've only seen him a couple of times, once when he arrived and once when I took him to one of the labs for some tests."

"Tests for what?"

"You'll have to ask the medical staff, sir."

The doors opened, and they stepped out onto the fourth floor.

"When I'm done, do I just walk back to the elevators and go down to the main floor and out the front door?" asked Weinstein, who was sure it couldn't be that easy.

"In essence, sir," said the sergeant. "I'll be standing outside Bartlett's room while you speak to him. The door will be closed, so neither I nor anyone else can overhear you. When you're through, just open the door, I'll escort you back down, you'll sign out, and I'll arrange transportation for you."

"That's very thoughtful of you."

The sergeant finally smiled. "Your tax dollars at work, sir."

They walked down the sterile, unadorned corridor, took a left, and stopped in front of a door.

"This is it?" said Weinstein.

"Yes, sir."

"Okay. I'll take it from here." Weinstein opened the door and stepped into the room. A very old man, who looked even older than his ninety-two years, sat propped up in his bed, watching a televised baseball game on the TV screen that hung on the far wall. He noticed Weinstein but didn't turn off the set or even lower the sound.

"Good afternoon, Amos," began Weinstein.

"Shut up!" said the old man. "There's two out and two men in scoring position."

Weinstein stopped speaking and looked around the room. The old man had a pile of books on his nightstand, and didn't seem to be attached to any monitoring devices. The place smelled of chemicals, cleaning fluids mostly, but then so did the rest of the hospital. There was a phone on the table, hidden behind the books, and a pair of glasses folded atop the stack of books. A window overlooked the parking lot.

"Damn!" muttered the man as the batter struck out, and the game ended. "Okay," he said, turning to Weinstein. "You're not a doctor or an orderly, so what do you want?"

"My name is Milt Weinstein, and I'm here to talk to you."

"You can tell Bucky Blackstone to go to hell!" snapped Bartlett. "I'm not saying anything."

"I don't work for Blackstone," answered Weinstein.

"Then what are you doing here?" asked Bartlett suspiciously.

"Like I said, I want to talk to you."

"Well, *I* don't want to talk to *you*." Bartlett folded his shriveled arms across his chest.

"Maybe if I tell you on whose behalf I'm speaking, you might change your mind."

"Maybe it'll snow in August, too," said Bartlett.

Weinstein pulled a chair up next to the bed and sat down.

"Okay, Mr. Bartlett. You don't want me here. I'd rather be three dozen other places. But this is my job, and I'm not leaving until I get what I want. How long it takes is up to you."

Bartlett glared at him. "All right," he said at last. "Who are you working for?"

"Ever hear of George Cunningham?"

Bartlett muttered an obscenity. "I *knew* it!"

"Well, at least you realize he's got the clout and the money to keep me here until I get what I came for." Weinstein smiled.

"Why can't everyone leave me alone?"

"Tell me what I want to know, and I'll see to it," said Weinstein.

"You're just a flunky. You can't make promises for him."

"You've only got one thing anyone wants, Mr. Bartlett. Once you tell it to me, the president's got no further interest in bothering you, and he can see to it that no one else does either."

"How?" demanded Bartlett. "This place is like a prison, and if I go back to the home, everyone will find me there."

"I'm sure we can arrange the equivalent of the witness protection program," said Weinstein. "New name, new state, all expenses paid for."

"They'd find me."

"They wouldn't even be looking for you. Besides, how old are you?"

"You're saying I'll die before they find me." Bartlett shrugged. "Probably you're right."

"Then shall we talk?" said Weinstein, pulling out a video device the size of a matchbook. "Don't mind this. It's just to make sure I don't misquote you."

"First things first. *Prove* you work for Cunningham."

Weinstein pulled out his ID card and handed it over.

"I could get fifty of these printed up in an hour's time," said Bartlett. "You must be able to get your boss on your cell phone. I want to see his face when he's answering you."

"I can't bother him in the White House just to prove I work for him," said Weinstein. "The man's got a country to run. This is small potatoes."

Bartlett stared at him for so long Weinstein was afraid he was going comatose. Finally, he nodded. "All right. Ask your questions."

"Thank you." Weinstein leaned forward. "You were on one of the Moon missions prior to Apollo XI, right?"

Bartlett nodded. "Yeah. I was the command module pilot for Aaron Walker. But you know that."

"Tell me about the mission."

Bartlett closed his eyes, sighed, then opened them. "Everything seemed in order. We took off on schedule, jettisoned our boosters on schedule, reached the Moon on schedule, orbited it the first time on schedule. It was a picture-perfect mission up to that point."

"Then what?"

"Then we orbited it again."

"And?"

"And again."

Weinstein grimaced. "What aren't you telling me, Mr. Bartlett?"

"Every word I've told you is God's own truth!" he snapped.

"I never said it wasn't," replied Weinstein. "I asked what you weren't telling me."

"I want a cigarette first."

Weinstein actually laughed. "In a hospital? Lots of luck."

"I want one!"

"I'm sure you do."

"And I'm not saying another word until you get me one."

"Then we're just going to stare at each other until one of us falls asleep," said Weinstein.

Bartlett stared at him. "Damn. You're smarter than *she* was."

"Who are you talking about?"

"Blackstone's spy." A pause. "Cunningham has more competent people than Blackstone does."

"Thank you for the compliment."

"I didn't say *good* people, I said *competent*," replied Bartlett.

"I thank you anyway. Six of one—"

Bartlett stared at him. "You have qualities. I'll bet you're great at rigging elections."

"Never tried," said Weinstein. "Can we get back to the subject?"

"Blackstone's lady?"

"The Moon flight."

"Aaron and Lenny are both dead, you know," said Bartlett. "I'm all that's left."

"I know."

"And look at me."

"You're doing okay, Amos."

"Sure I am."

"So what really happened up there?"

His eyes brightened. "What the hell. Maybe someone ought to know the truth while I can still tell it."

"Makes sense to me," said Weinstein encouragingly.

"All right," said Bartlett. "You want to know what happened? Blackstone already knows, but he can't prove it."

Weinstein wanted to ask if he meant that there was a landing, but he knew better than to say it first. Sooner or later, someone might claim that he was leading a senile witness. "So tell me, Mr. Bartlett."

"Call me Amos."

"All right, Amos."

"They took the lander down to the surface on the far side," said Bartlett.

Weinstein checked his video device to make sure it was working. "You want to say that once more, Amos?"

"They landed. I was left alone in the ship. I orbited eleven times, then they hooked up with me again. Never said a word about what they were doing down there. I knew it was hush-hush, and, of course, it had to have been planned all along. I never asked them why or what they had done. I couldn't be sure the ship was secure. When we got back, got away from everything, I asked, but they'd been sworn to silence, same as I had. After that, I never saw them again."

"Did they bring anything back up to the ship?" asked Weinstein. "Rocks, pebbles, anything at all?"

Bartlett shrugged. "I don't know."

"How could you not know?" persisted Weinstein. "You weren't at the controls twenty-four hours a day. You had access to the rest of the ship."

"Oh, they didn't bring anything aboard the ship," said Bartlett. "But I don't know what they might have left in the lander. I never got into it during the flight, and I never saw it again after we came home."

"That's very interesting, Amos."

"You think so?"

"Don't you?"

Bartlett shook his head. "I find it scary, not interesting. What the hell did they do that half a century later nobody knows anything about it?"

"That's what your president wants to find out."

"He's the president, isn't he?" said Bartlett. "Why doesn't he just order NASA to turn everything over to him? I mean, you can't keep secrets from your president when he wants them, can you?"

Only if his name is Ford, Reagan, Bush, Clinton, Bush 2, Obama, or Cunningham, thought Weinstein wryly. Then he remembered that he'd only gotten half his answers.

"I have another question or two, Amos."

"I know."

"You do?"

Bartlett nodded. "You want to ask about the earlier flight, Myshko's, don't you?"

"Yes, I do," said Weinstein.

"I don't know. They took off, did some orbits, came back, and there was never any indication anything unusual had happened. I didn't realize there'd been anything out of the way about the Myshko flight until they started talking about it a couple of weeks ago. If they actually went down, too, they sure as hell didn't tell any of us."

"Who told you not to say anything?"

"An admiral. Castleman, his name was. I wasn't to say anything to anyone. Not even let anybody know there was anything to tell. After that, no one ever mentioned the landings again. We had debriefings, and it was as if everything had proceeded according to the officially announced plans. I was told that everything that happened was top secret, and that if I divulged anything I'd be locked away for the rest of my life . . . but that's just what's happened to me now. And I'm tired of having this hang over my head." A rueful smile crossed the old man's face. "They won't believe you either, you know."

"One man will," said Weinstein, getting to his feet and walking toward the door.

"Who?"

Weinstein turned to face Bartlett. "The one who counts."

| 20 |

It was Jerry's first day on the job for Press of the Dells, a mid-size Wisconsin publisher. He hadn't sought the job; like all the others he'd been turning down until he realized he was running out of money, it had sought him—or his reputation, to be honest. You could fill a dozen books with what he didn't know about the publishing business—indeed, people already had—but at least it wasn't the government, and if he had to tell an occasional white lie, it didn't make him feel as if he was lying to the world at large about vitally important issues.

His job was loosely defined: at-large editor, which meant that he wasn't responsible for any particular line of books (the house published both fiction and nonfiction in various categories), and assistant to the publisher, which was even more loosely defined but essentially meant that he was the middleman in both directions between the literary press and the stockholders on the one hand, and Cliff Egan, the middle-aged publisher, on the other.

At least, he thought, *I'll be dealing with rational people instead of paranoids who see conspiracies behind every statement.*

That comforting thought lasted all the way until midafternoon of his first day, when Millicent Vanguard (which he was sure couldn't be her real name) burst into his office.

"Good afternoon," he said. "How may I help you?"

"It's happened again!" she snapped. "And it's got to stop!"

He looked past her, through the open doorway, into the hall. "Has someone been annoying you, Miss Vanguard?"

"Him!" she screamed, tossing a magazine down on his desk.

He picked it up. *Wisconsin Reviews Magazine*. "I'm not acquainted with this. Can you explain, please?"

"Harley Lipton!" she said. "That little carbuncle on the behind of humanity!"

"What exactly did this little carbuncle do?" asked Jerry.

"Just *read* it!"

He picked up the magazine. "What am I looking for?"

"Page twenty-seven!"

He turned to page twenty-seven, and began reading aloud. "I am as willing to suspend my disbelief as the next man, but when it comes to the sludge that passes for a Millicent Vanguard novel, I find I cannot suspend my appreciation of plot, characterization, and the proper use of the English language. Her latest, *Kiss These Dead Lips*, is even more ludicrous than her *Grave Lover*. If I may paraphrase the late, great Henny Youngman, take my Vanguard books—please!"

"Well?" demanded Millicent when Jerry had finished. "What are you going to do about it?"

He was at a loss for an answer. Finally, he said, "Are you asking me to edit your next book?"

"No!"

"Then what?"

"I want you to get Harley Lipton fired!" she screamed.

"Just because he doesn't like vampire romances?" he asked mildly.

"What better reason is there?" she demanded. "And they're *paranormal* romances."

"I can't get a man fired just because he doesn't like a book."

"But he hasn't liked my last seven!" said Millicent. "He's clearly prejudiced against not only me, but the entire paranormal romance field. He has no right to be writing reviews."

"Maybe you could speak to his editor," suggested Jerry.

"I did! The fool wouldn't listen, any more than you do!" She turned on her heel and stalked out.

Ah, well, they can't all be Ernest Hemingway or Joseph

Heller, he thought. Besides, would facing a drunken Heming-way, who was probably carrying a gun, have been any better?

Then he thought of Millicent Vanguard again, and thought, *Yeah, probably.*

The next day brought new interactions with the artists to whom the reading public had entrusted the preservation of the culture and the language.

First came a phone call from James Kirkwood, who was two years late on a biography of Wisconsin Senator Willis McCue.

"I wasn't aware of the book," Jerry had replied. "I've only been here a couple of days. But McCue is running for reelection next year, and he's down nine points in the polls. I think you'd better get it in fast, before he's out of office and people forget who he is, or was."

"You're supposed to encourage me, not depress me, damn it!" snapped Kirkwood.

"I *am* encouraging you," said Jerry reasonably. "I'm encour-aging you to deliver the manuscript."

"When I'm ready!"

"Remember what I said. I don't see how we can use it if you wait much longer."

"You sue me for nondelivery, and I'll sue you for harassment and mental cruelty!" yelled Kirkwood, slamming down the phone.

An hour later he got an e-mail from Melanie Dain, explain-ing that her eighty-five-thousand-word novel was two hundred thousand words and still going strong, but that her agent would soon be in touch about splitting it in half on the reasonable as-sumption that Press of the Dells would pay her double since it would now be two books. When he asked if the first book, or first half, or whatever they were calling it, would have a satisfy-ing conclusion, since not every reader would be buying both books, she explained that it could easily be done—for triple the advance. He explained that triple the advance for a single book that was running long through no fault of the publisher's was an unreasonable request, and she explained that she never talked money, that he'd have to speak to her agent.

"But you just *did* talk money," he pointed out. "You asked first for double, then triple the advance."

"That was a matter of *principle*," she explained archly. "My agent talks dollars and cents."

Suddenly NASA and Washington weren't looking all that bad.

Things went more smoothly for the next two days. Then Schyler Mulhauser, the award-winning science-fiction artist, delivered his cover painting for Richard Darkmoor's newest book.

"It's very nice," said Jerry, looking at the painting.

"One of my best," said Mulhauser.

"But I'm afraid we can't use it."

"Why the hell not?" demanded Mulhauser. "I worked three weeks on the damned thing."

"Schyler, you put a naked woman in the middle of the painting. She's absolutely beautiful, but she's absolutely naked."

"That scene's in the book."

"I haven't read it, but I'll take your word for it," said Jerry. "But we can't use it anyway."

"Why not?" repeated Mulhauser.

"Most of the distributors won't handle it because most of the stores won't display it."

"And you're going to let a bunch of middle-class churchgoing bigots tell you what to do?" demanded Mulhauser.

"Those middle-class churchgoing bigots probably constitute 80 percent of our population," answered Jerry. "We're in business to sell books; we can't sell what the stores won't take."

"Publish them as e-books and skip the stores."

Jerry was getting a little tired of artistes. "Good idea. We'd save the cost of printing, shipping, and cover art."

"WHAT?"

"Mulhauser, hang the painting at a convention's art show and sell it at auction, or find some publisher who hasn't figured out that busty naked ladies don't get displayed in bookstores, but I need some acceptable cover art, and I'm not okaying payment until I get it."

"I'll think about it," muttered Mulhauser. He turned and walked to the door, then turned back. "I don't like you much."

"I'm desolate," replied Jerry.

"Just remember: I'll be here long after you're gone."

"In Wisconsin?" said Jerry, as Mulhauser stalked out of his office. "I wouldn't be a bit surprised."

On Monday, the printer phoned to say the press he was using for
Jerry's books had broken down, which meant he'd be three days
late. Jerry had to call the trucking company, which wanted a fee
for canceling on such short notice, and 15 percent more than
usual for supplying trucks on Thursday on almost as short a notice, and one of the distributors explained that the science-
fiction, romance, and political-essay lines would probably hit
the stores two to three weeks late, despite only arriving at his
warehouse three days late. Of course, if Press of the Dells really
had to get the books out sooner, he was sure something could
be worked out. It was a phone call, but Jerry could almost hear
the distributor's hand stretching out to Wisconsin, palm up.

The next day, Jerry was eating lunch in a nearby sandwich shop
(which he had to admit gave him twice as much for half the price of
its Florida equivalents) when Sarah McConnell, one of the editors,
found herself in the same restaurant and sat down across from him.

"I hope you don't mind," she said.

"Not at all."

"I've hardly had a chance to get acquainted with you," she
said. "How do you like it here, after being on television every
day and hobnobbing with the rich and famous?"

"NASA scientists are neither rich nor famous," he replied
with a smile. "As for the job, I'm getting used to it."

"Good. I don't know how you can deal with those science-
fiction people. They're all crazy. And the mystery people . . . the
women want such neat, cozy, comfortable murders, and you get
the feeling the men really enjoy describing decapitations."

"Are *any* writers totally sane?" he asked with a smile.

"*My* writers are," replied Sarah.

"You're mainstream and romance, right?"

"Mainstream and paranormal romance," she corrected him.
"Plain romance is, well, *passé*."

"But women falling for werewolves and zombies isn't?"

"I'm talking about my writers, not the subject matter demanded by their readers."

"Okay, I see the difference."

"And my writers are absolutely normal. Well, as writers go, anyway."

"I met one of them my first day on the job," he said.

"Oh?"

He nodded. "Millicent Vanguard. She wants me to kill a reviewer."

"Well, Stanley *is* incredibly cruel to her."

"Stanley?" he repeated, frowning. "No, I think the guy's name is Harley someone-or-other?"

She laughed. "Harley Lipton?"

"Yes."

"At least he uses some wit. Stanley Pierson is positively vicious to her."

"If they all hate her writing, why do we keep buying her manuscripts?" asked Jerry.

"You mean, beside the fact that she's the best-selling writer for the entire publishing house?"

He sighed. "Give me time. I'm still new on the job."

"Isn't it the same everywhere?"

He shook his head. "Everyone can love a rocket's design and its cost, but if it won't get off the ground, we scrap it and try another approach."

"No wonder the country's so deep in debt," remarked Sarah.

"Wouldn't *good* be nice, too?" asked Jerry.

"Good is what pleases the public. We're just the conduit between the artists and the readers."

———————

Then, on his twelfth day on the job, a manuscript arrived. It went to the nonfiction editor, who walked into Jerry's office and tossed it on his desk.

"Here," he said. "This is much more your field of expertise than mine. Have fun with it."

Jerry looked at the title: *Reaching High: A History of Our Space Program*.

"Oh, Lord, another one!" he muttered, but, out of a sense of duty, he began reading at the top of page one, figuring he'd stop before the end of the prologue and send a little note saying that it was a nice concept, but others had thought so, too, and covered the same subject many times before.

But when he put it down to grab a cup of coffee, he realized that he was on page forty-three and was anxious to get back to it. He took it home with him, read far into the night, and finished it at his desk in midmorning. The second he was through, he walked into Cliff Egan's office and told him that he'd just read the best damned book on our space program he'd ever experienced.

"Who published it?" asked Egan.

"No one," said Jerry, surprised. "I'm talking about a manuscript we received."

"Oh," said Egan with no show of enthusiasm. "I'm glad you liked it."

"Everyone will like it once we bring it out. I'd like to be in charge of the publicity campaign."

Egan stared at him as if he'd lost his mind. "We won't be publishing it, Jerry."

"Don't you want to even read it?" demanded Jerry.

"I'm sure it's as captivating as you say," said Egan.

"Then why—?"

"You're new to the field, Jerry. We're in business to make money, and books about the space program just don't sell. Write the author a glowing personal rejection and suggest some other publisher, someone big enough to publish it for the prestige, knowing it's a loser."

"You won't even look at it?" persisted Jerry.

"Why bother?"

———

Ten minutes later, Jerry was on the phone to Bucky Blackstone.

"That job you mentioned a couple of weeks ago," said Jerry. "Is it still open?"

Five minutes later, he stopped by Egan's office to hand in his resignation.

21

Gloria checked her computer and turned to Bucky. "He's on his way up."

"Culpepper? Good."

"Do you want me to leave?"

Bucky shook his head. "No, *we're* going to leave. I want to show him around—especially the plant where we're working on the ship."

"Then why not meet him there?" she asked.

"Because he's been working in a place that's being starved for funding, and I want to impress the hell out of him by having him come up and take a look at the offices where he'll be working."

She stared at him. "You always have a reason for what you do, but I sure don't know why you want to impress him. I mean, hell, we've already *got* him."

"He's going to take over from Ed Camden as the spokesman for the Moon shot," said Bucky.

"Ed's not going to like that."

"We'll find lots of things for Ed to do, but Jerry has to be our public face for this project."

"Why?"

"Because he quit NASA as a matter of conscience rather

than continue lying to the public, and that makes him the most trusted and believable spokesman we could have."

"Most people don't know why he quit."

Bucky smiled. "They will," he assured her.

"Okay." She didn't always love the way Bucky's mind worked, but she admired its efficiency.

"And if we find what I expect to find, I need a spokesman whose veracity and integrity are above reproach."

She checked her screen. "He's here now."

"Let him in."

Gloria got to her feet, walked to the door, and escorted Jerry inside. Bucky found himself facing the man he'd seen so often on television: an inch or two under six feet, brown hair beginning to recede at the temples, intense gray eyes, a slender man just starting to add a little poundage with age.

"Welcome aboard, Jerry!" said Bucky, walking forward and extending his hand. "I can't tell you how happy I am to have you on the team."

"Thanks." Jerry shook his hand. "Sorry I couldn't get you any more information, but that publishing house took everything I had." He paused and made a face. "One more day there, and I'd sure as hell have killed someone."

"Anyone in particular?"

"About six in particular." Jerry smiled ruefully. "Maybe seven."

"Well, if you're going to work in an industry where the practitioners tell you up front that they're lying, you can expect that," replied Bucky.

"I'm just about ready to agree with you."

Bucky nodded. "Well, let me give you a little orientation tour. We'll start right here. This is my office . . ."

"I know that."

"And this"—he indicated Gloria—"is my executive secretary, Gloria Marcos, who's been with me longer than anyone else. If you need to contact me, she'll always know where I am, and if I've given orders that I'm not to be disturbed, she'll know how to circumvent them because I am always available to you."

Jerry nodded pleasantly to her. "We've met online."

"You know Ed Camden," Bucky continued. "There's a burly guy who pretty much leaves me alone in here but is my shadow everywhere else. You'll meet him soon enough. He's Jason Brent, my number one bodyguard."

"You have more than one?" asked Jerry curiously.

"I have eight."

"I knew you had a few enemies, but I didn't think that many people hated you," said Jerry with an attempt at levity.

"For every one who hates me, there are a dozen who'd like to kidnap me and hold me for ransom," answered Bucky.

"Of course. I hadn't thought of that."

"As I told you, if you need to dig up any information, especially information that someone doesn't want you to have, we've got a young woman named Sabina Marinova who's pretty good at ferreting it out. She's the one who was the first to have a face-to-face with Amos Bartlett." Bucky paused. "There'll be a few more people I want you to get acquainted with, but let's take a tour first."

"What did Bartlett say? Did he admit to anything?"

"You can draw your own conclusions, Jerry." He turned to Gloria. "See that he gets access to the video."

"Will do."

"Now, Jerry, let's go take a look at our transportation."

"The spacecraft?"

"Of course."

"Good! I'm anxious to see it."

"Let me show you where you'll be doing your most important work first," said Bucky, leading Jerry out of the office to his private elevator.

"My office?" asked Jerry, as they descended to the third floor.

"Your office is a minor part of it," answered Bucky.

The elevator came to a stop, and they got off. "That's yours to the left." Bucky indicated a large office filled with up-to-the-minute electronic equipment. "The one on the right belongs to Ed Camden. He may be a little upset for a few days, since you're replacing him as our spaceflight spokesman."

"I can do some other job . . ." began Jerry.

"Do you think you're the best at what you do?" demanded Bucky. "Tell me the truth."

"Yes."

"Okay, then—no false modesty. You're our spaceflight

spokesman, and that's that." He walked to a very solid door and opened it.

"My God, that's impressive!" said Jerry as he walked into a state-of-the-art video studio.

"It should have everything you need," said Bucky, indicating a number of digital cameras including 3-D, acoustical microphones, teleprompters, and lights, plus half a dozen video and audio recording and dubbing devices. "Our technicians can be ready to work on a moment's notice. We can broadcast you all the hell over the world on television, radio, the Internet, you name it. We can also transfer images from the ship, and from the Moon itself, and send them out from here. We have experts who can put together any kind of presentation you need on almost no notice."

"This is a far cry from where I was working at NASA," said Jerry, looking around.

"If there's anything else you think you'll need here, just ask for it. My priorities are different from NASA's"—he smiled—"or at least from those of NASA's boss over on Pennsylvania Avenue."

"I can't imagine that this studio needs anything."

"It needs the right spokesman," said Bucky. "And now it's got him." He paused. "You want to look around a bit?"

"I can do it later," answered Jerry.

"Okay, let's go look at my new toy."

They reentered the elevator and, to Jerry's surprise, descended past the ground floor and even the basement level, to the subbasement.

"What the hell's down here?" asked Jerry, as they emerged into a dimly lit area of concrete floors, walls, and ceilings.

"Transportation system," answered Bucky, leading him to a small vehicle that looked like a souped-up golf cart. It was parked next to a dozen identical vehicles.

"But why? I mean, all your buildings are on the same piece of property, right? I read that you own about two square miles."

"A mile and a half," said Bucky. "This is Jason Brent's idea. If they don't know where I am, it's hard to set a trap for me—or shoot me, for that matter."

"Why do they want to shoot you?"

Bucky shrugged. "Why did anyone want to shoot John Lennon? There are crazy people out there, and if you make the news, and I do, you're automatically a target."

"I guess you are at that."

"It shouldn't surprise you. Your previous boss is protected around the clock by the Secret Service."

"You expect a president to be a target," responded Jerry. "You don't think of it in terms of normal people."

"I won't even resent being called a normal person," said Bucky with a smile. "But consider this: In the almost two and a half centuries the United States has been in business, four presidents have been assassinated—Lincoln, Garfield, McKinley, and Kennedy. How many nonpresidents have been shot down in that same amount of time?"

"I wasn't arguing," replied Jerry. "I just hadn't considered it."

The route was well marked with glowing signs and arrows, and after a couple of minutes, Bucky came to a stop next to a freight elevator. They got out of the vehicle, walked over to the elevator, and ascended to ground level. There was an armed guard standing right at the elevator door, and others were posted at the various entrances and exits. Bucky nodded to him, which seemed to be all the guard needed to know about Jerry, and he stepped aside to let them pass.

They found themselves in a huge area, some two hundred feet on a side, forty feet high, with a number of cranes not in use lining the back wall—and right in the middle was the ship that would be taking Bucky and four others to the Moon.

It was a glistening white vehicle, slim and elegant, with more than a hint of raw power, pointing to the ceiling and, beyond that, the stars.

Jerry let out a low whistle of admiration. "Somehow I thought it would be bigger," he said. "It seems dwarfed in a place like this."

"I wish it *were* bigger," said Bucky. "I'm going to feel awfully cramped after a couple of days." Suddenly, he smiled. "I wish we could at least have added a flush toilet." He paused. "It takes off vertically and lands horizontally. The Moon lander lands and takes off horizontally. Everything's magnetized or somehow attached to the bulkheads since we're going to be out of gravity pretty soon."

"Where the hell's the booster?"

Bucky pointed to it. "It looks like it's part of the ship. But we'll be jettisoning it not long after we take off."

"I'm impressed," said Jerry.

"It looks even smaller when it's on its belly, which is the way it's going to touch down," replied Bucky. "I never know which parts of it they're working on from day to day, so I never know if it's going to be pointing to the ceiling or to a wall." Suddenly, he smiled. "We could make it bigger," he added, "but if we did, I don't know if we could get it off the ground."

"You know," said Jerry, "I've never seen one of these close-up, at least not before it's taken off and returned minus a couple of stages. I signed on after the last shuttle launch."

"It's not a shuttle anyway," said Bucky. "This baby was built to reach the Moon." He pointed to a smaller section of the ship. "And *that* baby was built to land on it."

"Well, I'm impressed," said Jerry. "I just think it's a shame that you had to do this yourself, that NASA couldn't get the funding."

"It's not a shame at all."

"Oh?"

"I'm a capitalist. I think it's a shame that we ever needed NASA in the first place, if in fact we did. There's money to be made up there, exploring the planets, mining the asteroids, building colonies."

"I agree with mining the asteroids, but when you talk about building colonies, you're making it sound like science fiction."

"Am I?" said Bucky. "As best we can tell, there are oceans hidden beneath the Moon's surface. If they're H_2O-type oceans, there's a lot of oxygen to be pulled out of them until we can create enough hydroponic gardens to sustain life for a few hundred or a few thousand people. You think five hundred heart patients wouldn't pay whatever it takes to live out their lives—their much-longer lives—in a low-gravity hospital on the Moon?"

"You'd make a profit from them?"

"Don't hospitals?" retorted Bucky. "Don't ambulances? If I invest a couple of billion, don't I deserve a return on my money?"

"That's why we have organizations like NASA, which *don't* exist to make a profit."

"They don't exist at all if the government doesn't take your money to fund them," said Bucky. "There's a little less charity in the world than you've been led to believe. But that's neither here nor there. There's a little less truthfulness, too. And that's why I'm engaging in this enterprise, and why you're going to be reporting it to the public, whatever the results."

Jerry sighed deeply. "There's no sense arguing about lunar colonies and hospitals, or about charities and economics. I'm here to help disseminate the truth about the Myshko and Bartlett missions, whatever that truth may be. And now that I *am* working for you, I'll tell you something else I've been able to find out: Just about every shot you've seen of the Cassegrain Crater taken since 1959 has been doctored."

"Cassegrain?" repeated Bucky. A grim smile crossed his face. "Damn! I *thought* it might be Cassegrain."

Jerry frowned. "What do you mean? Why Cassegrain?"

"It's the area with the smallest number of photos and almost no description of it."

"That's your destination?"

"That's right."

"What are you looking for—footprints?"

Bucky shook his head. "We'll look for them, of course, but I would imagine they were swept clean."

"It's a big crater, maybe forty miles across," said Jerry. "How will you know exactly where to look—and what will you be looking for, if not footprints?"

Bucky led Jerry around the ship to the smaller lunar lander. "Do you see this?" he said, pointing to a section of it.

"Yeah."

"That's a descent stage. If we're right about this, there should be two of them on the ground."

"Damn!" exclaimed Jerry. "I never thought of that!"

Bucky flashed him a grin. "I'll bet George Cunningham never thought of it either, or he'd find some obscure law to prevent us from taking off."

"So it's *not* going to be like looking for a needle in a haystack!"

"We probably won't be able to see them from orbit, but we'll have instruments that can find them and pinpoint their location. Then maybe we can finally find out why nine presidents in a row have lied to the American people."

Cassegrain. The word kept running through Jerry's head. And then he realized—"There's something else," he said.

"What's that?"

"There was a secret project back during the Apollo days."

"Really?"

"Its name has an echo."

"Its *name*?"

"They called it *Cassandra*."

Suddenly, Jerry began to feel very excited again. It was a feeling he hadn't experienced since he first began working for NASA. He'd forgotten the sensation, and now that it was back, he never wanted to lose it again.

| 22 |

"They've had the breakthrough, Mr. President. Wescott tells me, *assures* me, that the average American born this year will be able to look forward to a life expectancy almost twice that of people in the last century." Laurie Banner, his science advisor, was standing three feet in front of the president's desk. Abraham Wescott was a Nobel Laureate who'd been leading the charge toward extended life spans for years. He was known to be extremely conservative in his official statements. So if he said so—

Laurie was a tall, thin African-American, impeccably dressed, wearing a conflicted expression. Good news and bad news. They'd known this was coming, but Cunningham had hoped it would hold off until he was out of office.

"Well," he said, "I guess we should raise a toast to Professor Wescott."

"There's more," Laurie said.

"They're going to do resurrections as well?"

"Almost. He says they'll also be able to reverse the aging process. But we knew if they could do one, they could manage the other."

"Well, I'm glad to hear it." George simply would have liked it to come when someone else was in office. "Seniors also get a break."

"Yes. It's hard to believe, Mr. President." She walked over to the couch and sat down.

"When?" he asked.

"They'll be ready to start treatments in six months."

"How much will it cost? The individual, I mean?"

"Wescott promised it would be affordable for most people. He's estimating less than a thousand dollars per patient. For another eighty years of life."

"People playing basketball at a hundred and twenty."

"I know it will create some problems, Mr. President."

"We can't very well deny something like this to the poor. Everybody will have to get access."

"I know."

"Can't have a quarter of the population ageing twice as fast as everybody else."

"Do we have a plan to deal with it?" She'd understood the societal impact from the beginning. And she read the answer in his clamped lips.

"I'm working on it." Life extension was okay in small increments. But doubling the game. And some of the science magazines were saying that was just a start. Huge advances lay just ahead. "First thing, I guess, Laurie, will be to revamp Social Security."

She nodded.

The country would be faced with bosses who never retire. Politicians who never leave office. The population would double within a short time. The highways were jammed now. They'd need twice as much energy. Twice as many houses. And that was only the beginning. He was going to have to sell family planning, which would put him even more at odds with the nation's conservatives. And he could probably expect complaints from the union of funeral directors and embalmers. "Just in time for the election," he said.

"It's okay, sir. People are going to be very happy about it."

"At first. Within a few years, we're going to be asking people to do their patriotic duty when they hit the century mark and jump off a pier. "

"They're also getting serious about genetic manipulation."

"I know. Want a kid with double your IQ? We can handle it."

"I don't think they're going to be able to do that," said Laurie. "At least not for a long time."

"Well, that's a blessing, anyhow."

"They'll be able to give you a pretty good politician, though." She smiled. "Kidding. But they *will* be able to tinker with people's looks. What's that old radio show about the town where everybody was above average?"

Then there were the two wars in Africa, with local dictators massacring protestors while the U.N. debated the issue and half the country was enraged that Cunningham had not yet committed American forces. Group marriage had shown up in—where else?—California, and was now a constitutional issue. Cunningham's father had told him at the start of his presidential campaign that he couldn't imagine why anybody would want the job. Now, of course, he was locked in.

His phone sounded. He leaned forward. Pushed the button. "Yes, Kim?"

"They're here, sir."

"Thanks. I'll just be a moment." He turned back to Laurie. "Anything else?"

"I understand Maurice Barteau and his team have successfully cloned a child."

"Okay." He'd known that was coming, too. He had no control over the French, of course, but there were already storm clouds in the United States. It was just what he needed: one more major fight. "Thanks, Laurie. I think I'll just hide under the desk for a while."

She smiled. "One more thing, sir."

"Not sure I need anything more at the moment."

She cleared her throat. Looked at him oddly. "There are several research groups working on producing artificial semen. But they're probably six or seven years away. So it's not likely to happen on your watch."

"Artificial semen?"

"Yes."

"What's the point of artificial semen?"

"You have better control of the product."

"You mean the baby."

"Yes. Sorry."

"It's okay. But you're telling me that males are going to become irrelevant."

"I didn't say that."

"You implied it."

"Mr. President." She delivered a wicked grin. "I don't think you have to worry about guys becoming completely irrelevant. That's never going to happen."

In the face of so much turmoil, the Moon story should have been a light diversion, a bit of stand-up comedy delivered by an egomaniacal billionaire with too much time on his hands. But people were jittery. Too much was happening. The voters had reached a point that nothing surprised them anymore. They were prepared to believe anything.

Ray Chambers was standing in the doorway.

Cunningham waved him in, and they both took seats at the exquisitely carved round table he'd inherited from the Obamas. "Got anything, Ray?" he asked.

"George, it looks as if the situation in Utopia is working out." That was Ray's ongoing joke, implying that everything was fine save for one or two minor issues. "I understand we're going to live a lot longer."

"If not," said Cunningham, "it will at least seem that way. Is there anything new on the Myshko business?"

"Maybe," said Ray. "I still think we should just get away from it."

"What have you got, Ray?"

"We've been calling around. Jasper and I have talked to everyone we can think of who was ever associated with the Nixon White House. One of them was a staffer for Bob Haldeman. Her name's Irene Akins."

"Okay. What did Irene have to say?"

"That NASA saw something on the Moon. Before Neil Armstrong. She said it was a 'big deal' at the time."

"When was that?"

"She's not sure of the date. And she told us she wasn't supposed to say anything. She never did, never heard anything more, and eventually decided it was all a joke of some kind."

"So what did NASA see?"

"She never knew. And she never heard about any secret flights."

"Where does she live, Ray?"

"Apparently, she's still in the area. She's over in Alexandria."

"Bring her into the White House."

"George, that's not a good idea."

"Just do it, Ray. Try to get her here this afternoon."

Irene Akins had joined the White House in March 1965, and had remained until 1978, when the Carter administration was in place. Her name until 1970 had been Hansen. She'd received positive evaluations from four presidents, which suggested she hadn't been simply another political appointee.

At a quarter after four that afternoon, Kim informed him that Ms. Akins had arrived and was waiting for him, as per his instructions, in the Vermeil Room. The Vermeil Room had a fireplace, and the walls were decorated with portraits of five of the twentieth century's first ladies. Its name derived from the collection of gilded silver on display. Despite the glitter, it possessed a casual ambience. It was the place Cunningham always used when he wanted to put a guest at ease.

Ray was waiting with her when he entered. They were drinking coffee, and she was sitting in front of the portrait of Jackie Kennedy.

Akins was in her seventies. A small woman, with white hair and glasses. A walker stood to one side of her chair. Her face was creased, but she managed a delighted smile. "It's hard to believe this is actually happening," she said.

Ray did the introduction and turned to leave, but Cunningham signaled him to stay. "Is this the first time you've been back?" he asked her.

"To the White House?" Her eyes gleamed. "Oh, no. I've been here any number of times, Mr. President. Brought my kids on the tours. And *their* kids. I have a lot of happy memories here." The smile faded. "And some unhappy ones."

"Yes," said the president, returning the smile. "I know exactly what you mean."

One of the interns came in with more coffee. She refilled the cups. Poured one for Cunningham, asked if anyone needed anything else, and hurried out.

"It must have been difficult at times," he said. "Especially during the scandal."

"That's true. But I wasn't close to any of that. I didn't see President Nixon much. Just in the hallways once in a while." She stopped. Shook her head. "I know what they said about him. And I guess he had some faults. But I liked him."

"Ms. Akins, you know about the rumors? That there were early landings, not reported, on the Moon?"

"It would be hard not to, Mr. President. It's all over the news. But I don't know any more than I told that man on the phone."

"We thought that might be the case. But it seemed worth the effort to try. I'm hoping coming back here might jar your memory." He tried to keep his tone light. "While you were here, did you ever hear *anything* about special lunar missions?"

She shook her head. "No, Mr. President. Not a word."

He tried the coffee, but didn't notice the taste. "Irene—Is it okay if I call you that?"

"Of course, Mr. President."

"You said something on the phone about NASA's having seen something on the Moon."

"That's correct."

"But you don't know what it was?"

"No, sir, I don't."

"What actually did you hear?"

She adjusted her glasses. Brushed back a curl. She would have been, Cunningham decided, an attractive young woman in her day. "Mr. President, I wish I could tell you. But I really don't remember any specifics. Mr. Haldeman might have said something. And maybe Mr. Ehrlichman. In fact, yes, definitely Mr. Ehrlichman. It's fifty years ago. I just don't recall—"

"Okay. You also said they'd made a big deal of it. What did you mean by that?"

"Well, I didn't mean that they made a big deal about the Moon. Just that when I asked about it once, I was told there was nothing to it. And the guy telling me was really upset. It was the only time I can remember someone there losing his temper with me."

"Who was it? Who lost his temper?"

"Gordon Brammer. He was a special assistant to the chief of staff."

"Brammer?" said the president.

"He's dead now, sir. Died a long time ago."

"Okay. Thanks, Irene."

The president started to get up. But Irene was lost in thought. "There was something else," she said. "About Jack Cohen." She frowned. "Funny. I haven't thought of him for years."

That brought Ray into the conversation. "Who's Jack Cohen?"

"I don't know, Mr. Vice President. He was just somebody who was in the office a lot at the time. The only reason I remember his name is—" She smiled. "I had a boyfriend with that name once. A long time ago."

"And this was when? In 1969?"

"Well, it was somewhere in the late sixties when Cohen was hanging around the White House. Then I didn't see him for a long time. Two or three years. He showed up one day seriously upset."

"When was that?"

"That's easy. It was right before the Watergate thing blew up."

Three years later. It couldn't be connected. "Was he a consultant of some sort?" Ray asked.

"I really don't know. He just showed up at the White House sometimes. I don't know who he was coming to see. As I said, the only thing that stuck with me was the name. I don't even remember what he looked like."

"So what was his connection with the Moon?"

"He came in that one day, looking really freaked-out. This was, as I say, right before Watergate. Now that I think of it, I remember they hustled him right into the Oval Office. Later, one of the bosses, Ralph Keating, I think it was, said something about it's being that goddam Moon thing again. Forgive the language.

"The comment seemed so off-the-wall that I never forgot it. I never heard an explanation. But for the next couple of days, everybody looked really upset."

————————

Ralph Keating had been dead almost forty years. The official records contained no mention of a Jack Cohen who'd been connected in any way with the Nixon White House. The president was talking about it with Ray when Kim called to remind him of a 5:00 P.M. meeting with representatives from the National

Economic Council. Cunningham hated economics and relied
heavily on his treasury secretary to see him through discussions
on fiscal policy. But the long struggle to right the economy was
continuing, and his presence was necessary to demonstrate he
was a serious player.

When it was finally over, and he got back to the Oval Office,
it was after seven. Ray was waiting for him. He looked pleased.

"I found Cohen, George."

"Good, Ray," he said. "Who is he?"

"He was a friend of Ehrlichman's. They were pretty close.
Both World War II veterans. They flew together with the Eighth
Army Air Force, I think it was. He was an anthropologist.
Taught at George Washington University."

"Okay."

"Irene was right. He used to spend a fair amount of time in
the White House."

"Is he still alive?"

"Died in 1987."

"We just don't catch a break, do we?"

"Doesn't seem like it. By the way, there's something else that
connects him with Ehrlichman."

"What's that?"

"They were both Eagle Scouts."

"George," said Ray, "we have a call from Milt."

"Okay. Let's hear what he has."

"Go ahead, Milt. The President's here."

"Mr. President, Bartlett says they did it. They went to the
surface."

Cunningham took a deep breath. It had to be a missed communication somewhere.

23

Milt Weinstein thought that Ray Chambers and the president had lost their minds. Despite his conversation with Amos Bartlett, it was obvious to him that the entire affair was a chase after hobgoblins. It was so ridiculous, he'd wanted to tell his wife about it, but he'd been sworn to secrecy, and he knew his ability to keep his mouth shut was the critical reason he'd become Chambers's most trusted aide.

He and Sheila had been the classic high-school pairing. There'd never been another woman in his life, and he more or less regretted that now. Not that he regretted Sheila. She was all he could have asked for. But there were times when he felt he'd missed something. And he suspected she felt the same way.

She lurked in the background as he leaned over the keyboard. "Milt, if we're going to watch *In Harm's Way*, we should get started before it gets any later."

"Okay, hon," he said. "Be with you in a minute."

She came up behind him. Pictures of people dressed in clothes from another era lined the screen. "What are you doing?" she asked.

"This is *The Cherry Tree*," he said.

"The what?"

"It's the yearbook from George Washington University. Nineteen seventy-five."

"That's a little before our time, isn't it?"

"A little."

"Why are we interested?"

He shrugged. "Idle curiosity, babe."

She caught the code word. More secret stuff from the White House. "Okay," she said. "When you're finished, I'll be in the den."

He was looking at pictures from the Anthropology Department. Professor John C. Cohen, the department chairman, was at the top of the page, dressed in a dark pin-striped suit with a black tie, gazing serenely back at him. He wore a neatly trimmed black beard, and his expression suggested a kind of amused superiority.

Weinstein switched over to the bio. Cohen had been born in Israel of American parents, had served during World War II with the Army Air Force. He'd piloted a B-17 in the raids over Germany. His navigator had been John Ehrlichman. After the war, the two men stayed in touch. Cohen taught for several years at the University of Pennsylvania before moving to George Washington. When Ehrlichman came to D.C. with the Nixon administration, the two reunited and remained close until Cohen's death in 1987.

He frowned. Ray thought there might be a connection between Cohen and the Moon dustup. But it was hard to see what it could be. Well, what the hell. He'd give it his best shot. He went back to *The Cherry Tree* and recorded the names of the other members of the Anthropology Department. In addition, two students had received their doctorates that year under Cohen's supervision. He wrote their names down, too. Then he went into the den, got cold beers for himself and Sheila, and sat down to watch *In Harm's Way*. He loved John Wayne movies. He'd seen this one five or six times. It never got old.

———————

In bed, and again in the morning, he read everything he could find on Cohen, including a few of his academic papers, which were tough going. The guy had never married. He'd won a couple of minor awards. Had once stepped in to prevent an attack by a gang of thugs on a young woman after hours on the campus. (That had cost him a few stitches.)

He looked up the names of outstanding anthropologists of the last half century. Then he googled the 1975 GWU faculty members and the two then-new Ph.D.s. Forty-four years had passed and, surprisingly, one of Cohen's contemporary professors was still at American University. One of the Ph.D.s had died. The other was at Georgetown. He was able to reach both, identifying himself as a research assistant for a Dr. Frank Markaisi, who was working on a book about anthropological contributions to our understanding of the development of civilization. He was, he told them, especially interested in the work of Jack Cohen. Both remembered Cohen and said yes, of course they'd be happy to cooperate. He set up appointments.

Inga Wilson had been the Ph.D. candidate. She was in her grandmother phase now. "Hard to believe it's been so long," she said. They were seated in her office, with a view of the campus. Traffic moved slowly along O Street. "Professor Cohen was a good guy. Worked hard. Knew what he was doing. His students loved him."

Weinstein asked a couple of his prepared questions, about Cohen's interest in the development of language, his work on the evolution of religion. Then, offhandedly, he got to the point: "Inga, did you know anything about his White House connections?"

Inga was a bulky woman. Tall, almost as big as Weinstein. And surprisingly muscular for her age. Her features retained almost nothing of the attractive twenty-four-year-old woman in the yearbook picture. "Oh, yes," she said, "he was a friend of John Ehrlichman's. Watching what happened to the administration was very hard on him."

"He was that close to Ehrlichman?"

"Yes. Apparently. He made no secret of the fact that he thought Nixon and his people had been maligned by an unfair press. It was odd."

"Why?"

"Well, I don't know. He wasn't a Republican. I mean, he was pretty much apolitical. He had friends in both parties."

"How did you find out about his friendship with Ehrlichman?"

"He arranged to have John come in a couple of times to talk to classes." She smiled wistfully. "I was shocked when the Watergate scandal erupted. I wouldn't have believed they could be capable of that. At least, that Ehrlichman could. He seemed like such a decent man."

"It must have been hard to take."

"It hit him hard, Milt. Professor Cohen, that is. It seemed, I don't know, personal, maybe. Yes. It was *personal*."

Weinstein salted the conversation with more prepared questions, not wanting to seem unduly interested in the White House connections. But when Inga began looking at her watch, he asked whether she had a class coming up.

"In ten minutes," she said.

"Okay, Inga. Let me get out of your way then." He got up. Collected his briefcase. "One final thing. Were his interests limited primarily to his field?"

"Oh, no," she said. "He was as much a Renaissance man as anybody I've ever known. He was interested in everything. Politics, the sciences, philosophy."

"Then he must have been caught up in the Moon landings?"

"I didn't know him then. But I'd be surprised if he wasn't."

The professor who'd remained at GWU was a stodgy, hypercritical guy with a bushy mustache and a tendency to squint. Weinstein took him to dinner that night at a small restaurant near the campus. His name was Leonard Butcher, and he needed no encouragement to go on and on about the old days. Mostly he dedicated himself to pointing out how inept everybody else on the planet was. Humans, he said, were too stupid to survive the rise of technology. "We almost killed ourselves with the nukes," he said. "We survived that. But it'll be something else. Just a matter of time." At which point he stopped and asked Weinstein to repeat his name before launching into another diatribe.

The problem was that he barely remembered Jack Cohen. He'd once offered to help Cohen with a paper he was working on, a treatise on the development of Greek mythology, but Cohen had persisted in finding his own way and, as a result, the paper had gone unnoticed in the journals. Of course. "He was older than I was, so he tended to think I couldn't be of any assistance."

He'd also offered Cohen advice on handling his classes. Don't alienate the students. Don't preach. It's all show business. It surprised Weinstein, because Butcher obviously knew what he was talking about. Whether he practiced it or not, of course, there was no way to know.

Butcher had noticed nothing unusual about Cohen. He'd had no social dealings with him. "Professor Cohen took it upon himself to encourage me. Told me I'd make a mark for myself." He sat back with a satisfied smile. He had indeed, it suggested, done that.

"Why did he leave the university?"

Butcher shrugged. "Don't know. I assume he had a better position elsewhere. Why else does one ever leave?" He flagged down a waitress and ordered some dessert.

Weinstein was about to explain that he had to go. That he had a plane to catch. But Butcher broke in: "What's your connection with Frank Markaisi, Milt? He's a pretty big name in the field."

Ah, yes. The admirable and fictitious Professor Markaisi. "I'm an independent contractor. He hires me once in a while for assignments like this one."

"Well, you tell him I'd be happy to cooperate if he wants any more information." He pulled out his wallet and held out a business card. Weinstein took it, paid the bill, and said good night.

———————

He reported back to Ray Chambers that evening.

"So you got nothing?"

"Other than Cohen was upset when the Nixon administration started coming apart."

"Why?"

"I guess because he and Ehrlichman were such good friends."

"And that's everything?"

"There are a few other people who were his colleagues at GWU. But they're out of town. You want me to stay with it?"

———————

Margaret Haeffner lived with her son and his wife in Downers Grove, outside Chicago. She'd enjoyed a long career in the academic world. Currently in her eighties, she remained active in community life, directing the local arm of Blind Justice, which, naturally enough, provided support for persons with visual problems. She was also a volunteer for the Animal Welfare

League. She was waiting on the front porch in a hammock when Weinstein arrived in his rented car. Her hair was snow-white, and she was rocking gently back and forth. Nevertheless, she didn't look like the high-energy volunteer in the Google accounts. It was a windy afternoon. Branches were swaying and, in an open field across the street, a group of twelve-year-olds were laughing and yelling their way through a volleyball game.

"It's a pleasure to meet you, Mr. Weinstein," she said, signaling him to sit down in a rocker. "I hope you'll forgive me if I don't get up."

"Of course, Dr. Haeffner."

"Did I understand you correctly? You flew out here from D.C.?"

"Yes, ma'am."

"Just to see me?"

"No. Actually, I'll be talking to a couple of people."

"Oh." She smiled at him. They both glanced across the street in response to a loud whoop from the volleyball game. "So what did you want to know?"

Weinstein asked a few of his usual questions, concentrating on Cohen's interest in the development of language in the Middle East and in early Greece. Her eyes lit up, and he realized it was a subject she seldom got to talk about anymore. He made notes, nodded occasionally as if Haeffner's answers confirmed what he'd learned elsewhere. And, finally, when there was a lull, he asked about Cohen himself. "The man," he said, "what kind of person was he?"

"Very gentle," she said. "His students really enjoyed his classes. They were always full. He was easy to get along with. Self-effacing."

"Is it true he was a friend of John Ehrlichman's?"

"Yes, that's correct. I met Ehrlichman once when he came to speak at the school."

"I understand Cohen was something of a Renaissance man."

"Oh, yes. He was interested in everything. Art, music, politics, you name it." There was a bad moment when the volleyball got knocked into the street. It bounced out in front of an oncoming car. One of the kids, a girl, charged after it and almost got hit by the vehicle. It jammed on its brakes, and the girl jumped aside at the last moment. The ball rolled onto the lawn next door. The driver yelled something at the kid, then waved her across the street. "Sometimes, I think," said Haeffner, "they're safer with their computers."

"What else can you tell me about him?"

"Well, outside the classroom, he was probably the most disorganized person I've ever known. He was always losing things."

"Like what?"

"The keys to his car. His stapler. He was always losing his stapler. He published a lot, and he'd bring in the stuff he was working on so he could work between classes, and he'd lose his notes or the book he was reviewing.

"A big part of his problem was that he never threw anything out. His desk and his files were full of stuff, which would have been okay if he'd learned to actually file things. But he just dropped everything in a convenient place. He'd be looking for information on Rahrich and wandering around in his office trying to find his data."

"Who's Rahrich?"

"A German anthropologist."

"Were you at George Washington when he left?"

"Yes. I was there. We were sorry to see him go. Well, *I* was, anyhow."

"What do you mean?"

She shrugged. "It's a long story. The important thing about him is that he had a marvelous imagination, he was dedicated to his research, and he was a pleasure to work with."

"Tell me the long story."

She frowned. "Okay. He had a drinking problem."

"I wasn't aware of that."

"Occasionally he missed classes. A couple of times he showed up at school events when he, um, should have stayed home. So the rumor was they invited him to leave."

"I'm sorry to hear it."

"So were we. We lost a good man. Eventually, it killed him."

"I wasn't aware of that either. What happened?"

"Not sure of the details, but you know he took his own life, right?"

"No. I had no idea."

"What I heard at the time was that he was diagnosed with

clinical depression. I'd liked the guy. I flew out to the funeral.
People who were there say it all started at GW. That the alcohol,
and the mood swings, and the rest of it hadn't been there before
he went to D.C. Hell, Milton, the guy flew a bomber during
World War II. If he was going to get depressed, you'd think it
would have shown up before the 1970s."

"Maybe it was the work environment?"

"Not a chance. George Washington was an excellent place
to work. Good administration. Good kids. I never should
have left."

Marvin Gray was the last person on his list. He owned a home
in an assisted-living community near Cincinnati. He'd been retired almost twenty years when Weinstein caught up with him.
Gray's wife let him in, invited him to sit in one of the armchairs,
and told him that Marvin would be right there.

"You must be Teri," he said.

"Yes."

"Are you a teacher, too?"

"I was. High-school math." She smiled. "It's been a long
time."

The place looked comfortable, with paneled walls, lush curtains, pictures of kids and other family members scattered
around. As well as a few certificates. And a trophy.

"We play in the local bridge league," Teri said.

He heard movement in one of the side rooms, and a giant,
overfed man with a shining scalp and an unkempt black beard
came out through the door, straightening the collar of a Xavier
University pullover. He was carrying a magazine, which he put
down on a side table. "Milton," he said, extending a wrestler's
hand, "good to meet you. What can I do for you?"

Weinstein did his usual opening lines, made a few general-
izations about Cohen's contributions to the field, and saw a
skeptical look begin to distort Gray's features. He added that of
course there had been differing interpretations of his work.
"That's why I'm here." He expressed his hope that his host could
shed some light "on things." Teri left the room. "How well did
you know him, Professor?" he asked.

"Call me Marvin. Please." Gray shrugged. "I knew him from

a distance. He was okay. Apparently, he was pretty good in the classroom. The only time I ever really worked with him, though, I mean closely, was in the doctoral program. He took everything seriously. Never neglected his responsibilities." He paused, trying to frame what he wanted to say. "I guess the reality is that I'm surprised anybody would be classifying him among the top anthropologists of the century. And I told you that on the phone, so I'm actually surprised you wanted to come all the way out here anyway.

"He did what was expected of him. But he wasn't—wasn't brilliant. You understand what I'm saying? He was probably at my level. Wrote some papers and won some nickel-and-dime awards. Nothing major, though. He won the Ditko Award, I think, and one or two others, but he never showed up on the big stuff. I doubt Triple-A even knew he existed."

"Triple-A?"

"The American Anthropological Association."

"Well," Weinstein said, "sometimes people aren't appreciated until after they're gone."

"That's probably true of all of us."

Teri came back with coffee and cinnamon buns. Then she explained she had work to do and left them to themselves. Weinstein tried one of the buns. "Good," he said.

"I'm not supposed to eat them."

Weinstein grinned. Tried to think of something funny to say, but he decided Gray's weight was a minefield. "I understand Cohen was a friend of John Ehrlichman."

"Yes. He visited the White House a couple of times. Apparently, he got to see Nixon."

"Did he ever do any work for the White House? That you knew of?"

"I don't think so. But he sure as hell was broken up when they all got kicked out of office."

"That's what I heard."

"Yeah."

"Is that when his drinking problem started?"

"Well, I don't really know *when* it started. I wasn't paying that much attention." Gray picked up the magazine, opened it, turned a few pages, and handed it to Weinstein. It contained an essay by Cohen. "The Origins of Monotheism."

Weinstein glanced at it, and they were suddenly back talking about ancient languages. He took notes and cited a couple of favorable references to Gray's work, commenting that he'd wanted to talk to him because he had such a favorable reputation among his peers. "Everybody credits you with good judgment," he said.

"That's nice to hear, Milton."

He let Gray enjoy the moment, then went back to Cohen. "I understand he was interested in the NASA spaceflights."

"I suppose. Pretty much everyone was back in those years." Gray refilled his cup and offered to pour more for his guest.

"Sure. Please." While he poured, Weinstein asked whether he'd known Cohen when the Moon landings were happening. "The early ones," he added. "In—what was it—'69?"

"No. I was still in the Navy then." He glanced sidewise at a picture of himself, a much younger version, minus the beard, in a lieutenant's uniform. "Didn't get to GWU until 1972."

Weinstein asked about his service. He'd been on a destroyer in the Pacific for two years. Then two years with subs, operating out of Norfolk. "I don't guess, having been a naval officer, you had much tolerance for heavy drinkers."

"There's some truth in that. But I don't think it had much to do with my time in service." He sucked on his lips. "My father was a drunk."

"Oh."

He looked at his watch. "Anything else, Milton?"

Weinstein tapped his notebook with his pen. "Not really. Cohen's history seems to suggest he didn't have a drinking problem until he got to GWU."

"I have no idea." He pushed back in his seat. "I can tell you one really odd story about him, though."

"What's that?"

"We threw a farewell party one time for one of the people in the department. Lisa Rhyne. She was getting married, as best I can recall, and moving to Boston. I think she'd gotten a position at Boston College."

"And—?"

"Anyhow, on the subject of Cohen's reaction to Nixon and the scandal: We were all sitting around at the party. At one of the local restaurants. And Cohen had had too much to drink. At one point I heard him tell one of the women that *he'd* been one of the Watergate burglars."

"Say that again?"

Gray laughed. "That's right."

Weinstein wiped his mouth with the back of his hand. "It was a joke, Marvin."

"He wasn't smiling."

24

Jerry entered Bucky Blackstone's office, nodded to Gloria Marcos, and approached Bucky's desk.

"My, don't we look sharp today?" said Bucky with a smile. "New suit?"

Jerry nodded. "And tie."

"I hope you remembered to use the company credit card."

"I did. But I feel a little guilty about it."

"Why?" asked Bucky. "You billed the government for everything for years."

"Yeah," said Jerry. "But that was the government. You're a private citizen."

Bucky smiled. "The only difference is that I'm not seventeen trillion dollars in debt . . . yet."

"There is that," agreed Jerry. "Anyway, I stopped by to see if there's anything you want me to say or avoid saying. I won't ask every time, but this is my first press conference."

"Just answer their questions," replied Bucky. "Well, as many of them as you *can* answer. I have no secrets from you or them or anyone else. But if you've been told anything in confidence, about the crater or anything else, keep it in confidence. We're doing *them* a favor. I don't need publicity as much as they need something to write about."

Jerry grinned. "Now I *know* I'm not in the government."

Bucky chuckled. "Three billion dollars insulates you from a lot of criticism." He paused and continued smiling. "And the wild part of it is that I owe it all to one forty-two-inch bosom."

"Yeah, I heard about how you got your start—or how *Suave* did. Whatever happened to Miss 42-D?"

"I married her."

Suddenly Jerry felt very uneasy. "I didn't mean . . . that is, I . . ."

"It's okay," said Bucky easily. "It lasted fifteen months." An amused smile crossed his face. "I think the final nail in the coffin was when I ran Miss 44-Double-D on the cover."

"You've led an interesting life, Bucky," said Jerry.

"I've had my moments." Bucky checked his watch. "Yours is coming up fast. Want me to introduce you, or would you feel better if I was nowhere around?"

"You're the boss."

"Then I think I'll watch from here. If I introduce you, I don't think I could stop from saying that you quit NASA as a matter of conscience, and that's all they'd ask about for the next hour."

"Thanks, Bucky."

"Oh, you're not getting off the hook. I'd kind of like you to defend the guy who's paying your salary, and that's who they've come here to savage."

Jerry frowned. "Why? You're always a good news story."

"They've been told to, of course."

"By . . . ?"

"By the administration, of course."

"Come on, Bucky," said Jerry. "This is America. They can't tell people what to write."

"No," agreed Bucky. "But they can make access to the president damned difficult for anyone who doesn't play ball."

"You really think they would?"

"This wouldn't be the first White House, or the tenth, or the twentieth, to do just that," said Bucky with conviction. "All of which is academic. They're going to try to get you to admit that I'm an idiot or a madman." Suddenly he grinned. "Might be interesting to see their reaction if you agree with them."

"You really don't care, do you?" asked Jerry.

"If I cared what the press thought, I'd sit in splendid isolation and clip coupons. Now you'd better get down there."

Jerry turned and walked to the elevator, took it down to the studio, and was surprised to find the place totally empty. He was still looking around when Ed Camden walked in.

"Hi, Jerry." He extended a hand. "I just want you to know there are no hard feelings."

"Thanks, Ed," said Jerry. "I appreciate that." He looked around. "Where *is* everybody?"

"They get unruly if they have to wait, so we keep 'em outside until the spokesman is ready for them." Another man came in, and Camden nodded to him. "Okay, Harry—unlock the cages."

Harry radioed down to the main floor, and a moment later some forty members of the press, most of whom Jerry knew on a first-name basis, thundered into the studio.

"Please be seated," said Camden. "As soon as you're all comfortable and those with cameras have set them up, we can proceed. Everything said will be saved to video and audio and made available on our Web page tomorrow afternoon, which gives you a twenty-four-hour head start." He paused, waiting for them to take their seats and set up their cameras. "Allow me to present the newest member of Team Blackstone, Jerry Culpepper, who will be our spokesman on all matters concerning our pending Moon shot." He stepped aside. "Jerry, it's all yours."

Jerry came forward. "Good morning. I'm a little new on the job, so I may not have answers to every one of your questions, but I promise that anything I can't answer today, or at any conference in the future, I will answer within twenty-four hours. That said, I have a few brief announcements. First, it has been determined that the ship will take off and land at a private field owned by Mr. Blackstone. Maps will be available to you on your way out. Second, the launch will take place exactly four weeks from this morning."

"*That* soon?" asked *The Washington Post*.

Jerry smiled. "The technology has been available since the late 1960s, though of course we've improved upon it."

"How does it feel to be working for a nutcase?" asked *The Los Angeles Times*.

"I don't know," answered Jerry. "I've never had the experience."

"What does Blackstone expect to find up there?" demanded CNN.

"The Moon," answered Jerry, breaking the growing tension and eliciting some chuckles.

"Come on, Jerry," persisted CNN. "Isn't this whole business about bringing you in here just a stunt to get publicity for your boss's Moon shot?"

"He's the second-most-recognizable man in the country after President Cunningham," said Jerry, "and I don't think you can find a dozen citizens who don't know he's flying to the Moon, so why does he need to create false publicity?"

"Maybe because he'd be lost without it," said *The Chicago Sun-Times*.

Jerry forced a smile to his lips. "I think he'd say that *you'd* be lost without it."

He looked around the room and called on Fox News.

"Let me word this properly, so you don't give us another run-around answer," said the woman from Fox. "Once he reaches the Moon, what does he expect to find other than Moon rocks?"

"He doesn't know," said Jerry. "No one knows. That's why he's going."

"How many people will be on the ship?"

"Four or five. I don't believe it's been finalized yet."

"And he's definitely going to be on the landing craft?"

Jerry nodded. "He'll be on the ship. I don't know whether he intends to go down to the surface." Then: "I wish I was going, too." He surprised himself with the comment. Would he really have been willing to ride the rocket for a chance to go to the Moon?

"Is he planning more flights?" asked *The Miami Herald*. "Commercial ones?"

"I don't follow you," said Jerry, frowning.

"Well, there's no resort hotel on the Moon, but would it be terribly far-fetched to suggest he could get a few million per passenger to go up there, *especially* if he hints that there's something strange going on, something our government has been hiding."

"That's ridiculous," said Jerry. "For one thing, he'd have to charge close to one hundred million a ticket to break even. For another, he's simply not going to do it."

"Will he be transmitting pictures back to Earth, or does he plan to hang on to them and sell them to the highest bidder?" asked *The New York Times*.

"Wouldn't you consider that immoral?" asked Jerry. "Given the importance of what might be in those photos."

"Absolutely," replied *The Times*.

"But of course you'd bid for them anyway," said Jerry irritably. "Fortunately, Mr. Blackstone has no need of any more money. All photos and videos will be instantly posted on our Web page and can be picked up by any news publications and networks at no cost."

"It just doesn't make any sense," said CBS.

"Could you elucidate, please?"

"I've followed Bucky Blackstone's career for twenty years now, and he doesn't do *anything* that hasn't got a profit motive. The guy practically defines everything I hate about capitalism, and suddenly he's a public-minded citizen who's spending a goodly part of his fortune getting us back into space and perhaps clearing up a half-century-old mystery, just out of the goodness of his heart. I don't buy it."

"I'm sorry you feel that way," said Jerry, searching for a quip or a put-down and not finding one.

"You know what I think?" continued CBS. "I think he's doing this to embarrass President Cunningham, to somehow imply there's some kind of nefarious conspiracy concerning the Moon and the space program."

"Why would he do that?" asked Jerry.

"To enhance his chances when he runs for the presidency."

"I can categorically state that Morgan Blackstone has absolutely no interest in running for any political office," said Jerry, hoping that he was telling the truth.

"Then it doesn't make any sense!" snapped CBS.

"Of course it does," said Jerry. "Wouldn't *you* go to the Moon if you could? And if you were convinced something had happened up there, something the government has been hiding for half a century, wouldn't that be all the more reason to go? You're a journalist. That bespeaks some sense of curiosity. Why do you feel that Mr. Blackstone can't possess one as well?"

"Because everything he's claimed is contradictory to everything we know!" snapped CBS. "The government wasn't *hiding* Moon landings; it was *bragging* about them."

"Bragging, certainly," agreed Jerry. "And perhaps misleading as well."

"If Blackstone doesn't find anything up there that Neil Armstrong and Buzz Aldrin didn't find, will he buy another half hour of TV time and admit he was wrong?"

"I assume he'll do just that," said Jerry, trying to keep the uncertainty out of his voice. He glanced to his right, where Ed Camden was listening to his cell phone. Suddenly, Camden grinned, turned to Jerry, and raised a thumb in the air. "In fact," continued Jerry, "Mr. Blackstone has just confirmed it. If he can't find evidence of a governmental cover-up, he will go on TV and say so."

"If there *were* secret missions, they'd have taken place at the beginning of Nixon's first term," said *The Chicago Tribune*. "Now, we all know Nixon was secretive, and he had more than a few chinks in his moral code—but can you suggest any possible reason why he'd have secret missions just days and weeks after he took the oath of office? I mean, he had a government to set up, and a war in Vietnam to try to end. What the hell could divert his attention to the Moon and make him decide to keep whatever it was secret?"

"I don't know," admitted Jerry. "That's one of the things Mr. Blackstone hopes to find out."

"I have a question," said *The Christian Science Monitor*.

"Go ahead."

"Let's say that Mr. Blackstone is right, and something happened up there." He was almost shouted down by his own colleagues, but he waited patiently until the noise had died off and he could be heard again. "If Mr. Blackstone is right, clearly President Nixon felt there was a need to keep whatever it was secret." He looked around, waiting to see if he would be shouted and jeered down again, but his colleagues were listening, trying to see where he was going with this. "And if that is so, doesn't it imply that this was something that Presidents Ford, Carter, Reagan, Bush 41, Clinton, Bush 43, Obama, and Cunningham have all agreed was important to keep secret? And if every president was in agreement, then perhaps there's a pretty good reason *not* to try to expose what they are hiding."

How the hell do I answer that? thought Jerry. *It's the same question that's been bothering me when I go to sleep each night.*

"You know what a secretive son of a gun Nixon was," said NBC. "He'd probably never have told Agnew or Ford, so maybe it's not a conspiracy of presidents, but a character flaw of *one* president."

The journalists began arguing among themselves: Would Nixon tell anyone? Why would any president down the line feel compelled to keep Nixon's secret?

Jerry relaxed with a sigh of relief. The relief passed when he realized that it was going to be like this every day, that in fact they were probably taking it easy on him because it was his opening day on the job.

The conference went on another twenty minutes. Finally, as it began winding down, one of them asked if Jerry would be on a future Moon rocket.

Jerry shook his head. "To be honest, I don't even like airplanes. It's *terra firma* for me."

"Some spokesman for a space shot!" snorted a reporter.

"You didn't seem to mind my being a spokesman for NASA," said Jerry coldly. "I don't remember your minding my setting up some private interviews for you when no one else would go out of their way to do so."

The assembled journalists seemed to realize they'd pushed Jerry enough for one day, especially his first day, and they asked a few innocuous questions. Finally, Jerry said that he would take one final question and call it a day.

"Has the Moon rocket got a name yet?" asked *Newsweek*. "Maybe something like the *Enterprise*?"

"Yes, it has a name," said Jerry.

"Well, what is it?"

Jerry turned until he was facing the bulk of the cameras. "The *Sidney Myshko*."

And, twenty-eight floors above him, Bucky Blackstone smiled in satisfaction. "We hired a good one," he said to Gloria Marcos. "I guess we'll keep him."

25

"After all I've done for him," said the president. He watched with a growing sense of betrayal as Jerry Culpepper defended Morgan Blackstone and implied government deceit.

"Wouldn't you go to the Moon if you could?" Jerry demanded of the reporters. "And if you were convinced something had happened up there, something the government has been hiding for half a century, wouldn't that be all the more reason to go?"

Cunningham shook his head. "You can't trust anybody, Ray. If not for me, he'd still be impersonating a lawyer in TV commercials for an obscure Ohio firm, trying to persuade viewers that he was on their side, and that 'the team' at Carmichael and Henry would happily take on the big corporations for those who'd acquired a lung disease"—he couldn't remember which—"because of irresponsible construction work."

Cunningham had taken him on board in Ohio during a successful run at the governor's mansion and provided an opportunity for him to rise to national prominence during the 2016 presidential campaign. "Then I handed him the job at NASA. And this is how he pays me back."

Jerry had left the press area by then and was back inside the terminal at Flat Plains. It was just like Blackstone, naming the new vehicle for Sidney Myshko. It was a nice touch but pure theater.

Ray grunted his agreement. "I can understand why Jerry lost patience with NASA," he said, "but I'd never have believed he'd cross over and join that son of a bitch."

The president shut the screen down and sighed at the ingratitude of the human race. "People have short memories," he said. "Well, I shouldn't be surprised, I guess."

"He's not the guy you thought he was, George."

"No, he isn't." Cunningham dropped the remote onto a coffee table. Not worth being annoyed over. "Ray, are you sure you've checked with everybody about this? There must still be a few people around who would know if anything that big had happened."

"You mean the landings?"

"Of course."

"George, it's been a half century. The high-level people who were at the White House and at NASA simply aren't with us anymore. We've asked everyone we could find. Nobody knows anything. But almost all of them were staff assistants or secretaries. There's no reason to believe they'd have known about anything major that was going down."

"What about the intelligence agencies?"

"You know how they are. Everything's Top Secret Bimbo or whatever. They don't talk to one another, and I suspect they don't talk much to the directors. I don't think they trust anybody who didn't come up through their organization. The information doesn't get passed around. It's just put into a classified vault somewhere, everybody retires or dies, and pretty soon it just gets lost, and nobody knows it ever existed. I think that's where we are now."

"Ray—"

"Yes, sir?"

"You think it happened?"

"No."

"Why not?"

"Because there's no explanation that makes sense, George. We were in a race with the Soviets to see who could get there first. To the Moon. If we'd touched down before Apollo XI, can you imagine any kind of reason President Nixon would have had for keeping it quiet?"

Cunningham raised his arm in surrender.

"That's exactly right, George. It's ridiculous. The whole thing's ridiculous. And that's why—"

Cunningham heard the jingle of Ray's cell phone. The chief of staff took it from his pocket, lifted the lid, and glanced at it. "Milt," he said.

The president felt an odd reluctance. "Let's hear what he has to say."

He tied the phone into the speaker. "Hi, Milt," he said. "President Cunningham's with me. What have you got?"

"Ray, I can't find anything about Cohen's being involved in political activities. But he seems to have been hit pretty hard by Watergate. It looks as if he might have started drinking heavily at about that time. And something else: He took his own life."

"I didn't know that," said Ray. "Did he leave a note?"

"No. But I checked into it. People who knew him said he was despondent. Said he was *always* gloomy."

"How'd he die?"

"An overdose of sleeping pills. I checked out the police reports. They were satisfied there was no foul play. But what's interesting is that the description of his personality is so different from what I heard about him at George Washington. At least the early years there. He had a reputation for being easygoing. Casual. Everybody liked him. Life of the party. Then, suddenly, in the midseventies, it all changed."

"Maybe," said Cunningham, "his name was on the list of the Watergate escort service. He might have been worried about being exposed."

"Nobody I could find," said Weinstein, "thought he'd ever have screwed around with whores, Mr. President. Excuse my language."

"It's all right."

"Apparently, he had all the women he wanted. Didn't have to pay for them."

"Okay. It was just a thought."

"Anything else, Milt?" asked Ray.

"Yes. Speaking of the Watergate—"

"Yes?"

"It probably doesn't mean a thing. But I told you about the drinking problem. Apparently, he was overheard one night saying how he'd been one of the Watergate burglars."

"Well," said Ray, "I don't think I'd give that too much credence."

"I talked with some of the people who knew him after he retired. They said it was a kind of running joke. When he'd had too much to drink. And you're probably right, I doubt it means anything. Still—"

"Thanks, Milt." Ray broke the connection and stared at the president. "George, we have nothing."

Cunningham got up, looked at the time, looked at his chief of staff. "What do you think?" he said.

"I didn't hear anything that convinced me Cohen was anything but a drunk."

The president had a busy afternoon coming up. "I have to get moving, Ray."

"Okay, sir." Ray started for the door.

"Wait one."

"Yes, George?"

"Are any of the Watergate burglars still alive?"

Ray checked his BlackBerry. "One. Eugenio Martinez. Lives in Georgia."

"Okay. Let's have Milt talk to him. We need to get control of this situation."

"It's a long time in the past."

"I'm talking about handling Blackstone."

"Oh." Ray's face scrunched up. "If we want to get the FAA involved, it's getting late."

"No, we can't do anything like that. If we start throwing up obstacles, Blackstone will scream, and the media will be all over us. Why don't we try something different?"

"What do you suggest?"

"Talking to the happy billionaire."

"We've tried that."

"Let's try again."

"Okay. I guess we can't lose anything. You want me to take care of it?"

"Yes." He smiled. "You might try appealing to his patriotism."

Cunningham's afternoon was booked. There would be the weekly CIA briefing, and meetings with the Director of National Security, with members of the National Education Committee, with a planning group for the nation's highways, and with the Lone Eagles, who were advocates for wildlife protection. In addition, he'd be giving awards to several Afghan veterans. The big conference, though, would be tomorrow morning, when the World Committee for Safe Population Levels would be in town.

Global population was just beginning to get serious attention. Many nations had chosen to follow China's lead, limiting families to one child. The Chinese had instituted the policy in 1978.

One of the several consequences of this unhappy approach was that families tended to favor male children. They were aborting girls by the millions. Consequently, the world was facing a growing crisis: Males in large numbers around the planet, especially in poorer nations, were coming of age in a world that didn't have enough women. The conference would be an effort to—at the very least—sound an alarm. Millions of angry males without women. And probably without jobs. If that wasn't a formula for disaster, the president had never heard one.

After dinner, he and Lyra would be hosting an evening with Manny Garfield, the Pulitzer Prize–winning poet. He didn't particularly care to spend two hours listening to poetry he didn't even understand, but it was part of his responsibility as president. No way he could disappear from the proceedings. Next week, Maury Petain would be in to play his violin. Ray had warned the president against trying to pass himself off as a lover of the arts. Political enemies would accuse him of being an elitist. Cunningham had explained patiently: It wasn't a matter of passing himself off as a lover of the arts. It was a matter of serving as a responsible host.

And anyhow, he had a taste for Rachmaninoff. *What's wrong with that? I'm president of the United States. I'll listen to whatever music I want.*

26

"Blood pressure: 127 over 68 . . . pulse, normal . . . heart, missing."

Bucky sighed as he sat on the edge of his desk. "Most people get a doctor. Me, I get a comedian."

"Just repeating what I read in the papers," said the medic, with a smile.

"I thought it was my brain that was supposed to be missing."

The medic shook his head. "The White House is claiming you could have hired more than two hundred thousand men and women for the money you're spending on the Moon shot. That means you've cost two hundred thousand Americans and an unspecified number of illegal immigrants their jobs."

"They *really* said that?" asked Bucky, amused.

"Don't you listen to the news?"

"Not when I can help it."

"Well, you're a heartless, mendacious villain who's costing us jobs," said the medic.

"Can't argue with that, not when Cunningham's keeping a bunch of caddies and golf courses in business." Bucky began putting on his shirt. "So, am I fit to go?"

"You're fit to fly to Montana. You're even fit to breathe in that thin mountain air. I don't know if you're fit to fly to the Moon."

"I thought I passed all the tests back in your clinic last week," said Bucky, frowning.

"And you were fit to go to the Moon last week. As for today, I can't state it with certainty unless I run another barrage of tests."

"Fortunately, you don't have to. I'm the guy who makes the final decision." Suddenly he grinned. "Admit it. Would you rather it was my hand on the button?"

"I thought we got rid of all our nukes."

"Except for the ten or twelve thousand we held back for self-defense."

"You're really feeling your oats this week," said the medic. "I think maybe the best thing we can do with you is stick you on the Moon." He paused. "Do you really think Sidney Myshko landed there?"

"Absolutely."

"Why?"

"Ask me when I get back."

"If he *didn't* land, are you coming back?"

Bucky smiled. "I've been wrong before, I'll be wrong again. I'm not ashamed of it." His face hardened. "But I'm not wrong this time."

"I know you and the guy you hired away, Jerry what's-his-name, think the two of you know something the rest of us don't know. But answer me one question: If Myshko was the first man on the Moon, why the hell would he keep quiet about it?"

"That's what I plan to find out."

The medic shook his head. "You're not following me. I mean, if it was *me*, if *I* was the first man on the Moon, nothing in the world could have kept me from bragging about it."

"And nothing in the world *did* keep him from bragging about it," agreed Bucky. The medic looked at him questioningly. "Something on the *Moon* kept him from bragging about it."

"What?" insisted the medic. "Little green men?"

Bucky shook his head. "He'd have brought one back to show us. Or maybe they'd have kept him to show *their* people."

"Then what could keep him quiet?"

"Like I said, ask me in a month."

"You're a very frustrating man to speak with," said the medic grumpily. "I'll bet your blood pressure hasn't changed in an hour. Mine's probably gone up forty points just during this conversation."

Bucky laughed and put an arm around the medic's shoulders. "Then we'd better get you out of here while you're still alive," he said, walking him to the door. "And thanks for coming."

"Thanks for paying for the clinic's new wing."

"Well, you never know. I might get my face slapped by a beautiful redhead right in front of the clinic and have to come in to have you staunch the bleeding."

The medic turned to face him. "You are a loud, vulgar, arrogant, brilliant, manipulative, conscienceless man, and I wish I didn't like you so much, so that I could hate you just a little."

"Don't give up hope, Doc. Your day may come."

The medic left the office, and Bucky sat down at his desk.

"He's right, you know," said Gloria, swiveling her chair to face him.

"Are you going to start in on me, too?" asked Bucky.

"No," she said. "I happen to admire those qualities. It means the corporation won't go under anytime soon."

"I *knew* there was a reason I hired you, besides the way you look when you walk away."

"I haven't looked like that in twenty-five years," said Gloria. "Well, twenty, anyway."

"I have an active memory."

"But thankfully you don't have active hands, at least not around me." She smiled. "There was a time when I wondered why not, what was wrong with me."

He chuckled. "There was nothing wrong with you. You were just too damned valuable to me and this organization to take a chance of offending you to the point where you quit."

She smiled. "That's actually perfectly in keeping with my appraisal of you. You make selfishness a virtue."

"Funny. It doesn't sound like one when you describe it like that." He pulled out a cigar and lit it. "Don't tell the doctor."

"My lips are sealed," replied Gloria. "Don't blow it this way, or I'll have to seal my nostrils, too, and then how will I breathe?"

"Clint knows he has to be at the airfield at 3:30, right?" asked Bucky suddenly.

"That's the third time you've asked," said Gloria. "Yes, he

knows he's flying you and Jerry to Montana. The rest of your crew has been there since yesterday."

"Just anxious to be off," said Bucky.

"Why is Jerry going along? He's not part of the Moon shot, so he'll just have to come back once you take off."

"Clint's got to bring the jet back anyway, and we'll have some local cameramen, as well as the national news, covering the takeoff, and I want Jerry there standing next to the ship for everyone to see, just like I want him waiting for us when we land in Nebraska after coming back from the Moon." He paused. "You made a face."

"I wrinkled my nose."

"Same thing. What did I do wrong?"

"It's *liftoff*, not *takeoff*."

"Does anyone really care?" asked Bucky.

"The press will correct you."

He smiled. "Let 'em. The public holds them in less esteem than used-car dealers and congressmen. If they criticize me, it'll make me warmer and more human."

"Do you really think so?" she asked dubiously.

"Probably not. But it sounds good."

Suddenly, her computer came to life, and, a moment later, Ray Chambers's face appeared on her screen.

"Good afternoon," he said. "I believe you know who I am. I'd like to speak to Morgan Blackstone, please."

Gloria turned questioningly toward Bucky, who nodded and faced his screen.

"Good afternoon, Morgan," said Chambers's image.

"It's Bucky. What can I do for you?"

"I'm calling on behalf of the president."

"I'm astounded," said Bucky.

"Please, Mr. Blackstone," said Chambers uncomfortably. "You're making this very awkward."

"That's what happens when you agree to do the president's dirty work for him. Now, what is it that he can't speak to me about himself?"

Gloria looked surprised that he'd speak to Chambers in such a manner, but the more ill at ease Chambers looked, the more Bucky was certain that he'd hit the nail on the head.

"The president wishes you a successful trip and hopes you and your crew come back safe and sound," said Chambers.

"That's very gracious of him," said Bucky. "Please thank him for me." He resisted an impish urge to pretend he thought the conversation was over and break the connection.

"Uh . . . there's something more."

"Surprises never end," replied Bucky dryly.

"If you should find something up there . . . something, well, unexpected or unusual . . . I'm not saying you will . . ."—Chambers couldn't hide his fidgeting—"but *if* you do, we would appreciate it if you would say nothing in public about it until we can talk."

"What do *you* think I'm going to find?"

"Nothing," answered Chambers. "Absolutely nothing."

"Then isn't this call a waste of your time?" said Bucky.

"Why are you being like this, Mr. Blackstone?" demanded Chambers in frustration. "I'm not the enemy."

"You're also not the president," said Bucky. "And I don't admire cowardice in the leader of the Free World."

"He's an incredibly busy man," said Chambers. "Do you really think he's afraid to speak to you?"

"I think he's afraid of being recorded, and of course he would be, just as you are being," answered Bucky. "Now, have you got anything else to say to me?"

Chambers stared nervously at him. "Do we have a deal?"

Bucky laughed aloud. "Go tell your boss that you might have had a deal if he'd had the guts to call me himself."

"Is that what it'll take?" said Chambers. "I can see if he's able to tear himself away from his meeting . . ."

"You mean his putting green," said Bucky. "And no, you and he blew it. No second chances."

"I hope you'll reconsider."

"I'm sure you do."

"We'll be in touch again before you lift off."

"No, you won't," said Bucky. "Now go back to your boss and tell him he'd better hope I come back empty-handed."

Bucky broke the connection and turned to Gloria. "How'd I do?"

"Even if Cunningham himself had called, you wouldn't have agreed," she replied.

"Yeah, but then I'd have needed a different justification for turning him down." Bucky grinned. "This made it easier."

She stared at him for a long moment. "Why did you never go into politics?"

"Too much compromise," he answered. "I like doing things my own way."

"So I've noticed."

Bucky stood up. "Damn it, I'm tired of sitting around waiting! Tell Jerry we're leaving now, and have Clint meet me at the plane."

"He's filed a flight plan, Bucky," said Gloria. "I don't know if he can move it up at this late date."

"Tell him to try. I'll be there in twenty minutes. Have someone bring my bags down to the limo and have a driver ready."

He and Jerry had to kill two hours in the airport bar, but finally the private jet took off, and, four hours later, they had landed on Tabletop Mountain.

"Well, this is *it*!" said Bucky enthusiastically, as a car drove them to the hangar where the *Sidney Myshko* awaited them.

"The first step, anyway," agreed Jerry. Then: "I wonder what you're really going to find there."

Bucky's cell phone beeped, and he looked to see that the White House was calling though he couldn't tell if the call came from Cunningham himself or one of his underlings. He grinned and put it back in his pocket.

"You're not the only one," he said.

27

"Relax," said Cunningham. "He knows he's holding all the aces right now. And he doesn't have anything to lose. If he goes up there and finds nothing, which is what will probably happen, he's going to look like an ass. So he's enjoying it while he can."

"That's not the point, George. The guy's not even civil. And my personal feelings aside, I can't say I care much for the disrespect he's showing the White House."

Cunningham had not been present during the conversation. He'd expected that Blackstone would be difficult, and he didn't want Ray trying to handle him while his boss was looking over his shoulder. "I'm tempted," he said, "to have the IRS start looking seriously at his tax returns."

"I doubt they'd find anything, George."

"I know. But they could keep his accountants and lawyers pretty busy."

"Don't do it. It's beneath you."

The president nodded. "Moreover, it'll leak, and we'll get caught."

Ray chuckled. "My thoughts exactly." Then he grew serious. "You're not going to call him, are you?"

"I was thinking about it."

"Let it go, George."

"Look, the guy seriously irritates me. And I don't like his mistreating my people."

"George, he was just being what he is, a horse's ass. He *wants* you to call him. That's what that whole thing was about. To get you to call so he can tell you to—"

"I know. I understand that—"

"You call him, you're just giving him what he wants. Don't do it."

"You're right, and I know that. But—"

"You're the one needs to relax."

"Okay."

"Good. Now, I think you have some people who're waiting to meet you."

A Boy Scout troop that was visiting the White House. "Okay," he said. "Tell them I'll be right there."

| 28 |

Bucky was strapped securely into his seat, as were Ben Gaines, Marcia Neimark, and Phil Bassinger.

"All right," said Gaines, the pilot. "One minute to go." A pause. "Fifty seconds." Another pause. "Forty."

"I have a request," said Bucky suddenly.

"Let's take off first," said Gaines.

"This can't wait."

Gaines stared at him. "You're the boss."

"I've wanted to be on one of these things since I was a kid," said Bucky rapidly, aware of the clock ticking down. "Could you, just to make me happy, could you say 'Blast off!' rather than something like 'We have ignition'?"

Gaines smiled. "For the man who pays my bills? Sure. I've always wanted to say it anyway." He checked the clock. "Twelve, eleven, ten, nine, eight . . ."

Bucky looked out the window, trying to pick Jerry's and Gloria's faces out from the crowd a quarter mile away.

"Blast off!" bellowed Gaines.

The ship trembled. Began to move. Bucky felt as if he had the weight of a small piano on his chest.

"Goddamn it, that was fun!" laughed Gaines.

"Someone should start reporting back," said Bassinger. "We're on television all over the world."

"Marcia's our most presentable crew member," said Bucky. He turned to her. "Go ahead."

"I'd rather not," she replied. "I have three advanced degrees and ten years at M.I.T., and all they ever ask me is what I think about being alone with three men on the Moon." She snorted contemptuously. "I grew up with five brothers."

Bucky smiled. "They know what their audience is interested in. Okay, I'll talk to them." He stared at all the buttons, switches, and dials in front of him. "Which do I flick or press?"

Bassinger leaned over and pointed to one.

"Thanks."

"And remember," said Bassinger. "You're on camera, so don't pick your nose."

"You're fired," said Bucky. "Pack up your gear and get out of here."

Everyone laughed, and then Bucky opened communications. "Hello, receding world. This is Bucky Blackstone."

"The takeoff seems to have gone very smoothly," said a pool reporter. "Everything okay aboard ship?"

"It's beautiful up here!" Bucky felt magnificent. "I'm living every kid's dream! When I get back, we're going to have to start selling orbital flights. Everyone deserves the right to see what I'm seeing."

"But can everyone afford it?"

"Sooner than you think," said Bucky. "After all, I'm not the government, so I'm not hiring three thousand people I don't need and paying ten thousand dollars for toilet seats."

"You've just passed out of the atmosphere," said the reporter. "Does anything look or feel different?"

"Everything's fine." Bucky looked out the window at the Earth and then ahead, hoping to see the Moon. But the sky was clear.

"Are you all right, Mr. Blackstone?" said the reporter anxiously.

"Sure. Why shouldn't I be?"

"You went silent for about twenty seconds."

Bucky resisted the urge to say he'd been busy pinching

Marcia Neimark, if only because he didn't want her glaring at him for the duration of the trip. "Just looking back at where I came from."

"Are you ready to tell us what you expect to find on the Moon?"

"Why guess?" answered Bucky. "We'll know in a few days."

Another reporter chimed in: "Has anyone got any messages for friends or family?"

Bucky looked at his crew. All three shook their heads. "Nope. They're too busy keeping us afloat, or whatever the word is. I'm going to hang up now."

"You mean 'sign off,'" corrected the reporter.

"On your ship, you sign off," said Bucky with a smile. "On mine, we hang up." And he broke the connection.

"It's glorious!" Neimark's voice shook with emotion. She, too, was looking down at the home world.

"Look how bright the stars are," said Bassinger. "You don't realize how much the atmosphere hides until you see them like this."

"Okay," said Gaines. "We've got some mandatory tests to run now. Bucky, sit back and relax. Enjoy yourself."

"I could help," offered Bucky.

"I don't want to be too blunt about it," said Gaines, "but as far as the ship is concerned, you don't know your ass from your elbow. We've been training on it for several weeks. You don't even know how to unlock the hatch."

"Don't sugarcoat it," said Bucky, amused. "You can talk straight with me."

They all laughed. "Just relax," Gaines said. "You're the guy who's paying for all this, and the guy who knows what we're looking for, or at least where we're going to be looking. Let us underlings get you there."

"Fair enough," said Bucky.

The other three spent the next half hour checking gauges and readings, going through routine operations that seemed wildly exotic to Bucky, and, finally, everyone reported that all systems were functioning perfectly.

"Boss," said Bassinger, "or maybe I should say, Commander Boss."

"What is it?" said Bucky.

"I hate to interrupt your reverie, but you have the stupidest smile on your face."

"Just thinking."

"About what?"

"The truth?" replied Bucky. "I was thinking that if we don't find a damned thing on the far side, even if there's nothing there but craters and rocks and dust, it'll have been worth every penny."

"Even telling the people you were wrong?" asked Bassinger with a smile.

"There's nothing wrong with being wrong. As long as you don't persist at it. Besides, a week later, it'll be old news . . . and just getting back to the Moon should sure as hell encourage other entrepreneurs to do the same. Why *not* put a colony here? Why do cruise ships have to only cruise the oceans? People have been talking about the Man in the Moon for centuries. It's time to put a *lot* of men there."

"Are you saying you don't think there's anything up there?" asked Gaines.

"I'm betting a billion dollars that there is," said Bucky seriously. "But if there isn't, I'll still have gotten my money's worth."

He'd been awake most of the night, too excited to sleep, but after another hour, he dozed off. He awoke six hours later when Neimark prodded him.

"Are we there?" he asked, confused.

She shook her head. "Not even close yet. But if you'll look at the navigation display, you'll see something interesting."

"Better not be a bird," said Bucky, blinking his eyes and forcing himself to become alert. He looked over at the screen and saw a bright red orb topped by what looked for all the world like whipped cream.

"Mars?" he asked.

She nodded. "Indeed it is . . ."

"It's gorgeous," he said, staring at it.

"We've got the main scope trained on it."

He squinted and peered. "I can't make out the canals."

She smiled. "We're forty million miles away. But the colors are startling once you get the scope clear of the atmosphere."

He nodded. "Just as well I can't see the canals. I'd hate to think John Carter and Tars Tarkas weren't riding their thoats around, or that Eric John Stark wasn't off to some new adventure there."

"Well, I'll be damned!" said Bassinger. "The hardheaded businessman is a secret romantic!"

Bucky searched his mind for a caustic reply, but stopped when he realized that Bassinger was right, that he *was* a romantic at heart. Why else would he declare the trip a success a handful of hours into it when the Moon was still three days away?

After that first nap, Bucky slept intermittently during the next two days. He kept staring out the window, thrilled by the sights, reveling in the sensation of weightlessness. Finally, he fell into a deep sleep and woke up almost eight hours later, feeling totally refreshed and unbothered by the confined space in which he found himself.

As the *Sidney Myshko* neared the Moon, he still felt like a kid in a candy shop. He homed in on Mars again and spent a few hours studying and admiring it. Then he started spotting the bigger asteroids.

"We'll move into orbit in about twenty minutes," announced Gaines. "I've calculated it—well, the computer has calculated it—and this should put us right over the Cassegrain Crater when we're on the dark side." He paused. "Have you got *any* idea what we're looking for?"

"Not since the last time you asked."

"Could it be metal?" persisted Gaines. "We don't have to see the exact shape of whatever it is. If we have a hint of what it's composed of, we can run a spectroscopic analysis of the crater square mile by square mile and see if there's, I don't know, some titanium or steel there, something from Myshko's ship."

"We'll know soon enough," said Bucky.

"Not quite as soon as you think," said Neimark. "Before we land, we'll take a number of photos and videos with zoom lenses and transmit them back to Earth. Cassegrain Crater is maybe forty miles across. You could land in it and not see a brontosaur at the other end, let alone something the shape and nature of which you can't even guess at."

"I know." Bucky sighed. "It's just that I've been living with this for months, and I want to know what the hell made Myshko land, and especially what made him keep his mouth shut about it."

"*If* he landed."

"He landed," replied Bucky with conviction. "And I want to know why damned near every photo of the Cassegrain Crater during the sixties was doctored."

"Just because some unnamed source told that to Jerry Culpepper doesn't make it so," said Neimark.

"I trust him."

"Oh, I believe he was told that, and that he was honest with you. I just don't know if the source was honest with him."

"I'm supposed to be the doubter," said Bucky.

"Nonsense," she replied. "Scientists are taught to doubt everything."

"Rubbish," said Bucky. "They hang on to disproven and discarded theories like religious zealots."

"Only some of them," she said defensively.

"And only some religious people are zealots." He turned to Gaines. "Are we in orbit yet?"

"About ninety seconds."

"How long before we're over Cassegrain?"

Gaines shrugged. "I'd guess an hour and a quarter, but the computer can tell you to the second, always assuming we don't come face-to-face with too much space garbage."

"Garbage?"

"Meteor swarms, things like that."

"What about *our* garbage?" asked Bucky, remembering his half-eaten lunch.

"We hang on to it till we're back on Earth," replied Gaines. "If we jettisoned it, it would just take up orbit, around the Moon if we got rid of it here, around the Sun if we dumped it in transit, and as it picked up speed over the years, it could collide with some ship a century from now and wipe it out." He checked his instruments. "We're in orbit now."

Seventy minutes later, Cassegrain Crater came into view.

"Doesn't look all that special, does it?" said Bucky, somehow disappointed that he could not see something wrong, something askew, from that distance.

"We'll know soon enough," said Bassinger. "Got all the cameras working."

"And then we send the stills and videos back to Flat Plains?" asked Bucky. Flat Plains was his operational headquarters.

"Yes. The government—hell, a lot of governments, and probably some advanced labs—will try to grab them, too, but we've got them pretty well coded. By the time anyone breaks the codes and actually sees the pictures, we should be safely back on Earth."

"Yeah," added Gaines. "If there's really something down there, who knows? They don't have to be as big as Tars Tarkas to cause a panic. Even *little* green men will do that."

"Besides, the boss isn't into sharing," said Bassinger with a grin. "Until he makes his millions first."

"If we find anything but rocks there," promised Bucky, "you're going to see just how *into* sharing your boss is."

As they were speaking, pictures from the Cassegrain Crater were already showing up on the navigational screen. The regolith was flat and gray, featureless save for occasional smaller craters.

Then—

Bucky stared. "Son of a bitch!"

29

After the Watergate scandal, Eugenio Martinez had established a quiet career selling real estate and had eventually retired to a small town in southern Georgia. "It's not something I'm especially proud of," he told Weinstein, referring to his part in the burglary. "I don't much like to talk about it, but I guess I've gotten used to it. What do you want to know that hasn't already been reported in every newspaper in the country?"

He sounded annoyed. Weinstein sympathized. It would have been difficult to refuse to do something if the president of the United States asked for your help. "Mr. Martinez," he said, "first let me assure you that whatever you have to say to me will be held in the strictest confidence."

Martinez frowned. "They're not opening this thing up again, are they?"

"No, no. Nothing like that. It's just that we've heard a couple of rumors, and we'd like to get a handle on what really happened."

"Oh." He smiled. "I'm relieved to hear it. What are the rumors?"

They were sitting in Martinez's living room, facing each other across a sleek, square cocktail table. The walls were paneled with mahogany, and curtained windows looked out over a lake. A light rain was falling. "Did you know Jack Cohen?"

"Cohen?" He frowned. "I don't think so."

"The name doesn't ring a bell?"

"No."

Weinstein produced a photo of Cohen, taken during his days at GWU. "You don't recognize him?"

"Nope. Never saw him before."

"Well, it's been a long time." He placed the photo on a coffee table where Martinez could see it. "Let's try another question."

"Go ahead, Mr. Weinstein."

"Was there a sixth burglar?"

Martinez laughed. "A sixth burglar? Where on Earth did you hear that?"

"Was there?"

"No. Of course not."

"Mr. Martinez, if you're hiding anything, I can assure you there's no need. I can get you a letter from the president himself releasing you from any responsibility for withholding classified information."

"No need to bother. I'm not hiding anything. There was no sixth burglar." He paused. Looked out as a bolt of lightning flickered against the window. "You wearing a wire?"

"No."

"You mind if I have a look?"

"Go ahead."

Weinstein stood while Martinez did an inspection. "Okay," he said finally, "I guess you're clear."

"So what were you going to tell me that required a search?"

They both sat back down. Martinez studied him for several moments, making up his mind. Then: "Just for the record, I've never thought of myself as a burglar. We were the president's operatives."

"The fall guys," Weinstein said.

"No. *He* took the fall. The big one." He looked ready to call a halt.

"Was there anybody else at all involved with the break-in other than the people who came to public attention?"

"Why are you asking?"

"Look, Mr. Martinez, I'm not supposed to mention this, but it looks as if I have to: The president wants to know. Don't ask me why. There's reason to believe someone else was with you inside the Watergate."

Martinez took a deep breath. Picked up the photo and switched on the lamp behind his chair. Held the picture so the light fell on it. "It could be him."

"It could be who?"

"There's no way I can be sure. It's too many years ago, and I only saw him that one night."

"When you did the break-in?"

"Yes."

"So there *was* a sixth burglar. Is that what you're saying?"

"No. That's not exactly what happened. If this is the same guy"—he stared at the photo—"he's the reason we were there in the first place."

"Wait a minute, Mr. Martinez—"

"Call me *Eugenio* if you like."

"Why were you at the Watergate? You were sent in to bug the place, weren't you?"

Martinez took a deep breath. "Maybe I should get that release."

"I can arrange it."

He got up, walked over to the window, and stared out. The skies were gray. "I guess, after all these years, it won't matter."

"So what were you actually after at the Democratic National Headquarters?"

He was still holding the picture. "This guy's briefcase."

Weinstein stared at him. "Why?"

"There was a notebook in it. I don't know what it was about. They never told us."

"So how would you know it when you found it?"

"We had a description of the briefcase and the notebook. And the guy it belonged to was with us."

"The sixth burglar."

"Not really. We kept him outside. In the passageway."

"Do you know how this notebook came to be at the Democratic National Headquarters?"

"I've no idea."

"You say you had a description?"

"Yes. We knew what it looked like."

"Did you know what was in the notebook?"

"They told us it had a couple of pages in a foreign language."

"Which language?"

He shrugged. "I don't remember. I really don't. Sorry." Thunder rumbled in the distance. "We need the rain," Martinez said.

"Did you find the notebook?"

"No. The police got there too quickly."

"Why didn't they get the guy in the hall?"

"We'd expected to come up with it pretty quick. Actually, I think what happened was that when we didn't see it, we told him to take off. They told us to take no chances with him."

"Then what? You went back and looked some more?"

"We kept looking until we heard the cops were coming up. There was no way to get clear, so we switched to our secondary mission."

"Bugging the place."

"Yes."

"But you did that strictly—"

"To provide a cover story. As we were instructed to do."

"And you, and none of the other guys, ever gave the real reason for the break-in."

He shook his head. No.

Weinstein felt a sense of admiration. "You took all that heat."

"We were told to keep it quiet." He leaned forward, his eyes locked on Weinstein. "If this story ever comes out, I'll deny everything."

30

"I still don't know why I had to stay up here," grumbled Bucky. "After all, every Moon landing we ever had, two went down and just one stayed behind to pilot the ship. That's *you*."

Ben Gaines smiled. "Two went down. That's *them*."

"But you don't need me up here," continued Bucky. "I don't know the first damned thing about running the ship."

"You don't know the first damned thing about landing on the Moon and taking off from it."

Then came the final argument. "It's *my* expedition, damn it! I'm paying for it, so I should go to the surface if I want to."

Gaines chuckled. "There's the hatch. Feel free to leave."

"Maybe I should fire you for insubordination," said Bucky with a smile.

"Be my guest." Gaines returned the smile. "I'm tired of driving this thing anyway. You take over."

"Oh, hell, I guess you can stick around." Bucky laughed, and Gaines joined in. He looked at the numerous dials and readouts on the control panel. "Have they landed yet, do you think?"

"Soon," said Gaines. "Maybe another twelve or fifteen minutes."

"Good. I'm getting tired sitting here doing nothing."

"Well, we couldn't send them until we'd picked their landing spot."

"It seems so inexact," complained Bucky.

Gaines frowned. "They'll land within a few hundred yards of the descent modules."

"I don't mean the landing is inexact," said Bucky. "I mean we still don't know why Myshko and Walker went down there in the first place. Do you see anything else?"

"Not a thing, Bucky."

Bucky paused, staring out through the port. "Where the hell is the lander?"

"You can't see it right now," Gaines said. "We've got the wrong angle."

"Damn! I should be down there!"

"You're starting to sound like a broken record," said Gaines.

"They stopped making records before you were born," growled Bucky. "What do you know about it?"

"Hey, I still collect vinyl," said Gaines. "Not every record was transferred to CD or MP3 files. Especially old comedy records, topical ones."

"You really collect them?"

Gaines nodded. "Mort Sahl, the original Second City, Stiller and Meara—almost none of them made it to CD. Same goes for a bunch of old Broadway shows that weren't big enough hits to get revived. There's really quite a large market for that stuff."

"You live and learn," said Bucky. Suddenly, he grinned. "Here I thought I was putting you down, and you made a fool of me. I *like* that in an employee."

"So I get to orbit the Moon once or twice more before you fire me?"

"Maybe even three times." Bucky turned his attention back to the panel. "Have they landed yet?"

"Bucky, take a nap. I'll wake you when they're there."

"Shut up."

"Okay, then—go to the bathroom. By the time you get back in all your gear, they'll have landed."

"I liked you a lot better five minutes ago," said Bucky.

"Ditto," said Gaines.

"You wouldn't talk to me like that if we were back on Earth."

"Sure I would."

"You're a good man, Ben. I chose the right pilot."

"You didn't choose me at all," said Gaines.

"Maybe not, but I chose not to fire you a couple of minutes ago. That counts for something."

They kidded and teased each other for another ten minutes, and finally they got the message they'd been waiting for.

"We've touched down in Cassegrain Crater." It was Marcia Neimark's voice.

"Everything okay?" asked Gaines.

"No problems of any kind."

"You want to talk to the boss?"

"Sure—but it makes more sense for him to wait until we have something to tell him."

"Can you see the modules?" asked Bucky.

"Yeah. We're a good distance away, but we can see them."

"Is there anything else?"

"Negative."

"Can you see any reason why they might have gone down there?"

"Not yet, Bucky. But give us a chance to look around a little. We'll be climbing down out of the lander in a couple of minutes."

"Make sure you set up a video camera on one of the landing legs so we can see what's happening."

"Of course, Boss," she said.

"Just making sure."

"Bucky, that's the fifth time you've made sure today."

"Sorry." He was grateful that she couldn't see his guilty smile.

"Okay." Bassinger took over as the voice on the speaker. "Are we all set for a Moon walk?"

"Help me secure my helmet, and I am," said Neimark.

A moment later, they'd set up the video camera, and Bucky was able to watch them descend to the surface.

"It's a shame the people back home can't see this," said Gaines. "But we can't transmit this until we're on the near side of the Moon."

"Just as well," said Bucky. "I'd like to know precisely what we've got before we start announcing stuff. We don't want to get ahead of ourselves."

"Well, I don't think there'd be any problem showing them walking on the surface," said Gaines, "as long as we don't show what they're walking *toward*."

"We're not entirely *sure* what they're walking toward," said Bucky, staring at the screen.

"Oh, come on, Boss. What do you expect to find? A Russian base?"

"Save the sarcasm, Ben."

"Okay. Sure. But we can show them walking, right?" persisted Gaines.

"Ask me when we're in a position to transmit it."

Bucky leaned forward, concentrating on the two images on the screen. Like Neil Armstrong and Buzz Aldrin half a century before, they seemed suddenly unfettered by gravity, even by the weight of their assignment. They jumped up again and again, then trotted in huge strides that would have lifted them over high hurdles had there been any.

"My God, I feel reborn!" exclaimed Neimark.

"We haven't had any gravity in the ship for a couple of days, but it's not the same thing!" Bassinger could barely contain himself. "I never want to go back!"

"Use up all your oxygen, and you *won't* go back," said Bucky. "What can you see?"

"Bunch of rubble," said Bassinger.

"That's *all*?"

"Bucky," said Neimark, "try to be patient. Give us a chance to get to the modules."

"How close are you?"

"Maybe a quarter mile."

"I thought you were supposed to land closer."

"Oh, come on, Bucky—we've traveled 250,000 miles and landed maybe five hundred yards from our target. You can't get much more accurate than that."

"Okay, okay." Bucky looked at Gaines. "I knew I should have gone down with them." Then he leaned over the mike again. "Just get on with it. I want to know what's over there."

"There's probably nothing, Bucky. Except the descent stages."

"Just take a look, okay? There had to be a reason for the initial landings."

"We're moving as fast as we can, Bucky," said Bassinger. "Just give us a few minutes, and we'll settle it once and for all."

"Go ahead," said Bucky. He turned to Gaines. "I hate waiting."

Gaines grinned. "I would never have guessed."

"Can you blame me? I've bet my fortune and my reputation that there's *something* out there, something that the government doesn't want us to know about. Now we're so close . . . *Damn!* I just *hate* this hanging around!"

"Stop yelling, Bucky," said Neimark. "You're hurting my ears."

"Sorry," said Bucky with a singular lack of sincerity.

"Tell you what," she continued. "Count to two hundred, and by the time you get there, I'll be able to tell you what we've found. If anything."

Bucky immediately began counting.

"To yourself," added Neimark.

He nodded to no one in particular, and began counting again, moving his lips soundlessly. Finally, he reached two hundred and looked at the screen, hoping to see something—but the video camera remained stationary, and the two figures were much smaller.

"Okay, Bucky," said Neimark. "I am about fifty feet from one of the descent stages."

"Okay. Good. What else can you see?"

"The other descent stage."

Bucky was running out of patience. "Damn it. What else?"

"Nothing, Boss."

"Nothing at all?"

"Negative. We've got two descent stages from lunar landers. Phil is taking photos of them from every possible angle. They're about two hundred yards apart. And they're in beautiful condition."

"Why did they land there, Marcia?"

"Please!" said Neimark. "No yelling! It's hard on my ears."

"Sorry," he said, and this time he meant it.

"Okay, taking a bunch of close-ups right now," announced Bassinger.

"All right," said Bucky, suddenly resigned. He'd been right. He'd scored a victory over the president of the United States. But suddenly it was tasteless. "All right, Marcia. Make sure you get close-ups of any ID."

"Will do."

"Well," said Bucky. "At least I was right about the landings."

"Looks like you were," agreed Gaines. "Marcia, we're about to lose contact with you. Catch you on the next orbit."

"We'll have all the photos we need by then," she replied.

Then they were out of range, and Bucky turned his attention to Earth. "How soon before I can speak to Jerry?"

"Not long," said Gaines. "I'll let you know."

Bucky studied the video of Neimark and Bassinger jumping around as if they'd been suddenly freed from confinement, then watched it again, and a third time, rapt with fascination and a sense of resentment that he wasn't down there with them.

"Okay," said Gaines. "Jerry's trying to get through."

"Put him on."

"Video or audio?"

"Both."

"Hey, Bucky!" said Jerry excitedly. "Do you read me?"

"Loud and clear," replied Bucky. "We'll be sending you a video transmission in a couple of minutes." But Gaines was nodding at him, signaling that it had already been sent. "Hold on, Jerry. Ben tells me you should have it."

"Wait one, Bucky." He could hear voices in the background. "They're telling me we got it. Give us five minutes, and we'll know what you sent. I assume it's not just Moon rocks?"

"A fair assumption."

"If you don't mind my saying it, you look awfully smug," said Jerry.

"You'll figure out why soon enough."

Jerry spoke to someone off camera. "We'll have it decrypted and enhanced in about three more minutes."

"So how are the Giants doing?" asked Bucky.

"I assume you're not about to give me a hint of what's on the video," said Jerry. "Okay, New York or San Francisco?"

Bucky smiled. "I had in mind the giants of industry."

Jerry chuckled. "Well, the only one who counts is enjoying himself immensely by teasing his spokesman." He paused. "I wish I was on that ship right now."

"The ship? Or the Moon?"

"Either one. Ever since I was a kid . . ."

"Yeah, the whole world wanted to be Neil Armstrong."

Suddenly staid, unflappable Jerry Culpepper let out a war

whoop as he looked at something off to his left. "I'll be damned! You found the descent stages!"

"You knew we would," said Bucky happily. "It was the rest of the world that doubted it. Marcia Neimark and Phil Bassinger are next to them right now, taking close-ups. We'll transmit them on the next orbit."

"So far everything's been encrypted, including this conversation," said Jerry. "Let me know when you want everything released to the world."

"Now's as good a time as any," said Bucky. "Can you patch me through and send the visual and audio of what I say next out to everyone—media, computers, everyone?"

"Not a problem," said Jerry. "Wait for my signal." It took two minutes, then Jerry said, "You're on in ten seconds."

Bucky counted to fifteen on the assumption that the adrenaline he was pumping was making him count too fast, and then stared into the camera that was transmitting his image back to Earth.

"This is Morgan Blackstone," he announced, "and I am speaking to you in orbit around the Moon. I know a lot of you have decided that I'm some kind of publicity-seeking nutcase, and that, of course, Neil Armstrong was the first man to land on the Moon." He paused for effect, then a huge smile spread across his face. "Well, I'm here to tell you that the nutcase has found proof that Sidney Myshko was the first man on the Moon, predating Neil Armstrong by more than half a year, and that Blackstone Enterprises back on Earth is about to transmit videos taken from orbit that will confirm what I said. When we finish our next orbit of the Moon, which gives the administration time to tell you that these are phony, we'll be transmitting still photos taken from just a few feet away from the abandoned descent stages. I've told our team on the Moon to make sure that any identifying codes are clearly visible." Another huge grin. "This is the publicity-seeking nutcase signing off."

"Somebody in Washington's not going to love you," said Gaines with a smile as he broke the connection.

"I know."

"Then why antagonize them so?"

"To keep them busy while we accomplish our mission," answered Bucky.

Gaines frowned. "But we've already proven you were right, that Myshko and Walker really did land on the Moon . . . so what are you talking about?"

"You're brighter than that, Ben," said Bucky. "Use your brain."

Gaines was silent for a moment. "I still don't understand," he said. "We *found* the descent stage. We *know* Sidney Myshko landed. We've accomplished our mission."

"We've *justified* our mission, Ben," said Bucky. "We haven't *accomplished* a damned thing. With a little luck, that comes next."

Gaines shook his head. "I don't follow you."

"Think about it. We know Myshko and Walker landed on the Moon. There's no longer any question about it. We know that the government has kept it secret for half a century. There's no longer any question about *that*, either. Now we come to the real purpose of this mission, and with luck we can accomplish it before Marcia and Phil run out of air."

Gaines stared at him. "Boss, it was a stunt. A couple of guys who wanted to walk on the Moon. What else could it be?"

31

The population conference got off to a bad start. Everybody seemed to recognize the severity of the problem, and that in it-self constituted good news. The major powers understood the threat to peace presented by uncontrolled growth. But there were vast gaps in the proposals on how to deal with the issue. Cunningham's advisors were pushing for a combination of approaches, mostly aimed at spurring economic development. History demonstrated that population growth tended to level off with prosperity, and it did so without widespread abortions. But it meant making liberal education available, putting money and sound management into the economies and managing them rationally. No one had ever succeeded in dealing with the prob-lem on a large scale. In fact, nation-building had at best a weak track record. Even with the unified efforts of the major powers, Cunningham couldn't see its happening. And they were by no means unified. Some wanted, for example, simply to ignore the more desperate areas of the planet and concentrate on keep-ing weapons out of the hands of militants. That was another blind alley.

Later that afternoon, he'd be meeting with his conference representatives. He sighed. They needed a plan. He had nothing. And neither did they.

He was still agonizing when Ray showed up, looking rattled. Kim offered to get him a cup of coffee, but he passed on it. She closed the door, leaving them alone. "Bad news, looks like, George," he said. "The networks are announcing that Blackstone is going to be transmitting pictures from the Moon. He must have found something."

Cunningham was tired. After the frustrations of the conference, Bucky's Moon flight just didn't seem that serious anymore. "What did he find?" he asked.

"They're not saying. They just made the announcement a few minutes ago. They're going to start broadcasting in"—he checked his watch—"six minutes."

"The son of a bitch lives to play to his audience, doesn't he?"

"I'd say so, yes."

He picked up the remote and turned on the TV. CBS was running a crawl stating that there was breaking news from the Moon, while three or four of their newspeople chattered about what it could be. NBC had its news anchor going on about the *Myshko* and speculating on whether there had really been other landings. ABC was interviewing physicist Michael Shara in his office at the American Museum of Natural History in New York. Fox had a team on the ground at Flat Plains.

ABC's Mark Cassidy broke off his conversation with Shara and looked up into the camera. "ABC has breaking news. Taking you now to the Moon—"

Shara's bright functional office was replaced by Blackstone, seated inside the cramped spacecraft, wearing his customary self-satisfied grin. Except it had an additional dimension this time. He looked like a guy holding four aces. "This is Morgan Blackstone," he said.

When it was over, Cunningham simply stared at the screen, which had reverted to Shara's office, where the physicist and his interviewer were talking about what they'd seen. But Cunningham turned off the sound. "I don't believe it," he said. Laurie Banner had shown up at the office door, and the president turned toward her. "There's no way this could be a mistake, is there?"

She made no attempt to answer but only stood shaking her head. "Mr. President," she said finally, "you really don't know any more about this, right?"

"No, I do not," Cunningham said. "Of course I don't." He was still not certain why he'd allowed himself to get so caught up in this. He'd thought at first that he simply didn't like Blackstone, didn't want to see him come off as the guy who knew the truth when nobody else did, not even himself. He felt ridiculous. A president left out of the loop. He could, of course, pretend that he *had* known and had simply been keeping a closely held government secret all this time. He'd have to work, though, to come up with an explanation for that.

Nobody trusted the government anymore. And no matter how this played out, confidence in *him* was going to be undercut. Did he want to be an idiot or a schemer?

"You're assuming the descent modules are really there," Laurie said.

"What are you talking about, Laurie?"

"I assume all we're going to have is pictures being sent back by Blackstone."

Ray chimed in: "Right. It could all be a prank. Designed to elicit a statement from you. Then he yells, 'April fool.'"

"Sure," Cunningham said. "What are the odds of that?"

Ray looked over at Laurie. The science advisor kept her eyes straight ahead.

She had made her reputation in quantum mechanics. Cunningham had never been able to grasp precisely what that was about. Something to do with a single particle going through two holes at the same time. He'd brought her into the White House because she had a talent for explaining complicated ideas in simple English. But she'd never been able to explain the two holes. At least not to the president's satisfaction. She'd also been a Nobel Prize finalist two years before. "What do *you* think?" he asked her. "Any chance of a hoax?"

She turned those dark brown eyes on him. "Physically, sure. But—" She hesitated. "I believe I'll leave the politics to you, sir."

"That son of a bitch Nixon," he said. "Why in hell would he do something like this? It makes no sense." He turned back to the screen. The first pictures were showing up. An astronaut stood out on the lunar surface, posing beside something that looked very much like a descent module. It was the same color as the dark gray moonscape.

"They did what they could to hide them," said Laurie. "They'd have been hard to spot from orbit."

The camera swung away, and the vehicle passed out of the picture. They were looking across open ground. Then the second descent module appeared. There was no commentary by Blackstone, or by the astronauts. The pictures were sufficient.

The president grumbled something. Then: "All right, Ray. I don't think we have to worry about keeping a lid on this any longer. Somebody out there must know something. Find him. Or her. Check with anyone you can locate from the Carter administration. I don't care what it takes. Find out what this is about."

The voters were going to demand some answers, and he'd better damned well come up with some.

ABC was running his comment from the Beverly Hills fundraiser: "While you're at it, you might check with Mr. Blackstone to see if he knows what's going on in the Bermuda Triangle."

His press secretary called. "Mr. President," she said, "they're all over us. I think it would be a good idea if you talked to the reporters."

They'd already run the daily press conference that morning. "I know, Helen."

"Do we have any answers, sir?"

"We're a little short there."

Helen had started as a journalist herself. She'd had a remarkable career with CBS over a six-year period and had come on board at Cunningham's request when he took office. He was aware that Jerry Culpepper had hoped to land the appointment, but he was too laid-back. Helen was dynamite. "They're already piling in here," she said. "I won't be able to stall them long. What do you want me to tell them, sir?"

Ray was shaking his head. Stay out of the pressroom until we know what's going on. But he couldn't send Helen in there to make it up as she went along. He couldn't imagine anything that would scream *gutless* more loudly at the reporters. "I'll be down in fifteen minutes," he said.

The descent modules were, of course, the only story in town. Where was a good congressional scandal when you needed one? Everybody was speculating about the hidden missions. Chris Matthews wondered about aliens. Mike Huckabee suggested there'd been some sort of freelancing by astronauts anxious to be first on the Moon, and that afterward their silence had been bought. Chevy Johnson, on SyFy, claimed that if you looked closely at the pictures collected by Blackstone, you could see footprints in the regolith that were definitely not human. One of the televangelists proposed that the astronauts had gone down to the surface because they'd felt the presence of God. But they'd kept it quiet because they hadn't wanted to be laughed at in this society which, he said with sad emphasis, had abandoned the Lord.

Everybody was asking where Cunningham had been through all this. Diane Brookover of *The New York Times*, interviewed on *NBC Special Report*, shook her head. "How could we possibly have done something like this and the president didn't know about it?" The fact that it had happened fifty years ago seemed to go unnoticed.

Ray had people calling everyone who might have an answer. Responses never varied. Two CIA chiefs knew nothing. Two former heads of NASA denied it was even possible. One former NSA director pointed out that "we don't spy on ourselves."

People were still calling back when Cunningham got up and headed for the pressroom. "Don't do it, George," said Ray. "Best right now is simply to issue a statement. Tell them we're investigating and will have more as the situation develops."

Cunningham nodded, signaling he'd heard. "Let me know," he said quietly, "if we get anything."

This wasn't the first time, of course, he'd faced the media under trying circumstances. A strike against Somali pirates during his second week in office had gone wrong and eleven hostages, including five kids, had died. That one still kept him awake at night. Always would. And there'd been the FEMA lack of response when the quake hit South Carolina. Cunningham had put one of his staunchest supporters in charge, a guy he'd always thought competent but who, he realized belatedly, thought public relations was the solution to everything. And then there'd been the Ethiopian massacre.

The pressroom wasn't big enough to accommodate everyone. Reporters were standing in back, and the crowd had spilled out into the passageway. The place was buzzing when he came through the side door, but it immediately fell silent. He took his place at the lectern. "Good afternoon, ladies and gentlemen," he said. "I guess we all recognize that this story keeps getting stranger.

"At the moment, I don't have any kind of definitive statement to make, other than to admit that the images Morgan Blackstone sent back from the far side of the Moon are as puzzling to me as they are to everyone else. I don't know what this is about, or how those vehicles could have gotten there, or why the United States might have landed twice on the Moon in 1969 and kept it secret. We're conducting a thorough investigation in an effort to get some answers. And we *will*, I promise you, find out precisely what happened. In the meantime, we'll have to wait to see what Mr. Blackstone has." He looked into the TV camera at the back of the room, then down at Stan Huffman from the A.P., and smiled. "Keep in mind that I don't have any answers. Having said that, the floor is open to questions." Huffman's hand went up. "Stan?"

"We understand you have no answers, Mr. President, but you must have a theory. Assuming these flights actually happened, and it looks now as if Blackstone was right, and they really did, do you have any conceivable explanation, any idea at all, *why* NASA might have done this?"

"None whatever, Stan. I haven't heard one from anybody else, either. It's why I'm still not entirely sure I'm buying in."

"Follow-up please, Mr. President. You're suggesting Blackstone faked the pictures."

"I'm not suggesting anything, Stan. I just don't know. I feel as if I'm living in an episode of *The Twilight Zone*."

Bill Kelly of *The Washington Post* was next. "Are there any plans to have NASA send something to the Moon to confirm that the pictures we're getting are valid? That those descent modules are really there?"

"Not at the moment, Bill. I think we can be confident that Bucky Blackstone would not perpetrate a fraud on the American people. No, I'm pretty sure that he found precisely what he says he did." Rick Hagerty, of Fox News, caught his eye. "Rick?"

"Is there any kind of hidden vault that presidents have to keep secret information, and make it available to one another? Stuff that nobody else can see?"

"Is that a serious question?"

"Until these last few days, Mr. President, it wouldn't have been. But yes, is there anything like that? And if there were, would you be willing to tell us that it exists?"

"The answers to your questions are no and yes." He looked around the room with the boyish grin that had been so effective with voters. "There's no hidden vault. Look, everybody, I'm sorry to admit this, but I doubt many residents of the White House have been that good at looking beyond their own terms in office." He hadn't yet finished the sentence before he knew it was the wrong thing to say. But there was no breaking off, or calling it back. At least, they'd have to concede his honesty, and for a politician, that was a major benefit. Maybe worth the headline he'd just created.

Meredith Aaronson, from NBC, got the next question. "Mr. President, why has NASA sat back while a private company went to the Moon? Is our space program dead?"

"No, Merry," Cunningham said. "Maybe we don't need a government-funded system anymore. We built this country on individual initiative, and I think we owe Mr. Blackstone a debt of gratitude for the action he's taken." *And a good kick in the rear as a bonus.*

The press conference, he thought, went extraordinarily well. *The Florida Times-Union* even sympathized with him. "I'm not supposed to do that," Danny Link said, "at least not publicly. I'm assuming that, when you find out what it's about, you'll release the information."

That will depend. "Of course, Dan. I mean, anything fifty years old can't possibly involve national security."

Ray was happy with the outcome. "Considering what you had to deal with, you did about as well as you could, George. I suspect, though, that you won't be getting many invitations to the annual ex-presidents' barbecue."

Cunningham grinned. "I love barbecue."

Ray sat down. "Got a minute, George?"

"Sure. What's going on?"

"We heard from Milt while you were in there."

"Did he find out anything?"

"He says that, according to Martinez, they weren't really there to bug the place."

"Really?" That made no sense. "Then what was it about?"

"Cohen."

"Say again, Ray."

"Cohen had a briefcase with some notes in it. Apparently, part of it was in a foreign language. Anyhow, somehow or other, it got into the Democratic office at the Watergate. That's what the burglary was about. They were trying to retrieve the briefcase."

"Why?"

"He didn't know. But if we can believe Martinez, the administration took the heat for trying to bug the DNC headquarters rather than tell the truth."

Cunningham rubbed his head. "That would have been three years after the Myshko flight."

Ray held up his palms in surrender. "I don't see how it could possibly be connected."

"I don't either," said the president.

| 32 |

"So what the hell is happening down there?" said Bucky impatiently.

"We won't know for another few minutes, until we've gone a little farther around the back side," said Gaines. "Can't you just relax and spend a couple of minutes luxuriating over your performance? After all, you just called every president from Nixon to Cunningham a liar, and you did it in front of, I don't know, maybe three billion people." He smiled. "You want something to worry about? Forget what Marcia and Phil might find. Consider the fact that the U.S. and Russia may be in a race to shoot us down when we return. After all, Washington's not the only city that hid this. They had a lot of help from Moscow."

"I know," said Bucky. "I'm just eager to find out *why*, and I have a feeling we'll know as soon as we can contact Marcia and Phil again."

"In the meantime, just lean back and enjoy your notoriety," said Gaines. "I hate a nervous passenger."

"You're fired."

"You fired me a few hours ago. You have to rehire me to fire me again." Gaines looked at his instrument panel. "About five more minutes. We're in no-man's-land; can't signal to Earth, can't contact our people on the back side."

"Why do you call it the back side?" asked Bucky. "I always thought of it as the dark side."

Gaines shook his head. "It doesn't show itself to Earth, but it's not always dark. Now and then, the sun hits it."

"I didn't know that."

Gaines stared at him and grinned.

"What's so funny?" asked Bucky.

"I was about to say that we could probably fill a book with all the things you didn't know about the Moon, but you'd just fire me again, and that's getting tiresome."

Bucky smiled, closed his eyes, tried to relax, failed miserably, and finally sat up and stared at the panel, which remained incomprehensible to him.

"So how long now?"

"Maybe another minute," said Gaines.

"They've got to have found it!" said Bucky.

"Found what?"

Bucky shrugged helplessly. "Whatever *it* is. Whatever we've been hiding for half a century."

"What do you really think's down there?" asked Gaines.

"I don't know, but I'd guess that, whatever it was, they knew about it for years. It was in the photos as far back as 1959. That's why all those photos were doctored, and that's why Myshko was sent up here with orders to land and get a close-up. And then Walker's mission obliterated it."

"Why?"

"If I can't tell you what it is, I can't tell you why they got rid of it."

"Little green men?"

Bucky shook his head. "First, I think we'd welcome them, I really do, even back in 1969. And second, if we blew them away, don't you think they'd have retaliated? They've had a half century to do so."

"Yeah," agreed Gaines, nodding. "Yeah, I suppose so."

"If on the other hand, they were little blue men . . ." said Bucky, and Gaines doubled over with laughter.

"What's so funny?" said Neimark's static-riddled voice.

"Just telling dirty jokes to each other," said Bucky. "What have you got?"

"We're not exactly sure," she said. "I sent Phil back for the video camera. I want you to see this close-up."

"What *is* it?" Bucky demanded.

"Just be patient," she said. "It's difficult to describe." A brief pause. "Ah! He's coming this way. Shouldn't be another minute. Hurry up, Phil!"

"Camera's light as a feather," said Bassinger's voice. "But I'm still not used to walking across a rockpile in low gravity. Just want to be sure I don't trip and bust the damned thing."

"So where's the image?" said Bucky.

"I haven't turned the camera on yet," said Bassinger. "Wait'll we get to the spot."

"What spot?"

"Just be a little patient, Bucky," said Neimark. "It'll make more sense if you can see it while we're talking about it."

"I've got a question," said Gaines.

"Go ahead," replied Neimark.

"Is it green and does it move?"

"No, it's a very dull gray."

Suddenly, the image of Neimark's face appeared on the panel.

"Just focusing," said Bassinger.

"How far are you from the descent stages?" asked Bucky.

"Maybe three-eighths of a mile," said Neimark.

"They landed pretty damned close to it, given that they were a half century behind us in technology," added Bassinger.

"Close to *what*?" Bucky exploded.

"Okay, I'm about to show you." They pointed the camera down at the ground about ten feet away from him. "Do you see it?"

"I see a bunch of Moon rubble."

"Now watch," said Bassinger. "Okay, Marcia, give it a boost."

Neimark bent down, wrapped her fingers around *something*, something gray, and straightened up.

"It's some kind of alloy," continued Bassinger. "Super-lightweight, or she couldn't lift it, even in this gravity. But hard as steel and clearly part of a greater structure."

"*Structure?*" repeated Bucky. "I don't see any structure."

"It's mostly buried," answered Neimark, laying the panel

down. "I'd bet a year's pay that this wasn't manufactured on Earth."

"But it *was* manufactured," added Bassinger with absolute certainty.

"Oh, yes," agreed Neimark. "This kind of thing doesn't occur in nature."

"So what *is* it?" asked Bucky.

"We can't be sure yet," answered Bassinger, "but it seems to have been some kind of construction. I've brought along a shovel strapped to my back, and I'll start doing a little tentative digging."

"Will you have enough air?" asked Bucky.

"If we need more, we'll go back to the lander and get it. And I'll also bring back some instruments that should help me determine what the hell it's made of."

It took two more orbits, but finally Neimark was able to announce with certainty that the artificial structure had been a dome, and the photos they transmitted to the ship seemed to verify it.

"How big do you think it was?" asked Bucky.

"I don't know. The more we dig, the more we find. The ground's not packed here, it's just rubble, so we're not having any trouble uncovering it. So far, I'd say it's at least thirty feet in diameter—but that's a minimum. It could be—could have been—three times that big."

"Whatever it was, it sure as hell wasn't an outpost for observing us," said Bucky. "You could never see the Earth from there." He paused, considering the possibilities. "Could it have been made by men?"

"Not unless you think they reached the Moon before the dawn of the Apollo Program, erected whatever this structure was with materials the instruments still can't identify, and came back unnoticed," said Neimark.

"So it was an *alien* structure?" persisted Bucky.

"I'd say so, but nothing's definite this early. The pieces are all curved, all the same way. It was a dome. That's all we can be sure of right now."

"Were there any windows?"

"None that we can see."

"But if the dome has no windows, what's the point?" asked

Bucky. "I mean, you can't see through it." Suddenly he paused. "Or could *they*?"

"We don't know anything about any mysterious 'they,' " said Neimark. "But we've only uncovered one curved panel, maybe two. Have you ever seen an astronomical observatory, Bucky? They're not transparent. They have reasonably solid, opaque domes, with holes and channels where they can position their telescopes."

"But they can't see Earth from this side of the Moon!" said Bucky in frustration. "What in blazes were they looking at?"

"You're jumping to conclusions, Bucky," she said. "We don't know that they were looking at anything. Give us another few hours here, then we'll grab some food, take a nap, replenish our oxygen, and come back to explore the site further."

"If it's okay with you, Bucky," said Bassinger, "we're going to stop talking to you and get to work. We'll transfer all the stills and videos to you, and I already see a couple of pieces of whatever this is that are small enough to carry back to the lander and take up to the *Myshko*."

"Yeah, go ahead," said Bucky. "Besides, if you start using scientific terms, I'll think you've gone crazy from the gravity and are speaking in tongues."

Gaines broke the connection and turned to Bucky. "So what do you think?"

"Same thing as you. There was something up here that wasn't human, wasn't born on Earth."

"Is there a possibility we might have killed them?"

"I don't know," said Bucky. "My first inclination is to say we didn't. There aren't any bodies, and they wouldn't decay and vanish up here. And if they'd fired on us, don't you think President Nixon would have tried to rally the people to his side? I mean, this is a lot bigger than Vietnam." He paused, frowning. "And then . . ."

"And then what?" asked Gaines.

"Well, if we destroyed the dome, did we purposely or accidentally destroy whatever was in it?" He frowned again. "Myshko and his crew weren't twenty-year-old fighter pilots with no experience. These were mature astronauts, trained in the sciences. *Why* would they destroy it? And why would nine administrations in a row hide it? Or did the last eight not even know?

And if they didn't, why would Nixon keep it a secret?" He shook his head in frustration. "I get the feeling that I know less now than before we took off from Montana."

"By the way," said Gaines, "I assume you want me to send the photos and video of the dome back to Jerry."

Bucky shook his head. "Absolutely not. I don't want the White House or anyone else seeing any of this until we've had time to study and analyze them back home."

"I figured as much," said Gaines. "But they'll be encrypted."

"They'll be the most important thing ever sent from one machine to another. How long do you think it'll take the CIA or the FBI to break through the encryption after they've intercepted them?"

"What's the matter, Bucky? We've made the most significant discovery in the history of man, and suddenly you sound paranoid."

"We aren't the first to discover whatever this is," said Bucky grimly. "You're only paranoid if they're *not* out to get you."

33

Marcia Neimark and Phil Bassinger climbed into the command module and began removing their space suits.

"I wish I could say the air smells fresher," remarked Bassinger.

"Settle for there being more of it," said Bucky. He stared at the two of them. "I can't tell you how much I hate you for being the ones to land while I was stuck up here."

"Aw, that's sweet," replied Neimark.

"Really," said Bucky. "Just be ready to spend the entire return flight describing everything you saw, every step you took, every sensation you felt."

"Or you won't feed us?" asked Bassinger with a grin.

"For starters." Bucky's tone was so serious that they couldn't be sure he was kidding. Suddenly, he looked around. "Well, where the hell is it?"

"Come aft and have a look."

Bucky half walked, half floated to the back of the ship, where the two curved plates were secured.

"You know," he said, "if I saw these atop an ancient church or temple, or even an old, abandoned legislature building, I wouldn't give them a second glance." He paused and stared at the plates. "And yet they were responsible for three Moon flights and the expenditure of who knows how many billions of dollars. Why did we do it?"

No one had any answers, and, after a few moments, he made his way back to the front of the ship.

"So what do you think?" asked Gaines.

"Doesn't quite stir the sense of wonder the way *this* does," said Bucky, waving a hand at a viewscreen. "We're not Earth-bound anymore. *I* found a way; so will others. And now that I've shown that we don't need the government to do it, man is coming back out here again and again. The human race's greatest shame is that we turned our back on it for fifty years." He stared out at the stars. "Damn, I hope it *is* an alien artifact! Once we know for sure they're out there, nothing will hold us back!"

"Calm down, Bucky," said Neimark. "You'll have a stroke."

"No I won't," he said. "Once upon a time, when I thought I'd experienced and accomplished just about everything, I'd have accepted a stroke with equanimity. But now that I've been up here, now that I realize I haven't set foot on Mars yet but that I *can* during my lifetime, now that I've seen what we're carrying back home, I intend to die with the greatest reluctance."

"I'll drink to that," said Neimark.

34

Cunningham, like any president, had grown accustomed to criticism. But the flavor was changing. Usually, attacks charged him with bad judgment. Now they were suggesting he'd allowed himself to be deceived, that there was a conspiracy at the heart of the government, and he had no more sense of what was going on than the voters. Where was the president who'd campaigned as the man who could make government work?

Brian Colson ran a clip of the vice president, speaking barely a week ago, lamenting that many of our troubles would go away if people could just have a little confidence. "The biggest single problem we have," the VP had commented, "is that we've lost our willingness to trust the people we vote in. Don't ask me why. Maybe we all see too many conspiracy movies."

"I guess that's what it is, Jogina," Brian told his guest. "Too many movies."

The lead editorial in *The New York Times* delivered a lecture on presidential responsibility. "It's time, Mr. President," it said, "to go after the truth." *The Miami Herald* commented that he probably meant well but was simply out of touch. "What else does Mr. Cunningham not know?" *The London Times* admitted to being shocked that he had not, when evidence of the backdoor Moon flights—as they were now being called—first surfaced, asked a few hard questions "of the right people." The only media type he knew of who'd come to his defense was Harold Baskin of *Rolling Stone*, who suggested that maybe the president had been just as surprised as the rest of us. "It's not always easy for a CEO to find out what the techs are doing out back."

"That may be true," replied Len Hawkins on *All-Star Round Table*, "but I think I'd rather have a president who's trying to keep the truth from us, for whatever reason, than one who doesn't have a clue."

Lyra was waiting for him when he trudged up to his quarters for lunch after a painfully long morning. "Are you okay?" she asked.

"I'm fine." His tone suggested he didn't need any sympathy.

She didn't blink. "George, I know you've heard me say this before, but I'll say it again: I'm sorry you didn't go into accounting."

"Me, too."

"You know," she said, "they're all idiots."

"They think *I'm* the idiot."

"I'd like to see any of those people, see Blackstone, especially, come in here and try to deal with the problems you have to handle every day. He'd be a basket case by the end of the first week."

Harry Culver called. Harry was the senior senator from Ohio, who'd encouraged him to go for the White House. Who'd been his mentor when he was just getting started in politics. "Just ride it out, George," he said. "You'll be okay. You should be used to stuff like this. As soon as the next scandal hits, it'll go away."

But it wouldn't, and he knew it. The world had changed with the advent of electronic communications. Presidents, beginning with FDR, were on the record. Nixon, despite a long career of postpresidential public service, would never get past *You won't have Nixon to kick around anymore*. Or *I am not a crook*. Bill Clinton, who'd been a major contributor to global stability, would always be remembered as the guy who didn't have sex with that woman. Jimmy Carter's *crisis of confidence* comments, which had morphed into *malaise*, would live forever. And George W. Bush could spend the rest of his days rescuing kids out of burning buildings, but he'd never live down *Mission Accomplished*.

For Cunningham, the Bermuda Triangle remark had already become part of the media landscape. Yes indeed, *Ask Mr. Blackstone*—Worst of all, he was left with no answers. What actually *had* happened up there, Mr. President?

He had no idea.

When he got back to his office, he summoned Ray. "What do we have on Cohen's briefcase?"

"Nothing yet, George. To be honest, I'm not sure where to begin."

"Whatever was in there, Ray, Nixon apparently fumbled away his presidency trying to get it back."

He almost felt sorry for Nixon. He'd watched the old film clips, read Mason's biography *The Plumbers and the President*, and understood why the country had turned against him. The truth, he thought, was that Nixon had simply not been emotionally capable of handling the pressures at the White House. Nixon's basic problem was that he'd had a thin skin, and that's a serious handicap on the big stage. Especially when you're sending people into combat. And, of course, those were the Cold War years, when a misjudgment could have killed everyone on the planet.

The president's cell sounded, the old horse-race theme, "Bahn Frei." It usually fired up his circulation. But not this time.

The phone was lying on his desk, while the horses tore around the track. Ray disapproved of that particular ringtone. It sent the wrong message, he'd argued. Left people with the impression that Cunningham wasn't a serious person. But Cunningham was, of course, the president of the United States, and if he wanted horse races—

"Mr. President." It was Kim. "Admiral Quarles is here."

The African meltdown was intensifying. Quarles wanted to send in the Marines. The last poll indicated that 58 percent of the country wanted to do just that. It always amazed him how quickly people forget.

"Give me three minutes, Kim. Then tell him to come in." He turned back to his chief of staff. "Ray, we need to find out what was in that briefcase. Do what you have to."

"How do you suggest we manage that, George?"

"Track down the people who worked in the DNC office at the time of the break-in."

"That was Lawrence O'Brien."

"I know."

"He's no longer with us, sir."

"Damn it, Ray, don't you think I know that? But there must be somebody who was there. Somebody who remembers what happened. A secretary, maybe."

"Okay, Mr. President. I'll do what I can."

"Make something happen, Ray."

The admiral arrived with two aides and a complete digital show demonstrating why we had to intervene. People were dying. More massacres were coming. The entire area was falling apart. And there were strategic considerations.

Usually, in military matters, Cunningham maintained a calm demeanor, listened to the arguments, and explained why he was not going to commit U.S. troops. It was a downhill slide. Put those first guys in. That's the easy part. Then reinforce them. Then watch the other side show remarkable endurance. Fight until the country gets tired of it all. Then pull out and leave those who helped you in said country, your friends and allies, to be killed. The country had done it time and again since the end of World War II. Until it had left the U.S. financially drained and hopelessly divided. *Last Days of the Empire*, if you believed the title of a current bestseller. "We aren't playing that game anymore, Admiral," he said finally, letting his irritation show. "We are staying out."

Quarles was a small, thin man with an eagle's beak. His scalp was crowned with thick white hair. He had an uncompromising conviction that the U.S. should use its military to stop the assorted killers in power around the globe. He was unwilling to recognize that Cunningham's first obligation was to the citizens of the United States. "With all due respect, Mr. President," he said in an angry whisper, "the blood'll be on our hands."

He meant Cunningham's hands, of course. And he was right. The president would have blood on his hands whichever course he chose. "Thank you for the briefing, Admiral," he said. "I trust we won't see any stories in the media about grumbling among the top brass."

When it was over, and the military contingent was gone,

Cunningham switched on the TV and looked at the pictures that were coming in, of towns burned and people brutalized. Usually, it was hard even to find a motive for the killing.

And, of course, rumors of dissension at the Pentagon surfaced that evening.

———————

"We can't just stand by and watch," said Senator Brig Nelson. Nelson was chairman of the Senate Armed Services Committee, and a member of the president's own party. "It's time we took action," he continued, speaking on *Editor-at-Large*. "And do I think the president intends to move against these killers? I don't like to put words into his mouth, but I'd be shocked if we don't see something within the next few days."

Lyra sighed. "George, why don't we watch *Those Magnificent Men in Their Flying Machines*?"

They occasionally spent their evenings with a classic film, when the outside world permitted. They always went for comedy. But it didn't happen often. Usually, they were committed to a banquet or they were having one of their artist-of-the-month events or there was an emergency meeting of the Haubrich Commission, which was looking into the most recent breakdown of the nation's infrastructure.

"I don't think so," said Cunningham. He was too stirred up at the moment.

Lyra reached over and touched his shoulder, trying to remind him he wasn't alone. She still looked good. Beautiful eyes and soft brown hair and a killer smile. The media agreed she ranked right in there with Jackie, Laura, and Michelle. But one of the Fox commentators thought she needed to pay more attention to her wardrobe. And one of the women on NBC said she could be a bit more diplomatic. It was true that she tended to say what she thought, a definite drawback in the political world, especially when she noted that the Speaker of the House would probably not be so anxious to jump into a war if anybody in his family was in uniform. (The Speaker also belonged to the president's party.) And just last week, she'd commented that the people who opposed family planning should learn how to count.

"George," she said, "don't you get tired of being attacked by these morons?"

"Try not to take it so seriously, love."

She wanted to get rid of Nelson but couldn't locate the remote. "If we don't act now, and decisively," he was saying in that standard supercilious tone, "we'll pay a price for it down the road. And eventually we'll be trying to explain to our grandchildren why we stood aside and did nothing."

"His attitude might be different," she said, "if he'd ever had to stand out at Dover and watch the bodies come back."

"Lyra, *I've* never had to do that."

"And I think it's smart of you to keep it that way."

The host raised the issue of Blackstone's Moon mission. "They're almost home, Senator. What do you think it all means?"

Nelson came close to scratching his head. "I'll admit, Jules, that I'm baffled. And I'd bet the White House is as puzzled as the rest of us." He looked out of the screen, playing his customary role as the Sage of Washington. "But I'll tell you this: We'll be putting together an investigation to find out exactly what happened and what they were trying to hide."

"Right," said Lyra. "You know, George, I'd love to see some of these people come in here and make some decisions. Maybe—"

The racetrack music started. Lyra rolled her eyes. She didn't like the ringtone either.

It was Ray. "Mr. President," he said, "we've found somebody."

"From the DNC?"

"Yes. Her name's Audrey Conroy. She was a bookkeeper."

"Beautiful."

"She's retired. Lives in Washington State. You want me to send Melvin to talk to her?"

Cunningham thought about it. "No," he said. He was pleasantly surprised. He hadn't thought anybody would still be alive. "We don't have the time. Call her. *You* do the interview. Set it up so I can listen."

While he waited, he did a quick search. Conroy's stint with the Democratic Party had ended six months after the break-in, when she took a job with the Department of the Interior. About the time Jimmy Carter came to the White House, she met her future husband, a dentist who was vacationing in D.C. A few months later, they married, and she moved to his hometown of Walla Walla. Today, Audrey was a grandmother. Four kids. Seven grandkids.

Lyra was watching him sympathetically. "It's a wild-goose chase, George. You know that."

"Probably," he said.

"I hope your biographers don't find out about it." Her eyes grew very round. "I can see it now. Chapter 17: Chasing Watergate."

Editor-at-Large had gone to commercial. Lawyers appeared, reassuring the audience they would fight to the end for them.

Then Ray was back. "Mr. President, we have her."

"Good." He activated the Skype. Audrey Conroy appeared on the TV. She was seated at a table, looking a bit flustered, an understandable reaction from someone who'd just learned the White House wanted to talk to her. But she gazed directly out of the screen and kept her voice steady.

"Yes, Mr. Vice President. What can I do for you?" She was tall, with clear brown eyes and hair cut short. She wore a light blue blouse, and her expression reflected an amused awareness of her own disquiet. She did not look like a grandmother.

"Ms. Conroy, we've been trying to clear up a few details about the DNC operation at the Watergate."

"Really?"

"Yes. During the Nixon years."

Her eyes fluttered shut. Then she was looking out of the screen again. Taking a deep breath. "You're kidding."

"No, ma'am."

"There's another investigation going on?"

"No, no." The vice president was trying too hard to be reassuring. *Just ask the damned questions, Ray.* "Nothing like that."

"Oh. Good. That's a relief."

"Yes. We're just trying to set the record straight on a couple of details. Does the name Jack Cohen ring a bell?"

Her forehead creased. Then she broke into a big smile. "You mean Larry's old buddy."

"We're talking about Lawrence O'Brien?"

"Yes. Is that who you mean?"

"Yes. Of course."

The smile grew even wider. "Jack Cohen. Sure. This is the first I've heard *his* name in a long time."

"How well did you know him?"

She shrugged. "Not that well, really. He'd come into the office once in a while, and he and Larry would sit and talk." Cunningham could see her reaching back through the years. "He seemed like a nice guy. But he wasn't the quickest horse in the stable."

"How do you mean?"

"He was an academic type. Loved to talk about Egyptian tombs and stuff like that. I never understood what Larry saw in him. I mean, Larry was down-to-earth, you know what I mean?"

"Yes. Sure."

"Okay. Anyhow, Cohen was always in some other world. But Larry was a little bit like that, too. I mean, he had a good imagination. And he was smart. But Cohen always seemed kind of lost. I remember one time he'd promised Larry tickets to a play at one of the colleges. But he couldn't find them in his pocket so he started looking through his briefcase. And he came up with tickets but they were to a show downtown. *The Thurber Carnival*, I think it was. The tickets were ten years old. I remember asking him if something had happened because he hadn't used them. He shrugged and said how he didn't remember, it was too long ago."

"Did he find the correct tickets?"

"I don't remember. It's been a long time, Mr. Vice President."

"What else can you tell me about the briefcase? Did he ever leave it at the Watergate office?"

She thought about it. "Not exactly," she said, finally. "But there *was* an incident. How did you know?"

"Just a rumor we'd heard."

"Well, yes. He *did* lose it on one occasion." Her brow creased. "It's an odd story."

"Why? What happened?"

"Well, Jack Cohen and Larry went to lunch together a lot. Usually in the hotel restaurant at the Watergate. They were down there one day and afterward they came up to the office." She paused, trying to remember. "I think what happened was, they sat in his office and talked for a while. Later that afternoon,

Cohen called, saying he'd left his briefcase somewhere, thought it was probably with us. Would we take a look?

"I don't really remember the details. I don't even remember whether I took the call or Jessica did. I don't think Larry was there at the time it came in. But we looked around. Didn't see anything. When Larry got back to the office, he looked, too. Cohen came back around closing time and they hunted some more. It sticks in my mind because it was right around the time of the break-in."

"Did it happen that night?" Ray asked. "The break-in?"

She shook her head. "I just don't know, Mr. Vice President. It might have. Or maybe it was a day or two later."

"Audrey," said Ray, "did he ever find the briefcase?"

"Oh, yes. It turned out he left it in the hotel restaurant."

"I assume you returned it to Cohen."

"As far as I know. Larry would have taken care of that."

"Audrey, thank you."

Cunningham had a line into Ray. "Ask her if she has any idea what was in the briefcase."

He relayed the question.

Audrey nodded. "I don't remember any specifics, but he was a teacher, and I think it had something to do with his classes. But I don't know. Again, it's a long time ago. He seemed really flustered. But this guy was always like that. Larry said how he was brilliant, but you couldn't prove it by me."

"Ray, how did Blackstone know where to look for the descent modules?"

Ray looked puzzled. "What do you mean?"

"He seems to have known exactly where to go." It was apparently a question that hadn't occurred to the vice president. "The back side of the Moon has a surface area of about seven million square miles. Blackstone was looking for a couple of pieces of metal that blended with the ground. How could he have possibly known where to find them?"

Ray sucked on his upper lip and shook his head. "I have no idea. He must have gotten lucky."

"Sure he did. I think we should ask him."

"You know how he is, Mr. President. He won't tell us."

"I think he will. We'll have to put up with the gloating, though. I'll tell you what. Put a call through to Jerry. Tell him I want to talk to him."

Jerry looked nervous. The smart, friendly, easygoing guy who'd been such an asset on the campaign trail a few years back had gone missing. And Cunningham understood why: He'd gone over to the enemy. It was hard to understand how that could have happened. He knew Jerry had received plenty of job offers. Good ones. Cunningham had arranged a few of them. But Blackstone had undoubtedly outbid everybody. Had taken Jerry for the sole reason that his presence would embarrass the president. What a son of a bitch he was. And he wasn't really sure which of the two men he was thinking of at that moment.

"How you been, Jerry?" he asked, keeping the anger out of his voice.

"I'm fine, Mr. President." He looked off to the side, but Cunningham doubted anyone else was present. Jerry took a deep breath. Then the eyes came back. "What can I do for you, sir?"

"Congratulations on the *Myshko* flight."

"Thank you. I'll pass them on."

"I'm sure you will." Cunningham was seated on the sofa in his study. "How's the new job working out?"

"I'm enjoying it, Mr. President. It keeps me in the space program."

"Yes. Very good. I was sorry we lost you."

"I was sorry to go."

"Well, I guess these things happen." Jerry's eyes were locked on him now. He was probably expecting an offer to draw him away from Blackstone. "It looks as if you and he were right all the time."

Jerry managed a nervous smile.

Cunningham made no effort to put him at ease. "Got a question for you, Jerry."

"Yes, sir?"

"How did your boss know where the descent stages would be? How'd he know where to look?"

Jerry needed a moment to decide whether he was free to speak. He apparently decided he was. Or maybe he couldn't resist putting a needle into the president. "It wasn't really that difficult," he said.

Cunningham listened while Jerry laid it all out. Rumors of a "Cassandra Project." Photos from satellites and probes, both Russian and American, that had been doctored. He was about to add something, but he thought better of it and broke off. Held up his hands. "That's about it, Mr. President."

"The Russians were part of the cover-up?"

"Yes, sir. They must have been."

"You're sure about that? Absolutely positive?"

"I've seen the photos, sir."

"That sounds as if *you* put some of this together."

Again, the hesitation. "Yes, Mr. President. I guess I did."

And Cunningham knew what he'd been about to say. He hadn't been able to get anyone at NASA to believe him.

The president shook his head. What a bunch of damned idiots they'd been. Or maybe not. The story had simply been too wild to take seriously. "Thanks, Jerry," he said.

———————

Restoring good relations with the Russians had been one of Cunningham's core goals. And, at least on a personal level, the two countries had come a long way. There were still people in power in Moscow who disliked and thoroughly distrusted the United States. Just as there were angry voices in D.C.

But Dmitri Alexandrov, the Russian president, had been at the White House five months earlier. The meeting had gone well. They'd conducted a joint press conference in which they tried to make the case for getting rid of what remained of Cold War animosity. Alexandrov's support, against unhappy opposition at home, in joining the coalition to create a world free of nuclear weapons, had been enormously helpful in winning friends in the U.S. The problem was that too many people still thought that the White House, in getting rid of its atomic capabilities, was handing the world over to its rivals.

He checked the time. It was late in Moscow, but Alexandrov was not inclined to retire early. He picked up the red phone and pushed the button. It took a few minutes.

"Yes, George," said Alexandrov. The call was strictly audio. "You are calling about the Moon shot, no doubt?" Much of his education had taken place in London, and he spoke with an accent that was a mixture of British and Russian.

"How'd you guess, Dmitri?"

"It is all over the newscasts. What else could it be?" He smiled. "I should mention that taking a call on the red phone is not as alarming as it must have been in the old days."

"It's a better world, my friend."

"Yes. Thanks to you. So what *did* happen with the Moon flights? I trust there's no emergency."

"No. Everything is fine."

"I am glad to hear it. And I am very curious. Your country put two vehicles on the Moon in 1969, prior to Apollo XI, and told no one. Why did that happen? There was such intense competition at the time—"

"Dmitri, I was hoping you might be able to tell *me*."

He laughed. Then realized it was not a joke. "Why would you think that?"

"Photos from that era were doctored to hide the landings."

"So how does that involve us?"

"*Russian* photos, Dmitri. Yours as well as ours."

"Surely, George, you are joking."

"I have it on the best authority."

There was a long silence at the other end. Finally: "If I even try to look into it, I will be laughed at. Nobody would ever take me seriously again."

"I know. I have the same problem. I just thought you should be aware."

———

"So let me get this straight, love," said Lyra. "You think Nixon set up the Watergate break-in because an anthropology professor left his briefcase in the Watergate restaurant?"

"Yes."

"And this is because the briefcase had a connection with two Moon flights that we did in secret?"

Cunningham just looked at her.

"And all this happened three years after the flights in question?"

"That's what it looks like," he said.

"Okay. Can you tell me what this Cohen could possibly have been carrying around that was that valuable?"

"I don't know, Lyra. That's what we've been trying to find out."

"Why do you think there was something in the briefcase?"

"I told you about Irene Akins—"

"The woman who worked in the Nixon White House."

"Yes. She thought there was a connection with Cohen. And she said something about a set of notes. In a foreign language."

She looked at him. Shook her head. "You said he was a linguist."

Cunningham walked over toward the window. It was a bright, clear evening. The Washington Monument dominated the sky. And a sliver of moon was rising in the east. "Yes, he was," he said.

"So what's next, love?"

"Okay. Look, we know they were trying to hide something. Three years later, and they hadn't destroyed it."

"So—?"

"It was something they wanted to hold on to."

"So they hid it somewhere."

"Yes."

"All right. Where?"

"I can only think of one place." He looked at her for a long moment, picked up the phone, opened it, and waited. After a moment he spoke into it: "Ray, you think Milt's free tomorrow?"

35

Milt Weinstein pulled off Yorba Linda Boulevard into the Nixon Presidential Library and Museum parking lot. A white colonnade overlooked a long, rectangular pool and a beautifully landscaped rose garden, filled with shrubs, annuals, palms, and flowering trees. Birds sang, and a young couple sat contentedly on a bench, holding hands. Others wandered through the grounds. The place looked busy and simultaneously placid.

Weinstein got out of his rental car, followed a walkway into the rose garden, and went through the front doors into a large display room. Tourists were everywhere, taking pictures of a Nixon bust, looking at framed photos from his presidency, posing among bronze figures of world leaders from that long-gone era. He walked slowly among flags and tapestries. Posters provided a history of the thirty-seventh president, from his early days in Yorba Linda and Whittier College, to his election in the midst of the Vietnam War, his breakthrough with China, and the devastating experience of Watergate. And, finally, his years as an elder statesman.

There was a short line at the admissions desk. He waited his turn, then showed his White House ID and asked to see Ms. Morris. Michelle Morris was the director.

The woman at the desk frowned at the ID, then looked at Weinstein. "Is she expecting you, sir?"

"Yes," he said.

"One moment, please." She picked up a phone, explained that Michelle had a visitor, nodded, paused, and nodded again. "Mr. Weinstein," he said, "someone will be right out." Then she looked past him. "Next."

———————

A tall young man in a museum uniform appeared out of a doorway. "Her office is in back," he said. "Please come with me." On the way, he passed the 1969 Lincoln that had provided transportation for President Nixon and glanced into a replica of the East Room of the White House, which was used by the museum for appearances by celebrities, and to accommodate weddings and other special events.

Morris rose from her desk as he entered. "Mr. Weinstein," she said. "They told me you were coming, but wouldn't say why. Please have a seat." She was tall and blond, about fifty, wearing a dark jacket over a white blouse. The jacket had a Nixon Museum patch on its breast pocket. Behind her, visible through a set of curtained windows, was a small one-and-a-half-story cottage. Richard Nixon's birthplace, built in 1912 by his father, Frank. Somewhere in the immediate area of the house grounds were the graves of the former president and his wife, Pat.

"The museum is very impressive," Weinstein said.

"Thank you. We're proud of it." She flashed an automatic smile. *White House or not, I'm busy. Can we please get on with it?* "So what brings you—?"

"This is going to sound a little off-the-wall, Ms. Morris."

"We'll help any way we can."

"Good." He lowered himself into an armchair. "There's a possibility a message may have been left here for the president. Left by President Nixon, that is."

The smile widened. "I'm sorry," she said. "I don't think I quite understand—"

"President Cunningham thinks it might have been deposited here with instructions to turn it over to a future president if one inquires about it."

"Mr. Weinstein," she said, "you're not making sense."

Weinstein laughed. "I don't know what it's about either, Ms. Morris. But apparently there's reason to believe such a letter exists."

"If it does," she said, "it's the first I've heard of it. What's it about, do you know?"

"They told me that it might have something to do with the Moon flights."

She sat back in her chair and shook her head. "I'm sorry. I don't think I can help you."

"You're sure?"

She got up. Ready to move on. "Positive."

"There's not some sort of lockbox here?" Weinstein tried a grin. "A hidden vault, possibly?"

"No, sir. I'm afraid not. But you can tell your boss that I'll have one of the interns look around. Just in case."

———————

He called Chambers from the Rose Garden. "Negative, Ray," he said.

"Nothing at all?"

"No, sir. She laughed at me."

"Okay," said Chambers. "It was worth a try. Come on home."

"Ray, if you don't mind—"

"What, Milt?"

"What are we actually looking for?"

"Just come home, Milt. And thanks."

Chambers disconnected, leaving Weinstein staring across the grass at President Nixon's Sea King helicopter. Marine One. Or Army One, depending on the service branch of whichever pilot had been on duty when the president was traveling. This was the helicopter that Nixon had climbed into on that last desperate day, turning to wave a final good-bye to his presidency. A crowd stood around it, taking pictures of it, sometimes using it as background for family photos. Despite the dark history on display inside—the Watergate break-in, the Saturday Night Massacre, the enemies' list, the secret tapes, and the rest of it—the general aura of the museum left Weinstein with a sense that the former president had, after all, been an iconic figure. A man for the ages.

He knew better. Weinstein wasn't old enough to remember Nixon in the White House. He'd been in his teens when he'd learned about the man's anti-Semitism. That he'd thought Jews were running the country and would ultimately bring it down. Nixon's presidency had come to a sad conclusion, but it was hard to sympathize.

He turned away from the helicopter and began walking slowly back toward the parking lot.

Weinstein was on Route 55, headed south toward Santa Ana and the John Wayne Airport, when his phone sounded. "Milton?" Morris's voice. "This is Michelle. I guess I was wrong. I think we might have something." The formality was gone.

"A letter?"

"No. It's a small locked box. Instructions attached to it are exactly what you described. They say it's to be turned over to any president who inquires about it."

"What's in it?"

"I haven't opened it."

"Where was it?"

"Back in storage. It wasn't in the safe."

"Okay. I'm on my way."

"Milton, there's probably no point in your coming back here."

"Why not?"

"The instructions say it has to be delivered *personally*. I have to put it into the president's hands."

"All right. You want me to pick you up? You can fly back with me."

"I'm not exactly ready to go this minute."

"You're not going to keep the president waiting, I hope."

"Oh, c'mon. How urgent can it be? It's been here since the 1990s."

"Only thing I can tell you, Michelle, is that they're anxious to get their hands on it. When can you be ready to leave?"

| 36 |

"She's with you now?" asked Ray.

"Yes, sir. We're on our way to the airport."

"She has the box, of course?"

"Yes, sir."

Ray gave the president a thumbs-up. Finally, we're getting somewhere. The president nodded. "Have her open it."

"Tell her to open it," said Ray, tying his phone into the speaker so the president could listen.

Weinstein was gone for a minute. Then: "She said President Nixon left instructions it should be opened only by the president."

Cunningham sighed and spoke into the mike. "Milt, put her on."

Michelle responded: "Mr. President? Is that really you?"

"Of course it is, Ms. Morris. Would you tell us what's in the package, please?"

"Sir, I know it sounds like you, but I really can't be certain. I'm sorry. President Nixon wrote specific instructions that no one except the president should be privy to the contents."

"Strange phrasing," said Cunningham.

Ray grinned. "Presidents talk like that sometimes."

Cunningham raised a hand. "Okay, Michelle. Is it okay if I call you that? Don't open it. Milton will bring you here."

"Thank you, Mr. President."

She apparently handed the phone back to Weinstein. "You want me to bring her right in tonight?"

Ray took over: "Yes, Milt. Come directly here when you get in."

"Yes, sir. We'll be there as quickly as we can."

Ray disconnected and looked disapprovingly at the president. "What's wrong?" asked Cunningham.

He shrugged. "That was a mistake, George."

"What? That we didn't insist she open the package in the car?"

"Yes. Why wait six or seven hours until they get back here? We're getting hammered by the media, and we need some answers."

"Relax, Ray. First off, I'm not sure she would have acceded. In any case, no answer that we come up with is going to satisfy the media. We're just going to have to take the heat. At least for the time being. My primary concern right now is that we don't compromise anything. If Nixon thought nobody should see it except the president, we should trust his judgment. At least until we know what this is about."

"But Nixon was a paranoid. I'd expect him to be overly secretive about something like this."

"Something like what?"

Ray put his hands to his skull and squeezed. "I don't know."

"Okay. Then just go along with me, okay?"

"Okay, George. If you need me, I'll be in my office."

"No need for you to stay on, Ray. They won't be here until after midnight."

"I think I'll hang around. I doubt I'm going to sleep again until we get this settled."

————

Lyra was parked in front of the TV, watching the NBC news anchor report on the Moon mission. "—will be entering Earth orbit in another hour," she said. "NBC will be providing full coverage tonight, and we'll be there when the *Myshko* sets down. We hope you'll stay with us."

They went back to their regular programming, one of the evening panel shows. Angela Baker, an attractive blonde who usually supported the administration, was speaking with a guest, one of the network's "political contributors." Cunningham was never sure precisely what that meant.

Lyra looked up as he came into the room, walked over, and slid down beside her. "Not the best day at the office, I take it?" she asked.

He was about to ask why she'd drawn that conclusion when some statistics appeared on-screen:

CUNNINGHAM APPROVAL RATE DIPS TO 41%

"That's down sixteen points," Angela was saying, "just in the last twelve days."

"He's gone off a cliff," said the political contributor.

"Actually, love," said Cunningham, "we might have gotten a break finally."

"I mean," the contributor continued, "the president either didn't know, or he *did*."

"Where do they get these guys from?" asked Lyra.

"If he *didn't* know, he looks out of touch. If he *did*, then he's been lying to the American people. Either way—"

"Do you think he knew, Andy?"

Lyra touched his arm. "You're all over the Internet, George, and you're on every channel."

"No, I don't think he had a clue," said Andy. "Look, we're talking about the biggest bureaucracy in the world here. Things get lost. But that won't help him—"

Lyra killed the sound. "So what was the break you got?"

"It looks as if Dick Nixon might have left us a message after all."

"Really? Are you serious?"

"The director of the Nixon Museum is on her way here now with a locked box of some sort."

She smiled up at him. The tension was obviously wearing on her. Things had been going so well until this Moon thing had shown up. All she wanted was to get the world back the way it had been. Lyra had been dazzled at the prospect of living in the White House. Of being First Lady. Had it not been for her, Cunningham probably wouldn't have pursued it. He didn't have what the pundits liked to call the fire in the belly. He'd have been just as happy living on a mountaintop somewhere, living the casual life, reading, fishing, playing bridge on weekends.

But she'd insisted the country needed him. And she was right. When he'd assumed office, the United States had still been spread around the world, wasting resources trying to maintain an imperial status for reasons no one understood. President after president came into office, and nothing ever changed. The troops stayed in Germany. And Japan. And several dozen other stations around the world. And then Cunningham had arrived, and everything changed.

He'd resolved major disputes as governor of Ohio, and had gone on the *CBS Round Table* one evening, where he'd said that the country would not see prosperous times again until it took down the empire. "We're still positioned as if World War II hasn't quite ended," he told the host. "That needs to change." Next thing he knew, he was riding a tide that carried him all the way to the White House.

It had been a good run, culminating in the elimination of the world's nuclear arsenal. Ray hadn't approved of the antinuclear initiative. Nor had the party. In fact, neither party liked it. And opposing politicians used the issue to win back twenty seats in the House during the off-year elections. What happens, they asked, if one rogue nation succeeds in hiding a few H-bombs?

The answer, to Cunningham, was simple enough. The vast military the U.S. had at its disposal didn't need nukes to take down anyone on the planet. But it had been an emotional issue, a scary one, and as his advisors had expected, the fearmongers had won out. When people get seriously frightened, don't expect them to pay much attention to logic.

"She's flying in?" asked Lyra.

"Yes." He checked his watch. "She'll probably be here about two."

"Two this *morning*?"

"Yes. Sorry about that."

"George, couldn't it wait until tomorrow?"

"Probably." He leaned toward her. Stroked her hair. "Lyra, I need to find out what this is about."

"Okay. I'll have Al make something up for her." A door

opened in back. He could hear his sons talking. And the TV screen was suddenly showing a smug Bucky Blackstone. He reached for the remote, but Lyra restored the sound.

"—will be our guest," Angela was saying, "Sunday morning on *Meet the Press*."

"He's doing pretty well," Lyra said. She switched over to the Newshawk website, where three million people had posted thumbs up for Bucky.

Cunningham looked at some of the comments.

> *The most trusted man in America.*
>
> *You think we can talk him into running for president?*
>
> *What the hell were they doing on the Moon anyhow?*
>
> *You know what scares me? There's the biggest science project of the last century and the nitwit in the White House doesn't know anything about it.*
>
> *Give him a break, Harry. He's a government worker.*
>
> *Thank God for Bucky.*

The racetrack sounded. "George."

"Yes, Ray?"

"They're in the air. On the way back. I thought you'd want to know."

"Okay. Good. I assume Weinstein will check in again when they land?"

"Yes, he will."

"Are you actually going to stay on?"

"I'll be here, George."

"All right. When they're on the ground, let me know. Have we arranged a hotel for Ms. Morris?"

"It's pretty late. I thought we'd put her in the Lincoln Bedroom."

"Okay. That's a good idea."

"I was thinking, as an alternative, we could install her over at the Watergate."

Cunningham was silent for a moment. Then: "This is why you'll always have a job with me, Ray."

Jon Stewart started his show by assuring everybody that there was nothing to worry about, that the president had everything under control, had known from the beginning about the Myshko and Walker flights. Had undoubtedly known what Blackstone would find because, hey, do you think everyone in the White House is an idiot? Then he ran a clip from the Beverly Hills fund-raiser. A guy whom Cunningham remembered only vaguely, Michael Somebody, asking for his reaction to the Blackstone TV show. And the president's brush-off response: "Look, Michael, I really don't know how to respond to his comments. I think you'll have to ask *him*. While you're at it, you might check with Mr. Blackstone to see if he's figured out what's going on in the Bermuda Triangle."

And, of course, Stewart responded with shock.

It was certainly not the first time Cunningham had been a target on *The Daily Show*. There had been times when the president had said one thing and done another. Like during the campaign, when he'd blamed the country's economic woes on the sharp decrease in population growth at the same time he was arguing that overpopulation was draining the country's natural resources. And again, when he'd reassured the nation that blue sky science was part of who we were, then proceeded to delay funding yet again for the Webb Telescope.

Normally he was able to laugh off the flubs. A foolish consistency and little minds. Everybody understood that. But this one hurt. It wasn't really his fault that secrets had been kept. Nothing he could have done about that, no way he could have known. But nonetheless, he looked ridiculous at the moment.

Arthur Stiles, on *The Late Show*, commented that historians had recently uncovered evidence that an Englishman named Joseph Pettigrew had actually been the first European to arrive in America. "Almost sixty years before Columbus," he said, shaking his head in mock astonishment.

"Holy cats, Arthur," said his bandleader, who also doubled as a straight man, "how come we never found out about it?"

Stiles shrugged. "Apparently, Henry V—he was king at the time—wrote it down somewhere, then forgot about it."

"Well," said the bandleader, "I guess it could happen to anybody."

The audience broke up.

"Want some coffee?" asked Lyra, getting off the sofa.

"Please. And a donut would be good, too."

———————

Vanessa Hodge, on *CBS Late Night*, was also enjoying herself at his expense. "We have a late-breaking story," she said. "The White House has just announced that the Russians have the bomb."

"Now *that*," said Lyra, bringing in the coffee, "is clever."

Cunningham nodded. "I suppose."

"George, you need a better sense of humor. You know that?"

"I know, Lyra. And I don't mind getting bushwhacked when I deserve it. And sometimes even when I don't. But this thing has come out of nowhere. What the hell was Nixon up to?"

"We're also getting word," said Hodge, "that the administration won't have to worry about a negative reaction to canceling the funding for the Webb Telescope project. NASA is reporting they can't find the telescope."

"The only thing that makes any sense," said Cunningham, "is that Myshko and one of his partners, Peters, I guess, made an unauthorized landing. Wanted to be first on the Moon. Nixon was under a lot of pressure at the time, couldn't get clear of the war, so he panicked and ordered a cover-up."

"So what would have been the purpose of the second mission?"

"They went down and sprayed some kind of paint on the descent stages, made them the same color as the ground, and hoped they wouldn't be found. And they were right."

"So why did the Russians join in?"

"Damned if I know. They had nothing to lose. So they probably extracted some sort of deal. My guess is that when Nixon's lockbox gets here, we'll find out." He was surprised to discover he'd eaten the donut. He sipped the coffee, put it down, changed channels.

HBO had *The Greta Lee Show*. Greta, lovely dark eyes, black hair, enticing smile, looked directly out of the TV. "Well," she said, "so we got two missions to the back side of the Moon, which is nothing but a big parking lot. And I guess you heard that we've also developed artificial semen. And we wonder where the money goes."

Cunningham growled something and went to one of the

movie channels. He selected *Casablanca*, probably his all-time favorite film. "Okay?" he asked.

"Sure, babe."

"I wonder how Bogie would have handled this?"

Lyra raised her cup. "Here's lookin' at you, kid."

He kissed her. Started to unbutton her blouse. And, in his best Bogart imitation: "You too, sweetheart."

The racetrack sounded again. "George, they'll be on the ground in twenty minutes. Should be here in less than an hour."

37

"Canaveral has offered us its landing facility if we want it," announced Gaines, listening to the transmission from Earth. He turned to Bucky. "We might consider it. It's a hell of a lot better than Flat Plains in every respect."

"With one exception," replied Bucky. "We own Flat Plains. I won't be beholden to the government or to NASA."

"Are you sure? I mean, if we need medical care . . ."

"Do your job right, and we won't," said Bucky, ending the conversation.

"Bucky, you should be the happiest man alive," said Neimark. "Why are you so grumpy?"

"In a couple of hours, I'm going to face the cameras and tell the nation that my president is a liar or a fool. And while we've had our differences, I'm just enough of a patriot not to be looking forward to it."

"So let Jerry Culpepper do it," said Bassinger. "That's why you hired him, isn't it?"

"This is *my* operation," said Bucky firmly. "I'll make the report to the public. Which brings up another matter."

"Oh?" said Neimark suspiciously.

"Yeah. I don't want anyone making any public guesses about

what this . . . this *thing* is. Or was. We'll wait until our experts have examined it six ways to Sunday, and we're sure."

"Oh, come on, Bucky," said Bassinger. "It's an alien artifact. There's no keeping it secret, and I can't imagine why you'd want to."

"I'm not that sure, Phil," said Neimark. "We've got to run it through half a dozen tests at our lab first."

"What else *could* it be?" demanded Bassinger.

She shrugged. "I don't know. But it's always possible it was brought to the Moon not by aliens but by Sidney Myshko."

Bassinger gave her a look that implied he thought she might start foaming at the mouth at any second, then shook his head, folded his arms, and shut his mouth.

"What do *you* think it is, Boss?" asked Gaines.

"I don't know," admitted Bucky. "I'm no scientist, or metallurgist, or whatever the hell's required to tell us. But I know what I *hope* it is."

"Proof that we're not alone?" suggested Gaines with a smile.

Bucky nodded. "Got it in one."

"We're *not* alone," said Neimark.

"You *saw* aliens?" asked Bucky disbelievingly.

"No, of course not," she replied. "But do the math. There are one hundred billion G-type stars in the galaxy. At least ten billion are G-type stars like our sun. We're finding that just about every kind of star we've been able to observe through the Hubble or one of the other telescopes has one or more planets. Now, what are the odds that there are from one to maybe three billion planets circling G-type stars and not a single one of them has developed life?"

"Astronomical," admitted Bucky. Suddenly he smiled. "Maybe that's why they call it astronomy."

His three cabin mates groaned.

"Nobody laughed," he observed.

"Would you?" said Bassinger, making a face.

"You're all fired."

"Okay, give us our pay."

"I left it in my other pair of pants. I guess you'll have to stay."

"Just as well," said Gaines. "It's raining out."

"Raining?"

"Meteors."

Bucky looked out the window and watched a cloud of rocks sweep past. He kept his eyes on them until the storm dissipated a few minutes later.

"Well, now you can say you've been in one," said Gaines.

"And I'm not even wet."

"Or crushed, or shipwrecked, or . . ."

"Are these things common, these meteor storms?" asked Bucky.

"Not very," said Gaines. "You're as likely to get hit by garbage from the Apollo flights that's been in orbit for fifty years."

"Really?"

"Well, in theory. In practice, someone had enough brains to figure out what might happen, so they carried all their garbage back to Earth." Suddenly Gaines smiled. "But it's a pretty interesting notion, isn't it? I'll bet you could make a hell of a science-fiction story out of it." Suddenly, he tensed. "Oops. New transmission coming in." He concentrated on the message, then looked up. "The University of Nebraska is sending a team from their medical school, just in case. That's more generous than you might think. We won't touch down until close to eleven local time."

"The Cornhuskers must have had a good year," said Bucky with a smile.

"Cornhuskers?" repeated Neimark.

"Their football team."

Gaines thanked them and turned to Bucky. "We'll be entering the atmosphere in another twenty minutes. Anything you want me to say to Jerry?"

"Yeah. Have an armored truck on the premises, as well as our best security team."

"You expecting trouble?"

"I don't expect anyone to try to steal these pieces if that's what you mean," replied Bucky. "But I don't want the press touching them or photographing them until *we're* done with them." He paused. "There's only going to be one first photo and one first video of whatever the hell this is, and I want to make sure that the four of us are standing next to it and not some moron from CBS or NBC."

"Okay, makes sense," agreed Gaines.

"Also, nobody hitches a ride and sneaks into whatever lab we're using. We don't want anybody reporting our findings to the public before we do."

"You're the boss."

Bucky smiled. "That's the first time you've acknowledged it since we took off."

"Spend a week in space, and it makes you crazy." Gaines matched his smile.

Then they were in the atmosphere. The ride got choppy, and Gaines had to concentrate on his piloting. Bucky traded seats with Neimark, who was able to double as copilot, and before too long, they were on the ground and being towed to the hangar at Flat Plains with numerous spotlights and floodlights illuminating the darkened field.

"What the hell's *that*?" demanded Bucky as he saw perhaps three dozen trucks and vans forming an aisle for the ship to be pulled into the hangar.

"The press, of course," said Neimark. "You didn't really think they wouldn't be here to interview the first people to walk on the Moon in most of their lifetimes, did you?"

"No, of course not." Bucky frowned. "But I don't want them inside the hangar until we're out of the ship, and I've talked to Jerry Culpepper."

Gaines relayed the order, and they could see members of the press, and especially the cable news companies, arguing fruitlessly to be allowed in. Then Bucky saw Jason Brent directing his security team, and a moment later the press, sullen and resentful but no longer trying to disobey his wishes, backed off and took up positions outside the hangar.

The ship entered, and the doors closed behind it. A number of Bucky's closest associates were there, including Gloria Marcos, Sabina Marinova, and Ed Camden, but Bucky walked directly to Jerry, shedding his space gear as he did so.

"So what, exactly, have you brought back?" asked Jerry.

"I'll be damned if I know."

"Let me ask it another way," said Jerry. "Is it of human or alien origin?"

"Same answer."

"We'll have it analyzed as thoroughly as any object in history," said Jerry. "I've got all the experts standing by, and we've turned the old farmhouse into the most high-tech lab you ever saw . . . but you're going to have to say *something* to the press."

"Why?"

"Bucky, you've got the whole world talking about you. You're the first man, well, the first group, to go to the Moon in almost fifty years. You found proof that the history of our space program is, if not a sham, at least wrong. You as much as suggested that the government of the United States is in collusion to keep this a secret. They saw Myshko's landing stages when you broadcast them from the Moon. The administration's got the best video and computer people in the country trying to prove you faked that transmission, and they can't. You've hinted that you found something even more startling. How the hell can you just smile at the cameras, say you're off to have dinner and a shower, and you'll talk to them in a week or a month, when our technicians determine exactly what it is that you've brought back and refuse to share with a breathlessly awaiting public?"

Bucky stared at him for a moment, the hint of a smile playing about his lips. "You ever think of going into politics?"

Jerry returned the smile. "Sometimes I think I've been in it for years." Then: "So what are you going to do?"

"Well, I don't want them breaking down the door of my hotel room, so I guess I'll talk to them right here after all. Stick around; you get to clarify it all after I've had my say and left."

"You want to show it to them?" asked Neimark, emerging from the ship.

"No one will believe me if I don't," replied Bucky. "Have Phil and Ben bring the pieces around and set them up over there."

"Set them up?" she repeated, puzzled.

"Prop them up against a table or something. They'll be more impressive that way than lying flat."

Gaines and Bassinger, who knew where the pieces of the dome were stored, brought them out and leaned them upright against a long table. Bucky walked over and studied them. He was almost disappointed when there was no alien lettering engraved in the strange metal.

Jason Brent walked in through a side entrance and quickly slammed the door behind him. "They're getting restless," he announced. "And by the way, welcome back."

"Okay, let 'em in," said Bucky.

The doors were opened, and in less than a minute Bucky found himself surrounded by perhaps twenty reporters and cameramen, while smaller numbers concentrated on Neimark, Gaines, and Bassinger.

"What's *that* stuff?" asked one of the reporters, pointing to the dome segments.

"That's what we hope to find out," said Bucky.

"Did they come from Myshko's ship?" asked another.

"I've no idea."

"Oh, come on, Bucky," said a third. "Take a guess!"

"I'm no scientist," replied Bucky. "We have to subject these things to all kinds of tests."

"Okay, you don't know what they are. What do you *think* they are?"

Bucky stared at the assembled members of the press for a long moment, and then his natural flamboyance came to the fore. "I think they're part of a dome that was constructed on the far side of the moon, in the Cassegrain Crater."

"By Myshko?"

A brief pause. Then: "I doubt it."

"You're saying it was made by *aliens*?"

"I'm saying that I doubt Myshko built it. Who else might have?"

"Where's the rest of this dome?" asked another.

Good question, thought Bucky. He looked at the reporter. "I don't know."

"There's no weather on the Moon, is there?"

"Not the way you and I know it," said Bucky. "So to anticipate your next question, no, it wasn't destroyed by a tornado or a cyclone or an earthquake . . . make that, a moonquake."

"So are you suggesting that Myshko destroyed it?"

Bucky shook his head. "I'm not saying any such thing. In point of fact, I believe that Myshko's mission was to look at it."

"Now I'm really confused," continued the reporter. "You didn't find any aliens up there, did you?"

"I think you can be assured I would have said so if we did." Bucky smiled.

"Then if the Myshko mission didn't destroy it, and aliens didn't destroy it, who did?"

"I think there's only one possible answer," replied Bucky. "I think it was destroyed three months after the Myshko flight by the Walker mission."

Even the jaded reporters fell silent as they did a mass double take.

"Just a minute, Bucky!" said *The Los Angeles Times*. "Are you saying that there was a *second* Moon landing before Neil Armstrong?"

"Yes," said Bucky. "Weren't you paying attention? There were two descent stages left on the Moon."

"But if there were no aliens there, no trace of any aliens, just this deserted structure, why would we want to destroy it?"

"To coin a phrase, I'd give a pretty penny to find out. But I've already spent quite a few billion pennies, so maybe you guys can be of some service here."

"Us?"

Bucky nodded. "I can guarantee you that the answer's not on the Moon. Surely you can find the answer if it's here on Earth."

Great! thought Jerry Culpepper. *If the White House didn't hate us before, they sure as hell do now.*

"Are you saying the president is a party to this?"

Bucky stared at the reporter. "The president was six years old when Myshko landed. Do *you* think he was a party to this?"

"If Nixon kept it secret . . ." began the reporter.

"Not just Nixon," said another. "They couldn't have done this overnight. Look at the dates, and think of the preparation time. LBJ would have had to be part of it, too."

"Whatever," said the first. "If one or the other knew about it, and whoever was president when Myshko landed, it was definitely Nixon when—and *if*—Walker destroyed it. Did he just do it on a whim?"

"I doubt it," said Bucky. "For one thing, Nixon wouldn't have been the only person to know about it. If there hadn't been a hell of a good reason, why would Myshko never claim credit for being the first man on the Moon? Why would Walker and all the others keep silent? There was a reason, all right. I don't know if it was a good reason or a bad one, but it was one that they all bought into, which makes me think it was a valid one."

"So are you suggesting that Ford and Carter and Reagan and the Bushes and Clinton and Obama and Cunningham, they *all* knew about it?" said *The Chicago Sun-Times*. "It must have been one hell of a secret. I mean, if Nixon didn't use it to distract us from Watergate, and Clinton didn't reveal it to take attention away from his impeachment trial, just what could it have been?"

"Right," chimed in Fox News. "We weren't under attack. The discovery of alien life, and sentient alien life at that—after all, they traveled to the Moon and they built this structure—would have been something to get up on the rooftops and yell about, not hide."

"So maybe it wasn't alien life at all," suggested *The New York Times*. "All we have are a couple of curved metal plates, and the supposition of a wealthy playboy who hasn't been trained in any of the sciences."

"The wealthy I'll take full credit for," said Bucky. "The playboy I resent. Or at least I resent never having had the time to be one. Anyway, I am not stating any of this as a scientific certainty. I'm inclined to say you dragged it out of me"—he smiled—"but the fact of the matter is that what I've told you is all supposition. Logical supposition, I think, and I'd bet half my remaining fortune that we ascertain that this metal wasn't created on Earth, but we don't *know* anything except that Sidney Myshko and Aaron Walker did land on the Moon because we found the landing stages from their ships."

"Why would ten presidents lie about it?" asked ABC.

"I don't know," answered Bucky. He was losing patience answering the same question every two minutes. "And maybe *lie* is the wrong word."

"In what way?"

"When presidents keep various aspects of national security secret, no one accuses them of *lying*."

"Are you saying this is a national security matter?" demanded MSNBC. "That we are in danger of being attacked by alien beings?"

Bucky shook his head. "No. I'm not saying anything like that. I just used national security as an example. There are a lot of things that presidents, and senators, and representatives, and generals, and for all I know, blacksmiths, don't tell us about. Most of it isn't national security. I'm not in the panic business, and I think it would be a good idea if you weren't either."

The man from MSNBC didn't look as chagrined as Bucky felt he should have, so he stared at him until the reporter shifted uncomfortably and dropped his gaze.

"All right," said Bucky. "I've told you what I know, which isn't much, and I've suggested where you might look for answers, which, of course, is up to you." *Sure it is, with three billion people watching or listening to this.* "Now you are free to interview scientists Marcia Neimark and Phil Bassinger, and pilot Ben Gaines. When you're done, Jerry Culpepper, the spokesman for the Blackstone Enterprises space initiative, will provide you with more background for your articles and reports."

"Have you got anything else to say?" asked *The Wall Street Journal.*

"Yeah," said Bucky. He looked into the cameras. "Start saving your pennies, because when we and other companies begin offering commercial flights in space, whatever it costs, you'll get your money's worth. I've done a lot of things in my life, been a lot of places, but I've never experienced anything like this. I feel"—he searched for the words—"emotionally blinded and deafened just by being back on Earth." He pointed out the open doors toward the sky. "Now that I'm *here*, all I want to do is get back *there*."

Then, accompanied by Jason Brent and Gloria Marcos, he excused himself and left.

———

"Well," he asked, when they were all seated in the private office that had been constructed for him, "how'd I do?"

"I think if you wanted to make President Cunningham uncomfortable, you couldn't have planned it better," said Gloria. She paused and stared at him. "*Did* you want to upset him?"

"Not especially," said Bucky. "One thing not a single member of the press thought about, or more likely cares about, is that if all those presidents thought it was essential to keep this thing secret, they must have had a reason."

"Son of a gun!" exclaimed Brent in surprise.

"Five'll get you ten that not one of them considers that before they stake out the White House." A bittersweet smile crossed Bucky's mouth. "We've been on opposite sides of this, or at least not on the same side, but Cunningham's a decent man, and for all I know, he has an excellent reason for covering up the Myshko mission, though now that they know about it, they'll never leave him alone until they get the full story." He leaned back on his chair. "I feel sorry for the poor bastard."

38

Lyra had gone to bed. The volume on the TV was set low, and Cunningham was violating Secret Service protocols, standing near the curtains, drinking a rum and Coke, looking out at the sliver of moon hanging over the capital. Not much point being president of the United States if you can't look out the window. The Moon is one of those things everyone takes for granted. Like spaghetti and meatballs. Or most of the people in our lives. We don't notice them until they're not there anymore. Or they start causing trouble.

The Moon is for lovers.

Well. Maybe back in the old days. He raised his glass to it.

And, reluctantly, to Bucky.

Behind him, NBC was replaying the arrival of the *Myshko*. He could just hear Cal Peterson's voice describing the scene. He seemed awestruck. A reflection of the arriving lights moved across the window.

"Here it comes," said Peterson.

He sighed, lowered himself onto a chair arm, adjusted the volume, and watched. The night sky was filled with stars. Abruptly, the picture split in two, one showing the incoming spacecraft, the other a crowd of several hundred standing anxiously behind security lines. Not bad, Cunningham thought. It was almost eleven o'clock out there.

He was looking across an illuminated landing field, probably from a perch atop one of the hangars. The lights were growing steadily brighter, descending out of the night. Peterson kept talking about what a great moment it was for mankind, and what a debt of gratitude the nation owed Bucky Blackstone, and, by the way, tune in tomorrow for a complete recap of the mission.

It was hard not to be jealous.

It was too dark to be sure how close the *Myshko* was to the ground. Then, abruptly, it was visible in the field lights, its gray metal body sleek in the style of a corporate jet except for the twin rocket engines in the rear. The crowd began to applaud. The voice went quiet as the vehicle touched down, rear wheels first, then the nose, and the applause grew, turned into shouts and clapping and somewhere, out of sight, a band began to play "Fly Me to the Moon."

Yes, indeed. One of the great moments in history. He wondered how Bucky could have overlooked managing things so they'd have landed during prime time instead of an hour before midnight, 1:00 A.M. on the East Coast. He was probably not as good at public relations as people gave him credit for. Or maybe he just didn't give a damn. The president shook his head. He'd begun to think too much like a politician. Not a good sign, not for a guy who thought of himself as so much more.

The vehicle slowed and came to a stop. Then guys with lights fanned out onto the field, directing the pilot toward a pair of tow trucks. Peterson was going on about how a new era in space exploration had begun. The *Myshko* pulled in behind the trucks, lines were attached to the undercarriage, and they began pulling it toward one of the hangars. As it disappeared inside, a new voice, a woman's voice, broke in. "Cal," she said, "we'll be getting a statement shortly from Mr. Blackstone."

But first there were journalists interviewing each other. Magnificent day for the United States. Proud to be an American. Tell you the truth, Bill, it's an important day for the entire world. And what do you think about those descent stages on the Moon? Where'd they come from? Then doors must have opened somewhere and suddenly the president was looking at the interior of the hangar, dominated by the *Myshko*. Lights were on, and the astronauts, still in their gear, were standing near the ship while security people tried to keep order. Off to one side of the spacecraft, two pieces of curved gray metal rested on tables. Both had jagged edges, as if they'd been ripped from a larger piece. They were different sizes, but the curvature and the complexion looked identical.

"What's that stuff?" asked a reporter, pointing at them.

Blackstone came forward, carrying a microphone. "That's what we hope to find out."

"Did they come from Myshko's ship?" asked another. Cunningham recognized her as the A.P.'s Jenna Hawkins.

"I've no idea."

"Oh, come on, Bucky," said a voice from the crowd. "Take a guess!"

Bucky grinned. He was having the time of his life.

After Blackstone left, Jerry took his place, Jerry in his trademark suede jacket and dark brown tie, smiling, holding up his hands, asking for order, inviting more questions. He was still trying to quiet everything down when Ray called.

"George," he said. "You saw it?"

"Yes, Ray."

"The telephones are ringing. We're going to have to get a statement out posthaste. You want me to put something together?"

Ordinarily, the assignment to create a first draft would have fallen to the press secretary. Who was presumably home asleep. But Cunningham had neither the time nor the inclination for that. "This is kind of a special case, Ray. My God, *aliens*. Is that really what it was?"

"I don't know, George."

"I'll take care of it. I'll get something to you in a few minutes."

"Okay." He hesitated.

"What, Ray?"

"It could still be a hoax, George. We don't know they actually found those pieces of metal up there."

"I suppose that's possible. But what would Blackstone have to gain by making up a wild story that would fall apart so easily? He knows he'd be found out. No, I think we can believe what he's telling us."

"Okay. I hope we have it right."

"Ray, I'm not sure what I'm hoping for now. By the way, where's Weinstein?"

"Should be pulling up out front shortly."

"Okay. Let me get this press release taken care of, and I'll be down."

———————

Easier said than done. His first inclination was simply to proclaim that he was on the case. That the White House had been as surprised as anyone else at Blackstone's discovery but that he wasn't prepared to say more than that until he'd looked into the matter.

But that would have been a bad call. Michelle Morris would be here shortly with something from President Nixon that, he assumed, would provide an explanation.

What the hell had they stumbled into? The early flights had been made at the height of the Cold War. Had this been some sort of behind-the-scenes game between the U.S. and the Soviet Union? Maybe we'd wanted to set up a site on the Moon to launch missiles? Or maybe just get the Soviets to *think* we were doing that? So there'd been secret missions. Did that make any sense at all? Was it even *possible*?

No.

It had to be aliens. But Cunningham had grown up in a family of real-world skeptics. He'd spent a lifetime laughing at people who thought there was a major conspiracy about Roswell, who claimed they'd been kidnapped by UFOs.

He called Ray. Told him to wait in the Oval Office. Then he headed downstairs.

———————

"Tell them," Cunningham said, "that we'll be putting out a statement within the hour."

"Okay." Ray looked uncomfortable. "When we do, what will we be saying?"

"Depends on what Ms. Morris tells *us*."

"Suppose she has *nothing*? I mean, I hate to be negative, but it's not really likely Nixon's going to be able to shed any light on what happened tonight."

Cunningham shrugged. "If so, we'll just tell them we're looking into it. That we have no answers either."

"Yeah," he said. "I'd hate to have to do that, but I think we're in a situation where we might have to just fall back on the truth." He grinned. It was a line that politicians often used. "By the way, they're here. Security tells me they've just entered the grounds."

———

The Nixon Museum director, accompanied by Ray, came into the oval office and smiled nervously at the president, who rose from his couch. She was carrying the locked box. "Mr. President," Ray said, "I'd like to introduce Michelle Morris."

"Mr. President," she said, "I'm honored."

"The pleasure's mine." Cunningham extended his hand. The box was made of dark-stained wood. It was large enough to hold a couple of oversize books. It did not, however, seem heavy. She tightened her grip on it and clasped his hand. "Now," he continued, with a smile designed to put her at ease, "let's see what this is all about, shall we?"

She handed it to him. He set it on a coffee table ringed by three armchairs. "Please be seated, Michelle." He indicated one of the chairs.

A small padlock secured a hinged lid. Michelle showed him the key. He was reaching for it when a strange expression appeared on her face. "Is something wrong?" he asked.

"My instructions," she said. She reached into a pocket and produced a folded envelope. "Sir, they say nobody but you is to see what's in the box."

Cunningham held out his hand. "May I see that?"

She gave the envelope to him. He opened it and extracted a piece of letterhead stationery. Richard Nixon's name was printed across the top, above his San Clemente address. The document was dated April 30, 1990, and was signed *RN*. With a flourish.

It was addressed to the Director of the Nixon Presidential Library and Museum.

The attached package is under no circumstances to be opened except as provided below, nor is its existence to be made known save to your successor. It is to be kept in a secure location.

In the event that a sitting president of the United States inquires about a secret package, or indicates he is aware of its existence, or believes such a package may exist, and he stipulates a connection with the Apollo program, it may be turned over to him. But no one else, including the director, may be shown its contents save at the express pleasure of the president. He should be advised that it might be best to make himself aware of the contents before allowing anyone else to see them.

Michelle was looking directly at Ray. Cunningham showed him the letter. Ray read it, nodded, and got up. "Call me if you need me, Mr. President."

Michelle also started to rise. Cunningham signaled Ray to sit down. "I'm sure we can trust Mr. Chambers," he said. He turned the package over. "Michelle, you have absolutely no idea what's in here?"

"No, sir."

"How long have you known about its existence?"

"I just found out when your man came looking, and we initiated the search. It was in storage."

"The previous director didn't say anything?"

"No, Mr. President."

"Okay, thank you, Michelle. There's a lady outside who'll show you to your quarters."

She beamed. "I'm staying *here*?"

"Yes, ma'am. You will have one of our best rooms."

"I wanted to carry the box for her," said Ray. "But she wouldn't let anybody touch it."

"She takes her instructions seriously," Cunningham said. He inserted the key, twisted it, and listened to the lock click open. He lifted the lid and looked down at plastic packing material. Beneath it was a nineties-style videotape. It carried a label, marked simply *RMN*.

Beneath the videotape lay more plastic. He pulled it back, revealing a mahogany-colored plaque with a silver plate. No. Two mahogany-colored plaques with silver plates. Both plates were metal, and both were inscribed with several lines of characters. The characters were in a foreign alphabet. Or, now that he looked at it, different alphabets. Otherwise, the plaques were identical. "That one's Greek," said Ray.

The letters on the second one looked vaguely Hebraic.

"I think you're right." Ray frowned. "It shouldn't be hard to find out for certain."

Cunningham moved them under a table lamp. "The Greek one is seven lines. This one is eight."

"You think it's the same inscription?"

"Could be." He picked up the videotape. "I wonder if we have anything that will play this?"

"It's pretty old. We can probably find something in the morning."

"Ray—"

"George, this is old technology. But I'll send somebody out. See if we can find something. In the meantime, how about we do the press release? Let's just tell them we're looking into it." He took a deep breath. "Don't know about you, but I've about had it for the night."

| 39 |

The next night, Blackstone Enterprises threw a huge celebratory party in the Flat Plains hangar. Every member of the press showed up. ("Trust me," Bucky told Jerry, "these guys would *never* miss a free meal.") But they also had half a dozen congressmen, three senators, and two governors, a Medal of Honor winner, five all-pro football players and all-NBA basketball players, and the usual hey-take-my-photograph celebrity crowd.

"Airport must have been swamped," remarked Bucky.

"You said it." Gloria Marcos grinned. "They only have one runway and two gates. Your private airfield is every bit as big, and probably a lot more modern."

"You know, I've been asked to run for the presidency by members of *both* parties," he said. "I wouldn't want to be George Cunningham tonight."

"You don't look that happy," she remarked.

"He's not an evil man," responded Bucky. "I don't know why he lied about it—hell, I don't know why *any* of our presidents lied about it—but I'm sure he had his reasons." He paused. "He didn't try to stop me, you know."

"Could he have?" asked Gloria.

"He could have made it a lot more difficult." Bucky frowned. "I think I'll try to make peace with him in a few weeks."

"And not run against him?" she said with a smile.

"I'm an entrepreneur, not a president."

"Isn't that what almost every president is, too—in a way?" said Gloria.

"Stop right there." Bucky spoke with mock severity. "You convince me of that, and you might spend the next few years dealing with all those jackasses in Congress."

She turned and began walking away.

"Where are you going?" he demanded.

"To get some tape to cover my mouth."

"Good. I was afraid for a minute I'd said something to offend you."

She laughed. "If that was a quitting offense, I'd have been gone two hours after you hired me."

He winked at her and then went around the room chatting with everyone, endlessly explaining every aspect of the mission, taking an occasional sip of the Dom Pérignon and an occasional taste of the Beluga caviar his people had set out for the guests. After another hour, he was getting bored with the same questions, and tired of fighting off less-than-subtle inquiries about his politics and his willingness to run in next year's election (for president, for the Senate or the House, or for the governor's mansion once they could figure out where his legal residence was), and decided he needed a break. He knew that if he went to his own office, he'd be getting a visitor every two minutes once they noticed he was missing, so instead, he went to Jerry Culpepper's much smaller office at the back of the hangar.

He opened the door, stepped through into the semidarkened room, closed the door behind him, and locked it—and suddenly the lights went on.

He turned, startled, to see Jerry sitting at his desk.

"What the hell are *you* doing here?" said Bucky.

"I work here," replied Jerry with a smile.

"I mean, in your office."

"It's your party. I thought I'd let you bask in the glow and answer all the questions. Besides, I don't *like* mob scenes."

"Well, since it's your office, I can hardly throw you out," said Bucky easily. "I hope you don't mind a little company. I've had it with those . . . those . . ." He searched for the right word.

"Sycophants?" suggested Jerry.

"Yes. Except for the ones that plan to stab me in the back—figuratively, of course—as soon as they can."

Jerry indicated a chair. "Have a seat."

"I don't mind if I do," replied Bucky with a smile. He sat down and took a deep breath. "It's cooler in here."

"You're not sharing the air-conditioning with ninety other bodies," noted Jerry.

"And quieter."

The phone on Jerry's desk rang.

"Well, it *was* quieter," said Bucky.

Jerry frowned. "Who the hell would be calling me at ten o'clock at night on a Sunday?"

Bucky smiled. "Why don't you pick it up and find out?"

"Okay," said Jerry, returning the smile. "But given the day and the hour, I may charge you overtime for this." He picked up the receiver. "Hello?"

Bucky could tell someone replied, but Jerry merely frowned. "Who is this?"

Another pause while the man at the other end answered.

"I don't care what you think you know, I won't speak to someone who won't identify himself," said Jerry curtly. Then he paused. "NASA? What part of NASA?"

Bucky gesticulated wildly, and Jerry said, "Hang on. I'm going to put you on hold for just a minute."

He hit a button on the phone and turned to Bucky. "What is it?"

"This is a guy from NASA?"

Jerry nodded. "Probably."

"Probably?" repeated Bucky.

"He says he's a friend of NASA."

"There could be a lot of reasons he won't identify himself," said Bucky. "Put it on speaker, so I can hear it, too. I won't interrupt, but let's find out what he wants."

"A job, probably," said Jerry.

Bucky just stared at him.

"Okay, okay, you're the boss." He put the phone on speaker and took it off hold. "Sorry for the delay. Now, what can I do for you?"

"Nothing," said the voice. "But maybe I can do something for you, Mr. Culpepper."

"But you won't tell me your name?"

"Hear me out, and you'll know why. As I told you, I'm a friend of NASA. I think it's terrible the way they've treated the Agency—the way they turned their backs on the Moon half a century ago and even gave up the shuttle. Just terrible!"

"You'll get no disagreement from me," said Jerry. "Is that what this call is about?"

"That's the *reason* for it," said the man. "It's not the *gist* of it."

"I don't want to be rude, but it's after ten o'clock, and I was up half of the last two nights. I'm tired, and I don't even know who I'm talking to, so can we get to the point, please?"

"I'm coming to it, Mr. Culpepper. You know what they found on the Moon, right?"

"Of course I do," said Jerry in bored tones. "It's in the next room."

"Impressive, isn't it?"

Jerry frowned. "Yeah, it's impressive. So?"

"So do you know what it is?"

"Part of some kind of dome, probably," answered Jerry, starting to get annoyed. "You got any other questions?"

"Just one. Do you know what it really is, and why it's been kept secret all these years?"

Suddenly, Bucky leaned forward, and Jerry tensed.

"Why don't you tell me?"

"That would be too easy for you and too dangerous for me," said the voice. "But you can find the answer if you want it."

"Of course I want it."

"Good."

"So where is it?" demanded Jerry.

"It's well hidden," said the voice.

"Okay, it's well hidden," said Jerry. *"Where?"*

"Just think about it, Mr. Culpepper. If you had something that valuable, where would you hide it?"

"In my safe-deposit box," said Jerry.

"Don't be a fool, Mr. Culpepper. This is a matter of world-wide importance. Just ask yourself—"

"I told you: I'd put it in a bank."

"Let me finish," said the voice. "Banks get robbed all the time."

"Okay," said Jerry. "What should I ask myself?"

"What would Sherlock Holmes do?"

"He'd solve the problem," said Jerry irritably.

"Don't be obtuse, Mr. Culpepper. You have your answer."

"*What* answer, damn it!" snapped Jerry, but the *click!* at the other end of the line was audible even to Bucky.

Jerry hung up. "So what do you make of it?" asked Bucky. "Did you recognize the voice?"

Jerry shook his head. "No." He paused. "But it didn't sound like a crank call."

"I agree. In any case, we've got to follow it up."

"Follow it *where*?" asked Jerry in frustration.

"I don't know," admitted Bucky. "*Yet.*"

"I don't know where the devil we can start."

"With the clue," said Bucky.

"*What* clue?" Jerry practically yelled.

"You heard him: What would Sherlock Holmes do?"

"And you heard my answer: He'd solve the damned problem!"

"Ah . . . but *how*?" said Bucky. "*That* was the clue."

"I don't understand you any more than I understood him."

"It's fascinating, Jerry. I don't know what we've found, what we've brought back. A couple of curved metal panels, that's all. But there's an answer *somewhere*, and this phone call may be the key to it. In other words, it's a two-step process. First, we figure out what the hell he was talking about, where this mysterious *something* is hidden. Then we find it, get our hands on it, and hopefully solve the mystery of what they've been hiding from us all these years."

"You make it sound simple," said Jerry.

"It can't be simple, or someone would have figured it out in the past half century."

"Not necessarily," replied Jerry. "For most of that time, no one knew there was anything to be discovered, or that Myshko had landed on the Moon."

"Then, since *we* know it, it shouldn't be that difficult, should it?" said Bucky.

Jerry just stared at his employer. *Now I know why you're the billionaire, and I'm the employee,* he thought. *You love a challenge, you come alive with one, and I just want it to go away.*

"Have you read much Holmes?" asked Bucky.

"A little."

"And you didn't recognize the voice?"

"No," said Jerry, frowning. "Why?"

"Because if he doesn't know you, he can't assume you're familiar with the canon, that you know all the stories inside out. So that has to be a simpler clue than we thought at first."

"I don't see anything simple about it."

"What characters do you know from Sherlock Holmes?" asked Bucky. "Besides Holmes, Watson, and their landlord, what was her name? Ah! Mrs. Hudson! Okay, who else do you know?"

"Professor Moriarty, of course," said Jerry. "Irene Adler." He frowned. "Moriarty, Adler . . ." He shook his head. "That's it."

Suddenly, Bucky was grinning like the cat that had swallowed the canary.

"Son of a bitch!" exclaimed Jerry. "You *know*! Just from that, you know!"

"I think so," said Bucky.

"Well?" said Jerry. He could barely control his voice.

"I think almost everyone knows Moriarty and Irene Adler. A few might also know Colonel Sebastian Moran, but you didn't, and he couldn't assume you did. But even if you've never read the books, one or the other is in more than half the movies. Hell, they were both in a Broadway musical called *Baker Street* a few years before Armstrong landed on the Moon."

"How do you know that?"

Bucky smiled. "I've always had a passion for Mr. Holmes."

"So what's the answer?" persisted Jerry.

"Consider this: Moriarty was even more of an egomaniac than Holmes was. He never hid anything from Holmes. He wanted Holmes to know what he was doing and dared the detective to stop him. But Irene Adler, despite the fact that the movies loved her, appeared in only one story. She had some love letters and was blackmailing the king of Bohemia with them, and Holmes was paid to get them back. He failed."

"Why?"

"Because she was as smart as he was, and she realized that the very best place to hide something everyone's searching for is in plain sight." Bucky paused. "She had them stashed behind a sliding panel out in the living room, where you might keep a few glasses. The problem is that we need *your* brainpower on this, not mine. You're the one he spoke to, so the clue is for you."

Jerry sat motionless for a full minute. Finally, he responded. "Son of a bitch!"

"You *know*!" said Bucky excitedly.

Jerry nodded. "I think so."

"Well? Where is it?"

"Can your private jet get me to Huntsville, Alabama, first thing in the morning?"

"No," said Bucky, and before Jerry could protest he added: "But it can get *us* there."

"Okay, but I don't think they'll let you in."

"In where?" asked Bucky.

"The Huntsville Archives."

"Everybody knows you're working for *me* now. What makes you think they'll let *you* in?"

"Because I just may have a secret weapon. I'll let you know tomorrow morning whether I can manage it."

"What are you going to do?"

"Call Mary. My old boss."

"You think she'll help?"

He thought about it. "Yes," he said. "I'd be surprised if she didn't."

| 40 |

Jerry and Bucky drove up to the NASA Archives in a rented car.

"Jason Brent is going to kill me for leaving him behind if someone else doesn't kill me first," noted Bucky wryly.

"I'll see if I can get you in," said Jerry, opening his door. "It'll be easier if they don't recognize you."

"If they don't recognize me, I hate to think how many hundreds of millions of dollars I've wasted."

"No kidding, Bucky," said Jerry. "You're not the government's favorite person this week. Let me handle it."

Bucky nodded and fell into step behind Jerry, who climbed the stone steps and approached the two armed guards at the front entrance.

"May I help you, sir?" said one of them, with an expression that implied that helping the visitors wasn't first on his list of priorities.

"My name is Jerry Culpepper. I used to work for NASA. I believe Mary Gridley has cleared me to enter."

"I'll have to check on that, sir."

The guard pulled out a communicator and spoke into it in low tones, then waited for an answer. Bucky looked around at the utilitarian buildings of the Marshall Space Flight Center, their blandness contrasted with the rockets, the shuttle, and the landers on display.

The guard got his answer and nodded. "Welcome to the Archives, Mr. Culpepper. You have been cleared."

"I assume my assistant can accompany me," said Jerry, indicating Bucky.

The guard frowned. "I don't know anything about an assistant, sir."

"Damn it," said Jerry, trying to look annoyed rather than terrorized at the consequences of sneaking the notorious Morgan Blackstone into the building. "I expressly said I would be bringing him along."

"Hold on, sir," said the guard, pulling out his communicator again. "I'll have my superior check with Ms. Gridley."

"Good," said Jerry, wondering what the penalty was for lying to an archive guard.

There was a pause that stretched from one to two to three minutes. Finally the guard pocketed the device and looked up at Jerry.

"Ms. Gridley is away from her desk at the moment," he announced. He stared at Bucky, but there was no sign of recognition on his face. "All right," he said at last. "I suppose there's no harm. After all, he works for you, and you've been cleared."

"Thank you," said Jerry.

He entered the building, followed by Bucky.

"I thought this was a public building," said Bucky, when they were out of earshot. "Why do you need permission to enter it?"

"There's a ton of stuff that collectors would love to get their hands on," answered Jerry, "either to keep or sell on the black market."

"Makes sense," said Bucky, looking around.

"Okay," said Jerry, "I got us this far. Whatever we want is in the building—or at least is *probably* here." He grimaced. "But it's a big building. Where do we start?"

They looked around at cubicles filled with boxes and crates. "They must have a section devoted to the Apollo program," said Bucky.

They walked over to a backlit floor plan and located it.

"That was easy enough," said Jerry. "Look, they have a section designated *Myshko mission*."

He began walking, but Bucky stood still, lost in thought.

"What is it?" asked Jerry, returning to him.

"That's too easy," answered Bucky. "I've been telling the public about Myshko for more than a month now. We can look later if we don't find something, but all that's going to be is records of *our* Moon mission. And probably the controversy preceding it."

"Where the hell else would it be?"

"Not with Apollo XI," replied Bucky. "Everyone and his brother would have headed straight to that display."

"I don't know," said Jerry dubiously. "We're not here on a hunch. Someone called and told me to come here."

Bucky smiled. "He told you to go *somewhere* to find *something*. The rest was pure Holmesian deduction."

"Okay, Sherlock," said Jerry in frustration. "Where *should* we be looking?"

"I'm working on it."

"Let's at least walk over to the Apollo section while you're thinking. The farther we get from the entrance, the less likely they are to pull you out of here if Mary calls back and says she doesn't know anything about you."

"Lead the way, Watson," said Bucky.

They soon reached the lineup of Apollo cubicles, with crates filled with material, logs, helmets, photos, occasionally a captain's chair or a Yankees baseball cap or a Bible. Exhibits ranged from the first suborbital flight to the very last Moon landing. Jerry walked over to the Myshko area, scrutinized the content tags thoroughly, opened more boxes, but couldn't find anything out of the ordinary. The tags were accurate. "It's just what you said, Bucky. Could we have been wrong?"

Bucky shook his head. "You got the call last night. The government's had a month to go over every inch of the Myshko display, all the messages, transcripts, video coverage, everything. It was never going to be here."

"You suddenly look very smug," said Jerry. "What do you think you know?"

"The same thing *you* know," said Bucky.

"What?" Jerry almost shouted.

"There were *two* Moon flights involved in this. Walker's was probably given the job of destroying the dome."

"Walker!" exclaimed Jerry, snapping his fingers. "Of course!" They quickly moved to the Walker exhibit.

They scanned the content descriptions and again found nothing of immediate interest, and no indication of inaccuracy. "Damn!" said Jerry. "I thought we had it! But I just don't see anything."

"Don't be so sure," said Bucky. "What are we looking for?" Jerry looked blank. "I don't know," he admitted.

"Neither do I. So let's look for what doesn't belong."

They stayed in the Walker cubicle and began a methodical search. After another ten minutes, Jerry uncovered a rectangular cardboard box at the bottom of a black trunk that was supposed to contain exclusively navigation equipment. A paper label marked CASSEGRAIN was attached to the lid. It was about the size of a coffee-table book. "Bingo!" he whispered.

Bucky immediately joined him.

"I wonder what it is," mused Jerry. It was taped shut.

"We might as well take a look at it right here," said Bucky. "They're never going to let us walk out with it."

"Keep an eye out for the guards," said Jerry. He opened one end of the box carefully while Bucky turned his back to him and tried to conceal what he was doing from any hidden security cameras.

"What have you got?" asked Bucky after a moment.

"I don't know," said Jerry. "It looks for all the world like an antique plate."

Bucky frowned. "Like a dinner plate?"

"No, it's rectangular, and a lot longer. And there's writing on it."

Bucky reached into his pocket and pulled out his state-of-the-art cell phone. "Use this," he said, holding it behind him until Jerry grabbed it. "It's got to be better than whatever you've got. At least, for what it cost, it damned well better be."

"Nothing on the back," muttered Jerry. "I'll take one shot of that, and six or seven of the face with the writing."

"Face? There's a face?"

"I meant the front of the plate," said Jerry. And, after a moment: "Okay, done. Let me slip it back in its box . . . Putting the box back. All right, let's get the hell out of here."

"Give me back my phone," said Bucky, holding out a hand.

Jerry handed it to him.

"Okay, let's hit the men's room."

"Can't it wait?" said Jerry.

"No."

They found a men's room and entered, and Bucky immediately took off his left shoe.

Jerry stared and frowned. "You're a big man. Why the devil are you wearing lifts?"

"Everyone has a use for falsies," replied Bucky with a grin. He manipulated the sole, and suddenly a compartment opened in the sole and heel, and he inserted the thin cell phone. Then he closed the secret compartment. "You wouldn't believe how handy that's been on my trips around the world." He walked to the door. "Okay, let's go."

Jerry kept expecting to be stopped with almost every step he took, but they made it out of the building, and a moment later a government chauffeur brought their car around. They were at the Huntsville airfield in a matter of minutes, and three hours later they were in Jerry's office at Blackstone Enterprises with Gloria Marcos, Jason Brent, and Sabina Marinova, awaiting the results from the linguistics experts Bucky had hired to decipher the inscription on the plate.

Finally, the wizened little man who was in charge of the analysis effort entered the room, with blown-up copies of the photographs in his hand.

"Well, Peter?" said Bucky. "Couldn't do a damned thing with it, could you?"

"We translated it," he said.

Bucky frowned. "You translated a totally alien language in just a few hours? Why do I have some difficulty believing that?"

"It's not an alien language," replied Peter. "I wish I could have gotten my hands on that plate."

"For what it's worth, there were no marks on it," offered Jerry. "To tell you the truth, it looked, well, almost *new*."

"It would. No air up there. Nothing ages." He handed a sheet of paper to Bucky. "Here you go, with a copy."

"What language is it?" asked Bucky, staring at the paper. "It's all Greek to me."

The man smiled. "To me, too."

Bucky frowned. "What are you saying?"

"It's Greek. A form that was used about two millennia ago, maybe two and a half."

"Greek," repeated Bucky.

The man nodded. "Yes."

"You're absolutely sure?"

"There's no mistake, sir."

"Thanks, Peter. There'll be a bonus added to your fee."

"Thank *you*, Mr. Blackstone."

"The bonus is 50 percent for your work, and 50 percent for your silence. You never saw this inscription, never heard of it, until I say otherwise."

The man nodded. "Is that all?"

"Yeah. Good job."

The man turned and left the office.

"Jerry, buy me some airtime," said Bucky.

"When and how much?" asked Jerry.

"As soon as you can, and all that you can."

"I'll get working on it," said Jerry, without moving. "I assume you want to know what it says?"

"Yes. That would be nice."

Gloria was trying to get a look at the translation.

"Okay," said Bucky. He moved away from Gloria and looked again at the translation. "It seems to be a warning. It says that no civilization, anywhere—and I assume that means anywhere in the galaxy, or maybe the universe—has been known to survive the advance of technology." He read further, frowning. "They all collapse. They fight wars. Or they abolish individual death."

"Individual death?" repeated Sabina. "That's a *bad* thing?"

"Evidently it guarantees stagnation. I'm not sure. It's a short message. It doesn't specify." He paused. "Anyway, it says that no technological civilization, anywhere, has ever grown old."

"Gracefully?" asked Sabina.

Bucky shook his head. "At all. They say the oldest known high-tech society was extinct within a thousand years."

"That doesn't make any sense," said Sabina. "*They* survived. They did more than survive. They obviously had an interstellar ship of some kind."

"That's the end of the message," replied Bucky, staring at it. "They say they were looking for a place to start over again, that the world they came from is a shambles."

Jerry headed for the door. "That's enough bad news for one day," he said.

When he was gone, they were silent for a minute. Then Bucky, who had been sitting on the edge of his desk, laid the papers down and stood up. "Do you realize what that means?"

"That we've lived so long, we've beaten the odds?" suggested Jason.

Bucky shook his head impatiently. "Sabina? Gloria?"

He received two blank expressions.

"It means at least one of them visited the Earth," he said. "How the hell else would they learn ancient Greek?"

"That's right!" exclaimed Gloria.

"I'll be damned!" said Jason.

"We were too primitive for the message to have any meaning back then," continued Bucky. "I mean, hell, Moses or Caesar might have been walking around in those days. So they left it on the Moon. If we never reached the Moon, we weren't high-tech enough for the message to have any meaning. But if we found it . . ." He let his voice trail off.

"What happened to *them*, I wonder?" said Sabina.

Bucky shrugged. "Probably they found a more hospitable world. Better climate, better atmosphere, fewer germs and viruses that could wipe them out. I won't say we'll never know, but we won't know until we can reach the stars and find them."

"It's fascinating, isn't it?" said Sabina.

"Yes, it is." Bucky picked up the translation and handed it to Gloria. "Put this in the safe—the one in my suite."

"Right." She took it from him and headed off.

"Damn!" said Bucky excitedly. "Greek! Who'd have thought it?"

"We were actually visited," said Sabina. "Isn't that remarkable?"

"It's going to be more remarkable when I go on television and tell the world," said Bucky. "And prove to them that the White House is *still* lying to them!"

He went behind his desk, sat down in his leather chair, opened a drawer, and pulled out a cigar.

"Do you have to do that?" asked Sabina, making a face.

"I have a victory cigar about once every six or seven years," said Bucky, taking a puff. "And this is my biggest victory of all."

"Most people take victory *drinks*," she suggested hopefully.

"I want my head to be totally clear when I address the public," he answered.

Jerry entered the office, looking pleased with himself.

"Well?" asked Bucky.

"Nine o'clock tonight, Eastern time," said Jerry. "I bought you time on ABC; the other two majors won't change their schedules to accommodate you."

"They're going to wish they had," replied Bucky confidently. "This speech will demote them to the minors."

"Every cable network is covering it as a news event," continued Jerry. He flashed a sudden grin. "Even the SyFy Network wants to cover it. They have no idea what you'll be talking about—none of them do—but they're sure it's about the Moon."

"Sign 'em up," said Bucky. "Hell, they've always believed in this stuff. The rest of the world hasn't—but they will after tonight."

Gloria returned from Bucky's suite. "Okay, it's locked away," she announced.

"Good," said Bucky. "I don't figure to lose it between here and the studio down on the second floor, but I feel better with a copy of it there. I don't know who our secret benefactor was, but I'd bet half my fortune that if we went back to the Archives tomorrow, it wouldn't be there."

"What makes you say that?" asked Sabina.

"It wasn't *that* difficult to find once we doped out where to look," answered Bucky. "It couldn't have gone unnoticed all these years. My guess is that it's back where it came from, some attic or underground vault that maybe three people in the world know about."

"I hadn't thought of it that way," admitted Jerry. "But now that you say it, it makes sense."

"That's because you're not quite the devious bastard that I am," said Bucky with a chuckle.

"Thank goodness." Jerry returned his smile.

"Well," said Gloria, "I'd better make sure the studio's spick-and-span and ready for the press."

"No press," said Jerry. "This is going out on the airwaves. It's a speech, not an interview or a press conference." He turned to Bucky. "At least, I *think* that's what it is. You didn't say anything about wanting questions."

"That's fine. This announcement speaks for itself." Bucky frowned. "I'll show photos of the plate, of course—we'll have the lab make 'em even bigger before the speech—but I wish I had the plate as well."

"You know what would have happened if we'd tried to walk off with it," said Jerry.

"Yeah," acknowledged Bucky. "Everyone could visit us on Sundays for the next fifty years."

"The plate is secondary," said Sabina. "The important thing is the message."

"Yeah, of course it is," said Bucky. He smiled. "At least I'm not announcing their pending conquest of the Earth."

"Or that the Sun is going nova," added Gloria.

"Or that there really are four-armed green swordsmen on Mars," said Jason.

"Yeah, there are worse messages to read," agreed Bucky.

Then, suddenly, he froze.

"Bucky," said Jerry, "are you okay?"

"Leave him alone," said Gloria quickly. "I've seen him like this a couple of times before."

"He looks like he's having a stroke," said Sabina, also worried.

"He's all right, believe me," insisted Gloria.

"Damn!" snapped Bucky, coming back to life.

"Are you okay?" asked Jerry solicitously.

"I am definitely *not* okay," growled Bucky, starting to pace back and forth across the office. Suddenly, he stopped and turned to Jerry. "Cancel the telecast."

"Are you crazy?"

"You heard me. Cancel it. If ABC won't return our money, let 'em keep it."

"But—"

"Just do it! Gloria, contact my pilot. Have him meet me at the corporate jet in an hour. Then you'll have to make a very private phone call; I'll be here so I can cut in and vouch for who you are if necessary."

"Where are we going, Boss?" asked Jason.

"You're not going anywhere," said Bucky. "This is something I have to do alone."

41

"So what do you think, George? We should have heard something by now."

Cunningham sat back. He'd just finished a conference with the Pentagon people. The brass were unhappy. Tired of congressmen trying to force weapons they didn't need down their throats to keep the armaments people in their home states happy. "We need better detection equipment," General Maybury had complained. "For roadside bombs. Nelson tells us sure, they're getting to it, but let's concentrate for now on that new upgraded jet CRY has developed." He was referring to Brig Nelson, head of the Senate Armed Services Committee.

Maybury and his people knew Cunningham had limited control over the situation, but they needed to vent. So they brought it to him. One more advantage of divided government.

The president looked across the desk at Ray. "We'll be okay," he said. "Blackstone bought time on ABC tonight. So they're obviously on board."

"But he canceled."

"He's trying to make up his mind what he wants to say. Relax."

"Not till I'm sure we're clear of this."

"Hey, Ray, take it easy. You know, you tend to be a bit pessimistic. You didn't even think they'd bite." They'd just finished watching security-camera images of Jerry and Blackstone going through the archives. Taking pictures of the Greek plate. It was perfect.

Ray had a worried look in his eyes. "I knew we'd be able to manage Jerry okay. He tends to think well of everybody. I just had my doubts about getting it past Blackstone. That son of a bitch trusts no one. And I'm still surprised they figured out the Holmes reference. *I* wouldn't have had any idea what Lou was talking about."

Lou, of course, was the staff member who'd made the call. And the president couldn't resist gloating. "We couldn't just phone and tell him where to look. Too simple. It would likely have aroused their suspicions. I wanted Blackstone to lock onto something else rather than asking himself whether the call was genuine."

"I know all that, George. But what made you think he'd understand?"

"Bucky was once a member of the Tuscaloosa Baker Street Irregulars. No way he could miss it."

Ray sighed. "Well, you were obviously right. I'll tell you, I feel a lot better than I did this morning when we came in. I think we got lucky. I wasn't sure what we'd have done if he hadn't known what we were talking about. Or, worse, hadn't bought the story. If he came after us."

Cunningham didn't even like to think about it. This was not a good time. He was surrounded by problems. The deteriorating state of public education. The blowback from shutting down large chunks of military spending. Global epidemics. Widespread hunger. Problems with fresh water. Continuing climate deterioration. Still, for one day, *this* day, he could celebrate.

He looked across the office at the ancient VHS unit that had been brought in to play the videotape. The tape itself was now locked in the bottom drawer of his desk, along with the second plate. "He'll spread the story because he believed it. Because it'll make him look good. Proves he was right, and we were wrong. That's all he cares about. He doesn't give a damn about collapsing civilizations, or whether that knowledge might have had a deleterious effect on the nation. Whether it might have discouraged people already struggling with an apparently endless war, or whether right now it will have a negative effect on a nation still trying to get clear of this god-awful economy."

"Well, you were right, George. I just didn't think they'd buy it. The average guy in the street hears that worlds are falling apart everywhere, and he says it's a shame, but by the way, how'd the Giants make out last night? That's the way we are. And that's what I don't understand. If Nixon was going to make up a story, why didn't he do something that *would* shake everybody up? Like maybe a warning against an impending alien invasion?"

"Simple enough, Ray. He wanted to scare the Russians into keeping quiet. Alien invaders wouldn't have accomplished that."

"I still can't believe he thought it would work. But I guess it did."

"I doubt it would have worked with ordinary Russians, who would probably have responded the same way we would. But the leaders bought into it. Hell, Ray, Brezhnev and Kosygin were Communists. Materialists. Not politicians, like Tricky Dick. They'd come to power in a different way, and they apparently didn't know their own people very well. Anyhow, they wouldn't have liked the idea that we were on the Moon already, so sure, they had every reason to join in the cover-up. And nothing to lose."

The president stared at the ancient VHS unit.

Nixon had been seated at a desk in front of an open window. Palm trees were visible, and birds sang. Despite the placid environment, he was clearly troubled.

"Mr. President," he'd said, looking out of the screen, "I hope I haven't caused any undue difficulty for you, but I was forced to take action." He picked up a pen and put it back down. "As you may be aware, we learned from probes toward the end of the Johnson administration that there was a structure, a dome, on the far side of the Moon.

"I was informed by President Johnson during a conference in December 1968, during his final weeks in office. At that time, he indicated that he had been uncertain how to respond, that they knew there'd been no Soviet missions to the Moon, and that consequently there was only one explanation for the dome. We'd been visited.

"President Johnson had classified the information on the highest level and set in motion a secret lunar mission to deter-

mine the nature of the object. He did not know whether it could
be made to work. And he was leaving office. Ultimately it would
be my responsibility. Whatever my decision, whether I proceeded with it, or canceled it, he told me, I should feel free to
consult with him. He said he would render any assistance he
could. And he would support whatever decision I made."

The former president sat quietly for a moment, looking back
over that conversation. "I thought he was kidding. I really
thought it was some kind of joke. And he got annoyed. We were
alone in the Oval Office and he'd begun by congratulating me
on my victory, and telling me how he hoped I'd have better luck
than he did with the war. His voice shook when he mentioned
that. 'End it,' he told me. 'Doesn't matter how you do it, but get
out of that hellhole.'

"He told me he understood that our views of how the country
should work were at odds, but that he hoped I would not oppose
the Great Society measures he had taken. Then he told me about
the dome.

"I consented to the go-ahead order. On January 15, 1969, two
of our astronauts landed near the Cassegrain Crater and approached the dome. It wasn't especially big. About the size of a
single-story house. The astronauts, Sidney Myshko and Brian
Peters, walked right up to it. We have the videos from the landing stored at the museum, filed under *riverboat KYB*.

"The thing had a door. It looked as if one of them touched a
doorbell. I couldn't tell them apart in their space suits. But they
touched something, and the door slid up. Into the dome." He
looked almost dazed.

"It was dark inside. They flashed lights around, and we saw
a small table. Otherwise, the place was empty. Not a goddam
thing. So they walked over to the table. There was a plaque on
it. Silver-colored metal on a dark base. The lighting wasn't
good, and they were right on top of it before I realized there was
a message on the plaque. In a strange language.

"And that was all there was. They brought the table and the
plaque home. The table is located in a secure storage area at
the Presidential Library in Yorba Linda. They don't know they
have it, but its numerical designator is AY775. You already have
the plaque in your possession.

"Actually, there will be two plaques in the package. One is

in Greek, the other in Aramaic. The Greek plaque was put together by us for the sole purpose of getting the Russians on board. In the end, we didn't use it. I didn't think it would work, and it seemed better to tell them the truth. So that's what we did. When they learned what it was, they got seriously scared. They thought if the word got out, it might destabilize us. The last thing they needed was a destabilized United States. And in all these years, they've never said a word.

"The Aramaic plaque, of course, is the one we found. And the message is different."

Cunningham had a copy of the translation on his desk:

Intelligent life is rare. When we discovered your cities, your boats, your dwellings, we wanted to join with you in mutual celebration. Our first action was to send an ambassador. But you killed him. Without provocation. Our judgment was perhaps hasty. And in error. We should not have trusted you. Nevertheless, we wish you good fortune. By the time you reach this place, if indeed you ever do, we hope you will have changed.

"My translator," continued Nixon, "informed me that the language dated from about the first century A.D. And Aramaic, as you may know, was the language in Israel from about 500 B.C. to A.D. 70." He stopped and waited, as if Cunningham needed a moment to get the point. "If we had released that information, you know the conclusion people would have jumped to. We were already in the midst of a war, and the country was coming apart. The last thing I needed, on top of everything else, was to have a major religious battle break out. So I kept it quiet. NASA sent a second mission to destroy the dome, to blow it apart and bury it.

"If the truth hasn't already come out, Mr. President, I urge you to restrain it as best you can. For the good of the nation."

Cunningham had stopped it there.

"It was the right move," said Ray.

"I agree."

Ray was trying to appear reassuring, but Cunningham knew him too well. He was getting ready to attempt a sale. "Times have changed," he said.

"I suppose. We don't have a war on our hands."

"We have an obligation to be honest with the nation."

"No."

"You won't even consider it?"

"No. I won't."

"George, this is the scientific discovery of the age. You can't continue to hide this."

"Let it go, Ray."

"But why not do it? You wouldn't have to take a stand. Just release the data. People will draw their own conclusions about it. If organized religion takes a hit, so be it. It causes half the problems in the world, anyhow."

"And maybe eases the other half. Look, Ray, life can be a tough ride. For a lot of people, their religion is all they have to hang on to. We're not going to undermine that."

"It's going to happen eventually. You've seen the numbers."

"Fine. Whatever happens, happens. First off, we don't know the truth. Secondly, religion may or may not disappear from people's lives. But if it does, I won't be party to it."

"Okay. You're the president."

"None of this gets beyond this office. Right?"

"Of course not. I won't say anything. But be aware that the people at the Nixon Museum will almost certainly let the press know you got a package from Mr. Nixon. And that it had something to do—"

"If we have to take some heat, we will." Cunningham restarted the program.

Nixon straightened his shoulders. "One final point I'd like to make, Mr. President. When the plaque first came into my hands, I had to find someone to translate. We weren't even sure what the language was. John—John Ehrlichman—had a friend who was a professor at George Washington University. I forget his name. But he did the translation for us.

"He never knew how we'd acquired the plate. Or at least, he didn't unless John told him. But I doubt very much that happened." He thought about it. Shook his head. "No. No chance. In any event he—the professor—assured us that none of what he'd seen would go any further. But we didn't realize he'd made notes. Kept them, despite his assurances no written record would be made.

"We put the plate away, intending it should never see the light of day. I'd thought about destroying it, but that seemed inappropriate." He stopped, and he seemed focused on another time. Another place.

"In June 1972, I got a call from John. The professor had informed him that he'd lost materials relating to the translation. Worse, he'd been socializing with the Democrats. With Larry O'Brien, and he thought he'd left the briefcase in his office. At the Watergate. O'Brien claimed he knew nothing about it.

"I have no idea who I may be speaking to, or how long it has been since I left the stage. It may be twenty years. It may be centuries. But I want to make the statement to you that I could never make to the American people: The reason for the break-in had nothing to do with politics. It was for the benefit of the nation. For that reason and no other.

"I should add that O'Brien, it turned out, did not have the briefcase. The idiot professor had left it in the hotel restaurant. But the guys who went in, and paid the price, never said anything. They never mentioned the professor's notes." He looked out at Cunningham. "I owe them. The country owes them."

And the screen went blank.

Ray sat back in his chair. "So where do we go from here, George?"

"We've arrived at the last act, Ray. It's over. Blackstone will give the voters an answer. He knows we handed it to him. He won't be able to figure out why, but he's indebted to us, and he knows it. So I don't think we'll take too much heat from him." Cunningham got up and walked over to the window. The sky was heavy with clouds. No Moon that night. "We'll announce tomorrow that Blackstone probably has it right. The people from the museum will think that's what was in the package. And it's done."

"Well, I hope you're right." Ray extended his right hand. "Congratulations, Mr. President."

The president was going over legislation that had just arrived for his signature when Kim called him. "Mr. President," she said,

"Mr. Blackstone is on the line. I don't know how he got this number, but—"

"It's okay, Kim. Have him hold for three minutes, then put him through."

Cunningham went back to reading a bill to upgrade the national parks. Or, perhaps more accurately, trying to read it. He was uneasy about the call. And he was looking at his watch when the phone began blinking again. He pressed the button and Blackstone's image appeared on-screen. "Mr. President," he said. "We should talk."

| **42** |

Two Secret Service men ushered Bucky into the Oval Office, then took up positions on each side of the doorway.

"You don't want them here," said Bucky, indicating the two men. "What we have to discuss is private."

Cunningham, seated behind the large mahogany desk, faced the Secret Service men and nodded.

"But, sir—"

"He's an old friend," said Cunningham.

"Frisk me first if it'll make you feel any better," added Bucky.

"We already did, sir," said one of them.

Bucky looked surprised. "When?"

"Electronically," came the answer. "When you entered the White House, and again when you entered the office."

"Isn't science wonderful?" said Bucky. "Not only can we reach the Moon, but we can frisk a man without touching him."

The two men looked at Cunningham questioningly.

"It's all right," he said. "Leave us."

They exited, closing the door behind them.

"I'm not so naïve to think that this isn't being recorded on both audio and video," said Bucky when they were alone. "Just make sure you get to the tapes or disks or whatever the hell you're using before anyone else does."

"It can be arranged," said Cunningham. "Perhaps you'd care to tell me why you think it will be necessary. And please be quick about it. I have a meeting in ten minutes."

"Cancel it."

"No one gives orders to the president of the United States," said Cunningham firmly.

"Then I'm *requesting* you to cancel it. Please."

"Now look here, Mr. Blackstone—"

"Bucky."

"Now look here, Bucky, I'm giving you a private meeting on something like three hours' notice. There are senators who have been waiting four and five months for one. So let's get to the point. You made it to the Moon and you proved someone was there ahead of you. I congratulate you for your remarkable achievement, and I hasten to point out that I was as unaware of what you discovered as the rest of the world. Now, what is the purpose of this meeting?"

Bucky smiled. "Very well said. It really tempts me to vote for you next time." He indicated a chair opposite Cunningham's desk. "May I sit down?"

The president nodded.

"There's just one little problem," continued Bucky.

"Oh?"

"Jerry Culpepper got a mysterious phone call, directing him—and me—to the NASA Archives, where, thanks to his ability to decipher a really vague clue, we found a truly remarkable plate that Sidney Myshko reportedly brought back from the Moon in January of 1969." He pulled a folded paper out of the lapel pocket of his suit and placed it on the desk. "Here's a photo of it."

"Amazing!" said Cunningham, picking the photo up and studying it.

"You know what's the most amazing thing of all, Mr. President?" said Bucky.

"No. What?"

"It's a phony." The smile vanished. "And *that* means that the White House planted it for us to find."

"Damn it, Mr. Blackstone! I didn't know Myshko had landed

until you came back with the proof. I had no idea that there had been any deception, I didn't even believe in it until yesterday, and I had no previous knowledge of this so-called plate."

"Maybe some of that is true," said Bucky. Before Cunningham could protest, he continued: "Maybe *all* of it is. And do you know what, Mr. President? It doesn't matter. Who's the public going to believe? A government that's been lying to them for half a century, or a man who went to the Moon and *proved* they were lying? So let's talk turkey."

"Calm down, Mr. Blackstone."

"Bucky, damn it."

"Bucky," corrected Cunningham. "Suppose you tell me what you're talking about and why you think the plate is a fake."

"Ah, yes—the plate that no one spotted for fifty years but that took Jerry Culpepper and me less than twenty minutes to find and photograph."

"You're a bright man," said Cunningham. "The men and women who work at Marshall are minimum-wage civil servants."

"Rubbish," scoffed Bucky. "The men and women who work there are retired officers for the most part. Anyway, we brought the photos back to the office and had the inscription translated."

"And what did it say?"

"It was a gentle warning from a benevolent star-faring race, cautioning us against the dangers of technology, pointing out that advanced civilizations have a limited life expectancy. It was a very considerate, caring message. Almost pastoral, in a sense." He paused, and the smile returned. "And I almost bought it. I even reserved television time. And then it occurred to me: Why would anyone hide this message? Why would they lie about it for fifty years? Hell, why wouldn't any president drag it along to nuclear disarmament talks? You want to balance the budget? Show this to the public, and they'll beg you to gut the Pentagon. This isn't the kind of thing you hide, Mr. President. It's the kind of thing you display, and make political capital of. No president in his right mind would keep this secret." The smile became less amused and more self-satisfied. "And that means it was planted for me to find. Two thousand years old, my ass!" he snorted. "More likely it's two months old."

"Fifty years, to be exact," answered Cunningham.

"Fifty?" said Bucky, surprised not at the answer but that Cunningham was willing to give it to him. "What's really being covered up?"

Cunningham stared at him, as if trying to make up his mind.

"You can tell me now," added Bucky, "or you can tell the world after I go public with what I know."

Finally, Cunningham, his mind made up, nodded and pulled a very old VHS tape out of his desk drawer. "Go put this in the machine," he said, handing it to Bucky and indicating the tape deck.

Bucky inserted the tape, turned on the monitor, hit PLAY, and watched transfixed as Richard Nixon's image appeared and said, "Mr. President, I hope I haven't caused any undue difficulty for you, but I was forced to take action . . ."

———————

When it was over, Bucky sat silently frowning.

"Do you understand now?" said Cunningham. "I was only made aware of this yesterday, but I have to think he made the right decision."

"You know the odds against this *ambassador* being the person you think it was must be a couple of thousand to one," said Bucky. "They killed a lot of people back then."

"If you were Nixon, or me, would you take the chance?" asked Cunningham.

"I'm glad I'm not you," said Bucky earnestly.

"What are you going to do now?"

"I don't know," admitted Bucky. "I'll have to give it some thought—a *lot* of thought." He got to his feet and extended his hand to the man on the other side of the desk. "But believe it or not, I'm a patriot."

"I hope you are," said Cunningham.

| EPILOGUE |

Three days had passed, and Bucky stood in the studio of Blackstone Enterprises, facing more than two hundred members of the national and international media. Since meeting with Cunningham, he'd made a trip to Huntsville accompanied by Jerry Culpepper and Ray Chambers, called the Moon flight crew back from their vacations, and arranged, through Cunningham's influence, to get airtime on all the public and cable networks.

"Thirty seconds, Mr. Blackstone . . . twenty . . . ten . . ."

Bucky gathered Ben Gaines, Marcia Neimark, and Phil Bassinger behind him, and faced the cameras.

"Three . . . two . . . one . . . you're on."

Bucky blinked once as the lights became even brighter, then forced himself to relax.

"Good evening," he began. Then a smile. "I almost said 'my fellow Americans,' but that is far too limiting a term. What I have to say is for the entire world." He paused for effect. "We found something on the Moon, something I haven't mentioned until now, because first, I needed to have it authenticated, and second, because I had to discuss our find with President Cunningham before revealing it to you—or sharing it with you, if you prefer."

He turned, took the plate from Bassinger, and held it up for the cameras.

"While Marcia Neimark and Phil Bassinger were examining the find—the one you know about—in Cassegrain Crater, they came upon this plate in the ruins of the structure that had been there. The inscription—and copies and photos will be made available to all members of the press, as well as posted on the Internet—is in a very early form of Greek, dating from perhaps twenty-four hundred years ago, and yet, given where we found it, it was clearly not written by a human hand."

He waited a moment for the full meaning of that to sink in.

"Yes, the Earth itself has been visited by an alien race, the same race that created the dome whose remains we found in Cassegrain. And as the translation makes clear, it was—and hopefully still is—a decent and benevolent race, a race that cares about us and our future. As you will see, there is a warning on this plate"—he waited for the audible gasp from the press to subside—"but it is not a threat. It is a warning for our own good, a warning on how to avoid a disaster in the future. I felt my first duty upon returning was to present it to the president and ask for his guidance"—there were only three or four disbelieving chuckles and snickers—"and he agrees that since this is a message to the entire human race, and concerns the entire race, that we make it available to the entire planet, and that is what I am doing. The translation will be posted on the Web within the next five minutes, as well as photographs of the plate."

"So why was the discovery of the dome kept secret?"

"I suspect President Nixon was concerned that people would be frightened by the knowledge there'd been aliens on the Moon. It was, after all, a difficult time."

"What happens to the plate now?" asked a reporter.

"That's up to the president, but I imagine it will wind up in the Smithsonian."

"And what about you?"

Bucky smiled. "My crew"—he indicated them—"and I are returning to the Moon. Jerry Culpepper, whose help has been invaluable since he joined us and who is now my second-in-command, will be in charge of Blackstone Enterprises while we're gone"—*that's for your loyalty and for doping out the clue, Jerry,* thought Bucky as Jerry looked his surprise—"and will make any decisions that need to be made. We leave in seven weeks."

"Don't you mean seven *months*?" suggested another.

Bucky shook his head. "We're not the government. We don't need half a year of debriefing."

"So you're really going back?"

"We are," said Bucky. "It's a big world. Even Cassegrain Crater is a pretty big place. There may be other artifacts we missed." He paused, trying to contain his enthusiasm. "And this time, nothing's going to stop me from walking on the Moon."

"Really?" asked still another journalist. "But you're fifty-eight years old!"

"Then there's no time to waste, is there?" he replied with a happy smile.

"Aren't you at all apprehensive? You had a clean trip last time, but a lot can go wrong."

"True. But it could have gone wrong for you when you were driving here tonight." He paused and looked into the cameras. "It's 240,000 miles from here to the Moon. Last time I made it 239,990." A huge grin. "This time I'm going all the way—and just between you, me, and the three or four billion people who are watching and listening to us right now, I can hardly wait."